Praise for **THE FERRYMAN**

"A fantastic extravaganza all its own, with a plot that hinges on unpredictable twists that run far ahead of reader expectations . . . The result is a sensational speculative tale that is sure to get people talking."

—*Publishers Weekly* (starred review)

"A chilling, original, and immersive standalone SF tale perfectly rendered for our tumultuous times . . . This is a novel about storytelling, a meticulously built tale that begs the reader to allow themselves to be swept away, greatly rewarding those who surrender and trust the designer to sail them to the finish."

—*Booklist* (starred review)

"The twists in this novel are plentiful and authentically surprising, and although there are tons of moving parts, Cronin does a wonderful job handling them. . . . It's a hefty book that moves with an astounding quickness—yet another excellent offering from an author with a boundless imagination and talent to spare. . . . Twisty, thrilling, and beautifully written."

—*Kirkus Reviews* (starred review)

"A page-turner that is impossible to put down . . . A profoundly genius culmination of every twisty event and unveiled secret caps off this mind-bending masterpiece. . . . The velvety prose, the creepy heart-clenching suspense, and the meaning and emotion layered into every word all give rise to an incredibly thought-provoking sci-fi thriller from Cronin."

—*Library Journal* (starred review)

"Cronin's shrewd world-building allows us to have it both ways: We sink into aspirational fantasy even as we relish the author's sly commentary on a certain species of coastal elite. . . . [*The Ferryman* is] a careful book with a limited cast, animated by the bonds of parental and romantic love. An undercurrent of grief, organized around a pure, almost unobjectionable family tragedy, forms the book's emotional core."

—*The New York Times Book Review*

"[*The Ferryman* is] an intricate mystery that deals with loss and devastation on levels both personal and global. It's a love story as well, or rather a catalog of love stories."

—*The Boston Globe*

"*The Ferryman* is unique, spellbinding and utterly thought provoking. An emotionally complex journey, Cronin's new work will take you to the far reaches of your imagination, through his rich language and captivating scenes. . . . Part science fiction, part dystopian fantasy, *The Ferryman* provides an honest portrayal of humanity (at both its highest and lowest points) and the characters, although plentiful, are uniquely distinctive. . . . A standalone novel that will resonate with readers who are looking to make a connection with an engaging plot and relatable characters."

—*Mystery and Suspense Magazine*

"Complex and brilliant . . . Not just a novel, but an experience. A pivotal ride in such an unexpected scientific journey, this is the dystopian entertainment that many books strive to be. . . . The fantastic immersion of the story and what we discover is so creative and well-crafted that I was genuinely surprised at some of the outcomes."

—*The Fantasy Review*

"A wondrous epic both brilliant and terrifying . . . As complex as his imagined worlds become, Cronin is always reminding us, masterfully, of the simplest and deepest bonds. *The Ferryman,* to me, is a novel about love."

—Amanda Eyre Ward

"I've been anxiously awaiting Cronin's first new novel since the Passage Trilogy, and all of my sky-high expectations were smashed. *The Ferryman,* like the very best speculative fiction, is a transcendent meditation on the human condition, delivered through gorgeous prose, characters who steal your heart, and riveting storytelling that is guaranteed to put the rest of your life on hold until you've turned the final page. Fiction doesn't get better than this."

—Blake Crouch

"A mind-bending novel full of big ideas and a roller coaster's worth of twists and turns—so powerful and thrilling!"

—Andy Weir

"A brilliant hybrid of a novel, as tense as it is tender, as surprising as it is smart . . . Justin Cronin has an imagination as vast as dreams."

—Chris Bohjalian

BY JUSTIN CRONIN

The Ferryman
The City of Mirrors
The Twelve
The Passage
The Summer Guest
Mary and O'Neil

THE FERRYMAN

THE FERRYMAN

A NOVEL

JUSTIN CRONIN

BALLANTINE BOOKS
NEW YORK

The Ferryman is a work of fiction. Names, characters, places, and incidents are the products of the author's imagination or are used fictitiously. Any resemblance to actual events, locales, or persons, living or dead, is entirely coincidental.

2024 Ballantine Books Trade Paperback Edition

Published in the United States by Ballantine Books, an imprint of Random House, a division of Penguin Random House LLC, New York.

Ballantine Books & colophon are registered trademarks of Penguin Random House LLC.

Originally published in hardcover in the United States by Ballantine Books, an imprint of Random House, a division of Penguin Random House LLC, in 2023.

Library of Congress Cataloging-in-Publication Data

Names: Cronin, Justin, author.
Title: The ferryman: a novel / Justin Cronin.
Description: First edition. | New York, NY: Ballantine Books, [2023]
Identifiers: LCCN 2022020852 (print) | LCCN 2022020853 (ebook) | ISBN 9780525619499 | ISBN 9780525619482 (ebook)
Subjects: LCGFT: Novels.
Classification: LCC PS3553.R542 F47 2023 (print) | LCC PS3553.R542 (ebook) | DDC 813/.54—dc23/eng/20220502

LC record available at lccn.loc.gov/2022020852
LC ebook record available at lccn.loc.gov/2022020853

International ISBN 9780593722640

Printed in the United States of America on acid-free paper

randomhousebooks.com

9 8 7 6 5 4 3 2 1

Book design by Elizabeth A. D. Eno

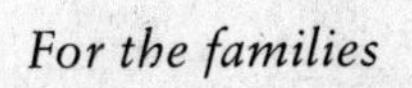

For the families

He pass'd the flaming bounds of Place and Time:
The living throne, the sapphire blaze,
Where angels tremble, while they gaze,
He saw; but, blasted with excess of light,
Clos'd his eyes in endless night.

—Thomas Gray, "The Progress of Poesy"

CONTENTS

THE FERRYMAN

PROLOGUE

Dawn is breaking when she creeps from the house. The air is cool and fresh; birds are singing in the trees. Everywhere, the sound of the sea, the world's great metronome, beating beneath a velvety sky of diminishing stars. In her pale nightdress, she moves through the garden. Her pace is not hesitant, merely unhurried, almost fond. How like a ghost she must look, this solitary figure floating among the flower beds, the burbling fountains, the hedges trimmed with creases sharp enough to draw blood. Behind her, the house is dark as a monolith, though soon its seaward-facing windows will swell with light.

It is not an easy thing, to leave a life, a home. The details dig trenches within one—scents, sounds, associations, rhythms. The creaking floorboard in the upstairs hall. The smell that greets one in the entryway at the end of a day. The light switch that meets the hand without thought in a darkened room. She could have stepped safely among the furniture wearing a blindfold. Twenty years. She would have twenty more if she could.

It was after dinner that she'd told Malcolm the news. A fine meal, one he loved: broiled lamb chops, risotto with cheese, asparagus grilled in a film of oil; good wine. Coffee and small crème pastries for dessert. They had decided to eat outside; it was such a beautiful night. A riot of flowers on the table, the tick-tock of the sea, candlelight glazing their faces. You will not know when it happens, she told him. I will simply be gone. Powerless, she watched him as he absorbed the blow, his face in his hands. *So soon? Does it have to be now?* Come to bed with me, she commanded—her body would say to him the things that words could not—and after, she held him as he wept. The dark hours passed. At last the lassitude of grief engulfed him. Wrapped in her arms, he slept.

Farewell, gardens, she thinks, *farewell, house. Farewell, birds and trees and long, unhurried days, and while I'm at it, farewell to all the lies I've had to tell.*

She is growing older. All the things a woman can do, she has done. The creams and extracts. The hours of exercise and meticulously observed diet. The small, discreet surgeries that even Malcolm does not know about. She has applied every resource to the slowing of the years, but that is at its end. She had decided to wait until someone remarked on it, and then, out of the blue, it happened.

"Are you taking care of yourself, Cynthia?"

They had just played tennis, the usual Tuesday group, a dozen women, all good; afterward, glasses of iced tea and salads everybody just picked at, no matter how hungry they were. She hadn't played well. She had played, in fact, quite badly. Her knees were sore and slow; the sun felt too strong, sapping her strength. It was time she felt in her limbs, its inexorable march, while all around her, in the bodies and faces of her friends, it moved at a genteel crawl.

But, the question. Her friend was waiting for an answer. Her name was Lauralai Swan. She was close to sixty but looked thirty:

skin taut; limbs lean with yoga-sculpted muscle; glorious, bountiful hair. Even her hands looked good. Was the question an expression of genuine concern or something darker? Cynthia had known this day would come, and yet she'd been caught by surprise, no answer at the ready. Her mind was sorting rapidly; just in time, it came to her. What she needed was a joke.

—Believe me, she said, if you were married to Malcolm, you'd look tired, too. The man won't take no for an answer.

She laughed, hoping Lauralai would laugh, too, and after a fraught moment, she did; everyone did; and soon they were all talking about their husbands, each woman raising the bet with every story that passed around the table, even comparing their men to former lovers and ex-husbands. Who was better, more considerate in bed. Who left his soggy jogging shorts on the bathroom floor. Who squeezed the toothpaste from the middle of the tube.

It was, in sum, a pleasant afternoon in the sunshine, all of them talking the way women liked to do. But inside herself, Cynthia felt something drop. *Are you taking care of yourself?* The thing that dropped: it was a blade.

Farewell to all of this and all of you, who gave me what passed for a life.

And yet: it is not the parties and concerts she will miss; not the good leather of her luggage and shoes; not the long dinners with beautiful food and good wine and sparkling talk until all hours—none of these. What she will miss is the boy. She thinks of two days, one a beginning, one an end. The first was the day he had come to her. She had expected to feel nothing; adopting a ward was simply one more thing a person in her position would do. The boy was, in that sense, a form of décor, like the couch in her living room or the art upon her walls. *Oh, you've taken a ward!* people would say. *You must be so thrilled!* They had seen a picture of him, of course. One did not choose blindly. Yet the moment Cynthia caught sight of him, standing at the rail of the ferry, something changed. He was taller than she had anticipated, at least six feet, his height amplified by his neutral, poorly fitting clothing, rather like pajamas or a doctor's scrubs. Though the wards were staring over the rail with a kind of unfocused blankness, he alone was looking about, taking in the sight of the crowd and the buildings of the city and even the sky, tipping his head upward to feel the sun on his face. His haircut, she saw, was awful. It looked like a blind man had done it. That was something she'd have to see to right away, getting the boy a proper haircut.

"Do you think that's him?" her husband said to her, and when she failed to answer, he addressed the adoption agent who had accompanied them to the ferry: "Is that our son?"

But Cynthia absorbed this conversation only vaguely. Her husband's voice; the buzz of the crowd; the sun and sky and sea: all seemed to pale by comparison to the sudden, vivid reality of the boy. Questions rose in her mind. What food would he like to eat, what clothes to wear? What music to listen to, what books to read? And what was this sudden impulse to wonder about these things? He was a presence produced entirely by paperwork. So why did she feel a rush of sudden tenderness toward this arbitrary being? The ferry completed its last maneuvers; the wards assembled at the top of the gangplank. Confined by a rope barrier, none of the guardians was permitted to approach. The boy—*her* boy—was first in line. ("Her" boy? Had it happened that fast?) He kept his eyes forward as he descended to the pier, his steps measured, his hands gripping the rail. He might have been stepping from a spacecraft onto the surface of an alien world, so methodical was each motion of his body. At the base of the gangplank, he was met by a man in a dark suit with a clipboard and a woman in a lab coat, holding a reader. The man in the suit did not speak to the boy; instead, he bared the boy's arm and held it out while his associate, presumably a doctor, inserted the wires into the ports on his monitor. A pause followed as the doctor examined the data; an anticipatory hush had settled over the crowd. At last she looked up, lifting her voice to the crowd:

"Will the guardians please come forward?"

The agent unhooked the rope, allowing Cynthia and Malcolm to advance; the boy did the same. The three of them met in the empty space between the crowd and the gangplank. The boy was the first to speak.

"How do you do?" he said, and smiled warmly. "I am Proctor, your ward."

He offered his hand. The gesture was something he had obviously been coached to do.

"Well, there you are, son," her husband said. Beaming, he shook the boy's hand keenly. "It's nice to finally meet you."

"Hello, Father," the boy replied, and turned to Cynthia, hand similarly extended. "And you must be my mother. I am very happy to make your acquaintance."

Your acquaintance! She wanted to laugh, and nearly did. Not a laugh of derision, but one of pure delight. How polite he was! How eager to be good, to please them, to make them a family! And his name. Proctor, from the Latin *procurator* (she was later to learn; her husband knew such things): a steward or manager, one who attends to the affairs of others. How perfect! She did not shake the boy's hand but, rather, wrapped it in both of hers and held it, feeling its warmth, its pulse of life. She looked into his eyes. Yes, there was something there, something different. Something . . . soulful. She wondered about the kind of man he'd been before. What had he done for a living? Who had his friends been? Had he had many wives?

Had he been happy?

"Cynthia, you can let the boy go now."

She laughed then, releasing him. *You must be my mother.* He was just a boy, newly reborn in the world—six feet tall but a boy nonetheless—and that's what she would be. She would be his mother.

It's true, she thinks now, making her way down the sloping lawn to the pathway. The sky is softening; the stars have washed away; at the horizon, a glowing margin of light has appeared. That was the day when she had taken the boy into her heart. And not just the boy, but Malcolm as well. This austere, moral creature, this lover of codes and protocols—it was as if a wand had been waved over his life, as if he were an adult-sized Pinocchio turned by sudden love into a person. The virile grin on his face as he'd shaken the boy's hand; the light of joy in his eyes when he'd shown the boy his room, with its matching teakwood bed and bureau and paintings of ships on the walls and the old telescope positioned on its tripod, facing the sea; how, at dinner, he'd fussed over everything, wanting the boy to feel welcome, and patiently guided him in the application of his knife and fork and napkin; and finally, at day's end, the muffled snap when Malcolm closed the boy's bedroom door, saw her standing in the hall, and held an upright finger over his lips: *Shhhhh.* How could she not feel something for such a man?

And the second day, years later. She had heard something once, long in the past, about love and letting go. She did not recall the words, only the idea: that loss was love's accounting, its unit of measure, as a foot was made of inches, a yard was made of feet. It was the boy's first year at university: a year of triumph, when a special gift emerged. He had told her not to come that day—it would make him nervous, he said, to know she was there—but still she had done it, taking a seat high on the natatorium bleachers where she could go unnoticed. The air was warm and wet, the acoustics disorienting. Far below her, the pool formed a neat rectangle of otherworldly blue. She watched with vague interest and a slow tightening in her chest as the various races came and went, until the boy's turn arrived. The 100-meter freestyle. He looked like all the other contestants—in their snug suits and goggles and silver caps, they were virtually indistinguishable—yet he alone was hers, his presence as particular as the day when she'd seen him at the rail of the ferry. He was standing by the pool, shaking his arms, rolling his neck. Watching him, she experienced a feeling of enlargement, as if he were an extension of herself, a colony or outpost. He made a little skipping motion and, with puffed cheeks, expelled a nervous breath of air. He was going into himself, she understood, like a man putting himself into a trance.

The signal was given; the swimmers mounted the blocks. As one, they bent at the waist, fingertips skimming their toes. The crowd tensed. For an interminable second they froze, and then the horn sounded, a sheen of noise, and ten hale young bodies launched through the air and were swallowed by the water.

Her heart leapt.

Her boy was in the third lane. A long subsurface glide and he emerged. She was on her feet now, shouting like a madwoman. "Go, go!" His strokes, impossibly long, propelled him through the water as if it were nothing. It was all happening so quickly, mere seconds, yet in those seconds she felt something infinite. He made his flip turn, pushed off, and surfaced once more, popping into second place. Two strokes and he pulled into the lead. What had seemed impossible was now about to happen. She was crying out, her heart flying with adrenaline. It was unfolding before her eyes: the greatest moment of his life.

The race was over before she knew it. One moment he was reaching out to touch the wall; in the next he was spinning in the water to look up at the clock, where his name shone beside his winning time. He raised a fist in triumph, his face glowing with impossible joy. She did not know it then, but he hadn't merely won the race; he had shattered the record by two-tenths of a second. The boy in the next lane slapped his upraised palm.

He broke away and looked up to scan the crowd. Suddenly Cynthia knew. His protestations had been a ruse. He had known all along that she would be there. It was as if his victory were a gift he had given her. But as she was rising to call out to him, a girl went tearing down from the stands to the pool deck. The boy hoisted himself quickly from the water. He stripped off his goggles and cap as the girl flew toward him, and then she was in his arms. Her feet actually lifted off the ground, so elated was their embrace. Without embarrassment he locked his mouth to hers in a long, deep kiss. The crowd cheered raucously; some in the stands began to whistle.

There had been girls, of course. He was a boy, after all, broad-shouldered and tall, with an easy smile and a way of looking at you when you spoke that said he took you seriously, that he was actually listening, not just waiting for his turn to talk, the way most boys would do. In other words, all the things girls loved.

But this girl was different. It was the kiss that told her so. Why had he never mentioned her? The answer was obvious. He hadn't mentioned her because the thought had never occurred to him.

She left the natatorium in a hurry, badly shaken. She felt banished, erased. Her boy was a boy no longer; he had taken his place at the table of life. As she exited the building, the afternoon sunshine hit her like a spotlight, all bright pain; she reached into her purse for her sunglasses and slid them onto her face. A portion of her had always held itself apart—the end had been ordained in the beginning, the way the final chord was built into the first measure of a symphony—yet nothing had prepared her for what she was experiencing now. How love had made a liar out of her! This was the thought that at last brought tears to her eyes, and she hurried down the steps and across the parking lot and onward, into the busy afternoon, alone.

All of it gone now; all of it lost.

At the end of the pier, the dinghy awaits. She lowers herself into it, sets the oars into their locks, and casts off. The sun has risen, shooting tendrils of pink into the sky above the placid sea. There is no wind at all. She permits herself a quiet moment, just drifting, then takes the oars into her fists and strokes away from shore.

The pier, the beach, the dunes, the house where she has lived for two decades: all grow smaller. The images blur into generalities, then are gone. Past the point, the ocean changes, becoming dark and wild. The sun has grown warm on her neck. Waves jostle her as the boat rises and falls into the troughs between them.

She's waiting for a witness.

She hears it before she sees it—a quiet, breathy buzzing, like a sustained "v" pushed through closed lips. The drone comes in low over the water on its dragonfly wings, decelerates, and moves into position above her. Made to resemble an insect but inarguably mechanical, it manages to look simultaneously natural and man-made and therefore neither. She lifts her face to look directly at it. From its shiny chrome underbelly, a glass dome bulges, holding the camera.

Who is watching her? She imagines a man, in the basement at the Ministry of Public Safety, sitting before a wall of monitors. He has been up all night; his eyes are tired and dry, his chin covered with stubble, his breath sour in his mouth. With his boots propped on the counter, he is penning in a crossword from a book of them. Something causes him to glance up. What have we here? A woman, alone in a rowboat. Odd, to see someone out at this hour, and is that a nightgown she's wearing? He punches a few keys. On a second screen, which shows the outline of the coast, a red dot appears to indicate the position of the drone. The woman in the nightgown is three miles from shore.

More keystrokes. Via the computer's facial-recognition system, the man gleans more data: her name, her husband's name, her address, and that she is fifty-one years old. Further, he learns that she is a former employee of the Board of Overseers' Department of Legal Affairs; that she is a member in good standing of the Harbor Club, the Union League, and the Opera Circle; and that she has received, in the last two years, six parking tickets, all paid. He learns the names of the charities to which she's given, the news organs she consumes, the contents of her bank account, her dress and shoe sizes (6, 8½), and the name of her favorite restaurant (Il Forno, on Prosperity Square; according to her credit card records, she eats there once a week). He learns, in other words, a very great deal about her, yet nothing that tells him why she's in a rowboat three miles from shore at 6:42 (he checks the time) on a Tuesday morning in July. Wearing a nightgown. By herself.

And what's she doing now?

Rubbing his eyes, he pushes his face closer to the monitor. From under the bench the woman has retrieved a small satchel. She pulls the knot loose with her fingertips and removes the contents, three items, setting each one on the bench beside her. A stick or dowel, about a foot long. A pair of wire cutters. And, sheathed in old leather, a knife.

The man at the monitor picks up the phone.

Indeed, it is only by viewing events through this imaginary man's eyes that Cynthia is able to do what comes next. While he watches with gathering anxiety, waiting for his superior to answer, she places the dowel into her mouth and pulls up the sleeve of her nightgown to expose her monitor port, a small rectangle embedded halfway between her left elbow and her wrist. She takes the knife in her hand. It is six inches long with a curved tip, of the type used to scale and gut fish. Three long breaths follow, her grip tightening on the knife. She places the tip of the knife into the small groove of flesh at the edge of the monitor, waits for the boat to still, and when it does, she shoves the blade into her arm.

The pain is astonishing, as is the volume of blood that erupts. The image on the man's screen has no audio; what he would hear is a series of strangled screams as she carves around the monitor's perimeter. The silence is, for him, a blessing, and Cynthia feels a twinge of pity for this unknown person, chosen by chance to endure this horrific scene. By the time she's done, her nightgown, the bench, the floor of the rowboat—all are drenched with blood. Her head is afloat in agony; she thinks she might have cracked a tooth. With a final plunge, she wedges the tip of the knife under the monitor. A ripping sound and a wet, hollow pop, and at last the device comes free.

Pick up, goddamnit, the man breathes into his phone. *Pick up, pick up, pick up.*

Two snips with the wire cutter, and she drops the monitor over the side. She removes the dowel from her mouth and tosses this into the sea as well. Specks of light, like fireflies, dance in her vision; she has begun to pant. A moment to gather the last of her strength and Cynthia reaches to the bow to free the anchor from its holder.

She begins to loop the anchor line around her ankle.

And this is when the man's superior finally answers the phone. Yes? he says curtly. What the hell is it? Why are you calling at this hour?

But the man at the monitor doesn't answer. He cannot answer. He can speak no words at all.

Cynthia rises. Her blood-soaked nightgown clings to her flesh. The boat jostles beneath her; she very nearly falls. Her limbs feel disconnected; her head is made of air, impossibly light. Still, she finds the strength to lift the anchor and hold it against her chest.

She tilts her face upward. Above her, against a blue morning sky, the drone hovers.

What is she thinking? But the man at the monitor cannot know; he couldn't even imagine. She is thinking of the boy and the man and their unlikely life together, too brief. *Goodbye,* she whispers. *Goodbye, my darlings, I never should have loved you but I did, I did.* And hugging the anchor to her chest—tenderly, like a mother with her child—she closes her eyes, rocks backward, and is swallowed by the water.

THE LAST BEAUTIFUL DAY

1

The dream was always the same.

I am swimming in the sea. Below the surface, breath held, I push my way forward through a liquid, blue-green world. My limbs feel clean and strong, my strokes effortlessly powerful; sunlight shimmers on the surface, far above.

On a trail of exhaled bubbles, I ascend. The sun is setting, making ribbons of color against a purpling dome of sky. Drawn by an unknown influence—my actions are neither voluntary nor involuntary, they simply *are*—I swim away from shore. Night falls slowly, then all at once, whereupon I experience a terrible sense of error. This is all a grand mistake. I pivot toward shore to find no lights anywhere; the land has disappeared. Panicked, I spin wildly in the water, all sense of direction obliterated. I am alone in an infinite sea.

"You don't have to be afraid, Proctor."

A woman is swimming next to me with a smooth breaststroke, her head held erect above the surface, like a seal's. I cannot make out her face; her voice isn't one I know. Yet there is something about her presence that fills me with a great calm. It is as if I have been waiting for her; at last she is here.

"It won't be long now," she says gently. "I'll show you the way."

"Where are we going?"

But she doesn't answer. As she glides away, I follow. There is no wind, no current. The surface of the sea is as motionless as stone, the only sound the gentle swish of water passing through our cupped hands.

She gestures skyward. "Can you see it?"

A single brilliant star has appeared. It's different from the others—brighter, more distinct, with a bluish tint.

"Do you remember the star, Proctor?"

Do I? My thoughts are diffuse, drifting like chips of straw in a current. They skip from point to point. The ocean, its impersonal, inky vastness. The star, piercing the sky like a beacon. All is known and unknown; all familiar, all strange.

"You're cold," she says.

I am. My limbs tremble, my teeth are chattering. She moves beside me.

"Take my hand."

I have, it appears, already done so. Her skin is warm; it seems to pulsate with life. It is a rich sensation, powerful as a tide. It flows through my body in a wave of softness. A feeling of homecoming, of home.

"Are you ready?"

She pivots toward me. For a moment her face is revealed, but the image is too quick, unable to be retained, and then she is kissing me, pressing her mouth to mine. A torrent of sensation barrels through me. It is as if my mind and body have suddenly been linked to infinite forces. I think: *This is how it feels to love. How have we forgotten how to love?* The woman's arms have coiled around me, pinning my hands to my chest. Simultaneously, I become aware that the character of the water is altering. It is becoming less dense.

"Time to wake up, Proctor."

I wave my legs frantically to hold myself afloat. But this is useless. It's as if I'm kicking air. I am held fast, barely able to move; the sea is dissolving, opening like a maw. Terror squeezes my throat, I cannot cry out . . .

Her voice is a whisper, close to my ear: "Look down."

I do, and with that, I plunge. *We* plunge, down into an infinite black abyss, and the last thing I think is this:

The sea is full of stars.

My name is Proctor Bennett. Here is what I've called my life.

I am a citizen of the archipelago state called Prospera. Located far from any landmass, Prospera exists in splendid isolation, hidden from the world. Its climate, like all things about it, is entirely beneficent: warming sunshine, cooling ocean breezes, and frequent, gentle rains. Island one, known as Prospera proper, is roughly circular, covering 482 square miles. It is here that all Prosperans reside. With its shorelines of crystalline white sand, interior forests abundant with wildlife, and inland valleys of the most fertile soil, it might be mistaken for a mythological paradise. Island two, known as the Annex, is home to the support staff—men and women of lesser biological and social endowments who nevertheless are, in my experience, wholly pleasant to be around. Roughly a quarter the size, it is connected to Prospera by a floating causeway, over which these helpful citizens travel daily to perform their various duties.

The last of the three islands is different from the others, in that we know very little about what occurs there, only that it does. This is known as Nursery Isle, or, more simply, the Nursery. Protected by dangerous shoals and towering cliffs, it might be likened to a floating fortress. There is only one way in, an opening on the eastern flank of the island, through which the ferry passes—a journey that each Prosperan takes twice per iteration, once at the beginning, once at the end. I cannot say who lives on Nursery Isle, though doubtless someone must. Some people say that the Designer himself resides there, overseeing the regenerative process that serves as the foundation for our exceptional way of life.

In this lush land, free of all want and distraction, Prosperans devote themselves to the highest aspirations. Creative expression and the pursuit of personal excellence: these are the cornerstones of our civilization. We are a society of musicians and painters, poets and scholars, artisans of every type. The clothes we wear, the food we eat, the social gatherings we attend, the spaces in which we work and rest and recreate—each facet of daily life is subject to the most scrutinizing curatorial eye. One might say that Prospera itself is a work of art, a canvas upon which each of our citizens brings to bear a single, exquisitely rendered brushstroke.

What is our history? How did we come to be? To these questions I haven't much to offer; even the year has become difficult to know. And what we know of the rest of the world's present state is, in a word, nothing. Protected by the Veil—an electromagnetic barrier that hides us from the world, and the world from us—we are spared this dismal tale. Yet one can easily imagine. War, pestilence, famine, environmental collapse; vast migrations and fanaticism of every stripe; a world de-civilized as the earth's peoples, sworn to competing gods, turned upon one another: such were the convulsions that inspired the Designer to build our hidden sanctuary in ages past. Rarely, if ever, do we speak of these matters, known collectively as "the horrors," because there is no profit in it. Which is, one might say, the heart of the Designer's genius and the whole point of Prospera: to shelter the best of humanity from the worst of it.

To leave Prospera is, naturally, forbidden. Word of our existence would threaten everything. But who could desire to leave such a place? From time to time one hears of someone—always a member of the support staff—who has foolishly attempted to journey beyond the Veil. But since none has returned, and our secret existence has remained intact, one can safely assume that these troublemakers have met with failure. Perhaps the seas have swallowed them. Perhaps they have found no world to receive them, civilization having finally consumed itself utterly. Perhaps, as in a tale widely told, they have simply sailed off the edge of the earth into oblivion.

As for myself: In my present iteration, I am forty-two years old. (Prosperans start the clock at sixteen, the approximate biological age of new iterants freshly off the ferry.) My current social arrangement, my first, is a fifteen-year contract of heterosexual marriage, renewable. After eight years together, I would say that Elise and I are generally happy. We are not the ardent lovers we once were, practically unable to keep our hands off each other. But these things soften over time, yielding at their best to an easier, more comfortable kind of partnership, and that is where we find ourselves. Our home, which Elise's guardians paid for—given my relatively modest salary as a civil servant, I could never afford such a thing on my own—sits atop a rocky promontory on Prospera's southern coast. Never have I seen Elise so blissfully in her element as during the two years of its construction. For hours every day, she huddled with the army of architects, artisans, and craftspeople, guaranteeing that her fingerprints lay upon even the smallest detail. I admit, my own interest was more tepid; I lack Elise's eye for these things and would have been content to take quarters closer to town. I was also concerned about her guardians' influence on our newly joined lives, her mother's in particular. But the house makes her happy, and therefore makes me happy, and it's there that Elise and I conduct our lives, all to the sound of wind in the palm fronds and the gnashing of white-toothed waves upon the beach below.

My job, as managing director for District Six of the Department of Social Contracts, Enforcement Division, is one that some people find unsettling, even a bit macabre. But the name "ferryman" is one I'm proud to wear. Sometimes the gears of emotion need grease to run smoothly, and I'm there to provide it—when, for instance, an elderly citizen, suffering the mental disturbances that often accompany the final years of iteration, cannot bring themselves to move on. These can be tricky situations. But most people, even when they resist the idea of change, can be brought around to see the wisdom of it. To embark upon a voyage to a wholly new existence; to put down the accumulated weight of life and wipe the slate of memory clean; to be reborn as a fresh-faced, bright-eyed teenager in perfect health. Who could fail to desire these things?

And yet.

There are times when the mind cannot help but wonder, to look askance at life. One thinks of the support staff. How different their lives must seem to them. To be born in the old-fashioned manner, shot into existence as a wet, squealing nugget, bathed in perfect innocence. To live one life and one life only, hemmed by swift time. To give one's days to earnest work of measurable results (the freshness of the mown lawn, the surgical spotlessness of the well-scrubbed kitchen, the farm field sown and reaped and sown again). To bear children of one's own and watch them stand, then walk, then grow into their lives. To pass fifty, sixty, seventy years upon the earth and then sail into thoughtless oblivion.

To believe in a god when there is no God.

In the abstract, their lives can make ours seem arid by comparison. I cannot help but feel a twinge of envy. But then I consider the heaviness and sorrows of such permanent entanglements. Love can fail. Children can precede their parents to the grave. The body collapses in a swift cascade of biological humiliations, a parade of pain. For the support staff, deprived of the blessings of reiteration, there are no do-overs, no escapes from the shocks and regrets of life. And so the envy dims.

Leaving what? An infinitude of perfect days, and a dream in which, pinned in the arms of love, I am plunging into stars.

A certain Wednesday, not so very long ago. A Wednesday in June, not because the date is important but because that's the day it was. The twisted, sweat-dampened sheets; the night's imagined terrors (sea, stars) dispersing; the morning's seaborne light, filling the bedroom like a golden gas; I, Proctor Bennett—Prosperan, husband, ferryman—open my eyes and know at once that the house is empty. I rise, stretch, don my robe and slippers; in the kitchen Elise has left a pot of coffee. Fresh ocean air washes through the house from the open patio doors. I pour myself a cup, add a dollop of milk, and step outside.

For some period of time I simply stand there, watching the sea. It has long been my habit to begin my days like this, allowing my mind to clear at its own pace. Sometimes my dream departs instantly, like a popping soap bubble. On such mornings I often wonder if I have dreamed at all and am simply remembering other nights of other dreams. Then there are mornings when the dream lingers in my mind as a kind of overlying, second reality, and I know that its images will color my emotions long into the day.

This is such a morning.

I have always been a dreamer—that is to say, a person who has dreams. As a general rule, citizens of our world do not dream. This is widely thought to be a by-product of the industrial poisons that once blanketed the planet, although a not-entirely unwelcome one. Why, when our waking lives are so satisfying, should we feel the need for such tortuous flights of storytelling? I say Prosperans do not dream, but that is not entirely correct. It is the oldest among us who do. In my line of work, I have seen the consequences many times. The restless nights and strange visions; the gradual disordering of thought; the final plunge into lunacy that is so painful to witness. Speaking for my profession, we try not to let things get that far, but that doesn't mean it never happens.

I've managed to downplay this part of my life for the most part—but this has not always been so. As a young ward, I was beset by nighttime visitations of such power that they often propelled me from bed to wander the house in a state of dazed unawareness, performing the most incomprehensible acts. Turning on all the taps. Mangling a light fixture. Making a butter-and-jelly sandwich and, perplexingly, hurling it out the window. (This was directly observed by my father; by that time, my guardians' practice was to leave me alone unless I was in danger of hurting myself.)

The thought may amuse now, but it didn't at the time. Eventually the situation so unnerved my guardians that my mother took me to a doctor. At the time I was just a year or two off the ferry. The world was still a new place to me, and apart from my daily ride to the Academy of Early Learning, I had yet to see much of the island. The shuttle took us inland, following a winding country lane through farm fields and orchards before letting us off at a nondescript office building in the middle of nowhere. By this time we were the only passengers. The structure was little more than a concrete cube, though pleasantly landscaped with flowering shrubs and a soft green lawn still wicked with moisture from the overnight rains. In the office, a woman took our names and told us to wait, though the room was otherwise empty. As the minutes ticked by, my waning excitement allowed the full measure of my anxiety to emerge. I was aware that my dreaming was a problem. Indeed, I did not *like* to dream. The broken images and powerful emotions troubled me profoundly. But even more concerning was the thought that I had disappointed my guardians, which I very much did not want to do. As I sat in the waiting room, my fears congealing like cold soup, an awful thought occurred to me. I was an embarrassment. Unless my dreaming stopped, my guardians would return me to the Nursery. Failing to live up to their expectations, I would be traded for some other, more worthy boy, like a poorly chosen present exchanged at the store for something more suitable.

At last, the door to the inner office opened. The doctor, a young woman in a white coat with bright blue eyes and brown hair fastened by a silver clip, introduced herself as Dr. Patty and invited us inside. The room was dispiritingly functional: windowless, devoid of any decoration, and containing only a padded table, a glass cabinet of instruments, and a chair for my mother. Dr. Patty asked me to remove my shirt and sit on the table, whereupon she examined me—checking my monitor, listening to my heart and lungs, peering into my eyes and nose and mouth—before taking up the question at hand. So, she asked me, dreaming, was it? (I nodded.) How frequently would I say that this occurred? (I wasn't sure. A lot.) And what, if anything, did I recall about these dreams? (They were scary?) She took note of my answers, jotting them onto my chart, including my mother's account of the butter-and-jelly sandwich. I was by this time a nervous wreck, on the verge of tears. Surely I had incriminated myself so utterly that I would be taken from her office straight to the ferry—that my present life, which had only just begun, was over.

But that wasn't what happened. Instead, Dr. Patty put my chart aside and gave me a look of utter reassurance. Well, she declared, I don't think there's anything to worry about. At my age, dreams like mine were uncommon, perhaps, but not unheard of. During the first years of reiteration, bits and pieces of a previous iteration might float to the surface. This could take the form of nighttime disturbances like those I'd described. Think of them, Dr. Patty said, not as dreams but as echoes. The source was gone, but the sound lingered, ricocheting through the mind until it, too, faded away.

And to her credit, this was, more or less, how the situation unfolded. Within a matter of months these episodes grew less frequent, then stopped altogether, and by the time I entered university, I didn't think about them at all. The whole thing was just one more oddball episode of early iteration, something to be joked about over a second cocktail or a third glass of wine. *Proctor, tell the story about the jelly sandwich! Your guardians must have thought you'd lost your mind!*

Or so I believed at the time.

But my memory of that morning does not end there. My mother and I returned to the shuttle stop. Although Dr. Patty's explanation made only partial sense to me (echoes in my head?), I felt tremendously relieved. I was normal; there was no reason to send me back to the Nursery. This thought put me in a state of giddy high spirits, yet my mother was silent, apparently unable to join me in my good mood. Sitting beside her on the bench, I attempted to cajole her with a chain of optimistic remarks, to no effect, until at last she turned her face toward mine and engaged me with a lengthy, searching look.

My mother was a pretty woman, much younger than my father. Only the tiniest lines fanned from the corners of her eyes and mouth; her hair, a rich cocoa, shone in the sun. It is true that I knew very little about her of a personal nature. I did not, for instance, know if my father was her first husband. (My father had been through three contracts before they'd met.) I had heard no mention of her own guardians; she'd never spoken of her own years of early iteration. There was, in sum, an atmosphere of wistful secrecy surrounding her—she was a woman about whom one longed to know more—and it was said by nearly all who knew her that she possessed an unusual quality of happiness—not that she herself *was* happy, which I now doubt; rather, that her presence had the power to arouse positive feelings in others. It was her special gift, one I can attest to.

Yet that wasn't what happened that morning on the bench. Her look made me afraid.

"You know I love you," she said, "don't you?"

On a day of strange events, these words to me were the strangest of all. Neither of my guardians had ever told me they loved me; parental love of the type practiced by the support staff for their biological offspring was neither anticipated nor required. Perhaps over time, as the three of us got to know one another, a deeper bond would form. But I saw no reason for them to love me.

"It's okay," she added, when I failed to respond. (I had no idea what to say.) "I don't mean to embarrass you. I just wanted to say it."

My bewilderment was profound. Why was she talking to me like this, in a manner so intimate—as if I were an adult? Yes, I was six feet tall, but what did I know about anything?

"You know, Proctor, I don't care what anybody says, I don't think it's a bad thing at all that you have dreams."

"You don't?"

"Actually, I think it's wonderful." She leaned closer. "I'll tell you a secret. You're not the only one."

I was taken aback. "I'm not?"

"Not at all. If you ask me, lots of people do it. They just don't *know* they do."

I considered this curious notion. "What about you?" I asked her. "Do you dream?"

She squinted into the distance again, as if the answer to my question lay elsewhere. "Sometimes," she said. "At least, I think I do. I wake up with this . . . feeling. Like I went somewhere else."

I understood what she meant: that sensation of travel, of having left this world for a different one. I asked, "Do you think they're good dreams?"

She shrugged lightly. "I really couldn't say." She looked back at me. "The important thing, Proctor, is for you to listen to what they're telling you."

"But I don't remember them."

"Maybe not. Maybe you never will, not the way you mean. But even if you don't, they're still inside you, something your mind made. They're part of who you are."

"I never thought of it that way."

Her expression grew more serious. "I meant what I said before. I hope that love is something that happens in your life. That you love somebody the way I love you. Always remember that, okay?"

She meant: *Someday I will leave you.* But I could not know that then.

Sounds behind me: Elise, returning from her studio over the garage. My cup of coffee, largely undrunk, has grown cold in my hand. I step into the house in time to see her deposit her portfolio on the dining table, move briskly into the kitchen, and open the refrigerator.

"*There* you are," she says.

Skin bright, eyes clear, her movements energetic; it has been a productive morning for her. She is dressed for the day in stretch pants and a loose linen blouse, the faintest touch of makeup, not that she needs it. Columns of silver bracelets, her only jewelry, jangle up and down her wrists. She commences hauling breakfast supplies from the refrigerator: carrots, celery, leafy greens, vitamin B complex, a lemon.

"You should eat something," she says, glancing my way.

Even by the lofty standards of Prospera, my wife is a strikingly attractive woman. Before she become a couturier, she had a highly successful career as a model, most notably for the Lifestyle Department's "Live Exceptionally" campaign, her face gracing the pages of magazines and smiling healthfully from billboards at passersby all across the island. People still recognize her—clients, guests at parties, even our plumber—their eyes lighting up when they make the connection. There are moments—such as now—when she can still take my breath away.

"Proctor, are you listening?"

I shake off my reverie. "Sorry." I hold up my cup. "The coffee's fine. I'll get something at the office."

She is dropping ingredients into the mixer. "What were you doing out here last night?"

"Doing?"

The mixer roars, then just as abruptly stops, carving out a deeper silence. Elise pours the concoction into a tall glass.

"I heard you banging around out here." She sips and makes a

roaming motion with her glass. "It must have been three o'clock in the morning."

This is, needless to say, unsettling. Is there some plausible explanation? Did I hear a noise and go to investigate? Raid the kitchen for a snack? Awaken to the sound of rain and rise to shut the windows? As far as I know, I slept straight through the night, dumb as a hammer.

"It must have been the wine. All that sugar. I couldn't sleep."

"Well, you certainly drank a lot of it." She polishes off her breakfast and deposits her glass in the sink. "Come on, I have something to show you."

In the dining area, she opens her portfolio to reveal four large pastel sketches, which she spreads over the table. Each shows the figure of a woman wearing a high-waisted, half-sleeved cocktail dress with a sharply pleated skirt and a velvet butterfly collar.

"For the new season." Elise steps back and folds her arms across her chest. "What do you think?"

Speaking honestly, I have no real opinion about the dress. Such things are difficult for me to imagine in the abstract. How would it look on an actual woman? It's very hard to say.

"I think they're terrific." I offer my best good-husband smile. "Maybe your best yet."

"Which one?"

"Which one what?"

"They're all very different, Proctor."

I see I'm not going to be let off so easily. I scan the images, hunting for differences, which seem so slight as to be inconsequential. I pick one and point, though my choice is arbitrary. "This one."

Elise squints her eyes dubiously. "Why that?"

I examine the image again. "I think it's the collar. It seems more understated."

"All the collars are the same, Proctor. They're the only thing that is."

A fraught moment passes; Elise begins roughly dragging the drawings into a pile.

"I might be wrong," I say. "Let me look at them again."

She shakes her head without looking at me, shoving her designs back into her portfolio. "No, when you're right, you're right. This is total crap."

"Elise, I didn't say that."

"You didn't have to. I don't know what I was thinking. I can't believe I just wasted my entire morning."

There's no point in offering further reassurances. After almost a decade together, I've learned that some version of this conversation is a staple of life with any creative personality and nothing to take personally; by afternoon Elise's spirits will brighten, and she'll be happily working away on something new. The constant struggle against self-doubt is simply a part of the process and amplifies her elation when everything comes together in the end (which it surely will; her designs go for top dollar at the best shops).

"Well," she sighs, rather hopelessly, "I guess I should get changed. I have an exercise class in an hour and a buyer's meeting at lunch. Not that I'll have anything to show for it." She gives me a guarded look. "You know, sometimes I worry about you, Proctor."

"Me? Why would you worry about me?"

"You just don't seem, I don't know . . . *interested* in very much these days. You're up half the night, you barely eat, you're not taking care of yourself."

"I'm fine, really. It's just a busy time at work."

"So maybe work is the problem. Maybe it's time to think about something else."

This, too, is an old conversation. "I've told you, I like what I do. People need me."

"And that's why you're at seventy-seven percent. And don't try to hide it. I checked the reader last night while you were sleeping. You left it in the bathroom."

She is speaking of my monitor. Every Prosperan has one: a small port embedded in our forearms, halfway between the inner elbow and the wrist. This is connected by a network of wires, one-tenth the width of a human hair and running along the bones, to a sensor array at the base of the cerebral cortex. It is our frontline tool for monitoring the constant ebb and flow of life—not merely our physical health but also the richer, more elaborate matrix that constitutes overall well-being. We are encouraged to check our number, measured in percentages, each evening, though the most ardently health-conscious among us are known to carry their readers with them everywhere they go. Generally speaking, my number has hovered in the mid-eighties since my early thirties, though lately I have seen the numbers decline, dipping a point or two every now and then and never fully recovering.

"Leaving it out like that," Elise says. "It's like you *wanted* me to see."

"It'll come up. I'm just tired."

"That's what I'm saying. The job's wearing on you. It hurts me to see you like this."

"What else would I do?"

Her face lights with a smile, meant to be encouraging. "How about painting? I think you'd be good at it. Or writing. You've talked about writing a book."

"Elise, I've never talked about writing a book."

She huffs a sigh; I'm not being a cooperative mate. "Well, *something* then. All those old people. Honestly, honey, I don't know how you face it all day."

"It's not like that. It's important, what I do. It makes me feel useful."

She looks at me pointedly. "Promise me you'll go see Warren, all right? Just to have yourself checked out. To make sure nothing else is going on."

Warren is an old friend; I've known him for years. A top official with the Ministry of Well-Being, Warren is a doctor in the same way that I am a traffic policeman—related professions, but hardly the same.

"Nothing's going on, Elise."

"Then that's what he'll say. I *care* about you, Proctor. I don't like to see you feeling down like this. Humor me, okay?"

A clean bill of health might at least put the conversation to rest. "I guess there's no harm."

"So, you'll go?"

I nod. "Fine, I'll go."

"Good." Smiling triumphantly—as if there were any doubt that she'd get her way in the end—she brings her face to mine and kisses me briskly on the mouth. "And for the love of God, Proctor, eat some breakfast."

She disappears into the bedroom and is out the front door before I know it. There's nothing more to say, really, about a situation that both of us know isn't likely to change. Nor does Elise actually need it to. It's all a game of sorts, whereby Elise expresses her concern about me and, having aired this thought, is free to move on. It's been my experience that a lot of human interaction comes down to just these sorts of exchanges, less an actual conversation than a form of parallel confession—the two parties performing their interior monologues, not really listening to each other but merely taking turns. I do not mean this cynically or as a statement of personal superiority; I'm as guilty as the next guy.

But beneath the conversation lies a second, unexpressed issue, one that has begun to weigh upon our union: the question of adopting a ward. Prosperans, unlike the support staff, can make no children of our own; sterility is a by-product of the reiteration process. This is a matter of mathematical necessity (we live on an island, after all) but also a generally welcome feature of our lives, as it allows for consequence-free sexual exploration while also sparing women the dangerous and disfiguring ordeal of childbirth. But adopting a ward is encouraged, and after eight years together, most couples would be well down the road to parenthood.

Yet somehow Elise and I cannot manage this. Generally, it's the wives who are the driving force, the husbands more or less willing to go along for the ride. But in our case, the opposite is true: I'm the one who wants to adopt. The strength of the impulse surprised me; it wasn't something I felt until I felt it, and I remember the moment this happened, not because there was some obvious stimulus but because there *wasn't:* I was relaxing on the patio on an unremarkably pleasant Saturday afternoon, Elise off somewhere, when out of the blue a sensation of incompleteness dropped into me that was so weirdly specific that I instantly knew what it was: somebody was missing. I was so excited to learn this about myself that I was ready to drive straight to the adoption agency and fill out the paperwork. But when Elise came home, and I told her what had happened, fully expecting her to join in my enthusiasm, I could barely get her to focus on the subject—I couldn't get her to focus at all. "Interesting," she said, not breaking her stride from patio to kitchen to living room. (I was actually following her, trying to make myself understood.) And: "I've really never thought about it." And: "Honestly, Proctor, when would we have time for that?" Words to that effect. I raised the matter again a day later, and then for several days after that, each time getting the same vague dismissals, and eventually I let the matter drop, hoping she'd come around to it on her own. But that hasn't happened, and I'm beginning to think it never will.

In the meantime, my low number warrants some attention. The morning has moved on, but as a managing director, I have some freedom in my comings and goings; I change into a swimsuit, grab a towel from the bath, and make my way down the long flight of stairs to the beach. The morning haze has burned off, though the light is still soft, with an appealing pinkish glow; the water is glassy-calm, as it always is in the morning, until heat building off the land draws in air from the south, bringing wind and surf.

I wade into the water and dive in.

I know what you are thinking: that I intend my morning swim

to deepen and extend my dream, to nudge its details to the surface so that I might, for instance, be able to see my mystery woman's face. And you would be partially correct. I do have a curiosity about these things. But I have always been a creature of the water. From early iteration, I have loved the ocean, and at university I swam competitively. I am hardly the swimmer I once was, of course—those days are gone, surrendered to younger men—but my spirit still feels at home in the sea as in no other place. (Odd to note that Elise is quite the opposite; the woman positively loathes the water. In all our years together, I've never once seen her so much as dangle her legs in a pool.)

I make my way outward, my muscles warming, my mind adrift on the metronomic rhythm of kicking and stroking and breathing. Beneath my face, fish wheel in vast schools, darts of silver in the blue; a carpet of underwater grasses undulates on the tide like a waving crowd as I pass. A quarter of a mile later, I adjust course to swim parallel to shore, proceed another quarter mile, and return to the beach, where I step from the waves to discover that I'm not alone.

A young woman is sitting on the sand, watching me. Probably a year or two off the ferry, she is slender and coltish, with white-blond hair in a pixie cut (a term I know from Elise, who briefly wore her hair this way), and wearing shorts and an oversized man's dress shirt. I know this girl, I realize—or, more precisely, know *of* her. How the story came my way I can't recall. But know her I do. I know her because of the scar.

New iterants do not arrive off the ferry in a state of absolute empty-headedness. Though their emotions are blunt, they possess working vocabularies sufficient to get them through the day, can perform pre-algebraic arithmetic, and have a basic understanding of the world's physical operations. Nearly all, for instance, can tell time, dress themselves, tie their shoes, and perform simple household chores, all without instruction. Others are capable of more complex tasks, such as riding a bicycle or using a telephone (though they have no one to call). That which they do not know, they quickly learn; they are voraciously observant, are natural mimics, pepper everyone they meet with questions, and gobble up information like starving people faced with the most glorious buffet. They also retain what might loosely be referred to as a "self." They express preferences and tastes—clothing, food, friends—and can be surprisingly dogmatic. They like to talk about themselves, like bores at a party. They are highly opinionated and frequently obstreperous, though also capable of astonishing bolts of joy. They are, in sum, very much like children, albeit large ones.

But, just like children, they have no sense. They are inveterate risk-takers, and their judgment is abysmal. That they don't all drown or get run over in the street is a miracle; one can hardly attend a social gathering without hearing a sleep-deprived guardian's white-knuckle account of death-defying foolishness. Usually these tales end well, with a punch line and an eye-rolling laugh from the other exhausted parents. But not always.

Thus, the famous scarred girl.

As our eyes meet, I sense immediately that my presence isn't altogether welcome. She is a girl alone, lost in her thoughts. But the beach is empty; we are, perhaps, the only two people on this strip of sand for miles in either direction, not ships passing in the night but vessels on a collision course. Some form of greeting is called for.

"Hello!" I call merrily. "Good morning!"

She says nothing back, though neither does she look away. I make my way up the sand. There is something forlorn about her, though the early years of iteration are, I know, a moody time. The scar, I see, is not quite as bad as I expected—a pink, puckered line that extends from below her left eye to the corner of her mouth. (An abrasion? A burn? I can't remember.) With a little concealer, it wouldn't be half so bad. The mark has the paradoxical effect of highlighting her otherwise perfectly proportioned face (wide, dark eyes, a pert and shapely nose, and a well-defined chin that she holds upward in a suggestively regal manner), while also reminding the observer how easily such a thing can be damaged—how chancy life is, in other words, no matter how hard we pretend otherwise.

"Mind if I rest a minute? I pretty much wore myself out."

I'm standing just a few feet away. She lifts her slender shoulders, her arms still encasing her folded legs.

"I never see anybody out here," I add, hoping to cheer her. "It's a beautiful time of day."

She glances past me toward the water, squinting against the morning light. "You swam a long way. I was watching you."

"Oh, it wasn't so far."

It is surely past nine o'clock. The fact that she isn't where she's supposed to be at this hour—school, obviously—occurs to me. But it's none of my affair, and I get the feeling that she'd rather be almost anyplace else.

"I can't swim at all," she offers neutrally. "We have a pool, but nobody ever uses it."

"That's too bad. They say that happens." I lower myself onto the sand. "I'm Proctor."

Another shrug. She is, like all young people, a master of shrugging. Her name, apparently, is not forthcoming.

"Why do you like it so much?" she asks.

"What's that now?"

"Swimming. You must *like* it, or you wouldn't *do* it."

Now I'm the one who shrugs. "I just always have. It makes me feel calm."

"What do you think about when you're doing it?"

I like this girl, her direct manner. "I guess I don't think about anything, really. That may be the point."

She weighs my answer, then looks once again into the distance. "Well, it must be nice," she says after a moment. "Not to think, I mean."

The situation is worse than I thought. Not that any of us

couldn't feel this way from time to time. I've done it myself on this very stretch of beach.

"You should give it a try," I offer, attempting to lift her mood. "I can teach you sometime, if you want."

She says nothing about this; she seems, in fact, not to have heard me. Another moment passes; then:

"What do you think's out there?" She lifts her chin toward the horizon. "Being the expert and all."

I turn my face toward the water: the sea, the sky, and the perfect, horizontal line of demarcation between the two. A circle wrapping the world.

"There's no way to know."

"But . . . something."

Her eyes grow more thoughtful, like she's trying to puzzle something out. I wish I had better answers for her.

"You're one of those guys who take people to the ferry, aren't you?" she asks suddenly. "A ferryman."

She must have heard her guardians saying something about me. "That's right."

"Is it sad?"

The question isn't accusing, merely curious. "Not really. Most people are glad to go when the time comes."

"Because they're old."

"There's that. But mostly it's the idea of what comes next. That they get to live a whole new life."

"What about you?"

"What about me what?"

"What's it like for you to take them? Do *you* get sad?"

It takes me a moment to process the question; it isn't something I've often considered or, for that matter, considered at all. I am performing a duty; the duty is useful; I'm good at it; people think well of me. It's the retiree's feelings that matter, not mine. This is the calculus by which I've measured my life.

"I wouldn't say so."

She looks at me pointedly. "I don't believe you."

"Why not?"

"You waited. You didn't answer right away."

I'm taken aback by her bluntness. Also the feeling that she might be right. "It was a complicated question. It's not really a yes or no thing."

The light has shifted toward midmorning, clean and bright, with a hint of a breeze off the water, making small, hissing waves upon the shore.

"I'm sorry to interrogate you like that," she says. "That was rude."

"No apology necessary." I smile to reassure her. "Those were good questions."

She scoops a handful of sand and begins to sift it through her fingers. "I'm not supposed to be here, you know."

"I had a feeling. I'm playing hooky myself, if you want to know the truth."

"You are?"

"It just seemed like too nice a day to be cooped up inside. But you might want to think about heading back. Your guardians are probably worried about you."

She gives a sarcastic little snort. "I seriously doubt that. I'm the last thing on anybody's mind, believe me."

"I'm sure that's not true."

"Yeah, well." She watches the last of the sand fall. "You're just going to have to trust me there."

A minute or two passes as, side by side, we watch the shushing waves. I'm out of my depth here; I know few if any young people; I have no idea how to advise her beyond the customary platitudes. *Look on the bright side. Tomorrow is another day.* Not wrong, but banalities just the same, which I sense she'd see through in a heartbeat.

"Well," I say, breaking the silence, "I have to get going." I rise and dust myself off. "It was really nice talking with you . . ."

"Caeli."

Caeli, from the Roman *caelus,* "from the heavens." It is a pleasant surprise to remember this from my brief and rather uninspired time as a student of classical languages. Also, the name seems to suit her, in the way that names sometimes do.

"It was nice talking with you, Caeli. Don't hang around too long, okay? I know you don't think anybody's worried about you, but they are."

She rolls her eyes at this. But she also smiles; my concern, rather parental, amuses her.

"Fine, if that'll make you happy." A pause follows, each of us uncertain how to steer things. "I guess I'll see you around, then?"

It's strange. From time to time one encounters someone with whom one shares an instant affinity. Who knows why this happens? And yet that is how I feel, this Wednesday morning in June. I feel as if I've made a friend.

"You bet."

I head down the beach. I don't look back; to do so feels as if it would be a violation of a newly established trust between us. But when I'm twenty steps away, she calls out to me.

"Did you mean it?"

I turn.

"About teaching me to swim."

The question reassures me. She is thinking about future days, something to look forward to.

"Sure," I say. "Absolutely."

She nods and looks out to sea once more. "Because I think I'd like to," she says. "I think swimming is something a person ought to learn."

At the bottom of the stairs I look up to see Doria, our housekeeper, waving urgently.

"Mr. Bennett! Mr. Bennett!"

I quicken my pace for the climb. "What is it?" She is a short, somewhat plump woman of indeterminate middle age.

"There's a man here for you."

"A man? Who?"

"He didn't say. He's waiting in the house."

Someone from the office, no doubt, come to reel me in. With a sigh, I take my towel from the piling and return to the house.

"Director Bennett?"

My visitor is standing in the middle of the living room—the precise middle, in fact, as if afraid to touch anything—holding a leather briefcase with the department insignia. Young as they come, clean-cut in the extreme, with flawless posture and an earnest, eager face, he is dressed in a dark suit and somber tie and shiny lace-ups.

"That's right."

"Jason Kim." He marches forward, hand jauntily extended. "I've been assigned to shadow you."

I'm thoroughly nonplussed. Mentoring a trainee: those days are long past for me.

"Let me just say, Director Bennett," he gushes, "what a great honor this is."

"I'm sorry, Mr. . . . Kim, was it?"

"Yes, sir. But please, call me Jason. Jason is fine."

"I'm afraid there must be some error. Nobody informed me about this."

Out it comes: the letter of appointment. I scan to the bottom for the signature. It's my own.

"When they told me I'd been assigned to you, I couldn't believe it. I've read all your case studies. Absolutely masterful."

I am, it seems, a victim of my own munificence. Some months ago, facing a decline in the retention of new hires, I sent a memo up the chain, proposing that we partner new recruits with senior enforcement officers. The idea was halfhearted, and I never expected anything to come of it. I certainly didn't intend to include *myself,* that's for sure. As for my signature: I sign dozens of documents every day with nary a glance.

"What would you like me to do first?"

I hand the letter back. "As you can see, Jason, it's been a busy morning for me." (Never mind that I'm standing in front of him wearing wet bathing trunks.) "Why don't I meet you back at the office? We can go over a few ground rules then. Two hours, say."

"I'm afraid that's not possible, sir." He reaches into his briefcase and produces a second letter, sealed in a blue envelope. "Your assistant told me to give you this."

Instantly I know what the envelope contains: a retirement contract. A ferry is scheduled to depart at one o'clock, and someone has made a last-minute decision to be on it. This isn't so unusual; for some, the decision to retire, once made, is best acted upon swiftly. Best to slip quietly away. I imagine I might feel the same when that day comes. What's done is done, even if it's everything.

What *is* unusual is the fact that the contract has come straight to me, rather than to a member of my staff—been brought to my home, no less, by an overimpressed, eager-beaver underling so freshly minted he smells like the ink on a new dollar bill.

"Wait outside at the car, please."

He looks at his watch. "But, Director Bennett—"

"I'm aware of the time, son. Here's my first rule. Are you listening?"

He stiffens. "Yes. Absolutely."

"Rule One: Do as I say, when I say. It's nothing personal, and it's not very complicated. Follow it, and we'll get along fine."

He nods vigorously, chastened.

"Off you go."

The front door clicks shut behind him. A sudden weariness punctures me; housebreaking a puppy isn't what I planned for the day. Nor do I look forward to managing a last-minute dash to the ferry. I might be dealing with a sudden impulse that, once the moment comes, evaporates in panic, making for an unpleasant scene.

Once the contract is signed, it can't be revoked; the retiree is going, like it or not. We have people to handle that, and it isn't always nice.

As for why the contract has come to me, I foresee two possibilities, neither welcome. One, the order is not voluntary. The monitor of the retiree in question had dipped below ten percent, mandating a judicial Writ of Compulsory Retirement. These are tricky circumstances. The retiree is probably no longer competent to act in his or her own interest, and other parties are likely involved: a spouse who cannot bring themselves to say goodbye or wards with a financial stake. In such instances, the oversight of an experienced ferryman, one at the level of managing director, is typically called for.

Or two, it's somebody I know.

Content to wait for the answer, I leave the envelope on the coffee table and prepare for the day. By the time I'm ready—showered, shaved, dressed in my own dark suit and well-shined wingtips—the clock reads 10:05. I discreetly draw the bedroom curtain aside. Outside, my shadow is leaning against the front fender of the car, a freshly washed department-issue black sedan. The tropical sun is pouring down; unless I miss my guess, the poor fellow is sweating profusely under his brand-new suit. He checks his watch (no doubt for the twentieth time) and puffs out his cheeks at the unremarkable news that time continues its forward march whether he likes it or not.

I return to the living room and open the envelope.

Replaying these events now, I pose the question:

Did I know?

Not merely the name on the contract; if I hadn't figured it out by then, I should have. Did I know the *rest* of it? Was that shiver I felt, as I unsealed the flaps, a premonition of all that was to come?

The mind works wondrously; it is capable of astonishing feats. It is the only machine in nature capable of thinking one thing while knowing its opposite. The bright, busy surface of life—that is the key. How easily it distracts us, like a magician who waves a wand with one hand while, with the other, he plucks a rabbit from his vest. Here is the golden morning, we say; here is the beautiful sea. Here is my beautiful home, my adoring wife, my morning cup of coffee, and my refreshing daybreak swim. We look no deeper into things because we do not desire this; neither are we meant to. That is the design of the world, to trick us into believing it is one thing, when it's entirely another.

I ask again: Did I know?

Of course I did. Of course I fucking knew.

2

It's past ten-thirty by the time we arrive. The crunch of tires on gravel and our slow, bumping passage over the potholed road, and then, all at once, the house appears: a sprawling, shingled structure standing with ramshackle dignity at the edge of the dunes. At the wheel, my shadow makes a little whistling sound—half admiration, half irony.

"Quite a place," he says.

It is. There are very few houses like it anymore, in this era of sterile lines and clean functionality. I instruct him to wait in the car. This obviously displeases him, but Rule One is Rule One. I haven't told him the name on the contract—the order went straight to my pocket a second after I read it—though it's possible he already knows. His arrival on this day of all days feels like no coincidence. Who is the babysitter, who the babysat?

"I mean it. I don't care if you see smoke billowing from the windows. Not one step from the car."

I exit the vehicle and approach the house. Time has not been kind. The paint is peeling off the trim in sheets; shingles have been stripped away by the ocean winds and never been replaced; a second-floor windowpane is cracked and held together by tape; a plastic tarp, weighted with bricks, blankets half the roof of the porch. Fifty yards to my left, partially obscured by vines, stands the tennis court, or what's left of it; the gardens look as if they've gone untended for years. The scene is thoroughly dispiriting, yet it is also home: the home to which my father brought his young bride over thirty years ago; the home where the two of them made a life together until its incomprehensible end; the home of my boyhood and its memories, for both good and ill.

As I mount the porch, the front door opens. A formal man, my father has dressed for the occasion, his outfit decidedly nautical: a navy blazer, crisp white trousers, and leather deck shoes. A handkerchief peeks from the breast pocket of his blazer, which bears the insignia of the yacht club where for many years he served as chair of the race committee. (Perhaps he still does; I wouldn't know.) Even at his advanced age—one hundred twenty-six—he is an impressive figure who occupies space with an air of ownership.

"Hello, Proctor." His eyes dart over my shoulder to the car and back again. His hair, as white and precise as his trousers, is damp from the shower and swept back off his forehead, the furrowed lines of the comb's teeth still visible against his pink scalp. "Thank you for coming so promptly."

We shake, like old friends. I detect a faint tremor in his grip—the kind of mild neurological unsteadiness that is typical of his advanced age. Three years have passed since we last saw each other, and even then, this occurred by accident—a chance encounter at a restaurant where Elise and I were dining with friends. (I might not have approached him at all if Elise hadn't made me go over to say hello.) It isn't ill will that inspired our estrangement, rather the tacit understanding that we were better off apart. My father, it must be said, is not a man to wear his emotions openly. In the aftermath of my mother's tragedy, I cannot recall that he shed a single tear or spoke a solitary word of comfort to me. Back then, this seemed a lack bordering on cruel, but such feelings have a way of moderating, and you can't say he didn't care very deeply for my mother—quite the opposite. Most men would have long since moved on to new arrangements. Yet twelve years later, here he is.

"Come in, won't you?"

He makes way for me to step into the entryway. Everything is just as I remember it, right down to the smell, a mélange of dust and general seaborne mustiness—a scent bomb that could send me reeling into the past, were I to permit this, which I have no intention of doing. I follow him to the living room. The space is so crowded with heavy upholstered furniture that it feels smaller than it is; white curtains, yellowed with age, billow in the open windows, like waving ghosts. The pair of us endure a silent moment, searching for words. From beyond the windows come the small detonations of waves.

"Would you like tea?" my father asks. "I was just about to make some."

I am mindful of the hour. If we don't keep moving, we might miss the ferry. But there is time enough for this. Tea, or champagne, or a strong whiskey: the ferryman does not decline such ceremonial, last-minute offers. This is a basic principle of the trade, one that mostly comes down to giving the retiree whatever he or she needs. In the last hours, most people experience a certain hesitancy. It is common to have doubts. It's no small thing to surrender all attachments—all the people and places and things that have served as ballast for the ship of life.

"Yes, thank you. A cup of tea would be nice."

He retreats to the kitchen. In his absence, I sit on the sofa and open my briefcase. Apart from my own report, there are two documents that warrant attention: the contract of voluntary retirement, by which my father will consign his physical person to the Nursery for reiteration, and the naming of his heir. Typically, all assets flow to a surviving spouse; when there is no surviving spouse, as is the case with my father, the entirety of the estate is absorbed by the Central Bank. In this manner, the wealth of

Prospera—and there's plenty to go around—doesn't concentrate within certain families. The retiree is allowed, however, to pass along a single item, as long as its value does not exceed two hundred thousand dollars. It is my responsibility as ferryman to act as the executor of this bequest.

The kettle whistles. My father returns, bearing a silver tray. His hands tremble as he sets the tray upon the table, making the spoons chime, the cups rattle in their saucers.

"Would you like me to pour?" I ask.

Too proud to accept, he waves my offer away. Thus, I am forced to watch with mounting anxiety while, with forced absorption, he goes about serving the tea. This unsteadiness an untrained person might notice. But there is something else—an intangible quality that my professional expertise has taught me to detect. One sees it in the eyes: a kind of metaphysical agitation, as if the retiree is attempting to tune out a sound that only they can hear, or to ignore a phalanx of hovering spirits.

The bad thoughts have begun.

There is, for every Prosperan, a number. It might be a hundred and twenty, or a hundred and thirty, or even, in rare instances, one fifty. It represents the number of years that a mind can carry before it breaks under the load. The genetic tinkering that blesses us with decades of healthful activity; the overall freedom from material want; the stimulating work we are encouraged to pursue; the rich communal matrix that binds us to the commonwealth; the romantic and sexual arrangements that stimulate and nourish us across the lengths of our iterations: none of these advancements to the human state can change one basic fact. Time itself has weight. It bears upon the mind—every joy, every regret, every minute of every day adding to the total—until the system by which we sort and file the data (I like chocolate; it's Wednesday; my ward is named Proctor; my wife, Cynthia, tied an anchor to her ankle and threw herself into the sea) collapses in a cascade of confusion.

There is no way to know when this will happen—until, as the

saying goes, you know. My father has not summoned me out of boredom. He isn't ill or in pain (at least not physically). He hasn't simply grown tired of life. I'm here because the world is no longer comfortable for him to live in. For my father, reality's gentle rain has become a bombardment. He might just as well be standing in a howling hurricane as spooning sugar into tea. Only by applying the most intense concentration is he able to maintain any sort of equilibrium, and the struggle exhausts him.

The tea, at long last, is successfully presented. We each take the opportunity to sip from our cups to make the effort of its delivery seem worth the trouble.

"Would it be all right if we got started?" I ask.

My father, silent, nods. Suddenly I am touched by the strangeness of it all. In almost two decades as a ferryman, I have performed this duty thousands of times. Perhaps a dozen retirees were people I might have called friends; acquaintances, another fifty more; the rest were total strangers. Never have I imagined doing it for my father.

"May I see your monitor, please?"

My father shrugs off his jacket and rolls up his sleeve. From my briefcase I remove the reader and plug it in. With a *ping*, the data starts to flow.

"Did I tell you I played tennis the other day?" my father says. "Not here, of course—at the club. The court—well, you've seen it. A total disaster. Do you remember our games?"

It's a pleasant memory I'm glad to share. "Yes, I do. Of course I do."

"The first time you beat me—I've never seen you so happy."

I send my mind back to that day. An improbable straight-set victory, 6–2, 6–3. The joy was like a flash of lightning.

"I think you let me win."

"Did I?" He purses his lips. "Well, perhaps I did. That nice new pro at the club, Javier. Do you know him?"

"I don't believe so."

"The nicest fellow. Absolutely the nicest. And that serve he has. Like a rocket."

I still play at the Harbor Club, and there's no one named Javier.

"I took the *Holiday* out afterward. Sailed it around the point like we used to."

His voice is distracted, his eyes damp and unfocused. More to the point, the *Holiday,* a twenty-two-foot racing sloop, has been gone for years. Perhaps he sailed a different boat and has simply confused the names. Perhaps he spent the day sitting in this very room, staring out the window, lost in the past.

"It was such a beautiful day," he says. "That's when I decided. I told myself, Malcolm, the next beautiful day, that will be the last one, and then you'll get on the ferry."

It is a sad thing to say; also, the right one. "I think that was a sound decision."

"Is that how other people do it?"

Many people pose this question, or some version of it. *Am I doing this right? Am I like other people? Is this normal?* We are herd animals, make no mistake.

"Sometimes. There's really no one way."

"And you don't mind? That I asked for you, I mean."

"Not at all. I'm glad you did."

The reader completes its work with a soft chime. His number appears on the screen: sixteen percent. Neither of us says a word—what is there to say? I unplug the wire from his arm—I'll download the full data later at the office—and put it away in my briefcase.

My father says, "It will be so strange, not to remember any of this."

"So you'll make new memories." I offer a smile. "That's the thing to focus on. Think how wonderful it's going to feel to be young again, your whole life ahead of you."

These are, of course, the durable talking points of my trade; I might just as well be reciting them out of a textbook for Human

Transitional Dynamics 101. They sound undeniably canned, but that doesn't make them any less true, or less helpful. (Back in the car, my shadow, whose name I've repressed, probably has a pile of flash cards in his jacket pocket with just these words. He probably quizzes himself on his lunch hour.)

"I know the house is a goner. I should have taken better care of it."

"You never know," I say. "Maybe somebody will want to fix it up."

"It just stopped seeming important somehow. I guess that's how this goes, isn't it? One day you just stop caring about things like that."

"Sometimes. Some people feel the opposite. Whatever feels best to you is the right way."

An empty moment follows.

"They say it's like falling asleep," my father says.

"That's right."

"Do you believe it?"

This, too, is a question commonly asked. "It's not something to believe or disbelieve. It's simply how it is."

"Lex non requirit verificari quod apparet curiae." He raises his eyebrows at me. "You don't follow?"

"My Latin is a little rusty. Why don't you tell me?"

He raises a finger and recites, "'The law does not require that to be proved which is apparent to the court.'"

"Ah."

"An idea that seems to have some bearing on today, though it only just occurs to me now." His expression softens. "You know, I always wished you'd taken that part of your education more seriously."

He isn't wrong; I was, at best, an indifferent scholar. It wasn't that books failed to interest me, only that my own thoughts interested me more.

He says, "Sorry, I forgot to ask. How's Elise?"

"Quite well, thank you. Busy, getting ready for the new season."

"Tell her I asked about her, won't you?"

"Absolutely. We are a little pressed for time, though. Should we take care of the contract now?"

He considers the question, then nods. "All right."

Perhaps this is the time to mention that my father is—or, rather, was—a lawyer, chief legal counsel to the Board of Overseers until my mother's death. It's entirely possible that the current permutation of the contract he is about to sign was, in fact, crafted by him. He hardly needs any instruction from me, in other words, but protocol is protocol. I need to read it aloud to him; I need to ask for his oral agreement; the contract needs to be signed in black ink (I carry a special pen for this; nothing is worse than having to scramble around for one at the last minute); I need to sign it as well, in my capacity as ferryman and legal witness.

We proceed. For some retirees, this is a tricky moment; a deeply human decision is being encoded into a wall of legalese. But not for my father, who speaks and loves the language of the law. As I recite my lines, his expression changes. There is a look of contentment, even nostalgia. For these few seconds, my father is a man in his element once again.

I reach the end. "And do you agree to all the terms as I've stated them here?"

"Yes."

My father takes the pen and quickly scrawls his signature. I do the same.

And just like that, it's done.

There's one last thing to see to.

I am his heir, of course; he has no one else. Ironic, and a little sad, that after decades of friendship and marriage and family and association, I am the only person left standing, like a last party guest who has failed to realize that his host is dressing for bed.

I ask him, "What would you like to bequeath?"

It would be easier, my father says, to simply show me. Without further explanation he leads me outside. A pathway of weathered planks guides us through the dunes and across a grassy estuary toward the beach. I am, by now, acutely aware of the time; once in the car, we will have to hurry. At the water's edge, standing on pylons, is the boathouse; that is where we are headed.

In the aftermath of my mother's death, my father resigned from his position as chief legal counsel to the board. It wasn't grief that caused this. My father cared deeply about the law, its intricate workings and ethical debates, and I think it would have softened the blow if he'd been permitted to carry on with his work. But for a man of his station, even a whiff of scandal could not be tolerated. For the better part of two years he did nothing at all, just moped around the house in his pajamas, filling in crossword puzzles and making everyone worry about him. But such a man could not stay idle forever, and as time went by, a hobby that had once served as a diversion from his job evolved into the thing itself—a wholly new career, as a builder of custom wooden boats. His designs became much sought after, prized for not only their seaworthiness but their attention to the grace notes: intricately carved bowsprits, decks and transoms of glossy teak, leather-wrapped tillers, brass hardware burnished to a blinding shine. It came as a pleasant shock to me, how the man I'd known as a rather dry intellectual transformed himself so completely into a craftsman—a man who actually *made* things that the world could put to practical use. Which only goes to show that people are more complicated than they let on, and that even tragedy (sometimes *only* tragedy) can open the door to who we really are.

My father's workshop faces the ocean, with a sloping ramp leading to the water's edge. We enter through a side door, into darkness. The air is rich with the smells of varnish and sawdust. My father fumbles for the light switch, and then, in a blaze, she appears.

A boat, of course—but what a boat. Even I, who lack my father's appreciation for nautical design, know exactly what I'm looking at: the man's crowning achievement. The vessel is not especially large. Twenty-five feet long, maybe a little more, seven or eight at the beam; a single sail, gaff-rigged, with a wide cockpit and a tiny cabin; no keel. A boat for the days like the ones we used to share, the three of us, sailing out to the point for a picnic lunch or a late-day jaunt (my parents called them "cocktail cruises"—a thermos of gin and tonics for them, orange juice for me) to enjoy the evening colors. A memory returns to me, vivid as a waking dream. The wind on my face and the snap of the sail; the firm heel of the hull and the taut, salty mainsheet in my fist; the lighted tips of the waves and the warm sun falling over us like a benediction; my parents seated in the stern, my father holding the tiller, my mother beside him, nestled under his arm, the wind tossing her hair, just a bit of it caught in the corner of her mouth as she laughs at something he has said and plucks the strand away. Why do certain arbitrary images stay with us, branded upon the walls of memory, while others sink forever into time's abyss?

I step forward. Resting in the cradle, my father's boat shines like a jewel upon felt. The urge to touch her—to run my fingertips along her hull—is so strong I actually do this. Even the lines look handmade.

"How long did this take you?"

"Two years."

In the presence of this magnificent creation, my father seems different, more himself. Banished for the moment is the air of distracted resignation. I know without being told that I stand in the presence of an additional, deeper truth. This is what my father was really waiting for; this is the last beautiful day. The day he finished *her.*

Circling the hull, I come around the stern. There, etched into a wooden plaque, is the vessel's name. *Cynthia.*

"I'm afraid I didn't have time to tidy up," my father says. "I hate leaving things a mess like this."

I understood what my father had done. His bequest is not for me, not truly; I am merely its handmaid. My mother's body was never recovered—just the rowboat, drifting in the tide, the anchor gone, the benches spattered with blood; no note. The last was, in a way, the hardest thing of all. Her death created an empty space with nothing to fill it, not even final words. It was a break in the natural order of things. In the eleventh hour, my father has attempted to correct this. His boat; his *Cynthia.* It is his way of putting her back in the world.

"Promise me you'll sail her."

"I will. Absolutely I will."

He falls silent a moment, feet shifting on the floorboards, hands buried in his pockets. "I know I didn't do the best job with you. Especially after . . ." He shrugs. "Well. What happened."

There is no conversation I want to have less right now, or ever. "It's all right. It's over."

"I just want you to know how sorry I am." He takes a long, heavy breath. "This is all my fault. There were things about her, son, things you didn't know."

The door opens behind him: my shadow. He's panting for breath; probably he ran through the entire house, looking for us. I could strangle him on the spot.

"I thought I told you to wait in the car."

"I'm sorry, sir. It's just, the time? I didn't think you'd want me to wait any longer."

I glance at my watch. It's a little past noon; the ferry is forty minutes away, more in traffic. And suddenly it hits me, like a blow to the chest. My father is going; my father is nearly gone. And once he's gone—when I stand on the pier and watch the ferry churn away—I will be the last of us. All the memories of the things that happened will be mine and mine alone.

"Give us a moment," I tell him.

But my shadow just stands there, fixed as a fencepost. I am, at this moment, capable of just about anything, including doing him bodily harm. But before this can happen, my father intervenes, turning to my shadow with his hand extended.

"How do you do? I'm Malcolm Bennett."

The look of shock on the boy's face is undeniable. So, he didn't know. As the two of them shake hands, his eyes dart to me, then back at my father. "You're . . . ?"

"That's correct. You work with my son, I see."

"Yes, sir. I'm his trainee."

"How fortunate for you. And your name?"

"Oh. Sorry. Jason Kim."

"Thank you for reminding us of the hour, Mr. Kim. We were just reminiscing a bit here and lost track of time."

"Sure." My shadow swallows laboriously. "I mean, of course."

"Excellent." My father beams a smile so disarming it's like a spotlight shined straight into the boy's face, and at once I see what the man's doing. Somebody needs to take the lead, to get us out of here and into the car, and I am proving myself utterly incapable. I'm on the verge of humiliating myself in front of a colleague two decades my junior, and this my father can't allow. It's enormously touching and sad to realize this fact.

My father swivels his smile to me. "Thank you for indulging an old man, Proctor. It was good to talk like this."

I can only nod.

"So?" he says, and rubs his hands together. "Shall we?"

My father and I ride together in the backseat. This is protocol—the ferryman doesn't let the retiree be alone, not for a second—although I would do this regardless. The roads are nearly empty—it is as if the world understands the gravity of our mission and has paused for us to pass—and my heart begins to calm. My father gazes out the window. I suppose he is saying goodbye to the world, though of course he'll be seeing it again, through fresh new eyes. His legs, in their crisp trousers, are elegantly crossed. His hands have stilled their nervous working and rest serenely in his lap. From time to time, he takes a sip of water from one of the bottles we keep in the car, but this is his only movement.

Clouds have rolled in off the sea, softening the light, banishing all shadow. As we cross the city's perimeter, traffic slows, but unless something unusual happens, we'll be on time. Around us, the buildings thicken—apartment complexes, offices, shopping establishments. Pedestrians appear as well: men and women in business attire, hustling to their various urgent destinations, or wearing exercise clothing, their faces radiant with exertion. At a shuttle stop, a group of young iterants in their academy uniforms—a plaid kilt and Peter Pan blouse for the girls; for the boys, khaki shorts and a blue polo shirt with the school insignia on the breast pocket—laugh and talk and jostle shoulders, the boys nervously watching the girls, the girls watching back, an ocular dance of youthful curiosity and desire that has been the same since time's beginning.

"It looks like rain," my father remarks—his first words since our departure.

Indeed, it does. The clouds have fattened, their gray underbellies hovering over the city. We enter Prospera's stately core. The car glides past Prosperity Plaza, with its vast green lawn and web of concentric pathways and central fountain, the great stone heart of the city. Drones buzz overhead, bobbing in the unsettled air, observing all. Hemming the plaza on two sides are the ministry buildings (Well-Being, Labor, Finance, Interior Works, Public Safety, and Human Resources, where Social Contracts is located); at the top of the square, like a patriarch presiding over a holiday gathering, sits Overseers Hall—a grand neoclassical structure with columns thick as tree trunks and an ascending runway of marble steps so numerous as to make even the fittest person pause at the top for breath. It is there, within its stately chambers, that the Board of Overseers goes about its mysterious, indispensable business; there that my father, for sixty years, arrived each day at 7:30 on the dot to compute and parse the law.

"Not long now," my shadow reports from the front.

The pier is located at the western edge of the U-shaped harbor.

The final leg of our journey takes us along Shoreline Drive, past waterfront apartments and restaurants and the busy marina. The beach is empty except for a few lone stragglers, organizing their towels and chairs and making their way to their cars. A gust of air buffets the vehicle. The silence of the car has begun to feel oppressive, though there's nothing I can, or should, do about this. The hour is not mine.

And it's at this moment that the worst begins to happen. My father begins to mutter.

Strange words, garbled words. Or perhaps not words at all, rather a phonetic expression of pure confusion. He looks frantically about, his head jerking like a bird's. I've seen this kind of thing before, always in retirees below ten percent. The gathering stress of the day—we're within sight of the ferry now—overwhelms their psychological defenses. The mental barricades they've constructed to maintain their equilibrium, to stay focused on the present reality, begin to collapse. It's like watching a dam burst.

"Dad, look at me."

He's breathing very fast; guttural syllables pour from his lips. One hand plucks at his seatbelt, the other at the door handle. My shadow's eyes dart to the rearview mirror. "Everything okay back there?"

"Malcolm Bennett," I command, *"look at me."*

I take his chin in my hand to steer his face toward mine. His eyes are damp and wide and full of terror. But in the next moment, something happens. My father breaks into a smile. It's unlike any smile I've seen before—glowing with wonder, almost beatific. It's as if a great happy light has switched on behind his eyes.

"Proctor?" he says. "Proctor, is it really you?"

"Do you need me to stop?" my shadow asks. "He doesn't sound okay."

"Keep driving."

"Proctor," my father says, "it's so good to see you." He wraps my hand, the one holding his chin, with both of his. His gaze is intent as a laser. He leans forward and lowers his voice. "Have we arrived?"

"Almost."

He nods. "Because I would very much like to arrive soon."

"Just keep your eyes on me. Everything's going to be fine."

"I'm cold," he says, and shivers. "I'm so very, very cold."

The car halts; my shadow pops from his seat and comes around to wait by my father's door. The lot is full of long black automobiles. Though I can't take my eyes off my father, lest my hold on him be lost, I sense, around us, the presence of a crowd—friends, families, associates from every branch of life, come to see their loved ones off, to bid them fond farewell. Watchmen in their blue uniforms and tall leather boots hover amid the throng.

"We're going to get out of the car," I instruct my father. "Can you do that with me?"

His expression sours. He shakes his head gravely. "The world is not the world."

The worst is upon me. I am losing him; he is sinking into madness. "Just stay with me. I'll be right here with you."

"You're not . . . *you.*"

My shadow opens my father's door, too soon. In a burst of panic my father is up and out of his seat before I can stop him. With astonishing strength, he shoves the door wide, hurling my shadow to the ground, and takes off running.

"Goddamnit!"

I emerge just in time to see my father disappear into the crowd at the top of the wharf. My shadow is sitting on the ground by the car with a dazed look on his face.

"I'm sorry, Director Bennett. He caught me completely by surprise."

"You fucking idiot!"

I launch after my father. The commotion at the car has not gone unnoticed. Three watchmen have joined the pursuit. Cries of alarm volley over the wharf. There's nothing more disturbing to our citizens than the scene that is now unfolding before their eyes; it is nothing less than the desecration of a temple. I am pushing, shoving, yelling for people to let me pass. Other ferrymen—colleagues all, men and women I will have to face in the hallways—are pulling their clients away, shielding their faces, telling them not to look.

My father reaches the top of the pier. It's the end of the line; there's no place left for him to go. Beside me, the ferry's engines catch with a roar and a gurgling swish of foam. Everything is automated; the boat doesn't even have a pilot. It leaves at one o'clock precisely, like it or not.

I won't be the first to reach my father. One of the watchmen has caught up to me. He is young and strong, a man eager to prove himself. Ropes of brawny muscle bulge beneath the blue fabric of his uniform. His leather belt creaks with gizmos—handcuffs, a shocker, a long, retractable baton. Why would such a man care that I've pulled my badge from my suit coat and held it high, that I have identified myself as a ferryman at the level of managing director, that I have ordered him to stand down? He is simply incapable, a dog cut from his leash. He applies a final burst of speed, and as my father turns to face his attacker, the watchman tackles him, the two of them hurtling to the concrete, and out comes the shocker, which he presses against my father's throat.

There's a god-awful crackling sound.

My father convulses once, his body stretched into grotesque rigidity as it arcs above the pavement, then collapses like a deflated balloon. The rest is a blur of heedless violence. Even as I enact it, I am aware that it will come back to haunt me—everything is being recorded by the drones that hover overhead. I reach down, yank the watchman by his belt to pull him off my father, wedge his neck into the crook of my elbow, and squeeze, compressing his carotid artery. He begins to fight me, clawing at my arms, but surprise is on my side, and I am no weakling. His life means nothing to me. He is, as far as I'm concerned, perfectly free to die. At the periphery of my awareness, the other watchmen stand motionless. Perhaps they have finally computed the meaning of my badge (now on the ground somewhere); perhaps they are simply too stupefied to act.

Somehow, the better part of wisdom triumphs. I release the watchman, who slithers to the ground, out like a light. Despite the chaos, retirees have begun to board the ferry, which issues a tart blast of its horn: the three-minute warning. I kneel beside my father. His eyes are open and blinking. Blood creeps along his hairline; one sleeve of his blazer has separated at the shoulder. His trousers are wet with a spreading stain of urine. How small he seems, how ruined! His dignity is gone, stolen from him at the last minute; all that remains is this frail, used-up body, this broken carriage of a man. His lips work soundlessly, fighting for speech. I bend to listen. A single word takes shape.

"Oranios."

The word is nothing I recognize. It isn't even a word, just the random babble of a disintegrating mind. "Dad, look at me." I cup the back of his head with one hand, his chin with the other, steering his face. The nature of the gesture is not lost on me. I have become the parent and he the child, another indignity I cannot spare him. The ferry's horn sounds twice. Two minutes.

"Don't you see?" he says. "It's all . . . Oranios."

I look up. My shadow has joined the two remaining officers, his face a portrait of mute incomprehension and shock. For the life of me I can't call up his name, though he repeated it less than an hour ago. The boy's out of his depth here, and I don't want his help anyway. I pull my father to his feet, position his left arm over my shoulder, and begin to half-drag, half-carry him down the dock. I am utterly nauseated; my limbs feel insubstantial as gelatin.

"Oranios," my father murmurs. "Oranios, Oranios, all Oranios . . ."

We reach the base of the gangplank. Retirees are gawking from the rail. A horrified silence has settled over everything; even the sky, churning with unfallen rain, seems to taunt me. I carry my father aboard. The wind has picked up; waves are slapping at the hull, making the lines creak in their cleats. The deck shifts drunkenly underfoot. I ease my father onto a bench and crouch before him. From somewhere a bottle of water is passed into my hand; I hold it to his lips. He manages a small sip, though the rest dribbles over his chin.

Three quick blasts. Thirty seconds and the ferry will pull away. Thirty seconds in which to say any final words that need to pass between us. And yet I can find none.

"Proctor?"

"Yes, I'm here."

"I'm frightened."

He shivers. The engine roars, then settles on its idle. I take his hand and hold it as the countdown commences. Ten. Nine. Eight.

"I understand."

"I just didn't want to forget her."

There are seconds that aren't seconds, not at all. They open around us like the bellows of a great cosmic accordion; within lies an infinite expanse, or so it feels. It is within this space that revelations come, and mine is this: there's only one thing I can do to help my father now, something I have never done before. I kiss him on the forehead.

"I love you," I tell him.

Seven. Six. Five. The engine's gears engage; the gangway is retracting. I will have to jump.

"I'm sorry, but I have to go."

Four. Three. Two.

One.

And gone.

Time passes mysteriously. One moment, it seems, I am on the ferry; the next, I am standing on the pier. The ferry recedes into the grayness of the water and the sky. The crowd dribbles away until I am alone. There comes a moment when I realize that the object of my attention is no longer visible; the ferry and all aboard it have been subsumed into a vast beyond.

From the far end of the pier, four figures approach. The first is my shadow, whose name, I suddenly recall, is Jason. Behind him are two of the watchmen; they, in turn, are assisting the third—the one I nearly strangled. I wait, hands in my pockets, as they make their way toward me.

Jason is holding my badge. Saying nothing, he hands it to me. As the watchmen move by—hoping to avoid me, no doubt—I order them to stop.

I mean these men no harm. That urge has passed. But neither do I wish them well.

"The three of you," I say.

They meet my eye with guilty expressions. They no longer seem like the brutes I recall from ten minutes ago. They are just boys doing a job, aware that they've flubbed it.

"You're fired."

Jason and I return to the car. I get in the front seat beside him. When he asks me where to go, I tell him to head back to the office. I need to file an incident report; it's best if such things are attended to quickly, while the memories are fresh. The last thing I want is for any aspect of my story to contradict the recordings made by the drones.

"What was that all about?" he asks me.

The world is not the world. You're not you. They are statements lacking any context; they float like orphaned atoms in a vacuum. Yet the order of their delivery implies a chain of thought. They relate, but only to each other. *Oranios. It's all Oranios.*

What is Oranios?

We proceed toward the plaza in silence. The pedestrians have thinned—the lunch break is over, and rain is moving in. As I note this, as if by celestial agreement, lightning forks the air above the harbor. A sporadic tapping on the roof of the car, and then the rain begins in earnest—a hot, pointy, tropical rain that sends the last people on the streets scurrying for cover. Café awnings. Office doorways. The shelters of shuttle stops. A few soldier on, holding briefcases and newspapers over their heads. It is a pleasant scene, one to excite the actions of memory. A rainy morning doing a jigsaw puzzle with my mother, and my delight in finding a single, perfect piece of sky. An afternoon when, walking home from a friend's house after school, I was caught in a sudden shower and, rather than seek cover, stood for many long minutes with my head rocked back to feel the rain on my face. A night in early marriage when Elise and I made love and went to sleep and awoke to a storm and, under its magical spell, turned to each other without words and made love once more to the sound of rain. I tell Jason to stop.

"Right here? It's pouring."

"Just pull over, please."

He draws to the curb.

"Take the rest of the afternoon off," I tell him.

"What about the report?"

"It can wait." He says nothing, just stares at me. "It's all right," I assure him. "You did fine. Just go."

I climb out; the car pulls away. Instantly, my suit is soaked. People are hurrying past, giving me curious, sidelong glances; others observe me skeptically from the awnings and doorways where they have taken refuge. Who is this man, standing in the rain? What is wrong with him? Does he have no sense?

News travels fast. Within hours, a day at most, word will go around: something awful happened at the ferry. But for now, I am no one to these people, a perfect stranger, which is all that I could wish for; and as I begin to walk, I draw up my collar and hunch my shoulders against the rain, so that they will not see me weeping.

3

The trip, Thea knows, is unwise.

At Prosperity Plaza, she catches a shuttle to the transfer station. The storm has moved through, the sun returned. Its tropical rays ricochet blindingly off the pavement and buildings and the leaves of the trees, which dribble with fat raindrops. At the station, she waits five minutes and then boards a second shuttle, the Annex Direct Line. Eyes flick up and then away as she takes a seat at the front; around her, conversations sink to a murmur. The shuttle is half full: men in their work clothes, slumped in their seats and reeking of sweat; women in the plain white costumes of maids or kitchen workers; a scattering of technical aides and clerks, the advantaged few, chosen for more challenging work.

With a pneumatic hiss, the doors close; the shuttle glides away from the station and down the hill. The ride to the causeway takes twenty minutes. Conversations gradually resume as her fellow passengers adjust to her presence. It's not as if Prosperans never visit the Annex, only that this happens rarely, and that when it does, they travel in groups and under some official imprimatur. Government fact-finding tours. Charity missions. (Prosperans delight in charity of all kinds.) Tourist excursions to satisfy the morbidly curious, who will *ooh* and *aah* over each charmingly squalid detail. A lone Prosperan, a woman no less, on the Annex Direct: she's like a single bright flower in a muddy field. Her shoes, with their three-inch heels and open toes, are in no way appropriate for the mucky streets of the Annex; her handbag costs what her fellow travelers probably make in a month. What's she doing here? What could such a woman intend, venturing into the Annex unescorted?

Four stops, each taking on more passengers; soon every seat is filled except the one beside her. More people are standing in the aisles. Progress slows as the shuttle pulls into a line of other vehicles at the base of the causeway. Thea's pulse quickens. Beads of sweat form in her armpits; her throat is suddenly parched. The confines of the shuttle feel unnaturally close. She knows how to handle herself, she has done all this before, but the body's response is beyond logic, wholly involuntary. They are third in line, then second. The remaining shuttle pulls away, revealing the guardhouse and gate. Three watchmen in tight blue uniforms are backed up by a pair of stripped-down, weaponized facsimiles—security faxes, they're called—human-sized and vaguely human-shaped but otherwise lacking any visible humanity. They are machines of pure utility, all gleaming rods and motorized pneumatics and pulsing interior lights. Everything they do makes noise.

The shuttle pulls to the gate and stops.

The watchman who boards is typical of his breed. Like the facsimiles, he possesses a mechanical aspect, nothing wasted: pale hair worn in a brush cut, stiff as wheat; a face of pitiless angles; muscles swelling inside his uniform like pressurized air. The leather of his boots and belt squeaks as he mounts the steps.

"IDs out."

The watchman glances at her—a quick, sidelong shifting of his eyes—as he passes. Row by row he examines the passengers' badges and runs them under the red beam of his scanner. All of this he performs with an air of oppressed loathing.

Thea is the last. The watchman's expression takes on a more ingratiating manner—*These people, can you believe them?*—though still possessing an inner hardness.

"Madam, good afternoon. May I see some identification?"

She opens her purse and hands him the document, which he scans.

"Very good, Ms. Dimopolous. May I ask the purpose of your visit to the Annex today?"

"I'm an art dealer. I'm here on behalf of a buyer."

"Art. Like . . . paintings?"

"Some of it is quite interesting, actually. In a primitive sort of way."

The notion amuses him. "Primitive," he repeats. "I'll just bet it is." He returns her ID. They are friends now, of a kind. Players on the same team. "Would you like me to call ahead for an escort?"

"That's kind of you, but no."

He eyes her with concern. "If you change your mind, let someone know. And I wouldn't advise staying after dark."

"Thank you, Officer. I don't intend to."

The ride across the causeway takes three minutes. In that brief span, one world is exchanged for another—spacious, manicured Prospera for the cramped confines of the Annex. Thea disembarks at the station and makes her way down the street. Even the weather seems different, the sunshine a force of exposure. The overstuffed apartments of drab concrete; the crowded market stalls of cast-off goods; the packs of children always underfoot; the stoops and corners where men idly linger, their eyes tracing her course.

It is dirty. It is dangerous. But it's alive. That's the word that Thea thinks of. The Annex is alive.

That's when she sees it: the first *A.* Painted on the side of a building in broad, dripping strokes, it's at least six feet across. A watchman stands guard over a pair of men in jumpsuits who are attempting to scrub it off with long, soapy brushes. Their efforts will come to nothing; the brick has already absorbed the paint into its pores. Whoever is responsible, they knew what they were doing. The whole wall will have to be painted over.

What does it mean? Thea has heard the stories; everyone has. Put more than two Prosperans in a room, and it's the first thing out of anyone's mouth. Domestics calling in sick. Road crews half-staffed. Listless efforts by janitors and gardeners and cooks. Not a general strike, yet; the term, for now, is "slowdown." No one can say how or even when it started.

"Hey, Mrs. Rich Lady."

The voice is a young boy's. He materializes in front of her, skipping backward to match her pace. A tangled mop of black hair, bare feet caked with mud, a cunning smile: he looks ten but could be as old as thirteen. Thea knows there are others waiting in the wings; he is merely the point man.

"You prossie?" he asks.

She doesn't slow her pace; neither does he. They proceed down the street in tandem, like a couple tangoing across a dance floor.

"You can tell your friends I see them."

"Friends? What friends?" Still grinning, he gives a little bow. "Antone Jones, at your service."

"I see. And what would your services include?"

"Whatever you might need! Antone will take care of it."

"For a fee, no doubt."

His eyes widen. "No fee! But whatever you can spare, I'd be much obliged."

They are approaching the end of the block. "Actually, there is something. A man is following me. Don't be obvious. See him? He's wearing a blue jacket and sunglasses."

Antone's eyes dart past her. "Everybody knows that one," he says. "Named Hanson. He's a big suit around here."

A suit: Shorthand for an agent of the State Security Service, or S3. He's been trailing Thea since she stepped off the shuttle.

"Maybe he is, I don't really know. But I want you and your friends to occupy him. For such a service, I'll pay you ten dollars."

"Twenty-five."

A shrewd one, this Antone. They are nearing the intersection, her moment to act. She withdraws a bill from her purse.

"Twenty. My final offer. Do we have a deal?"

The boy snatches the bill, whistles through his teeth, and is gone. Thea doesn't look back. At the corner she quickens her pace and turns right, then left, ducking into an alleyway, finally emerging into a busy marketplace of crowded stalls. Some people stare; others look away and step aside to let her pass. She turns into another alley, screened by tall tenements. Halfway down she comes to a door—heavy steel set into brick. Thea knocks three times, pauses, and knocks twice more. The sound of unbolting locks and a sliver of a man's face peers past the chain.

"I'm looking for Stefano."

"Who?"

"Mother sent me."

The door closes; the chain comes off.

"Inside," the man says. "Quickly."

Thea enters. A small room lighted by a single window of wired glass. In the corner is the cot where the man sleeps and, adjacent, a makeshift kitchen with a hot plate.

"Were you followed?" He is thick and muscular, with a smooth bald head and heavy eyebrows.

"I was, from the shuttle depot. I lost him in the market."

"What do you need?"

"Clothing. An ID."

"Let me see what I've got."

While she undresses, the man rummages through a packing crate. Thea selects a pair of cotton pants that tie with a string, a loose-fitting blouse, and a pair of leather boots. The clothing smells of sweat and age and work. She has brought her own makeup: some red and purple dabbed around her eyes, a flesh-toned liquid to blanch her lips, a yellowish powder to wash out her complexion. Her hair, with its delicate highlights and meticulous layers, can only be concealed; she ties it up and stuffs it under a man's cap.

"So?" she says.

The man regards her a moment. "Keep your head down, you should be okay. Let's take your picture."

A sheet is hung against the wall; Thea stands before it. A flash and the photo ejects from the bottom of the camera. The man disappears into a second room and returns shortly, carrying Thea's new ID badge, still warm from the laminator. Thea puts it in her pocket and opens her purse.

"You know Old Fred?" he asks.

Thea nods. Everybody knows Old Fred.

"I'll leave your things at his stall."

What he means is: Don't come back. He walks Thea to the door and draws back the bolts.

"Arrival come," he says.

"Arrival come."

She walks with her head down, staying out of sight of the drones and cameras. Of the man who had been trailing her, she detects no sign. She keeps her route circuitous, and by the time she arrives at her destination, the shadows have begun to lengthen. She's near the docks on the east side of the island; the air is rank with the smell of fish. Boats bob at the pier, the men unloading the day's catch into baskets. Some will go to the Annex; the best will find its way onto china plates in the homes and bistros of Prospera.

She takes the key from its hiding place behind a loose brick in the wall and lets herself into the building. After the drabness of the Annex, it's like stepping into a jungle, so alive is the room's interior with color and form. Huge painted canvases hang on every wall; others stand on easels dispersed throughout the space. Their brushstrokes are wild and bold, rich with emotion, yet somehow communicating great control and intention. The calm after rain. The sorrow of missing someone who departed long ago. The spark of a first, surprising love.

"Pappi," she says.

The old man is seated in front of a canvas on the far side of the room, his face pressed close to the surface. So intense is his concentration that he takes no notice of her approach.

"Pappi, it's me."

The spell breaks; he swivels his rigid face toward her. "Thea?"

His eyes are like clouded marbles; his hair, what's left of it, is a wild white mane. She steps into his warm embrace.

"What are you doing here?" he asks, grinning.

"You're not supposed to ask that."

"I'm assuming you're here to see Mother," Pappi says. "Well, she's not here."

"Actually, I came to buy some paintings." A joke, but not entirely. "I'm telling you, I can make you rich."

He laughs lightly. "That's all I need, somebody picking out my work to go with the sofa. 'Do you have something with more beige in it? How about cats? Do you have any paintings of cats?' "

Thea looks more closely at the canvas. "I see you've been doing the faces again."

It's a subject he returns to, again and again. No, not a "subject"; Pappi's paintings *have* no subjects. The word Thea would choose is "presence"—a subterranean stratum just visible below the surface of the work. Faces in the water. Faces in the clouds. Faces in the walls of buildings. A thread of faces, woven through the fabric of the world.

"Tell me what you see."

It's a game they play. Thea looks at the painting, letting her eyes travel its surface, drawing in the feeling of it.

"Solitude," she says after a moment. "No, that's not right. Loneliness. But a certain kind. You're awake in the middle of the night, but no one else is." She looks at him. "So?"

"You really got all that? I thought I was just kind of fucking around here. Say you're staying for dinner."

"I have to be gone by dark."

"So we'll eat early."

She should refuse. Time is short. Yet she cannot make herself do this. To stay for dinner, what's the harm? Just the prospect lifts her heart in a way that nothing has for months.

She kisses his bald head. "We'll see."

Pappi smiles; the matter has been decided. "Oh, Thea. Our Thea. The cousins will be so happy to see you."

She lets herself out through the back, into a second alley, filled with trash and weeds. She walks its length, comes to another door, and lets herself in. The odor is stronger here; the building was once used for fish processing. Long steel tables, meant for cutting and gutting, are pushed against the walls. At the rear, there's a hatch, flush to the floor. Thea hauls it open and descends into a basement hallway illuminated by a single weak bulb. The walls sweat, smelling of mildew and damp soil. She comes to another door. A camera, aimed downward, is positioned above it. She knocks and looks up at the lens.

A disembodied voice says, "Who goes there?"

"For fucksake, Quinn, open up."

"Hang on a second."

It takes more than a second—more like two minutes. Just as Thea is about to lose patience, the door opens.

"Wow," Quinn says, "dressing down, I see."

He doesn't look so hot himself. Somewhere north of forty, with pasty skin, eyes pulled in a permanent squint, and a poorly tended beard, he has the appearance of a once reasonably attractive man worn down by a long, exhausting illness.

"That's all you have to say? I thought we were friends."

"It's dangerous to have friends, haven't you heard? Did Mother call you?"

"I came on my own. Something happened at the ferry today."

He opens the door wider to let her through. "Let's see what you've got."

She enters a complex of cramped spaces. A room of bunks for movement members. A small kitchen, which doubles as an infirmary. And the centerpiece: the room known as "the lair."

Not more than fifteen feet square, it acts as the hub of the movement, its cerebral cortex. The room has the appearance of some kind of mechanical brain, packed with terminals, panels of lights and switches, jury-rigged tubes of conduit running everywhere, on the walls and floor and ceiling. Thea doesn't know what half of this stuff does.

Thea asks, "Can you call up today's drone feed from the pier?"

"What time?"

"A little before one o'clock. Say, twelve-fifty."

Quinn sits at his terminal. For a couple of seconds, he positions his hands above the keyboard, like a pianist preparing to unleash a storm of notes; then he begins to type. Data from the Central Information System flies up the monitor, a wall of letters and numbers, neon green against the black screen.

"Ta-da," Quinn says.

A window appears on the screen and, within it, a moving image. The pier, seen from above. People are filing aboard the ferry. A time stamp reads 12:53.

Quinn leans forward, pointing at the lower left corner of the monitor. "Is that you?"

"Yeah."

"What were you doing there?"

"Taking a walk on my lunch hour." She shrugs. "I go there sometimes."

"Pretty morbid way to spend your lunch hour."

"Never mind that. Just watch."

From the left side of the frame, a figure enters. He's running, somewhat clumsily, down the pier. Three more race after him—watchmen, shockers drawn—followed by a fourth figure in a dark suit. The drone swivels its eye and zooms in on the first man. He has nowhere to go; his flight is pointless. At the end of the pier he stops and turns toward his pursuers. He holds up his hands in a gesture of self-protection but then the first watchman tackles him to the ground and shoves the shocker to his throat. The man's body stiffens and goes limp.

"Nice fellow," Quinn says. "Hasn't anybody ever told him to respect his elders?"

The scene continues. The ferryman arrives, yanks the watchman up by the belt, and wedges his elbow underneath his chin.

"Now," Quinn says, tapping the glass of the monitor, "I do believe he's about to strangle that man."

It looks that way. Several seconds pass, and the guard's body slackens. The ferryman releases him; he falls to the ground.

"Aw, nuts," Quinn says.

The ferryman drops to his knees beside the old man and cups his head. The gesture is in a decidedly different key from what preceded it. It's tender, almost loving. The old man's eyes are open and staring at the sky. His lips begin to work.

"Freeze that," Thea says.

Quinn strikes a key and turns in his chair. "Is that who I think it is?"

"Yeah, and that's not all. The ferryman? I think that's his kid."

"Holy shit."

"Can you give me audio? I need to hear what he's saying."

Quinn rewinds, pauses at the moment where the ferryman kneels, fiddles with the audio, and starts again. The words are still lost in a wash of background sounds: the cries of the crowd, the rumble of the ferry's engines, the wind of the approaching storm.

"Can you clean it up somehow?" Thea asks.

Three more passes. Each time the sound improves, but only

slightly. The man's words still elude them. Quinn leans back and rubs a hand over his face. "There's just too much ambient noise."

"Do it again, but slowly. Frame by frame."

Quinn backs up and starts again.

"There," he says, and points at the man's mouth. "That's an *O*."

"*O*'s easy. Keep going."

"A?" Quinn asks.

"No," Thea says. "See how the muscles of his jaw tighten?"

"If you say so."

"That's an *R*. *O*, *R*, then *A*."

Quinn looks at her intently. A silence passes. "What the fuck," he says.

They move forward, but there's little need. They know what the man is saying.

O-R-A-N-I-O-S.

Oranios.

"I've been trying to get past that firewall for years," Quinn says, "and then the old guy comes along and says it like it's nothing."

They are sitting in the kitchen, drinking tea. The door opens behind them. Jess.

"Thea," she says happily.

Thea rises; the two women embrace.

"Mother's not here," Jess says.

"So I'm told."

When they part, Thea looks at her friend. The Jess that Thea met ten years ago was quite striking; she could have easily passed for a Prosperan. The beauty is still there, but with a leaner, harder edge. The face of a woman to whom much has happened, who lives on belief. Her hair, once long, is cut close to her scalp.

"And you?" Jess asks. "Are you all right over there?"

Thea shrugs. "I get a facial once a week. I'm working on my backhand."

"Did Mother call you?" Jess says.

"I came on my own," she says. "You need to see this."

In the lair, they show Jess the drone footage. "Right there," Quinn says, tapping the screen with a fingernail. "That's when he says it."

Jess drops into a chair. "Good God." She looks at Thea. "How did you find out about this?"

"I was there. I saw the whole thing, and I wasn't the only one. Half the island's heard the story by now."

Jess shifts her eyes to Quinn—all that's required. "I can keep an ear on traffic," the man responds. "We should learn soon enough."

She turns to Thea again. "What else do we know about the ferryman?"

"Quinn pulled up his personnel file. He's been with Social Contracts since he finished university. His position in the department is pretty high up, managing director for District Six. Probably he's in line for something bigger, given his wife's connections."

"Oh? Who's the wife?"

Thea tells her.

"Well, that's just *peachy*. Anything else?"

Thea shrugs. "They've been under contract for eight years but haven't taken on a ward. Given their position, it seems a little odd."

"So, a power couple, devoted to their careers," Jess suggests. "Could explain it."

"That, or trouble on the home front. Maybe they don't like each other very much."

"The big question is what *else* the old man might have said."

"Was he under surveillance?" Thea asks.

Jess thinks a moment. "He was, but it's been a while. A cook, I think. When he fired her a few years ago, Mother let it go."

"Why would she do that?"

Jess shrugs. *Who knows why she does what she does? She's Mother.*

"So we have no idea if this is his first . . . episode," Quinn says.

"We know shit, is what we know."

"Are you going to tell her?" Thea asks Jess.

"You want the job?" When Thea doesn't answer, Jess shrugs again. "Yeah, I'm gonna tell her."

Thea asks. "What do you want me to do?"

Jess considers the question. "We need to get close to the ferryman. Find out what he knows."

"I agree."

"Quinn?"

At his terminal, the man shrugs. "I should be able to come up with something we can use."

Jess gives Thea a sober look. "This is obvious, but I'm going to say it anyway. We're not the only people looking at that recording. The S3's going to be all over this, especially with everything else that's going on."

"I saw one of those *A*'s right by the shuttle station. It was kind of hard to miss."

"Yeah, and it's hardly the only one. Those things are popping up all over."

"Do we know who's doing it?"

Jess makes a face of demurral. "Nobody in the movement, as far as we know. At least, no one's taking responsibility. Whoever they are, they're stirring up a lot of trouble. The board's not going to let this thing go without a response. You'll want to watch your ass over there."

"Don't I always?"

"I'm just saying." Jess takes a long breath and lets it out. "I can't believe it. Fucking *Oranios*."

And then, for an hour, Thea gets to be a person.

All the cousins are there. They aren't actual cousins, of course. A collection of castoffs, street kids, they come and go, their numbers always changing. Pappi presides at one end of the table, his wife, Claire, at the other. She is a bountiful woman—bossy and bustling, like a warm hearth around which others gather. Chaos at the table, everyone talking at once. Antone is the last to arrive, sliding into the chair next to hers.

"I can't believe you tried to shake me down like that," Thea tells him.

"Took care of the suit, didn't I?" He is grinning ear to ear. "Besides, I got people. Things have to look a certain way."

"Like I'm a fool."

"Your words, prossie, not mine."

"You know, I wouldn't mind if you stopped calling me that."

Pappi taps his water glass with the edge of his knife, silencing the table. "Okay, everyone, you know the drill."

They all join hands, making the circle. Antone is on Thea's right, Quinn on her left, Jess across from her. She bows her head and closes her eyes.

"Great Soul, fashioner of the earth and heavens, thank you for your blessings and your watchful aid, and especially for Thea's presence at our table today. She is one of your bravest servants, a sister in our struggle to know the fullness of your Grand Design. Hold her safe in your hands so that she may do her vital work. Till arrival come."

A chorus from around the table: "Till arrival come."

Pappi raises his face with a grin. "And now that that's out of the way," he says, "we eat."

The plain fare of the Annex: loaves of rough, warm bread, a stew of cabbage and root vegetables, pitchers of water with slices of lemon and orange. As the food is passed around, Thea wonders, as she always does: Did the prayer make her feel something? Feel *anything*? She is touched by Pappi's words, even a little embarrassed, but is that all? She would not say that she is a true believer, exactly. Many times, she tried to will herself into the faith, hoping that it could offer her some comfort and direction—that it might fill the hollowness she feels. But despite her best efforts, this has failed to happen. It's Pappi's paintings she believes in, the sensation they arouse of a deeper dimension to life. It's as if there's no canvas at all, no paint; she is looking through a window, and what lies beyond that window is a more authentic reality, the true shape of the world.

But even as Thea thinks this, she puts the thought aside. Perhaps there's a Grand Design, perhaps not. It's the circle that saves her: the faint, almost electrical pulse that passes hand to hand. It's the only happiness she's ever known. That is the plain truth of the hour: she is happy.

"Slow down, Antone. You're going to make yourself sick."

The boy is using a slice of bread like a trowel to gobble up the stew. Before Thea knows it, his bowl is empty.

"Here," she says, and slides her bowl toward him, "take mine."

"You too good for it? Probably you eat nothing but cake."

"I'm not too good for it, Antone. I'm just not hungry."

He begins to work on the second bowl, speaking around a mouthful of stew. "Just making fun. Don't worry. You one of us."

The hour goes by too quickly. In the kitchen, where Thea has gone to help with the dishes, Claire pulls her aside.

"Are you really all right?" the woman asks her. "I'm worried about you. Pappi, too."

They are passing plates. "Honestly, I'm fine."

"Thea, I know you. I can see it."

"What do you see?"

The woman stops and studies her face. "Exhaustion. Worry. Loneliness. I don't know what Mother has you doing over there, and the less I know the better. But maybe it's time to just live your life. You've certainly earned it."

"She needs me."

"I'm sure she does. We all need you, Thea. Pappi most of all."

The guilt stings. Her face must show it, because Claire says, "Sorry, that wasn't fair of me."

"It's okay. It's nice to be needed."

"All I'm saying is, be careful."

"I know what I'm doing. You don't have to worry."

"Of course I do. Worrying's my job." Claire gives a tired smile. "That and keeping everybody fed."

The dishes washed, Thea says her goodbyes. She's cutting it close; darkness is minutes away. Old Fred's stall is closed up, his wares stored for the night. She uses Stefano's key to let herself in and finds her belongings in a paper sack. She changes quickly and reaches the station just as the last shuttle is boarding.

"A productive day, Ms. Dimopolous?"

It's the same watchman from earlier. Thea looks at his smug face.

"Yes, thank you," she says, and smiles. "I do believe it was."

For Callista Laird, chair of the Board of Overseers for All Prospera—sixtyish, toned, manicured, highlighted; slim gray pencil skirt, matching jacket, heels—the day has not gone well.

It began with the report from the Ministry of Labor. Callista was hoping for good news, but it was just the opposite: week to week, worker participation had declined an average of four percent over the last thirty days. People are beginning to notice, and those that haven't will soon enough. Garbage reeking uncollected at the curb. Farms and factories sitting idle. Restaurants without enough waiters and busboys, where it can take you an hour to get a table.

And now this . . . ugly business at the ferry.

The minute Callista heard, she imposed the usual media blackout, but the horse was already racing from the barn. The place is one big gossip factory; by dinnertime, nobody will be talking about anything else. *Have you heard . . . ? How terrible, what a shock, I can't believe nobody told you . . .* And Malcolm Bennett, of all people. You had to feel for the man, but honestly, why was he even still around? He should have been put on the ferry years ago.

A rap on the door and her aide appears. "Madam Chair, the minister of Public Safety has arrived."

"Thank you, Sacha. Send him in."

She rises to greet her visitor. "Minister Winspear. It's good of you to come at this hour."

"Not at all, Madam Chair."

"May I offer you something? Coffee? Tea? Something stronger, perhaps?"

"Not just now, thank you."

They sit. Callista takes a moment to regard the man across from her. About her age, he is trim and well built, with sharp cheekbones and a head of meticulously trimmed silver hair and a beard to match. Despite the late hour, his suit looks freshly pressed.

"I'm sure you know why I called you."

Winspear nods.

"Have you seen the drone footage?"

"Naturally."

"No one else?"

He shakes his head.

"And what is your impression?"

Winspear pauses, touching his beard. "The footage is . . . concerning."

"Don't bullshit me, Otto. Did Malcolm say it or not?"

"The audio isn't clear, but he may well have. We're interviewing witnesses now."

"How many are there?"

"Fifty-six, not counting retirees. Most were at a considerable distance, however. I don't think we need to be terribly concerned about them."

"Who do we need to worry about?"

"Besides Proctor? I'd say his trainee."

"I wasn't aware Proctor had one. Who's the trainee?"

"Jason Kim."

Callista's stomach tightens.

"The boy was just assigned," Otto continues. "This very morning, in fact."

Callista gives herself a moment. Isn't it somebody's job to catch these things before they happen?

"Madam Chair, if I may—" Winspear bends in his chair and removes a file from his briefcase. "After reviewing the footage, I did a little digging. This is a report from the Ministry of Well-Being, dated twenty-four years ago. Proctor's guardians brought him in for a full, unscheduled health assessment."

This is news to Callista. "What was wrong with him?"

"He was dreaming." Winspear places the file, open, on her desk. "Not only that, he was acting out. Quite dramatically, in fact."

Callista picks up the file and reads. *Subject Bennett, Proctor, age I+2, Guardians Malcolm and Cynthia Bennett. All monitor readings WNL. Subject complains of frequent and unsettling dreams though does not retain specific memories of their contents. Episodes of somnambulance described by maternal guardian, including destruction of household property.*

"As you can see," Winspear continues, "Proctor's been echoing practically since he got off the ferry."

Good God, how did they miss this? "Was there any follow-up?"

"Not that the record shows. He was young, these things do happen. Dr. Patty didn't make very much of it at the time."

Callista rises and turns to face the window behind her desk. Through her reflection, she sees the lights of the city and, beyond that, a trail of moonlight glowing on the surface of the outer harbor.

"Madam Chair—"

She holds up a hand. "Please, Otto. We've known each other too long."

"All right. Callista, then. I know this is personal for you. It always has been. But this . . . this is a *problem.*"

"Maybe Malcolm didn't say it."

"Maybe. Maybe he did and Proctor won't think anything of it. It was a stressful situation, he may have already forgotten all about it. Has Elise said anything to you?"

"Such as?"

"Any sort of change in the man's behavior. Difficulties at home, perhaps."

"She hasn't mentioned it. I'm not sure she would."

"And she seems well?"

She turns from the window.

"I'm sorry to press, Callista, but I need to keep on top of these things. I'm assuming you saw the new data from Labor?"

"What has that got to do with Proctor?"

"I'm afraid it has everything to do with him. Unrest is growing in the Annex. These Arrivalists—"

"Malcontents," she scoffs, tossing a hand. "Religious fanatics. We've dealt with their kind before."

"True. A certain amount of this kind of thing is to be expected, and we've always been able to manage it. But this is different. *Arrivalists,* Callista. Surely this choice of word hasn't escaped your attention."

"It could mean a lot of things, Otto."

"Yes, it could. But I don't think so, and I'll go out on a limb and say that neither do you. Somebody over there *knows* something. They may not *know* they know—at this point it's just a feeling—but it's spreading quickly across the Annex. There's talk, even, of a general strike." Otto pauses, settling back in his chair. "So along comes Malcolm Bennett and his little . . . episode on the pier. Proctor talking about it to his friends at the country club is one thing. Talking to the staff—that would be quite another. Whatever the man heard or thinks he heard, I'm sure these Arrivalists would be just as interested as we are."

"We still don't know if Malcolm said it."

"I concede that could be the case. The question is: Can we take that chance?"

Callista turns back to the window. Really, how magnificent the view is, how beguiling. The hour is just past seven; everywhere else, the people of Prospera are readying themselves for the evening, bathing and dressing and mixing cocktails and worrying about their dinner reservations.

"I thought, maybe just this once . . ."

"That the problem would fix itself?" Otto says. "You and I both know that's not how this works."

A silence passes.

"I almost forgot," Callista says, still facing away. "I understand you've engaged a new contract, Otto. Congratulations."

"Thank you. That's kind of you to say."

"A lovely girl, from what I hear. Still, she's a bit on the young side. You're going to get some stares." Before he can respond, she turns to face him again. "Thank you, Minister. I appreciate your coming in on such short notice."

"If you want me to speak to our friend—"

She stops him with a hand. "That will be all."

Winspear regards her a moment, his expression unreadable. Then he rises, takes up his briefcase—he rather pointedly leaves the file on her desk—and nods.

"Madam Chair."

Alone again, Callista crosses the room to the bar and pours herself a whiskey. Winspear is a cold fish; just being around the man always unsettles her. And the things that go on at Public Safety: well. Even Callista is a little vague on the subject.

She returns to the desk and sips the whiskey. What's on the docket for tonight? Probably they have tickets to something; they nearly always do. Just about now Julian will be pacing the floor, checking his watch every five seconds, wondering where she is.

A quiet knock on the door and her aide's face appears. "Madam, will there be anything else?"

Callista's thoughts have drifted far away. "That's fine, Sacha. You can go."

"Good night, Madam Chair."

A good girl, her Sacha. Polished, punctual, discreet to a fault. Sitting at her desk, Callista polishes off the whiskey. The phone is right there, waiting. Goddamn Malcolm Bennett. Goddamn Otto Winspear. Goddamn Proctor and goddamn this job and goddamn fucking all of it.

She knows what she has to do; it's just a matter of making herself do it.

4

"Oh, Proctor, I'm so, so sorry."

Standing in the foyer, Elise threw her arms around me.

"I came home as soon as I heard. Where have you been? My God, you're soaked."

Indeed, where had I been? It was as if the afternoon had unfolded in a state of only partial reality. Getting out of the car, the rainy streets, a city transformed. Walking, directionless, for miles. The sun emerging from the clouds, blindingly bright, scalding my eyes. At some point I'd found myself—and I use the phrase literally; I had no idea how I'd gotten there—outside the gates of the academy, wondering in some half-formed way if Caeli had ever made it to school (why should I do such a thing, why should I care?); then later, as evening came on, standing on the same strip of sand where she and I had met that morning, the scene in temporal reverse: the sun behind me now, tipping my shadow toward the water; the sky striped with color above the darkening sea; the air without motion, static as held breath; and the small curls of waves falling onto the wet margin of sand. *What do you think's out there?* Standing at the water's edge, I was taken by a sudden urge. I stripped to my shorts, placing my rain-soaked suit, folded, upon the sand, walked to the ocean's edge, and plunged into the waves.

Now, inexplicably, the day was over; I was home.

"It must have been terrible for you," Elise said.

"How did you hear?"

Even as I asked the question, I realized how stupid it was. She knew because everyone knew.

"I heard it from a buyer. I didn't know it was you, but then somebody called me from your office."

"Was his name Jason?"

"I think so. He said he was your trainee. I didn't even know you *had* one." She drew me into an even deeper hug. "At least you were there. I know how much it must have hurt to see him like that. But at least it wasn't a stranger with him, at the end. That's the important thing."

"Probably you're right."

She drew her face back, and I saw that her eyes were glassy with tears. Shouldn't I have been the one crying, touched by the love of my wife, comforting me in my hour of need? And yet I felt none of it. I wasn't feeling anything at all, except exhausted.

Elise said, "I'm sorry about this morning. I was so short with you. I only want you to be happy, Proctor. And then a thing like this happens . . ."

"I know you do. I'm sorry, too."

A final squeeze. "Let's get you out of these clothes."

Elise drew a bath while I undressed. Only as I sank into its warmth did I fully realize how cold I'd been, wandering all afternoon in my sopping suit and squishy shoes. I was tired to the bone. I remained until the water grew tepid, and by the time I emerged, three things had happened. My thoughts had cleared. Elise had made dinner. (I smelled garlic and wine.) And I had decided to quit my job.

To be a ferryman was to accept a certain role. We were meant to comfort, to calm. We were the shepherds of emotional order in one of life's most challenging moments. Six hours ago, in full view of a crowd of horrified onlookers, I had nearly asphyxiated a fellow public servant. In one thoughtless instant, I'd given the lie to everything I stood for; I'd brought dishonor to myself and my profession. It was entirely possible, now that I considered the matter, that I was about to be fired—or if not fired, shunted into some lesser role that would dwindle over time, a death by a thousand paper cuts. *Oh, former director Bennett? Down the hall, take a left, you'll find him in the storage closet next to the toilets.*

Not a prospect I relished. Better to fall on my sword like the warriors of old. Yes, I told myself, the time was at hand to move on.

I dressed and headed to the kitchen. Elise was putting the finishing touches on dinner. The table was set, the candles lit, our custom. An open bottle of wine and two glasses were sitting on the counter.

"Feeling any better?" she asked me.

I nodded. "I didn't realize how chilled I was."

Shaking out a colander, she tipped her head toward the wine. "Pour me one, would you?"

I carried our glasses to the table. The wine was a good, snappy red, made by someone we knew—a friend of Elise's who had taken over her guardian's winery on the island's north side. The climate there, drier in the summer and with more rainfall during the cooler months, was said to be the best for the richer varietals. Maybe I could be a vintner?

Dinner was served. For a while, we ate without speaking. I couldn't account for the strength of my appetite—I was ravenous—until I realized that I hadn't eaten a scrap all day. My plate was clean before I lifted my eyes to find Elise looking at me with tender concern. This good, kind woman. Why couldn't I fully embrace the fact of her? Did this happen to all married couples—that we became, over time, a union not of choice but of habit? I was glad for all of it—the consoling embraces, the cocoon of a warm bath, a nourishing dinner served by candlelight—yet the day's events made everything feel less solid to me, more contingent. It's as if they were aspects of a life that wasn't entirely mine, or was mine no longer. I thought of Caeli, my surprising new friend. Perhaps the trauma of the afternoon had distorted my sense of the encounter, but it seemed a harbinger of some sort. I was about to say something about it to Elise—"I met the most interesting girl today, it's quite a story, you may have heard of her, the girl with the scar"—when an uncomfortable thought stopped me. Antsy, middle-aged man plus pretty, troubled girl: the math did not look good. My interest in her could have easily been misconstrued. If the story had been about somebody else, I might have jumped to the same conclusion.

"Proctor? Okay?"

"Sorry." I managed one of those smiles—half bemusement, half apology—that I always seemed to be offering the world. The food on Elise's plate, I noticed, was more rearranged than eaten. "Just woolgathering. It was a pretty strange day."

"Would it help to talk about it?"

"I'm not sure what to say."

Elise reached across the table and took my hand. "You know I only want what's best for you."

"You don't have to say it. I've given it some thought. You were right this morning. Today made that pretty clear."

Her face lit with a delighted smile. "Proctor, that's wonderful. I'm so glad to hear you say it."

"It'll take a few weeks to wind things down. A month, maybe. I don't want to leave the department in the lurch. But once that's done, I'll ask for a leave of absence. Probably that would be the most graceful exit. It's not like I haven't accrued the time."

Elise was nodding along. "That makes a lot of sense. I think that's an excellent plan."

"I doubt I'll get any pushback after today. Probably it's what they'll want. I'm just saving them the trouble of saying it."

"Well, you're the best at what you do. Everybody says so. No shame in moving on while you're on top. A leave will give you time to consider your options."

"Actually, I have. I was thinking maybe teaching."

"Teaching." Elise nodded neutrally. She'd been hoping for something more adventurous, perhaps. "You mean, at the university level."

"I'm not sure." Which I absolutely was not. Teaching? Where the hell had that come from? And what would I have to teach anyone? "Anyway, it's just an idea I have."

"So maybe teaching. Maybe something else. The important thing is for you to figure out what you really *want* to do. Take me, for example. All I ever wanted to do was be a designer."

"You're certainly good at it."

"And you'd be good at *lots* of thing. So take your time. Enjoy yourself. There's no hurry." She jostled my hand. "And don't worry about the dishes. I want you to rest."

"Thanks, I am a little tired."

"It's the least I can do. You just go take it easy, okay?"

I carried the last of the wine to the patio, where I engaged in the project of polishing it off, watching the sea. It throbbed like a heartbeat, powering the earth. How strange it all was. A beautiful night, clear and full of stars, yet my father was nowhere in it.

That night, the dream was different.

I awakened to discover myself wandering an unknown street. Where was I? How had I come to be here? There were no houses, no lights anywhere. I was wearing my robe—beneath that, nothing at all. Somehow, in my fugue state, I had at least possessed the presence of mind to cover myself. A madman's modesty! At least I wouldn't be arrested for public indecency, merely insanity.

The night's events returned. Getting sloshed on the patio. Elise coming up behind me, taking my hand, leading me to bed. The closeness of the covers and the smoothness of her flesh and then the softness of her mouth on mine. The gathering heat and the familiar rhythms and the lassitude that came after, pulling me down and down.

The night air was shockingly cold; wispy clouds scudded across a silver rind of moon. The hour, unknown, felt late. I recognized nothing at all. Which way was home? What if someone saw me? How could I possibly explain myself, roaming around in the middle of the night in my bathrobe?

I chose a direction and began to walk. Dense vegetation hemmed the road on both sides, forming impenetrable walls. The minutes ticked by and still I saw nothing to tell me where I was. I had about given up hope, thinking dawn would find me exposed, when I came upon a rutted driveway. Such was my desperation that I decided to risk disturbing the house's occupants.

I followed the driveway into the foliage; at length, the house appeared. No lights glowed inside, but at such an hour, why would they? As I neared, discouraging details emerged. The lawn was badly overgrown; shades were drawn over the front windows; a downspout had peeled away from the side of the house. I tried the bell but heard no sound; the ringer was broken. I knocked to no avail, then again, more insistently. "Hello?" I called. "Is anyone home?"

Silence. I was becoming increasingly frantic. I was also freezing. When had the nights become so cold? I tried the handle, discovering that the door was unlocked. "Hello, I'm coming in!"

The air in the foyer was close and damp, with a faint tang of mildew. By this time the idea had begun to register that the house was deserted. I moved farther in. There was no furniture, no art on the walls, nothing to say that people lived here. I searched for a phone, but of course there was none. By the appearance of things, the house had been abandoned for years.

A sliding glass door opened from the living room onto the backyard. By this point I was looking just to look. I stepped through and found myself on a patio of uneven stones, weeds poking through the cracks. Beyond it lay a dark, open space.

It was a swimming pool. Just a few inches of fetid water, choked with debris, lined the bottom.

What had happened here? Where had the occupants gone? And why was there such a feeling of sadness to the place, of bitter loss and sudden flight?

That was when I saw the man.

He was standing at the edge of the patio, facing away, his head tipped skyward, like a stargazer's. He, too, was wearing some kind of dressing gown. I was in luck! A fellow wanderer, cast from bed by restless dreams to prowl the night as I did. I cleared my throat and, when he failed to stir, called out, "Excuse me, sir. I was wondering if you might help me."

Still, he said nothing. I approached him from behind. "I seem to be in need of assistance." Not wishing to alarm him, I stopped a few feet away. "You see, I'm rather lost."

Silence. Then:

"The stars are wrong."

What a peculiar remark. Was I hearing him correctly?

"I can't believe I never noticed before. Do you see?" Still facing away, he raised an arm and swept it over the sky. "The stars aren't right at *all*."

I felt suddenly, profoundly uncomfortable—almost afraid.

"But you've known it your whole life, haven't you? Time to wake up and smell the coffee."

He spun to face me. My limbs turned to gelatin; all strength left me. It was as if I were floating, unbound from the earth. A nightmare in which I was flying but could not make myself land and would float away forever.

The man was me.

"You've forgotten, haven't you?" He seized me by the shoulders, his grip firm as iron. "You sad fuck, you've forgotten everything."

My body was shaking. I could not form words.

"Open your eyes!"

"Please," I stammered. "I don't understand."

He reared back and slapped me across the face. The pain was immense. "Open them, I said!"

He slapped me again. I was whimpering like a dog; I had no strength to resist.

"Hey, sleepyhead!"

And again.

"Open your goddamn eyes!"

"Open your eyes, sleepyhead."

The cool sheets, the sun in my eyes, a face hovering above me. Elise.

"There you are," she said, smiling.

I blinked the dream away. Dressed for work, Elise was sitting on the edge of the bed, like a nurse about to take my temperature.

"What time is it?" I asked.

"Nine-thirty? Closer to ten."

This seemed impossible. My wife had been up for hours—risen, worked in her studio, exercised, eaten, bathed, and dressed, all without my being aware of it. A whole morning transpiring without me.

"I called Oona and told her you weren't feeling well. Stay and rest. I have things to do in town."

Oona was my assistant—though in reality she played a much wider role, more like a second-in-command. Possessing a head of flaming red hair and a brisk, no-nonsense manner, she was far too smart for her job. For years I'd expected her to move on to something more worthy of her talents, but so far she hadn't.

"Okay, but I still need to file my report."

"Really, Proctor? I'm sure someone else can do it."

"It doesn't work like that." Elise looked at me pointedly. "Okay," I said, "message received. But I'll have to do it sooner or later."

My answer seemed to satisfy her. She leaned down and pressed her mouth to mine, letting the kiss linger. "You were lovely last night."

Did she mean the sex? Or had I dreamed that as well?

"You, too."

She rose from the bed. Her outfit, I saw, was more polished than usual: a cream-colored silk blouse, open just enough to expose a bit of décolletage, a short, snug skirt, and high heels. A woman dressed for war. She must have had an important meeting with a buyer.

"Don't forget that thing tonight," she said.

I searched my memory but came up empty. "I'm sorry, you'll have to remind me."

She sighed. "The concert? My parents?"

My in-laws were devoted patrons of the arts. The opera, the symphony, the theater—they sat on all the boards and had season tickets to everything. They often invited us to accompany them.

"Right. Sorry I forgot."

Elise's smile returned. "It's just the stress," she said. "I totally get it." She bent down, kissed me again. "I'm so proud of you, Proctor. We'll get that number up. This change is for the best, you'll see."

I listened to the crunch of gravel as she pulled out of the drive—glad to be alone again, but also not. In the bathroom I used the reader to check my number: seventy-five. Not as bad as I feared, but still. What a state I was in! A state of dreams from which I awoke to find myself in yet more dreams. The notion ramified disturbingly. Who was to say I wasn't still asleep?

The day could be avoided no longer. I cleaned up, dressed, thought about breakfast but had no energy to actually do anything about it. I was sitting at the table, nursing a cup of coffee, when the doorbell rang. I assumed it would be Jason, whom I'd send packing, but it wasn't.

"Wow," Caeli said. "You totally forgot, didn't you?"

She was standing in the doorway, wearing a yellow terry-cloth dress over her bathing suit and carrying a woven bag.

"I didn't know you meant *today.* I don't remember agreeing to anything that specific."

"You said you'd teach me to swim. So, here I am."

"Shouldn't you be in school?"

"Totally overrated." Her eyes slid past me. "So, where's your wife?"

"She's at work."

"What does she do?"

"If you must know, she's a fashion designer."

"Fashion," Caeli echoed. Coming from her mouth, the word seemed patently ridiculous. "Like, dresses and stuff?"

"Yes, like dresses and stuff."

She nodded coolly, tucking a strand of blond hair behind an ear and wrinkling her nose. "One thing I should mention before we get going. I'm actually sort of afraid of the water."

"Oh? Why's that?"

She angled her head and gave me a look of pure condescension. *God, these adults, they're just preposterous, who put them in charge?* "I dunno, Mr. Ferryman, like maybe because it wants to drown me?"

"The ocean doesn't *want* anything. It just kind of *is*."

She smiled victoriously. "Well, there you go, I'm learning something already. I'll just wait here while you get ready."

It was true. She wasn't just afraid. She was terrified.

"No fucking way."

We were standing in water up to our waists. "Hey, watch the language."

Her jaw was trembling; all the color had drained from her face. "I mean it, this was a stupid idea."

"Have you ever even *been* in the ocean before?"

"Define 'been in.'"

"So, no."

"You could say it's something I've been meaning to get around to."

"This would be the part where I push you in."

"You wouldn't."

A shove and in she went. A second later she emerged, flailing and sputtering.

"You asshole!"

"You can stand there, you know."

She glared at me. "I know I can *stand.* I was just getting to that."

She rose.

"So," I asked, "how was it?"

"Horrible, thank you very much."

"I meant calling me an asshole."

She considered this. "Okay, that was pretty satisfying."

"Let's start with something easy to get you used to it. Can you hold your breath for twenty seconds?"

"Five?"

"Let's say ten. Come behind me and put your arms around my neck."

I crouched as she climbed aboard. "This is weird," she said.

"Not really. My mother taught me this way. Ready?"

"You're kind of freaking me out."

"Keep your eyes open. That's the fun part, seeing what's down there. Deep breath and . . . now."

Headfirst, I slid beneath the surface and pushed forward, pulling her like a cape. Two strokes, three, and I was piloting along the bottom. Tiny fish darted around us, a swirl of color. It was the moment that one loves, that *I* loved, the feeling of submergence in this hidden world of beauty and life. They moved by instinct, without thought. What did a fish care about anything, besides being a fish? What did the world above the surface mean to such a creature? Did it even exist for them, or was it just a heavenly glow they could not enter? I counted off the seconds, and when I reached ten, I pushed off the bottom and ascended, back into the sunny morning.

"Holy shit!"

I couldn't tell if she was amazed at what she'd done or angry with me for making her do it.

"Pretty cool, isn't it?"

"What were those things? Were they fish?"

"You're kidding, right? You've never seen fish before?"

"On a *plate.*" She came around behind me again. "Okay, Mr. Ferryman, time for another pony ride."

I couldn't stop myself from smiling; this was more fun than I'd had in a long time. After yesterday, who would have thought that I'd be giving a swimming lesson to the world's moodiest teenager? Again and again we dove under, gradually moving outward into deeper water. On our last trip I instructed her to let go and pull herself up. She popped to the surface, elated.

"Now for the real stuff," I said.

For an hour or so I guided her through a basic freestyle stroke. Her motions were poorly coordinated at the start—she stopped kicking whenever she turned her head to breathe, which made her sink like a rock—but bit by bit she got the hang of things. By the time we took a break it was nearly noon, the sun high in the sky, the two of us a pair of jolly co-conspirators in a scheme to thwart all institutional obligations for the day.

"Thanks for teaching me," Caeli said.

We were sitting on our towels with our backs against the rocks, pleasantly exhausted, our skin sticky with salt.

"Actually, I'm the one who should be thanking you."

"Oh? What for?"

"Yesterday you asked me if I got sad. It made me think. You were right, I do." I shrugged. "Or did."

"What do you mean, 'did'?"

The morning had put me in a mood of self-disclosure. "Something happened at work yesterday. I won't go into the particulars—it's too long a story. But I decided it was time to do something else with my life."

She looked at me skeptically. "So, you're not a ferryman anymore?"

"Well, for a little while longer. These things take time to sort out. But then on to something else, I guess. Got any suggestions?"

She considered the question. "Well, you're a pretty good swimming teacher. Is there money in a thing like that?"

"Ha-ha."

"Oh well, can't say I didn't try."

It came to me then. What had I said to Elise? *I was thinking maybe teaching.* Perhaps, unconsciously, I'd been speaking of Caeli, of this day.

"Something I don't get," Caeli said. "If it made you sad, why did you become a ferryman in the first place?"

Always my inquisitor. "Well, it didn't, not always. I helped a lot of people. I was good at it, too. You know what A-lines are?"

She squinted. "Some kind of test?"

"That's right. Your first year at university, you take a bunch of them. Based on how you do, your adviser helps you pick the kind of job you'd be best at. They're not tests of what you know, more like *how* you know. Things like 'shapes and spaces' and 'signs and semiotics.' Turns out I was pretty bad at those."

"I seriously have no idea what you're talking about."

I laughed. "Honestly, I didn't either. But one category made sense to me. It was called 'emotional intelligence.' Basically, it means the ability to understand what other people are feeling. That was my highest score."

"So, your adviser told you to be a ferryman?"

"Actually, no. He told me to be a lawyer. Which was, believe me, the last thing I wanted." I glanced Caeli's way just in time to catch her finishing up a yawn.

"Sorry, go on," she said.

"This is a boring story, isn't it?"

"A bit, yeah. I'm kinda sorry I asked. I like the part about understanding people's feelings, though. That sounds like a nice thing to be good at."

There was more to it, of course. A lot had to do with my mother, though I was too young to comprehend this at the time. Even though her tragedy lay years away, I've come to believe that even then I'd sensed the seed of woe that lay within her, and that my becoming a ferryman was a symbolic effort to forestall its flowering, to crack the code of her mysterious inner life so that she might not be alone with it.

"Can I ask you something else?" Caeli said.

I nodded at the sea.

"How come you've never said anything about my scar?"

The question took me by surprise. I'd long since ceased thinking of her in those terms. "To tell you the truth, I've kind of forgotten about it."

She rolled her eyes. "Oh, please."

"Honestly, it just doesn't look that bad to me."

"Then you would be the one person who thinks so."

"Lots of people have scars, Caeli. Maybe you can't see them, but they're there all the same."

"So, what's yours?"

"My mother killed herself."

I'd spoken thoughtlessly—that is to say, without thought. It was the great unmentionable, yet it was the core of my life, and I'd be lying if I didn't admit that there was comfort in confessing it: the comfort of shared pain. My crime was one of audience, choosing a child to hand this to.

"Wow," Caeli said. "You totally win."

"That wasn't fair of me. I apologize."

"I'm the one who asked. Why do you think she did it?"

"I wish I knew." *Proctor,* I thought, *what's wrong with you? Telling this tale to arguably the most depressed girl on earth?* "Listen, I'm serious. Forget I said anything. I was wrong to bring it up."

"You must be pretty pissed at her."

"Do you really want to talk about this?" When Caeli just looked at me, I shrugged. "Sometimes I am. Mostly I wish I could have done something to help."

"Like what?"

The answer came to me, stark in its clarity. "Told her I loved her, and please don't kill yourself."

We sat quietly for a time, watching the waves shush in and out.

"I'm really sorry," Caeli said.

"That's okay. It was a long time ago."

"It wasn't your fault. You may think so, but it wasn't."

I turned my face toward her. She was staring at the ground, idly carving figures in the sand with her finger. Circles within circles within circles.

"It was just a stupid mistake." Her voice was distant, airy. It was as if she'd gone away, into some abstract realm. "If she'd thought for even a second how it would make you feel, she never would have done it."

I was stunned. No one had ever spoken these words, or anything like them, to me—not ever. How might my life have gone differently if my father had said them? And the sad fact struck me: I hadn't said anything to him, either.

"Maybe so," I said. "I hope that's true."

Another silence descended over us, deeper than the first. The day was barely half over, yet it felt as if we'd been there much longer. I would have been thoroughly content to stay on the beach all day.

"Well," Caeli said finally, "I guess I should be going." She rose, jammed her feet into her sandals, and gathered her things. "Another lesson tomorrow?"

"Caeli, this has been fun, but I really think you need to go to school."

"Not really my thing."

"Yeah, I get that. But aren't you going to get in trouble?"

She looked at me for a few seconds and sighed with exasperation. "Fine, whatever you say."

"Honestly, it's not that I don't want to. It's just . . . there are rules. There's a way to do things."

"I said okay, didn't I? Go to school. Got it."

I felt kind of awful. On the other hand, how long could this last? She was someone else's ward, after all. With defeat in her stride, she made her way to the base of the path, where she stopped and turned to look at me. Not look: stare.

"Do you think we used to know each other?" she asked.

I understood what she meant. There was a theory, commonly held, that we were drawn to the people who had been important to us in previous iterations. "Convergence," this was called. It was said to create a sensation rather like déjà vu—a fleeting, dreamlike sense that one had lived all this before. People liked to joke about it. *I think I married you once! Maybe we slept together—I hope it was good!* Fun and games, but possessing an undertone of seriousness: the wish that our past lives might not be completely lost to us.

I smiled at her. "Maybe so."

"Because it kind of feels like it."

"We're friends now. That's the important thing."

She hoisted her bag higher on her shoulder. "Anyway, I just wanted to say that. Thanks for the lesson."

She began to climb the bluff. The girl wasn't wrong; I'd felt it, too. I knew convergence to be an entirely psychological phenomenon, nothing to trust or do much with; yet, watching her go, why did I feel such an acute sense of loss at her departure, a kind of instant loneliness? I realized that in all our hours together, I'd learned nothing substantive about her at all; I simply hadn't thought to ask. Our time together felt hermetically enclosed, sealed off from the rest of the world.

The footpath switch-backed up the bluff; her progress was slow, as if she were reluctant to leave, though probably this was just the steepness of the grade. At the top, she turned, saw me watching, waved. Hello? Goodbye? Both? I waved in reply.

I was still watching when she disappeared.

5

Thea arrives at ten-thirty to open the gallery.

DIMOPOLOUS GALLERY, MONDAYS–THURSDAYS, 10–5, FRIDAYS BY APPOINTMENT: so reads the sign, with a number to call. Located in a fashionable neighborhood of boutiques and specialty stores, it is flanked by a millinery on one side and a bookshop on the other; across the street stands a bakery that floods the block each morning with the aromas of baking bread and sweets. Thea disarms the sensors and turns on the lights; in the workroom, she heats water for tea. Her head is throbbing like an engine. She carries her tea to her desk in the gallery. It's what she needs, something warm to hold in her hands, though she'd rather have a drink—something strong to take the edge off her nerves.

She has three appointments scheduled, though her real task today is to bide her time until she hears something from Quinn that will put her in the path of one Proctor Bennett, ferryman. Guest lists, memberships, tee times; virtually everything is there, Quinn's told her, if you know where to look. One time, the man managed to figure out that a certain deputy underminister of Finance, his marital contract recently expired, took the air each day at precisely 12:30, always following the same route from his office. Thus, the broken strap on Thea's handbag, spilling its contents onto the pavement at his feet.

Where will Quinn's message come from? There's simply no way to know. Mother's people could be anyone, anywhere. Housekeepers, janitors, landscapers, waiters. They move through Prospera with their eyes and ears open, noting who plays tennis with whom, picking papers from the rubbish bins, eavesdropping on conversations as they pour the wine and pluck the dirty dishes from the table. Others, like Thea, go deeper. They aren't pouring the wine; they're drinking it. Nights of shameless flirting. *You work at the security service? I've always wondered what that's like, it must be so fascinating, tell me more . . .* while, beneath the table, a hand finds someone's knee.

Beyond the windows of the gallery, pedestrians flow obliviously past. How happy they all seem, how abundantly healthful and positive. Prosperans don't just meet the new day; they storm it like an enemy trench. "Live Exceptionally!" The messages are everywhere—on billboards, in the pages of magazines, between programs on TV. "Express Your Potential!" "Be Your Best Self Today!"

Thea doesn't feel like her best self. When she returned to her apartment last night, she was half-expecting to find a couple of suits at her door. The flash of the badge, the hand on her shoulder—it's the fear she lives with every day, like a scene from a movie always playing in her head. By the time she stepped off the elevator and turned the corner, keys in hand, she was actually surprised to find nobody waiting for her—only a note from a neighbor asking Thea if she could check on her cat over the weekend. ("Plenty of food in the bowl. Going to the country with friends. Hope you don't mind!")

The silence of her apartment nearly undid her. How awful it

was, to be alone with one's thoughts. Lying on the couch with the lights turned off, she thought of Proctor Bennett. Who was Proctor Bennett? Just another cog in the machine, but there was something about the man. Something . . . different. Thea replayed the video in her mind, frame by frame. The commotion on the pier and the jolt of the shocker; the old man stiffening and Proctor with the watchman's neck in the crook of his elbow; the exchange of whispered words and Proctor hoisting the old man to his feet and wrapping his arm around his waist to bear his weight; a pause in the action as, preparing to make a dash for the ferry, he adjusted his balance and pivoted his face to the sky.

Freeze it.

The face that Thea saw was not unhandsome. Dark hair swept back from his temples and a slightly expanded forehead; a sturdy brow and jawline; a small, though full-lipped, mouth. His strength was evident in the bulk of muscle straining the shoulders of his suit jacket. He presented, in sum, an appealing if generic specimen of midlife Prosperan manhood: well groomed, well exercised, and well constructed, fighting the good fight and mostly winning.

But that wasn't what the man's face *said* to her.

Not his face: his eyes. He'd looked up at the drone—the gesture was involuntary—yet he didn't seem to be looking at anything at all. It was as if he were beaming his thoughts to some invisible realm from which some aid or comfort might be coming. *Help me,* the man's eyes said. *I don't know why I'm doing this. Help me understand.*

After that, she drank. A glass became two, then three, which became, in due course, the entire bottle, and the next thing Thea knew, she was lying on the sofa in her clothing, sunlight pounding her eyes.

She casts her bleary eyes around the walls of the gallery, which only makes her feel worse. How boring it all is, how lifeless, how stale. Sunsets. Mountain vistas. Still lifes of bottles and flowers and fruit. Somebody's dog.

Thea sighs. These squares on the walls: they're not paintings. They're paint.

She's filing invoices in the workroom when the bell rings: her first appointment. She checks herself quickly in the mirror and steps into the gallery, where her visitor is waiting, holding a cardboard tray of coffee in paper cups.

"Sandra!"

"Thea!"

A quick embrace, made awkward by the coffee and the obligatory air kisses. Sandra, in black leggings and ballet slippers and a long-tailed shirt of shimmering fabric, has come straight from the yoga studio down the street. Her hair is clipped back, her face damp and flushed with high-minded health.

"I brought you a latte," she says and pries a cup from the tray. "Soy, yes?"

Thea hates soy; it tastes like paste. She's not much of a coffee person, either. But the customer is always right. She sips, scalding the tip of her tongue. "Thanks, I needed that."

"Rough night?"

"Does it show?"

Sandra licks foam from the rim of her cup. "The single life. Enjoy it while you can, believe me."

The travails of Sandra's marriage constitute the backbone of her major talking points. Her speech on virtually any subject is peppered with allusions to her husband's tiny crimes: late arrivals, insensitive remarks, forgotten occasions, clumsy sexual performances. Thea's sense of the man is assembled entirely from these complaints. She doesn't even know his name.

Thea smiles. "It has its perks."

"You really should come to class with me. This morning? I checked my monitor? Ninety-two! Ninety-two, at my age!"

Thea has no idea how old Sandra is. She's met septuagenarians who could pass for fifty, or even forty-five. The woman could be a hundred for all Thea knows.

"The studio has this great new instructor," Sandra goes on, a little breathlessly. "He did this thing, I'm not kidding, where he did a headstand holding himself up with his fingertips."

"Wow," says Thea.

"Plus he throws in a lot of Zen stuff, getting in touch with universal consciousness, that sort of thing." She rummages in her purse, comes up with a folded piece of paper, and reads: "'As a bee gathering nectar does not disturb the color and fragrance of the flower, so do the wise move through the world.'" She looks up. "Inspiring, am I right? I made him repeat it after class so I could write it down."

Thea nods agreeably. "He sounds interesting."

"A little woo-woo, okay, but when you think about it, it makes a lot of sense. Plus he's super cute. Like, *gorgeous.*"

On to business. Sandra explains what she's looking for. Not for herself; she's a decorator, with a list of well-heeled clients. Her current project is a large apartment near the opera house—sleek, modern, lots of glass. They move through the gallery, Sandra taking notes, and then look through the catalogs of the artists she likes. By the time they're done, it's nearly lunchtime. At the door, more hugs and air kisses; Sandra extracts Thea's promise to try her new yoga instructor, whose name is Raymond.

"I mean, imagine what the man could do with those fingers of his. Oh," she says, "I almost forgot." From her purse she produces a small envelope, which she holds out to Thea. "For you," she says.

How odd; the encounter has suddenly acquired a perplexing new dimension. Thea opens the envelope. A ticket.

"A mutual friend thought it might be something you'd enjoy," Sandra says.

Thea looks up. Ditzy Sandra! Who would have thought?

"Thank you," Thea says. "That's very thoughtful. I'm sure I will."

Sandra breaks the tension with a gleaming smile. "Well, super!" At the threshold she turns and gives Thea a knowing wink. "And don't forget what I said about Raymond. I swear, if somebody else doesn't fuck him, I will."

Thea locks the door behind her and draws the shade. She

makes two quick phone calls, begging off her afternoon appointments, then two more, to the nail shop and the salon. *It's Thea Dimopolous, short notice I know, but can you squeeze me in? That's wonderful, you're an angel, I can't thank you enough . . .*

She tucks Quinn's envelope into her purse and exits the gallery. The lunch hour is in full swing. She takes a moment just to breathe and then steps forward into the river of humanity flowing past and down the busy street.

6

It was a little past two when I returned to the house—time enough, I thought, to get the worst part over with.

Showered and dressed, I made my way to the shuttle stop at the end of our street. The schedule on the glass said I had ten minutes to wait. It had been years since I'd ridden one. As a ferryman at the level of managing director, I had a car and driver at my disposal at any hour of the day. But if I was to live without such perks, I thought, best to get used to it now.

And, come to think of it, just how long had it been? Try as I might, I could recall no occasion more recent than the morning my mother had taken me to see Dr. Patty. Surely this was not the case, yet it seemed so. My mind went back to that day. *You know I love you, don't you?* Sitting at the shuttle stop, I suddenly missed her intensely, though the emotion was different from sadness. There was a peacefulness to it, as if, via this small reenactment of our day together, I had awakened a dormant feeling within myself—the feeling of being her son.

The shuttle arrived. At this hour of the day, it was occupied entirely by support staff. I walked down the aisle and took the first available seat, beside a man in brown coveralls. The air around him was a rank zone of stale sweat with a fecal undertone. The jumpsuit swam on him, though he possessed an aura of sleek strength. I was suddenly aware of myself in a not entirely comfortable way. Like many Prosperans, I'd never crossed the causeway to the Annex, having had no occasion to do so, and my experience of the support staff was limited to a handful of individuals and couldn't be called even remotely personal. To ease the awkwardness, I decided to speak.

"How's your day going?" I asked him.

Eyes staring forward, he shrugged. "Okay."

"What kind of work do you do?"

Another extra beat. Everything about him said he didn't want to talk to me. "Sewers," he said.

Thus, the smell. "That sounds like challenging work."

"I guess."

Why was I doing this, making this poor fellow think about his day, wading in waste? A person could learn a lot just by looking at our shoes: his bulky work boots, unlaced to let the heat escape, next to my polished loafers.

A dumb thing to say, but I said it. "I'm sorry."

He turned his face toward me. His teeth were stained and oversized, crowding his mouth; sometime in the past, his nose had been nearly demolished.

"What are you sorry about?"

"Forgive me. It was a stupid remark."

His eyes traveled the length of my body, like a butcher sizing up a side of beef. The balance of power had reversed; he was now my inquisitor.

"I don't want your pity," he said.

"That's not what I meant."

That was when I saw it: in his eyes, a glow of pure disdain, like a pilot light burning in the furnace of his brain. This man: he hated me!

"So what *did* you mean?"

"I didn't mean anything. Forget I said it."

"You're the one who brought it up. You said you were sorry, so why don't you tell me? Exactly what are you sorry for, prossie?"

The word was like a siren going off. All chatter ceased among the passengers. It occurred to me that I had wandered into dicey territory. From what I knew of the Annex—again, not much—fights were common. Words were exchanged, emotions ran wild, and the next thing you knew there was blood on the walls and a body on the floor. My seatmate didn't outweigh me, and I was more than capable, but his strength was earned—a crucial difference. Through the rearview mirror, the driver shot me a glance of warning. *Mister, what are you doing? Shut the hell up.*

"I was trying to be nice. If I've upset you, I apologize."

"You don't know the first thing about me. Maybe I enjoy shoveling your shit. Maybe I think shoveling your shit is the greatest thing in the world."

"Okay, maybe you do. That's your business."

"You should try it sometime. You might like it."

This ride couldn't end fast enough. What had I imagined would happen, attempting to engage him? That the two of us could have a jolly chat about our days? To be hated—I simply had no experience with this.

The bus stopped and a man got on. A lanky, bearded fellow, somewhat disheveled, with tired, squinting eyes. He took the seat across the aisle and opened his shoulder bag, from which he removed a book—slender, with dark covers. He folded one knee over the other, settled the bag onto his lap, and opened the book, exposing its mysterious title: *Principles of Arrivalism.*

"Hey, prossie," my seatmate said, "want to hear a story?"

"What?" I was thoroughly rattled. Beyond the windows, the outer suburbs flowed past.

"I'm sure you'll find it interesting. So my wife, Tess, she's a maid. There's this lady, rich person like yourself, Tess helps out with all her parties. She's done it for years, the two of them are like old friends. With me so far?"

"Your wife's a maid," I repeated, idiotically.

"Exactly. So, one night, Tess is working in the kitchen while the lady's getting ready for her party, and wouldn't you know, she can't find a necklace she wants. It's something old, probably worth a bundle. She makes a big deal about the necklace, goes tearing through the house. 'Where's my necklace, where's my necklace?' Know what she does when she can't find it?"

I saw where this was going, and it wasn't good. "She accuses your wife of stealing it."

He grinned a mouth of ruined teeth. "Now, that's the first *intelligent* thing you've said. Forget she's worked for the woman for years. Next thing you know, there's a car in the drive and the watchmen are hauling her away. Still with me, prossie?"

I was, though I could think of nothing to say in the presence of this ghastly tale. I glanced up to see the man across the aisle watching me. His eyes met mine in a manner that suggested more than a casual interest—something more personal, as if he had a stake in the outcome.

My seatmate went on: "Of course, I didn't know anything about this. I don't hear anything at all for four days, until Tess comes home. I almost don't recognize her. Face beat to a pulp. But her face wasn't the worst thing."

The man across the aisle finally spoke up: "Friend, why don't you leave the man alone?"

My seatmate ignored him. "Want to know what they did to her?"

I absolutely did not.

"Go on." He nudged my side with his elbow. "Take a guess."

The other man said, more forcefully, "I think that's enough."

My seatmate shot him an icy glare. "You mind? I'm telling a story here."

I felt almost ill. "I don't know."

My seatmate held up his right hand, folded his thumb into his palm and made a flapping gesture with his fingers. "What they do to a thief is, they cut off a thumb. Pretty much all she can do now is wave." He drilled me with a diabolical smile. "So, what do you think of my story?"

I was struck silent, aware that he had told me this grisly tale because I was implicated in its cruelty. As far as he was concerned, the woman with the necklace might just as well have been me.

"Cat got your tongue, prossie?"

What I came up with, laughably, was "Did they ever find the necklace?"

"Sure they did. I was just getting to that. The lady found it in the couch cushions. Wrote Tess a nice note of apology. We hung it on the fridge."

Now I really *did* feel sick. Saliva washed down the sides of my mouth; a taste of bile burbled in my throat. "That's . . . horrible."

"You're damn right it is. Want to know the best part?"

Good God, there was more?

"I made the whole thing up. I don't even have a fucking wife." He erupted in laughter. "You should see your face, prossie."

I was shaking with anger; I could feel the pulse in my neck. "You bastard."

"You said you were sorry. I wanted to give you something to be sorry about." He turned his face away. "You people, what a bunch of phonies."

And that, mercifully, was the end of it. We sat in silence for the rest of the ride, each of us pretending the other wasn't there. *You heartless prick!* I wanted to shout. *What gives you the right to do that to someone?* By the time we reached the plaza, my head felt like it was going to detonate. I launched from my seat like a sprinter from the blocks, strode down the aisle, and descended the steps to the sidewalk, where I was met with a blast of sunlight so intense it felt like a slap. I was heaving for breath; my heart was lurching in my chest. What the hell was wrong with me? In the space of just twenty-four hours, I was coming totally unraveled.

"Citizen, may I assist you?"

I was bent at the waist with my hands on my knees. I lifted my eyes to the source of the voice. A fax. Gender ambiguous, with an articulating wheeled platform below. They were called "helpers," these models. They zoomed around the streets of the city making themselves useful—offering directions, opening a door for a woman with her hands full of packages, directing traffic when the need arose. Just the sight of its ersatz expressionless face filled me with revulsion.

"Are you in need of medical attention, citizen?"

I drew myself slowly upright. "No, thank you."

"Proctor Bennett, I would be glad to call for assistance if that is what you require."

How did it know my name? But of course it knew my name. Connected to the Central Information System, the fax had scanned my face and run the image through the database. Probably the damn thing knew what I'd eaten for breakfast. (Nothing.)

"That's not necessary. I'm fine."

It skipped a beat and declared in an androgynous monotone, "I am equipped with a full suite of medical diagnostic software."

"Are you listening, you stupid machine? Go away."

"If you will permit me access to your monitor—"

I placed a hand against its metal chest and shoved, hard. "I said leave me the fuck alone!"

The fax rolled backward and stopped. Another beat—I could practically hear its circuits whirring—and it spun in a one-eighty and whizzed away in search of other people to harass with mindless generosity. I watched it go, full of contempt. Whose idea had it been to make these bogus monstrosities, these parodies of people? And why had I failed to notice this before? Just as I'd failed to notice the barely bottled hostility of those common men and women among us who were forced not merely to perform the lowliest sorts of tasks all day but also to endure our pity for the very chores we asked of them.

"Friend, are you okay?"

It was the bearded man from the shuttle. He produced a water bottle from his bag and held it out. "Here, take it. It's unopened."

Who was I, at that moment, to decline such a kindness? I cracked the seal and sipped.

"I'm not such a fan of those things myself," he said. "Pushy bastards."

I handed back the bottle. "Thanks."

"Don't mention it." He returned it to the pack. "That guy on the shuttle was a real asshole."

"I appreciate your trying to help."

He shrugged. "No trouble, friend. Not that it did any good."

I recalled something. "What was that book you were reading on the shuttle? I didn't recognize it."

He grinned through the pocket of his beard. "You must be a well-read man, to know every book."

"I meant that word in the title, 'Arrivalism.' I'm not acquainted with it."

He swung his bag around again, reached inside, and produced the slender volume I'd seen him reading. He held it out for me to take.

"What's it about?" I asked, turning it in my hands.

"More like, what isn't it? Think of it as a whole new way of seeing things." He tipped his head. "Keep that if you like. I've got others."

It was more like a chapbook than an actual book—twenty pages, if that—with a cheap, homemade feel. Somebody's crackpot philosophical tract, whipped up in a basement.

"That's kind of you," I said, and handed it back. "But my plate's a bit full at the moment."

I expected him to protest—in his genial way, he seemed quite insistent that I have it—but he accepted it without hesitation. "When you're ready, then." He returned the book to his bag and regarded me an extra moment. "That guy was pretty rough on you. You sure you're okay?"

I told him I was, which was true. The man's concern had revived me. I had been the victim of a cruel prank, but that was all, and I could even imagine how the whole thing might make a funny story, later. *This awful man, he told me the most outrageous story, I can't believe I fell for it . . .*

"Really, you've been more than kind," I told him.

"No trouble at all." That smile again. "Arrival come, friend."

I watched him amble away, my mind full of his oddness. "Arrival come"? What could he mean? Arrive where? And "friend": the way he'd said it, it hadn't come across as insincere—just the opposite. As if the two of us were, indeed, friends, just by his saying so.

My plan was to be in and out of my office quickly, without drawing too much attention to myself. Social Contracts was located on the north side of the plaza; as with all ministry buildings, its lobby was a grand affair—a soaring, window-lit space with enough marble in it to make the smallest sounds ricochet for half an hour. I showed my credentials at the desk and rode the elevator to the sixth floor, where District Six was housed. Gone was the showy splendor of the atrium, replaced by bland functionality: acoustic-tile ceilings, industrial lighting, neutral carpeting. The place was quiet, as I'd hoped; a lot of people had already left for the day. But Oona was still sitting at her desk outside my office. She startled at the sight of me.

"Director Bennett? I thought you wouldn't be in today. Your wife called this morning."

"Don't believe everything you hear. Can you get my father's paperwork? I need to file the incident report."

"Of course." She rose from her desk. "I just want to say, Director Bennett, how sorry I am about . . . what happened."

"Thank you, Oona."

I was stepping into my office when I realized that I'd left my reader in the car the day before. I'd been so turned around I'd forgotten it completely. "Is Jason here?"

"I haven't seen him since this morning. I think he went home."

It was just as well; I had no appetite for dealing with him. "By any chance did he leave my reader with you?"

"No, but I can ask around."

I went into my office to wait. It was the largest on the floor, with a comfortable sitting area and a pleasant view of the harbor. On the clearest days, it was possible to catch a glimpse of the Nursery at the edge of the horizon. But not today. I thought about my father, and what was happening to him there. Were retirees made to wait, contemplating what lay ahead, or was the process over for him already, his body restored, his beloved memories wiped away? This seemed like something a person in my position should know, and yet I hadn't the foggiest.

A few minutes later, Oona returned, carrying the file. "This is strange," she said, and placed it on my desk.

The file was stamped CLOSED. I opened the cover. There it was, the incident report, but somebody had already filled it out, including my father's data from the reader. In the section for "narrative description," it read: *Subject experienced mild disorientation. Assisted by Social Contracts personnel. Boarded on schedule.*

That was it, just three sentences. No mention of his mad dash across the pier, or the shocker, or my practically strangling the watchman. I should have been relieved—a duty I dreaded had been lifted from my shoulders—but that wasn't how I felt. Something had been stolen from me, something I didn't even know I'd wanted: the truth of what had happened.

"Proctor, what are you doing here?"

Amos Cordell, deputy minister of Social Contracts, was standing in the doorway. A large, affable man, he was my direct superior; we'd known each other for years.

"I came in to file the IR on my father." I held up the file. "Do you know who filled this out?"

He cleared his throat. "Ah, that." He turned to my assistant. "Oona, could you give us a minute, please?"

She stepped out and closed the door. Amos said, "First of all, let me just say how sorry I am. You never should have been put in that position."

"So *you* filled it out."

He held up his hands in surrender. "Okay, you caught me. Honestly, Proctor, I thought you wouldn't mind."

"It was my responsibility."

"And believe me, I know how seriously you take that. I just couldn't see making you do the paperwork after what you went through."

"I'm fine, Amos. It wasn't great, but I did my job."

"And no one's saying otherwise. But under the circumstances, I thought it best to move on and be done."

"So, we're just going to sweep this under the rug."

"You make it sound sinister, Proctor. I was only trying to help." He pulled my reader from his jacket pocket and deposited it on my desk. "You forgot this in the car. Motor pool found it."

I could tell I had injured him; I felt a stab of remorse. We were friends, after all, and he'd meant the gesture as a kindness. "Amos, I'm sorry. I'm overreacting. It was nice of you to do it."

An uncertain moment passed, and then he shrugged. "Forget it. Everybody understands. I'd be a mess if it were me." He looked up, brightening. "Tell me, how's Elise?"

I was glad to change the subject. "Half out of her mind. She's got a big show coming up."

"Good for her. The woman's quite a talent. Olivia can't get enough of her designs."

"That's nice to hear. I'll pass that along."

"You should. The money we've spent, you could probably build a wing on your house." He made for the door. "And for godsakes, Proctor, get out of here. Go home to that gorgeous wife of yours."

I called for a car (no chance I was riding the shuttle again), and by the time I got home, Elise was already there.

"Proctor, where on earth have you been?" She spoke to me through the mirror of her dressing table, where, in a black cocktail dress, she was putting on her jewelry: earrings, a silver charm bracelet, a necklace of blue stones. Under the pressure of an evening with her parents, the warm mood of our morning interaction had fled. "Never mind," she added, "I don't even want to know. For goodness' sake, just get ready. We're going to be late as it is."

Dressed for the evening, we took the car into town. (Elise insisted on driving, making me feel, once again, less like a husband than a patient.) At the Cultural Center we parked and made our way across the lot to the auditorium with the other concertgoers, a well-heeled, slightly older crowd.

"I forgot to tell you," Elise said as we entered the atrium, "Warren's going to be joining us."

I paused in my tracks.

"Don't be like that," she said. "I ran into him today, that's all. I thought you'd like seeing him." Without waiting for my answer, she lifted her eyes to search the crowd. "Warren!" she called, waving. "Over here!"

And before I could say another word, there he was, striding toward us through the throng: my old friend Warren Singh, wearing a broad, full-lipped smile and a sharp black suit, his wavy hair combed dashingly back. He kissed Elise on both cheeks ("Hello, gorgeous"), and then turned my way to wrap my outstretched hand in a solemn masculine shake that he employed to draw me into a one-shouldered hug and a cloud of his cologne.

"Proctor, buddy, I don't know what to say."

Warren's being there was obviously no accident. In what capacity had my wife invited him? Old chum concerned for my welfare? Medical professional? Third-party witness to my mental disintegration? Our relationship, though affectionate, was not without its complexities. There had been a time, before I came on the scene, when Warren and Elise were an item. Elise had assured me that their relationship was both brief and unserious, a matter of exactly zero consequence. Still, it's not an easy thing to watch a man kiss your wife and call her gorgeous when at some time in the past, he's done these things to her in bed. Warren was also more handsome than anyone I knew, with a playboy's insouciant confidence and vast personal reservoirs of erotic exploits. Of all my friends, he alone had never engaged a marital contract, preferring the life of a free sexual electron. A parade of women, each more beautiful than the last, marched through his life like models on a runway.

"So, where's your date?" I asked him.

Still gripping my shoulder as if I might float away, Warren grinned, displaying a fence line of sparkling teeth. "Can't you tell? I'm with him right now. Elise said she was willing to share you for the evening." His smile faded. "Seriously. It must have been awful for you."

"Thanks for saying so."

His gaze was so laden with concern it embarrassed me. "He was a good man, Proctor. And you, put in that position. It's a shame things had to end like that."

"That's what I keep telling him," Elise offered.

"You mustn't blame yourself," Warren continued earnestly. "I know you did everything you could. And I want you to know that I'm here for you, pal. I'm with you, whatever you decide."

I looked at Elise, who said, with a sheepish little shrug, "I might have mentioned something about it. Your new plans, I mean."

"Mentioned?"

"Okay, fine. I told him. It just kind of slipped out. But it's *Warren,* sweetheart. He's our friend."

"And I think it's great," Warren said. "Really great. Now," he went on, "I want you to come see me at the office. Before you object, I know, I know, you're perfectly fine. But it couldn't hurt to get yourself checked out, could it?"

"That's just what I was telling him," Elise chimed in.

I shot her another look. "You told him about my number?"

"She was only expressing her concern, Proctor." Just when did Warren plan on releasing my shoulder? "She loves you. As do I, incidentally. Tomorrow morning, first thing. I'll send you a car."

It was masterful. The whole thing was like a play. I could practically hear the two of them running their lines over salads and chardonnay, sitting in some bistro for their weekly meeting of Project Mopey Proctor. Where had I been when all this was going on? Giving a swimming lesson.

"So *there* you are, darling."

My in-laws had crept up on us. Were they, too, actors in this scripted drama? Never mind—their presence liberated me for the moment. I broke away from Warren, shook Julian's hand (his eyes, dewy with sympathy, instantly told me that he, too, had heard the news), and, turning to my mother-in-law, went in for the customary kiss.

"Callista, hello."

Perhaps at this point I should mention a particularly salient fact: that my mother-in-law, Elise's guardian, was none other than the Honorable Callista Laird, chair of the Board of Overseers for All Prospera. In other words, not merely the boss of my marriage but the boss of everything.

"Proctor, how *are* you?"

My patience with this question had run its course. But before I could answer, Elise interjected, "We were just talking about the future."

Callista glanced at her daughter and then returned her eyes to me, offering a measured smile. A measured woman, my mother-in-law, brisk as an ocean breeze, precise as a freshly sharpened pencil, of a certain age but still possessing a frank, somewhat bossy sensuality. She was dressed for the evening in a sleek ankle-length gown with a low-scooped neckline, tastefully understated jewelry, a light fur wrap suitable for the overworking air conditioner of the concert hall. A faded rose, perhaps, but not without thorns. I should have been afraid of her—Julian was terrified—but I had somehow never managed this. To the contrary: her candor, though often brutal, could be a real time-saver, and I liked to think that we shared a measure of mutual respect. I had, after all, something she did not: her daughter.

"The future—now, that's interesting," Callista said. "What has everyone decided?"

It was Warren who stepped in, rocking on his heels with his hands in his trouser pockets. "Just that it contains so many possibilities, wouldn't you say?"

Callista said, warmly, "Warren, I didn't know you'd be joining us. How wonderful."

"Elise twisted my arm. Tell you the truth, you ordinarily wouldn't catch me dead at one of these things. I'm a bit of a heathen."

"It's true, I did," Elise said, more brightly than the situation called for. "Who needs wine?"

I did, that was for sure, ideally served in a glass the size of a flowerpot. Warren and Elise headed to the bar to do the honors, leaving me alone with my in-laws—one more maneuver that had happened too quickly for me to react.

To fill the silence, Julian said, "I've heard wonderful things about the performer."

Of all of us, my father-in-law was the one person who might have actually cared about the music. I, for one, had no idea what we were seeing, or even what instrument he or she would play. It could have been a harmonica for all I knew.

"Julian, why don't you go to the bar to help them?" Callista said.

"It's just a few glasses."

She looked at him pointedly. "I'm sure they could use an extra set of hands."

Julian opened his mouth to say something but at the last second thought better of it. "Fine," he grumbled, and off he went into the crowd.

That poor man, I thought, watching him go. One time, after three particularly hard-fought sets of tennis and just as many gin and tonics, he'd confided in me that he was counting the days till his contract expired.

"Proctor, I wanted to speak with you privately," Callista began.

"So I see."

"I know how difficult this must be. No one could be more sympathetic."

"There's a 'but' in there."

"'But' nothing. I'm worried about you. You've been through something horrible. *Two* somethings. Anyone would feel spun around."

It was unlike her to raise the subject of my mother. We had entered new territory.

"I'm all right, Callista. Really."

"And no one's saying otherwise. You did everything you could."

"So, you've seen the footage. Tell me, how's the kid's neck?"

She took me by the elbow. Why did everyone suddenly have the urge to touch me? "Don't make too much of it, is what I'm telling you. The man was out of his head. Now," she went on, "my daughter tells me you're thinking of taking some time off."

"For Pete's sake, is there anyone she *hasn't* told?"

"She's concerned, Proctor. She wants you to be happy. And I want you to know, you have my full support, whatever you decide. It goes without saying, but you're like a son to me."

I was hardly like a son to her. Something was coming; I was being led down a path.

"We need to put this behind us. Just one thing, Proctor, and I have to ask. What did he say to you? The footage wasn't clear."

Ah, I thought. *Here we go.*

"Your father was an important man. He was privy to a great deal of confidential information. I know I can count on your discretion, but if he said anything improper, there's always a chance someone else might have heard."

"It wasn't anything, really. Just a bunch of nonsense."

"So, nothing in particular stood out."

The world is not the world. You're not you. It's all Oranios. Did she know? Her officious tone, her careful emotional maneuvering, her mention of my mother: all conspired at that moment to make me fiercely protective of my father's final minutes. "To tell you the truth, I don't even remember it all that well. He was out of his head, you said so yourself. If there was something more, I'd tell you. I just want to forget the whole thing."

Another few seconds, and the woman released me. "Well. No doubt that's for the best. But if anything comes to you, anything at all, promise you'll come see me, all right? A thing like this," she said, and shivered faintly, "it's disturbing to people. Ah," she added, looking past my shoulder, "here we are."

The drinks had mercifully arrived. Simultaneously, a soft chiming filled the hall, summoning everyone to their seats.

"Bottoms up, everyone," Warren said, passing glasses around.

He didn't have to tell me twice.

The instrument was a piano—huge, black, gleaming under the spotlight like a shark in a tank; the performer was a woman with a pale oval face, dark hair in a French twist, and dramatic lipstick. The music was dense, difficult, somewhat atonal; her fingers sailed over the keyboard in a blur, too quick for the eye. Beside me, Julian was practically clawing himself with pleasure, yet I found myself increasingly repulsed. There was something profoundly mechanical about the woman's playing, almost industrial. It was like watching someone perfectly hammer nails into a board. Four pieces, each earning exultant applause, and she glided into the first one I recognized, from my required music-appreciation course at university. Franz Liszt's Hungarian Rhapsody no. 2: lush, emotive, completely cornball but nevertheless a touchstone of romantic feeling. Under the woman's hands, it was dead as wood.

At the forty-minute mark, I could take it no longer. In the

wash of applause between songs, I nudged Elise and whispered, "I need some air."

I was up before she could object, climbing over my father-in-law to stride to the rear of the auditorium and out the doors. The atrium was nearly empty—just a few support staff cleaning up and a lone bartender, who was dunking glasses in the sink. I could still hear the woman banging away. The sound had become hateful to me; it filled me with dread. I needed to be rid of it, and her, completely.

I ascended the stairs to the hospitality area, which opened onto a balcony with a view of a small, manicured garden: hedges, seasonal flowers, a burbling fountain. I stood still a moment, just breathing. Frogs were croaking in the trees, a pleasant sound—an antidote to the woman's playing if ever there was one. How long could I hide out here before Elise came to reel me in?

The door opened behind me; an unknown woman stepped through. Perhaps sensing my desire to be alone, she didn't acknowledge my presence. But the balcony was small; we could avoid each other only so long. She moved to the rail, where she opened her clutch and produced a small, tubular device, which she held up to show me.

"Do you mind?" she asked.

The latest health craze; it was known as "clouding." A flavored liquid, infused with essential nutrients, was heated to produce a vapor that the user drew into the lungs. It was said to be relaxing.

"By all means."

She brought the tube to her mouth and inhaled. A great plume of fog, sweet and spicy, spilled from her lips, attached to the breeze, and washed straight over me.

"Sorry." The woman winced, embarrassed. "Maybe we should trade places."

"No need. It's nice. What am I smelling?"

"It's called 'peace torte.'" She sidled toward me and offered the clouder. "Want to try?"

The light from the doorway caught her face: pretty, though in a slightly unconventional way, less calculated and fussed over than most women's. Hair the lightest possible brown, with hints of amber; the redhead's fair complexion, lightly dusted with freckles; a pert, slender nose and softly rounded cheekbones; pale, almost invisible eyebrows. She was wearing a simple silk sheath of cobalt blue.

"Here, like this." She guided my hand around the tube. "All you have to do is push the button and inhale."

I did as she instructed. A faint sizzling, and the vapor flowed comfortably into my lungs. As I breathed out, the tastes of fruit and pastry coated the inside of my mouth.

"Not bad," I said, and passed it back. "Maybe I should take it up."

My companion drew on the device again and exhaled. "So, what did you think of the performance?"

"I thought she played . . . very fast."

She laughed lightly, ejecting little puffs of steam. "It's kind of horrible, isn't it?"

"I thought I was the only one who'd noticed."

"Believe me, no. Want to hear my theory?"

"A woman of theories."

"Everyone notices. They're just so eager to impress each other that they don't *know* they notice."

I gestured at the clouder. "May I?"

I inhaled again, held the vapor in my lungs for a few extra seconds, and let it out slowly. It hovered before my face, expanding lazily, then, latching onto a current of air, zoomed away.

She offered her hand. "Thea Dimopolous."

We shook. Her hand was small and strong. "Proctor Bennett."

We were silent for a time, passing the clouder back and forth. It was true what people said: under the vapor's influence, the world seemed more manageable, even enjoyable.

"So, what do you do, Proctor Bennett? That's what people ask, if I'm not mistaken."

I usually did my best to deflect this question. Ninety percent of the time, telling people what I did for a living was a conversation killer if ever there was one. But now—and perhaps it was the effect of the clouder—I dropped my guard.

"Social Contracts," I said, and then, to clarify, "I'm a ferryman."

"I see," she said, nodding equably. "Sounds intriguing."

"It doesn't bother you?"

"I don't know, should it?"

"It's just that most people would be running for the exit about now."

She gave a wry smile. "I guess I'm not most people, then."

"It's not as exciting as you might think. There's a ton of paperwork involved." A memory rose. "Dimopolous. Haven't I seen your name somewhere?"

"Perhaps you have."

"I don't know where, though."

She opened her clutch, removed a business card, and handed it to me. DIMOPOLOUS GALLERY, FINE ART, with an address not far from my office. I'd seen the sign on my way to the bakery across the street.

"You're an art dealer."

She rolled her eyes. "Allegedly."

"Oh?"

"Frankly? Most of it's awful. Like that woman's playing. No *there* there."

"Surely not all of it's that bad."

"You should come in sometime, judge for yourself."

"You think I'd like it?"

"I couldn't say." Our eyes met and held. "What kinds of things do you like?"

A crackling pause followed. It was like a contest, who would look away first. No one had flirted with me like this in a long time. It was immensely enjoyable, like picking up an old hobby after years away.

"Real things, I suppose."

"So, you're one of *those* people."

"Who do you mean?"

"You know." She smiled. "The ones who think for themselves."

Voices drifted up from the courtyard. Men and women in evening dress were filing out of the auditorium, going in search of drinks or dinner.

"Looks like the show's over," I said reluctantly. "I should probably go."

"Ah," she said. "Yes, probably you should."

"Aren't you with someone?"

"Oh, him? Stood up, I'm afraid."

"That's hard to believe."

"It's just as well. He's one of the other kind. I like talking to you much better." She angled her head toward the door. "It's all right. I don't want you to get in any trouble."

"Already in it." The last thing I wanted was to leave, to break the spell. "Well," I said, and nodded from the chin, "it's been nice talking with you. I hope I'll see you again."

"You have my card."

In the atrium, the departing crowd had thinned. I saw Warren and Elise waiting by the bar, now closed.

"Sorry," I said, striding up to them.

Elise nailed me with a hard glare. "Proctor, where have you been?"

"Getting some air, like I said." I scanned the room. "What happened to your parents?"

"They went ahead to the restaurant. Honestly, Proctor. Leaving me stranded like that. It's embarrassing."

"You had Warren to keep you company."

My friend held up his hands in comic surrender. "Don't look at me, buddy. This is your fight, not mine."

"It's not a fight." I looked at Elise again. "Do we really have to go to dinner? I'm exhausted."

"What am I supposed to say to that?"

"'No, we don't have to go'?"

"Don't be ridiculous. They're *waiting*."

What could I do? The evening had to proceed as planned. The three of us walked to the parking lot, which was nearly empty. At our car, Warren said good night.

"You're not coming?" I was suddenly desperate for his company.

"Are you serious? Callista scares the living shit out of me. No offense, Elise."

"None taken."

He was leaving us, of course, because he had a better offer. Why should a man like Warren Singh be saddled with an evening as dull as ours? Probably a woman was already lounging in his bed, clad in a combination of high-dollar silk and nothing at all, listlessly paging through a magazine while she wondered what was taking him so long.

"So, I must be off," he said, and planted yet one more stagy kiss on Elise's cheek. "And as for you," he added, wagging a finger in my direction, "don't forget your appointment tomorrow. I'll be waiting, and I don't make house calls."

We watched him amble off to his vehicle, a handsome convertible roadster—the car of the unfettered. He hopped in, lowered the top, and with a toot of his horn zoomed away, off to a night of adventure.

"I'll drive," I said.

Elise eyed me dubiously.

"Really, I'm fine. It'll help me clear my head."

Hardly a case for taking the wheel, but with a sigh, Elise surrendered the keys. "Just please don't get us killed on the way to the restaurant," she said.

We got into the car. It had taken all of twenty-four hours to exhaust my wife's patience with me completely. A dreadful dinner loomed (rapturous encomia for the music, a lengthy disquisition from Julian on the art scene, gossip about people I knew or didn't but either way couldn't care less about); but right then, sitting in the car, that wasn't what I was thinking about at all. My thoughts were on the woman, Thea. The volleying conversation, crisp as a baton passed between runners. The frisson of sex as we traded the clouder back and forth. Our eyes daring each other to break the gaze. *—You think I'd like it? —I couldn't say. What kinds of things do you like?* How long since something like this had happened to me? Years. Ages. As I started the engine, I glanced out my window toward the balcony, wondering if Thea might still be there, but of course she wasn't. She had exited the scene just as she'd entered it: as if by magic.

"Proctor, are we leaving or not?"

"Right. Sorry." I put the car in gear.

This night of music. Elise. Warren. Callista. Thea, sprite of the balcony. And Caeli—this strange, bossy, woebegone girl who had insinuated herself into my life.

It was all right there. I just couldn't see it.

II

THE STORM

7

Friday morning: I awakened, once again, in an empty bed. In the kitchen, I found Doria unloading groceries onto the counter.

"Mrs. Bennett asked me to tell you she's gone to the country. She didn't want to wake you."

Things kept happening while I was asleep. "When was this?"

"Just now. To work on her show."

"Did she say when she'd be back?"

"For the weekend, she said. She left you the car."

Elise's trip was not without precedent. Many times, in the run-up to an important show, she'd left for the weekend to clear her thoughts and make final preparations. She had plenty of friends with country places who were only too happy to let her use them.

"Would you like me to make you breakfast, Mr. Bennett?"

"Thank you, Doria. Some eggs would be nice."

Fed, washed, dressed, I was waiting in the driveway when Warren's promised car arrived. The driver, an older woman, wasn't one

I knew. It was only after a few minutes had passed that I realized we weren't headed into town, but away from it.

"I think there's some mistake. I'm going to the Ministry of Well-Being."

The driver glanced down at her clipboard. "That's not what it says here."

She passed the clipboard over the seat. The address, far out of town, felt familiar, though I couldn't place it.

"Do you want me to take you someplace else?" she asked.

"No, that's fine," I told her, and handed it back. "I don't want you to get in any trouble."

We drove on in silence. By the time we arrived, almost thirty minutes later, I'd figured out where we were going. The driver pulled up to the entrance.

"I'll wait for you here, sir."

The building was just the same as when I'd visited Dr. Patty, all those years ago. Inside, the lights were off; there wasn't a soul in sight. The check-in desk was barren, lacking even a telephone. I was about to call out when a door opened and Warren appeared, wearing a lab coat over a polo shirt and slacks.

"About time," he said cheerily. "I was going to send out a search party."

"This place looks abandoned. What are we doing way out here?"

"Oh, we still use it sometimes. I thought you wouldn't mind a little extra privacy. So, what do you say? Let's do some doctor stuff. I've got a tee time at noon."

He followed me into the examination room—the same table, the same glass cabinet of instruments, the same windowless, artificial light—and handed me a small paper bundle.

"Be a good fellow and put on this sexy nightie."

I disrobed behind a curtain. The gown left little to the imagination, and I was instantly freezing. What sadist's idea was it, to make a doctor's office so cold?

"All right, handsome, up on the table."

Warren went about examining me—the usual stuff, peering and poking and listening, all the while nodding inscrutably. When this was done, he exited the room and returned with a reader.

"Okay, let's get a peek at that monitor."

He plugged me in. The reader was larger than a typical home model, or even the one I carried for work, capable of extracting vastly more specific information. While the data flowed, Warren peppered me with questions, jotting down my answers on a clipboard.

"Exercising?"

"I swim most days."

"Good for you. Alcohol?"

"Maybe a couple of glasses of wine each night."

"I know you, you're as straight as they come, so I won't ask about other drugs." Check mark, check mark. "Elise says you've been a bit down lately."

I shrugged. "Maybe a little."

"I'm sure that thing with your old man didn't help. How about sexual activity? How are things in that department?"

"Are you seriously asking me that?"

Warren looked up from the clipboard and grinned, enjoying himself. "The question is right here on the form. Want to see?"

"I'll pass, thanks."

"Strictly *entre nous*."

"*Entre nous,* none of your business."

Warren said nothing, merely stared at me with a doctory gaze. Was it something they learn to do in school?

"Okay, fine," I said. "Things are fine."

"Now, how hard was that? Glad to hear it, by the way." He jotted something down. "How about headaches?"

"None to speak of."

"Intrusive thoughts?"

"Such as you asking about my sex life?"

"I'll take that as a no. How are you sleeping?"

"All right."

"Seven, eight hours?"

"Something like that."

"How about dreams? Any of those?"

I froze. Warren looked up from the clipboard. "I read your records, Proctor. I have to ask. It's no big deal."

"No."

"None at all? Or none you remember?"

The lie came quickly. "The first."

"Your chart says you used to sleepwalk. Some pretty nutty stuff, too. What did that sandwich ever do to you?"

"I was a kid, Warren."

"So, nothing like that going on now."

This line of questioning had grown irksome. Also, I wasn't entirely sure what the truth was. "I told you, no."

The reader chimed; Warren unplugged me. "Why don't you get dressed? I'll run the data and be right back."

I was shoving my feet into my loafers when he returned. "So, are we done?" I asked.

But his face told me we weren't. "I'll be honest, Proctor. Your number concerns me. Seventy-two is too low for a man your age."

Down another three points. "You sound like Elise."

"The woman's not wrong. You're showing signs of acute mental and physical stress. You need to take it easy."

I was relieved. "That's all? Just take it easy?"

"Not quite. I'd like to give you something, should put a spring back in your step. Hop back on the table and roll up your sleeve."

The obedient patient, I did as he said. Warren drew a rolling chrome tray up to the table and from the pocket of his lab coat produced a small steel box. Inside was a hypodermic needle—enormous, with a gleaming chrome plunger and a fat glass tube of yellowish liquid.

"What the hell is that?" I asked, appalled. "It's the size of a sword."

Warren snapped on gloves and swabbed my arm with alcohol. "Oh, this is one of the little ones. You should see the extra large."

"What's in it?"

"You know, medical things." He held up the needle and flicked it with his fingertip. "Relax, Proctor. Have a little trust. It's vitamins, okay?"

"That's a lot of vitamins."

In the needle went, buried to the hilt in my upper arm.

"Fuck!"

Warren pushed the plunger. My arm felt like it was being pumped with cold cement. When the plunger reached the bottom, he withdrew the needle and handed me a square of gauze.

"Press this against it."

I was too startled to speak. Warren capped the needle, put it aside, and taped the gauze in place.

"There now," he said with a merry smile. "That wasn't too bad, was it?"

"It hurt like shit."

"No need to thank me." He tossed his gloves into the bin by the sink and began to wash his hands. "It might be sore for a little while. Leave the bandage on until you go to bed. Soap and water after. You should feel the effects in a day or so."

I rolled down my shirtsleeve. My whole arm was throbbing. "So, that's it?"

Warren turned off the faucet with his elbow and shook off his hands. "Not unless you want a high colonic. I know a woman who does those. Not bad-looking, either."

"I'll take a rain check."

"Can't say I didn't make the offer." He angled his head toward the door. "Now go on, get out of here. And learn to relax, will you?"

I returned to the house to find a department sedan parked in the drive. Jason was sitting at my kitchen table, energetically forking scrambled eggs into his mouth.

"What are you doing here?"

Like a kid caught in the commission of some minor crime, he just about leapt from his chair, simultaneously wiping his mouth on a napkin. "Good morning, boss."

So it was "boss" now, was it?

"I hope you don't mind," he went on with the hallmark breathlessness that had yet to charm. "Your housekeeper offered to make me eggs."

"That was nice of her. Were we out of lobster?"

He looked confused. "Um, I don't really like seafood."

"It was just a joke, son." Why did I take such delight in tormenting the poor kid? And yet I couldn't seem to stop myself. "So, did the office send you, or did you just decide to drop in on your own?"

"I thought you might want a driver for the day."

"I'm on vacation, in case you hadn't heard. Doria, could you give us a minute?"

She disappeared deeper into the house. I took the seat across from him.

"Okay, why don't you tell me what's really on your mind?"

The boy shifted in his chair. His shirt collar, I noted, was half an inch too large. That, or he'd shrunk since Wednesday.

"They talked to me, sir. About . . . you know. What happened."

"Who's 'they'?"

"There were three of them. Two were from Internal Audits. I wrote down their names." He withdrew a notepad from his jacket pocket. "Chase Smith and Jennifer Bodine."

"I know them. They're all right." I helped myself to a slice of his toast. "Who was the third?"

"That's the thing. He didn't say. He didn't ask me any questions either, he just sat there. It was kind of creepy." He lowered his voice. "I think he might have been S3."

S3: State Security Service. Why would they be involved?

"What did he look like?"

"I didn't really get that close a look. Silver hair? With a beard? He was sitting off to the side."

"What makes you think he was S3?"

"It was how the other two were acting. They were as nervous as I was. Like anything I said could get them in trouble, too."

"What did you tell them?"

He shrugged. "Nothing, really. Just that everything was going fine, then your father got upset and ran from the car. I didn't tell them about the things he said. I would never do that."

The boy learned fast. "So, what did you hear, exactly?"

"The stuff in the car. 'You're not you.' 'The world is not the world.' All that."

"What about on the pier?"

He scrunched up his eyes. "Something about . . . Oranios?"

And just like that, my shadow morphed into a being of three dimensions. He was part of this thing now, like it or not.

"And you didn't mention this?"

He shook his head.

"In the interview or to anyone else? Girlfriend, boyfriend? Take a second."

"I don't really have one of those."

No clarification followed, not that it mattered. It could have been both for all I cared. "Well, keep it that way."

His eyes wavered. "Sir?"

"Sorry. Not the girlfriend-boyfriend stuff. Have as many of those as you want. Don't tell anyone what you heard, is the point I'm making."

He nodded vigorously. "Absolutely, boss. You can count on me."

"One other thing. You can stop with the 'boss.'"

"Really?" His face lit up. "You want me to call you 'Proctor'?"

"No, Jason, I do not. What I want you to do is wait outside while I think a minute."

Thus, for the second time in our brief association, I ejected young Jason Kim from my house to stand around in the tropical sun and contemplate his life. I was no fan of the S3. Every society produces such men: the ones who dwell in the shadows, who live on suspicion, whose project in life is to tighten the air in every room one notch, just by breathing it. The S3 was a necessary evil, perhaps—someone had to do the dirty work—but an evil nonetheless.

I was at a loss, however, to account for their interest. My father's final moments hardly seemed like a matter of state security. Nor could I account for the fact that they had interviewed my assistant but not me, the principal actor. All of which my mother-in-law had failed to mention.

I stepped outside to find Jason waiting at the wheel. He rolled down the window at my approach.

"Give me the keys," I told him.

"Director Bennett, I just want to say—"

"Forget it, son."

"It's just that, all I've ever wanted is to be like you."

Believe me, I thought, *you don't.*

"Really?" Jason said. "We're stopping *here*?"

We were parked at the curb along the east edge of the plaza, across the street from Overseers Hall.

"Yes," I told him. "We are. Wait in the car."

It was possible I'd be summarily turned away; one didn't just drop in on the chair of the Board of Overseers unannounced, even if the chair was one's mother-in-law. I rode the elevator to the top floor, where a young woman was manning the desk outside Calista's office. She examined my credentials and looked up with an empty smile.

"How may I help you today, Director Bennett?"

"I'd like a few minutes of the chair's time."

"Madam has a full schedule this morning. Perhaps you could make an appointment."

"It's all right, Sacha." Callista had appeared in her office doorway, dressed in a chic gray suit I recognized—it was one of Elise's designs. "Proctor, how lovely. To what do I owe this visit?"

"We need to talk."

"Of course." She waved me in. "Sacha, hold my calls, please."

Her office was grand on a scale befitting her station. At the far end, her desk, a mahogany monstrosity the size of a billiard table, floated in regal isolation. She directed me to a sofa and took a chair across from me.

"I'm glad to see you," she said. "Can I offer you something? Coffee? Tea?"

"Not just now, thank you."

She sat back, crossing her elegant legs. "So, tell me. Did you remember anything more about what happened on the pier?"

"No, and that's not why I'm here."

"Oh?"

My feelings had sharpened on the drive over. The S3's involvement seemed less a mystery to be solved than an offense to be met with equal force. "Why is Otto Winspear interrogating my trainee?"

"Ah, I see." Her face was a rictus of professional control. "Jason, is it?"

"Jason Kim."

"First of all, let me assure you that nobody's interrogating anyone. A few questions, that's all. Minister Winspear was there simply as an observer."

"Not the way Jason tells it. The boy was scared shitless."

"And that's unfortunate. I'll look into the matter, I promise. But I thought you understood the situation."

"Maybe you could explain it again."

"You're angry. I understand that. And I'm glad you care so much about your trainee. But in a case like this, a formal inquiry is simply de rigueur. I couldn't stop it if I wanted to."

"Should I be expecting a visit, too? Hell, bring in the goons right now. I have nothing to hide."

"Nobody's saying any different, Proctor. And if you must know, the S3 did want to interview you. I instructed them not to."

"Oh? And why would you do that?"

Her face drew back. "Proctor, I'm surprised at you. And a little hurt, frankly. We're *family.* Of course I'd go to bat for you. And not to make too fine a point, but I've technically impeded an official investigation on your behalf. I think a little gratitude would be in order."

I had to hand it to the woman. Ten seconds ago, I'd been riding a wave of pure self-righteousness; now I was the one who owed the apology.

"You're right," I said. "I'm sorry."

Her expression softened. "Really, you mustn't worry. I'm on your side here. Lots of people are. My daughter, for one. Did I hear you have an appointment with Warren?"

Nothing I did seemed to be a secret. "I saw him this morning."

"And what did he have to say?"

"He said I needed to take it easy."

"Well, there you go. That sounds like excellent advice." She looked at me seriously. "It's not an easy job, what you do. It takes a toll, and not just on you. I've kept my distance for Elise's sake, but her happiness means everything to me. I hope you understand that."

Here was the Callista I knew only too well. The woman was like cake frosting on a bar of iron. "It's important to me, too."

"I know it is. Which is why I'm advising you not to overthink things."

There was a rapping on the door; Callista's assistant peeked through.

"Madam Chair, pardon the interruption, but the labor minister's office just called. He's on his way up to see you."

Callista sighed theatrically, and entirely for my benefit. "Can't it wait?"

"He says it's urgent. Something about the slowdown."

I looked at Callista. "What slowdown?"

"I'm surprised you haven't noticed. Labor participation is down sixteen percent."

"You mean . . . the staff aren't showing up at their jobs?"

"It happens. We've dealt with things like this before." She rose from her chair. "Duty calls, I'm afraid. Let me show you out."

She walked me to the door. "I'm glad you stopped by," she said. "Have I put your mind at ease at least a little?"

Not hardly. "Yes, thank you."

She flashed a quick, disarming smile. "Just remember, Proctor, we're all on the same team here."

I was halfway across her outer office when an uncomfortable notion stopped me. I turned. "How exactly do you deal with it?"

Callista paused at her door. "Deal with what?"

"The slowdown. You said you've dealt with it before."

She gave a careless wave. "Oh, little of this, little of that. It's mostly a game, like everything else. Everything will turn out fine, you'll see."

Outside, Jason was standing by the car, attempting to talk a traffic enforcement officer out of writing us up for parking in a loading zone.

"I'm sorry, Director Bennett, I didn't know what to do, you told me to wait—"

I flashed my credentials at the man. "Go away," I said.

Chastened, the man scurried off. I took the keys; Jason and I got into the car.

"Here's Rule Two," I told him. "Don't apologize every ten seconds. It's annoying."

"Right." He nodded ardently. "Got it. Don't apologize."

"Also, stop repeating everything I say."

"Is that Rule Three?"

I looked at his sweet face.

"Yes," I said, and pulled away.

Thus, to the Central Library.

Within its vast, dimly lit maze lay the collected knowledge of the ages—the apex of human civilization, from a time before "the horrors." The reference room was suitably majestic, like a cathedral or a medieval dining hall. Iron chandeliers hung on black chains above the rows of tables, where students and scholars were earnestly reading and scribbling. The acoustics were so magnifying that even the smallest sound volleyed like a gunshot; one could hardly clear one's throat without earning a nasty glance from the librarian, who presided from a raised platform at the top of the room. And sure enough, we hadn't made it ten steps before the man's eyes bored into us: the same heavy-eyebrowed homunculus I recalled from my university days—a man whose censorious glowers had made my insides twist back then and still did. I told Jason to wait for me and approached the platform.

"Is there a CIS terminal available?"

Again, I displayed my credentials. The librarian examined them with bunched lips and, after a sufficient number of seconds had passed to make the point that this was his kingdom, not mine, reached below his desk to produce a key on a heavy wooden fob.

"Down the hall, third door on your left."

The room, barely larger than a coat closet, contained only the terminal, which rested upon a small table, and a rickety wooden chair, obviously meant to discourage dawdling. The space was lit by a naked lightbulb hanging on a wire. The Central Information System was not available to the general public, of course. Even I, a managing director, had only limited access. Still, I hoped it would prove sufficient to my purpose.

I took the chair—it was as unpleasant as it looked—logged in to the system, and typed:

SEARCH > ORANIOS

CIS replied:

ORANIOS > ?

So, there was something here; the system had recognized the word. I typed:

ORANIOS > FILE

A second passed.

ORANIOS > NO FILE

So, not a file. It was something else.

QUERY > ORANIOS
ORANIOSSYS LOGIN >

It wasn't a data file, it was a system command. Not a noun, a verb. I typed:

ORANIOSSYSLOGIN > PBENNETT8759476

CIS said:

PASSWORD >

I had only one, not very imaginative:

PASSWORD > ELISE

A pause; then:

PROCTOR, I AM PROCTOR.

What in hell . . . ?

OPEN YOUR EYES, PROCTOR.

OPEN YOUR FUCKING EYES.

Before I could process this, the words disappeared, replaced by:

PBENNETT8759476 > AUTOLOGOUT

What in God's name had I just seen? I logged back in to the system and tried again.

ORANIOSSYSLOGIN > PBENNETT8759476

PBENNETT8759476 > AUTOLOGOUT

I made two more attempts with the same result. Was I imagining things? I lifted my gaze from the screen, now blank. Was it just my eyes, smarting from staring at the monitor, or had the room altered somehow? It seemed closer, more confining; the light was oppressively uneven, as if the bulb over my head were subtly pulsing. And the cold. The air was frigid; I could almost see my breath. My shirt, damp with sweat, swathed me like a cocoon of ice. I lifted a hand before my face. My hand, yes, but there was something weirdly arbitrary about it. Its existence at the end of my wrist felt foreign, as if it might just as well have been someone else's, or had only recently been placed there.

I exited the room quickly, close to panic. My heart was surging; I felt on the verge of some kind of attack. I was so disturbed that when I emerged into the reference room, its quiet orderliness shocked me. What had I been expecting? A hall of fun-house mirrors? A jungle habitat of swinging monkeys?

"Director Bennett, if you please?"

The librarian was staring at me. I held out the key, which he accepted with a goblinous glare, and went to find Jason. The boy was sitting with his feet propped on one of the tables, paging through a sporting magazine.

"Director Bennett, are you okay?"

My face must have shown something. My heart had calmed, but the chill of the room lingered; my fingers were actually numb.

"Did you find anything?"

"Not really." It was the easiest answer. "Come on, I've got another idea."

The library had many dictionaries. Simple ones for new iterants, complete with pictures, all the way up to the granddaddy of them all, the *Wells-Gifford Lexicon and Concordance of the English Language and Its History.* I led Jason through the stacks at the back of the room, located the correct volume, laid it open on a table, and paged to the entry I was looking for.

> Oranios (ō-ˈran-ē-əs): var. of the Greek οὐράνιος (Ouranios, Oranos, Uranos); the sky personified as a god and father of the Titans in Greek mythology; celestial, i.e. belonging to or coming from the heavens; the stars.
>
> Roman equivalent: Caelus.

Caelus, I thought.

Caeli?

8

The day had grown gloomy by the time we pulled into the drive. There it stood, my father's house, like the lone survivor of some great catastrophe. We exited the car, mounted the porch—it was reassuring, after so many years, to find the key still under the mat—and stepped inside.

Jason asked, "What are we looking for?" We were standing in the foyer.

"Good question."

Indeed, it was. What was I to make of the fact that my father's final utterance and the name of the world's gloomiest teenager were variations on the same classical deity—that is, basically synonymous? I was struck, yes, and who wouldn't be, but I was also perfectly willing to chalk it up to coincidence, as any halfway sensible person would.

And yet.

We moved deeper into the house. What a haunted stillness there was to the place! Just two days since I'd taken my father to the ferry, but it felt far longer, as if he'd been gone for years. I stood for a moment at the threshold of the living room, trying to inspect it with fresh, neutral eyes, which proved difficult: everything I saw was so laden with memories that it was like trying to view them through a cloud of past events.

"Go check the kitchen," I told Jason.

I moved about the room. Nothing seemed odd or different; the place seemed merely neglected, though there were also sad little signs of my father's last days, things I'd failed to notice before: a book of crossword puzzles, splayed facedown on a side table; a pair of bedroom slippers in front of his favorite chair and a glass of watery whiskey on the table; a stack of unread mail. (Who bothers with the mail when they're planning to retire? No one, that's who.)

Jason returned. "Find anything?" I asked him.

"Just some dirty dishes in the sink."

The leavings of my father's last meal were nothing I needed, or wanted, to see. "Come with me."

My father's study, behind a pair of curtained French doors, was reached by a short hallway off the foyer. Even now, I hesitated before entering; it was my father's private domain, a sacred, masculine space to which I had been invited only rarely and always on the occasion of some solemn moral instruction. My initial impression was that everything was in order, though there had been changes. The wall of legal tomes was still there, but his desk, which used to be in the middle of the room, had been shoved under the windows and replaced by a drafting table. Upon it lay a large nautical blueprint, held in place by bulky glass paperweights. A sailboat, of course. There were three views: a side angle of the vessel with its sails raised; a cutaway of the hull; and a layout of the boat's interior spaces—saloon, galley, sleeping quarters forward and aft, and an engine room. The whole thing was fantastically detailed, right down to the minutest specifics of its rigging. The boat was also immense. According to the scale, the damn thing was over eighty feet long.

"Was it something your father was building?" Jason asked.

"I don't see how he could."

"So why would he draw it?"

To that I had no answer. I stepped to the bookshelves. Most were occupied by legal volumes of one kind or another, though others were devoted to the sea: maritime history, naval architecture, ocean adventure tales, celestial navigation. These were interspersed with an assortment of nautical artifacts. A ship in a bottle. A gimballed compass floating in a handsome wooden box. A sextant. I ran a fingertip along the shelves. It came away clean and, when I held it to my nose, smelled of furniture polish.

"Let's check upstairs," I said.

We looked in my parents' bedroom first. The room was amply sized, with windows looking over the east lawn and gardens on one side and the ocean on the other. The bed was roughly slept in on one side; heaps of clothing were strewn over the floor; drawers stood open; dirty plates and half-drunk cups of tea teetered atop every surface.

"It kind of stinks in here," Jason said.

It did, and it wasn't just the food. The old-man smell: that was the first thing I'd noticed. A warmly biological odor, like sour breath. We started with the closet: on one side, my father's clothing, the blazers and suits and pressed cotton slacks he favored; on the other, my mother's dresses and blouses, slowly deforming upon their hangers from their own weight. I checked the shelves; I rifled through the bureau drawers; I dropped to all fours and scanned beneath the bed—nothing but dust balls—and when I rose, I realized something sad. The half of the bed that was unmade: it had been my mother's. My father had been sleeping on her side.

"Is this her?" Jason asked.

He was looking at a small framed photo atop my father's bureau. I took it in my hands. The two of them, posing together at a party: my father, much younger, wearing a tuxedo; my mother in a slim red dress, the two of them close together and smiling. The picture had been taken before I'd come along.

"She looks like a nice woman."

It was a touching thing to hear. "Well, she was. She had a lot of friends."

"How did they meet?"

"My mother worked for him. She quit, though, after they adopted me."

I considered slipping the photo into my pocket, but what would be the point? It would only depress me. Also, taking anything from the house was illegal. The photo, like all my father's personal effects, was part of his estate and now property of the Central Bank.

I returned the photo to its place on the bureau. "Let's keep looking."

The two guestrooms told us nothing; they looked like nobody had set foot in them in years. All other options exhausted, we followed the back hallway to the bedroom that had once been mine. I wondered why I'd saved this for last, and then I knew. I'd saved it because of the telescope.

It was the oldest memory I possessed with any clarity. My first day off the ferry, when everything was strange: my father had led me to my bedroom, where, among an array of unfamiliar items, I beheld a beautiful, arcane object: a long slender tube wrapped in leather, with shiny brass fittings and a tripod of polished mahogany, standing in the curved bay window. My attention went to it instantly, as if pulled by a magnetic force. *What is it?* I asked this man who had told me he would be my father. *What does it do?* And with a look of delight in his eyes—he'd been hoping I would ask this very question—he explained the action of the lenses, and how a telescope could make small objects seem large, distant objects seem close, and that it was something seafarers had once used, to see the things of the world and know where they were going. I liked the way he said this, though I did not fully understand it—not until I lowered my face to the eyepiece and from the blue blur of the ocean beheld the crystalline image of a sailboat, far out to sea. The sight seemed miraculous, a thing of purest wonder, and I sensed that my father was telling me via this bit of mechanical instruction how it was that a person—me, in other words—ought to conduct the affairs of his life.

For a time, the telescope had been a source of endless enchantment. For hours I'd peered through its eyepiece, taking stock of the world I was now a part of: the white-tipped waves; the sailboats tacking muscularly across the wind; the moon with its features so facelike as to seem to be looking back at me, acknowledging my existence; the stars. Eventually, of course, other interests had intervened, and the telescope became a glorified clothes hanger. Still, it remained in my memory as a totem of my boyhood and its marvels, when I was a fresh new person, stepping into life.

But when I opened the door to my room, it was gone. As was everything else. The room was empty, no furniture at all.

The sight stopped me in my tracks. I thought, with a flash of sadness, that perhaps our estrangement had been so painful to my father that he'd emptied the room as a way of erasing me from his life. But the man I'd sat with two days ago did not seem like such a person.

"What do you smell?" I asked Jason.

He thought a moment. "Fresh paint?"

I picked a wall and ran my hand along it; the surface was perfectly smooth. I dropped my gaze to the floor. Scattered along the baseboard were small white droplets.

I turned back toward Jason. "At the interview, did they ask anything else about my father?"

He struggled briefly with the question. "I'm sorry, Director Bennett, I just don't remember. The whole thing kind of freaked me out."

"And the third man. You're positive he didn't say anything, ask you any questions."

"It was like I said. He just sat there." He squinted at me. "You think the S3 did this?"

"I don't know, but the paint's barely dry. I don't think we're the first people to come in here."

I stepped back to scan the walls. Something was here, I could feel it. And yet I could see nothing.

Back at my house, I told Jason to return the car to the office and go home.

"You're sure? There's nowhere else you need to go?"

"It's fine. Have a weekend." I got out of the car and bent to the driver's window. "One last thing. Don't talk about today, not to anyone."

"What if it's the S3?"

"Especially the S3. You hear from them, call me right away."

He was silent a moment, looking over the wheel. "I just want to say, Director Bennett, I'm really sorry about your dad."

I'd heard these words repeatedly over the last three days. They were what one said, the common analgesic. Yet coming from him, they sounded like more.

"Thank you, Jason. I appreciate your saying so."

"My guardians retired together three years ago. Maybe you remember them? Frank and Leonie Kim."

Suddenly, I did. Though I hadn't been the ferryman assigned to the case, it had come under my review because it was a dual retirement—rare, but not unheard of. The couple had been together through three contracts, almost sixty years; Frank, who was older than his wife, had been having some difficulties. There was some special paperwork involved. They had a ward at university, a boy.

"Did we meet?"

He nodded. "It was at the house the day they left for the ferry. There were a lot of people there, but you took me aside and shook my hand. You told me how brave I was."

"I said that?"

"Yeah. It was really nice of you."

All this time, he'd been waiting for me to recall this. "Jason, I apologize. I should have remembered."

He shrugged. "That's okay. You've had a lot on your mind."

It didn't feel okay at all. I tapped the roof of the car and backed away. "I'll see you Monday."

I watched him drive off and went inside. The empty house felt wrong until I recalled that Elise had gone to the country. I checked my messages, but she hadn't phoned—which, upon reflection, was just as well. What would I have said to her? How could I explain the events of this peculiar and troubling day?

I mixed a drink and repaired to the patio. Thick clouds were moving in from the sea, the temperature falling; sitting in a deck chair, I was actually shivering. I retrieved a blanket from the bedroom, yet even this failed to warm me.

I was stepping inside to refill my glass when the phone rang. Elise at last, I thought, calling to reassure me that I was still in her thoughts. But hers wasn't the voice I heard.

"Catching you at a bad time, Mr. Ferryman?"

"Caeli?"

"Let me check. Yes, it's definitely Caeli."

I was, needless to say, caught completely off guard. "How did you get this number?"

"Um, the phone book? So," she went on, "the reason I called. You said the missus was . . . a designer, was it? I was thinking. Maybe she could design something for me? Plus, I'd like to meet her. Since you and I are friends and all."

"Caeli, do your guardians know you're calling me?"

She sighed. "This again."

"I really don't think this is appropriate."

"You're really not making it easy."

"Making what easy?"

Her voice became frantic. "This! The whole thing! I'm only trying to help!"

It occurred to me that the girl might be having some kind of episode. "Caeli, are you okay? Is anyone there with you?"

"You said you were sad. I'm trying to cheer you up. *Duh.*"

"I'm fine, Caeli. That's nice of you, but I'm perfectly well."

"So, I can meet her then?"

"I guess. At some point."

"Do you think she'll like me?"

Why this was a matter of such importance to her, I couldn't fathom. "I don't see why not."

"Because it would really suck if she didn't. Also, I wanted to tell you that you might not be seeing me around for a while."

"Oh? Where are you going?"

"Not up to me. I just thought you should have the heads-up. In case you were, you know, worried."

I had no idea what to make of this abrupt declaration. "Well, thanks for telling me," I said, when she added nothing further. "I'm sorry to hear it."

"Anyway," she said, "that's all I called to say. Good night, Mr. Ferryman."

She hung up before I could say anything else. For some period of time, I just stood there in utter confusion. Was she in some kind of trouble? The call had possessed a strange encoded quality, as if she were trying to tell me something without coming out and saying it.

The phone rang again.

"Mr. Bennett? It's Thea Dimopolous."

It took me a moment to reorient my thoughts. And "Mr. Bennett": the woman's gambit was plain. If Elise were listening in, the call would sound harmlessly official.

"I hope you don't mind my disturbing you at home."

I didn't; far from it. The day had left me lonely and disturbed; I did not like being alone with my thoughts. "That's perfectly fine," I said, then added, "I'm here by myself, actually."

"I enjoyed our conversation last night. As it happens, I have some new work coming in that I thought might interest you."

"Oh?"

"So, I was wondering, and short notice, I know. But might you be free for lunch tomorrow?"

9

There was a time when Elise and I were genuinely happy together. More than happy: from our first meeting, our relationship felt like something fated. This happened at a black-tie benefit to which neither of us had brought a date, and from the moment we took our seats and introduced ourselves, I simply couldn't take my eyes off her. It wasn't that she was beautiful, although she was; rather the feeling that something life-altering had occurred, as if I'd discovered a key to a long-locked door. This feeling only grew as the evening went on, the two of us locked in conversation of such mutual intensity that the room around us seemed to vanish. When the band struck up the first song, and I rose from my chair and offered my hand, she accepted it without words, only a knowing smile; she, too, had felt it. I led her to the dance floor, and that was the first time I held her in my arms.

We danced the night away.

Our courtship transpired in a happy haze. Everything about her fascinated me: her view of life, her career, her stories of her past. It was as if I'd found the one person on earth who was truly meant for me. My job seemed not to trouble her in the least; on the contrary, she questioned me in detail about it, and professed great admiration for what I did. With Elise in my life, anything seemed possible; I couldn't believe my luck. On a sunny afternoon two years exactly from the day we met, we signed our contract (fifteen years; I would have happily signed for a hundred, but fifteen is standard for first arrangements, and we could always renew), and under a torrent of rice and the good wishes of family and friends, off we went into married life.

Yet something nagged at me. It is impossible, of course, to completely know another person; we are, in the end, prisoners of our own minds. But in Elise's case—and this is where my professional training played a role—I began to sense something more formidable at work, a hidden sorrow that all the smiles couldn't quite hide. I would, for example, catch her staring out the window with a look of puzzled pain upon her face, as if she couldn't quite fathom the source of her distress; at other times, she would simply recede into an airy distractedness that could go on for hours or even days. Had something happened to her, something bad? Was there a trauma in her past so deeply buried that even she couldn't fully access it? Yet when I probed her on the subject—always with the utmost caution—she would swear to me that nothing was wrong.

But something *was* wrong; I felt the gap between us widening with every year that passed, and my enthusiasm for taking on a ward only made matters worse. (I wondered if some or even most of this impulse came from my hope that a ward would draw us closer. The opposite proved true.) There was no outward friction between us, at least nothing serious. As I've said, we were generally content, and you can't expect the flames of passion to blaze forever. But Elise and I were adrift, and it made me feel deeply alone.

I say these things not to exonerate myself for what happened, because nothing can, only to describe as accurately as possible the state of mind that led me, that June afternoon, to descend the stairs to a certain out-of-the-way basement bistro to dine with a woman not my wife. All of which is just to say: this is the part of the story in which I am no hero, not at all.

Imagine it. The windowless dining room below street level, a zone of permanent night; the permissive languor of a summer afternoon—the day was scorching, the hottest in months—and the tinkling of glass and silver and china wrapping the space in a hush. I'd arrived ten minutes early. Was I nervous? Who wouldn't be, marooned at an empty table, nursing a glass of water while contemplating the betrayal of his marital vows? I'd spent the morning in a state of complete moral agitation; many times I'd contemplated calling to cancel (though I still hadn't done it). The restaurant held just a dozen tables, and of these, only four were taken—their occupants, all couples, locked in the sort of intimate conversations that such a place encouraged. Were any of them like me? Was I the lone would-be adulterer in the room, or was a midday assignation at Malvolio's Café a well-understood shorthand among the faithless? What the hell was I doing here? Perhaps, I thought, I had the situation all wrong. I'd been out of the game for a while; maybe I'd misread the signals. I was married, middle-aged, arguably depressed. I had the gloomiest of all jobs. Why would a woman like Thea Dimopolous take the slightest interest?

All these thoughts were wiped away when, at the stroke of precisely five minutes late, Thea entered the room.

I got to my feet as she strode toward the table. She was just the same, which is to say, mesmeric.

"Am I late?" she said, a little breathless.

"Not in the least." An awkward pause ensued—how was I to greet the object of a fifteen-minute flirtation I'd tried not to think about for days?—until Thea rescued the moment by leaning forward for us to exchange brisk, airy kisses on each other's cheeks.

"Have you been here before?" she asked as we took our chairs. It was she who'd selected the restaurant.

"Yes, but I don't remember when."

"It's a favorite of mine. I like how cozy it is." She darted her eyes toward the waiter's station, instantly drawing the man to our table.

"How can I start you off, madam?" he asked, lighting the candle on our table with a long wooden match. "A cocktail? Wine, perhaps?"

Thea gave me a mischievous look. "What do you think? Is it too early?"

I ordered a bottle, which arrived, or so it felt, by magic. All the rituals of label and cork were obeyed with a kind of knowing discretion. *Sir and madam are having a rendezvous, are they?* The waiter generously poured the wine into our glasses, big as fishbowls, as if filling them with a golden light. We took a moment to sip, though I was having some trouble. It was hard not to stare. What was different about her? The word I thought of was "presence." She simply seemed more *there* than other people. The thought both saddened me (where had my wife gone?) and simultaneously deepened the woman's almost magnetic hold on me.

"So where should we start?" she asked.

"You mentioned some new work."

She laughed lightly. "I did say that, didn't I? Clever of me. The truth is, I just wanted to have lunch with you."

"I sort of guessed."

"Good boy."

"So, to be clear, there *isn't* any new work."

Thea sat back. "Oh, there's always new work. How do you feel about a cat on a windowsill? I have a couple of sentimental seascapes you might like."

The waiter returned to take our order. We picked something. Food, I think it was. I couldn't have cared less, caught as I was in the spell of her.

"I'll tell you something, though," Thea went on. "There's good work to be had. It just doesn't come from anywhere near here."

"No?"

"It all comes from the Annex." She read my expression. "You're surprised?"

I was thinking of the man on the bus—his filthy hands and teeth, his coarseness, the glow of loathing in his eyes. "A little. I always thought—"

"You and everybody else. Trust me, it's not what you think. There's a painter there, we've gotten to be friends. The man's an absolute genius."

"That's a bold claim."

She sipped her wine. "Maybe, but not wrong. You should see his work. Intense, disturbing, totally brilliant. Also, not for sale. I've asked a hundred times."

"Doesn't he need the money?"

"I'm sure he does, but I don't think he cares."

"He sounds like a saint."

"Or a madman. A bit of both, probably." She paused. "Can I ask you something?"

"All right."

"Why did you hate the concert so much?"

I laughed. "That's easy. I was bored."

"Bored is one thing. Hating it, that's something else. I saw it, you loathed every second. You couldn't even stand to be in the room."

"How did you know that?"

"Because I was seated right behind you."

It took a second for her words to sink in. "Are you saying you . . . followed me?"

"'Followed' is a strong word. Sounds a bit creepy, don't you think?" She tipped her head and smiled. "Okay, shoot me, I followed you. Stalked you all the way to the balcony. I wanted to know more about this man who hated that woman's ridiculous playing as much as I did."

I wasn't sure how to assess this. On the one hand, it disturbed me to think I'd been so obvious. On the other, I could hardly complain about the consequences. It had been years since I'd felt like this, so caught in the vortex of another's personality.

"Well, you're right," I said, "I did hate it. It just seemed so . . . empty. Inhuman, even. All the notes, perfectly played, but with nothing behind them, no actual feeling."

"As if nothing real had ever happened to her in her life."

"Exactly." I shook my head at the memory. "I used to like going to things like that. Or, at least, not mind them so much. Now I can't imagine why."

"So, one day your feelings changed, just like that."

"I hadn't thought of it that way, but yes. Was it the same for you?"

She considered the question. "Yes and no. It started early, though I didn't know it at the time. My guardians took me to everything—museums, concerts, operas, plays. And not just the pablum they dish out for new iterants. I'm talking heavy cultural fare. One time they made me sit through, I'm not kidding, Wagner's entire *Ring* cycle, all four days of the fucking thing."

"It sounds miserable."

"To be fair, they meant well. And it made me feel *very* grown up. Which was the problem. I didn't understand, let alone actually like, any of it, but I was an expert at pretending I did."

"Were your guardians some kind of artists?"

She laughed. "God, no. My father worked for the Ministry of Finance, my mother rode horses all day."

"So, the gallery . . ."

"Overcompensation. At university, I majored in 'creative expression and aesthetics.' I thought it might help me crack the code, why people thought some things were beautiful and others not, but it actually made me feel worse. All this high-minded talk—what did it have to do with anything? Do you know who Picasso was?"

I sipped my wine. "Somebody famous?"

"Spanish painter, twentieth century. He invented something

called Cubism. It's hard to describe, you'd really have to see it, but basically, he took all three dimensions of an image and showed them at the same time so you could see it from different angles simultaneously. When you look at one of his paintings, it's like looking at everything in a truer way you never thought of, a kind of off-kilter dream world. It's not pleasant, or even comfortable, but that's the point. The truth isn't always nice. After that, I decided to open a gallery when I graduated. I wanted to find other artists who could make me feel that way, because there had to be some, didn't there? Not everything was pictures of flowers and fruit." She gave a defeated shrug. "Turns out, I was wrong. That's just what everything is."

"Except for your friend in the Annex."

"Exactly." She raised her glass in a little toast. "Except for him."

I thought a moment. "Do you go there a lot? The Annex, I mean."

"I wouldn't say 'a lot.' But I do go."

"So, you have friends there."

"I'd say so." Her eyes narrowed on my face. "Why do you ask?"

"I met a man the other day. Well, not met, exactly. We were talking at a shuttle stop. I think he was support staff. He was reading a book, *Principles of Arrivalism.* Do you know it?"

"I've heard of it. You see it over there. I don't know very much about it, though."

"But something."

She sipped her wine and returned her glass to the table. "It's a religion, basically. The central tenet is something called 'the Grand Design.' A heavenly reward for earthly toil, that sort of thing. The righteous ascending to a mythical promised land. Illegal, of course, but pretty benevolent."

"Do they have some kind of god?"

She nodded. "They call him 'the Great Soul.' Or her. Or it. Honestly, it's all pretty vague."

"Are there a lot of followers in the Annex?"

"Hard to say. They're a pretty secretive bunch."

"What about your painter?"

"I don't know. I never asked."

It was strange: I'd given the encounter virtually no thought since the day it had happened, and yet something about it had obviously stuck with me, to prompt me to raise it now.

"The man I met. He kept calling me 'friend.'"

"Sounds like a nice guy."

"It wasn't so much what he said as the way he said it. 'Arrival come, friend.' Arrival where?"

She smiled. "That's always the question, isn't it? Wherever we're going, I guess."

We left the matter there. Our lunch arrived—fish, it turned out. We ate and talked, the subjects roaming around comfortably, the wine bottle growing lighter.

"I need to be honest with you about something, Proctor." We were splitting a pastry; the restaurant had emptied out. "You may want to stick me with the check when you hear it."

"I doubt that."

"Don't be so sure." She took a long breath. "There's another reason I followed you. I was on the pier last Wednesday. I saw what happened."

I was dumbstruck.

"I sometimes go there when I know a ferry's leaving. I can't explain it, really. Something about watching all those people just . . . giving it all away."

It was as if she'd alerted me to a whole new track of existence, parallel to, but wholly separate from, my own. "So, this whole thing—it was just to satisfy some kind of morbid curiosity?"

"I was curious, I'll admit that."

"About what?"

"You, of course. The whole ferryman thing. I always thought you people were, I don't know . . ."

"Ghouls?"

"That's a bit strong. But basically, yeah." She looked at me intently. "The expression on your face. The way you were with him. It wasn't what I expected."

"How was it different?"

She considered the question. "Gentle, maybe? No, that's not right. Something more, something deeper. Did you know him?"

"He was my guardian."

Thea took this in. "I see."

"We'd been out of touch awhile, though."

"So maybe that explains it. All that lost time. It must have been hard for you to say goodbye. Hard for you both."

All that lost time. She meant the years my father and I had mislaid, each of us foolishly thinking the other would prefer it that way; but I also heard, in her words, something more. For decades I had been sleepwalking through my life; I'd chosen basically nothing that hadn't already been chosen for me; I'd spoken with others' words in my mouth, like an actor reciting his lines. It was what the world taught us to do, but it was no way to live, and now, for the first time, I felt like I was waking up.

I said, "You know, you kind of remind me of a friend of mine."

"Who's that?"

I shrugged. "Just a girl. I met her on the beach the other day. She doesn't let me get away with any bullshit, either."

"She sounds like a good friend to have." Thea paused, then said, "Anyway, then I recognized you at the concert, and, well . . . you know the rest." She eyed me cautiously. "So. Did I blow it?"

"Not at all." I smiled to underscore the point. "I'm glad you told me. It's good to talk about it like this."

"Honestly, you mean."

I nodded.

"One last thing, speaking of honesty. Your wife—"

"Ah."

"Does she know you're here?"

I shook my head. "Gone for the weekend."

"So being here with me—"

"Isn't something I'm going to discuss with her, no."

We paid the check and left. Out on the sidewalk, the light blasted our eyes; the heat washed over us in a white sheen. The air was so scorching I shivered.

"God," Thea moaned. "This is horrible. Who broke the weather?"

I checked my watch; it was a little after three.

"I have an idea," I said.

"Proctor, it's beautiful."

"'She,'" I corrected.

Thea raised her eyes.

"That's what you call boats," I explained. "Boats are always 'she.'"

She moved deeper into my father's workshop and slowly circled the hull. When she came to the stern, she looked up. "Who's Cynthia?"

"She was my mother." How much should I say? "She's been gone awhile now."

"So, your father built a boat and named it after her."

"That's right."

She gave a bright smile. "Well, I think that's lovely. And we're actually going to sail her."

"That's just what we're going to do."

I winched up the cradle; the two of us pushed the bow, and my father's boat slid stern-first on its rollers out of the shed and into the water, meeting it with a soft splash. Once the hull was fully afloat, I rolled up my trousers, took her by the painter, climbed onto the dock, and guided her to the end, where I tied her off and lowered myself into the cockpit. There was a steady breeze now, coming from the southeast. While Thea watched from the dock, I attached the rudder and tiller, released the centerboard, and hoisted the sail. The canvas was crisp and brilliantly white.

"How do I get in?" Thea asked.

"I'll help you."

I held out my hand. She sat on the edge of the dock, found the deck with her feet, gathered her nerve, and stepped down into the cockpit.

"We'll be going off on a starboard tack," I told her.

"A what?" She was smiling, as was I. I hadn't sailed since my mother's death; just to be aboard felt like a homecoming, a return to a more natural condition. One more pleasure I'd lost track of.

"That means the sail will be on the left side when you're facing the bow," I explained. "That's called the port side. The starboard side is to the right. That's where the wind will be coming from."

"I see," she said, nodding with mock seriousness. "Very technical."

"For now, it means sit over here."

She took a place on the bench. I shoved off, moved to the stern, pulled the tiller toward me, and drew in the mainsheet until I felt a tug of resistance. With a little snap, the sail filled; we were moving away.

"You make it look easy," Thea said.

"It's pretty simple, actually."

"Not from where I sit." She closed her eyes and tipped her face toward the sky. "The breeze is nice."

"That's one of many upsides."

She gave a backhanded wave toward the bow. "Take me away, skipper," she said and, on second thought, added, "I think that's the right term, yes? You're the skipper."

"A quick study."

"If I'm not mistaken, that makes me first mate. I rather like that."

As one moves out to sea, the world's dimensions change. While things on land grow distant, the sea increases in its expanse, made bluer and wilder; there is a taste of something grand in it. It makes one seem small but also connected to larger forces, part of a great planetary flow. I felt deeply inside the present moment, as if I'd entered a more authentic state of being. *It's impossible to feel bad on a boat,* my father often said, and that was true, or true for me. Here I was, after the most horrible week, a tiller in my hand and the breeze filling my sail, in the company of this magnetically clever woman who made no bones about her interest in me—a totally renovated reality I could never have anticipated.

"I can see why you like this," Thea said. Her voice was dreamy.

"Would you like to steer?"

She looked doubtful; also excited. "Kind of?"

We traded places on the bench; I guided her hand around the tiller.

"We're on what's called a reach," I said. "That means the wind is coming more or less straight over the side. Here, do this." I shifted the tiller back and forth a little, tightening and loosening the sail as I pointed the bow on and off the wind. "See how it moves?"

She smiled with delight. "Like magic."

"Physics, actually. Want to know how it works?"

"Not this minute." She wrinkled her nose. "I don't want to wreck it."

I released the tiller. "Okay, she's all yours. Just hold it steady for a while, get the feel."

We continued outward. Her concentration was fierce, her eyes pointed over the bow. I walked her through the different relationships the boat could take to the wind and how to trim for each.

"Ready to tack?" I asked her.

"Shouldn't you be the one doing that?"

"You have to learn sometime."

She took a breath. "Okay, here goes nothing."

She pushed the tiller away. My father had constructed the *Cynthia* for grace, not speed; the process unfolded in genteel slow motion. The boom swung overhead as we pivoted across the wind. A pop of canvas and we were off and running again.

"Expertly done."

We were far from shore now. The sea had grown choppy, the wind more robust. The Nursery was within sight, about a half mile off our port bow. I didn't recall having ever been so close to it, not even when I'd sailed with my parents.

"Want to take a closer look?" I asked Thea.

I took the tiller from her and sailed toward it. The island possessed a blocky appearance, like a giant cube of rock; the reefs surrounding it on all sides created a zone of crashing whitecaps.

"Will we see a ferry?" Thea asked.

"Not today. The next one is Monday."

The currents had stiffened; swells from the reef jostled the boat. Once again, I was struck by a feeling I had failed to anticipate. In the abstract, I knew the Nursery to be a place of beginnings, an almost holy mystery, but the reality—the stern, off-putting appearance of the island—created a different effect: more solemn, even a little frightening. Things began there, but they also ended.

"It's kind of giving me the willies," Thea said.

"I know what you mean."

She pointed. "Here come the drones."

There were four. Moving in a tight formation, they swooped in low and fast over the water toward us. At a distance of a hundred yards, they peeled off from one another, decelerated, and took up hovering positions on all sides of us.

"Try to look innocent," I joked.

Thea gave them a mocking wave. "Maybe we should go?"

Who was watching us? By now we'd been identified via the drones' facial-recognition system, our personal data racing up somebody's screen. Proctor Bennett, managing director of District Six, but what was he doing in a boat with this woman, Thea Dimopolous—a woman not his wife?

"I think that's a good idea."

I reversed course. For a few minutes the drones maintained their positions around us; then, when a certain distance from the Nursery was reached, they popped skyward and zipped away.

"I hate those fucking things," Thea said.

We sailed on, toward the distant shore. The bright mood of the afternoon had dimmed and, with it, the weather; clouds had moved in, smothering the sun. My mind tossed with recrimination. Was it possible that the S3 would investigate and, in the course of their investigation, tell Elise what they'd seen? *Mrs. Bennett, if you please, could you tell us a little bit about the woman in this photo? And what is her relationship to your husband?*

But that wasn't my only worry. The weather was quickly falling apart. The wind had increased; the seas were building. Two feet, then three, carving deep troughs that sent tendrils of cold spray splashing over the boat. The *Cynthia,* with her fat, heavy hull and overlarge mainsail, was not made for serious weather.

"Should I start to be scared?" Thea asked.

I forced a smile. "Just part of the fun."

We were heeling hard; the rudder was fighting me, requiring all my strength to manage. I glanced astern. What was I seeing? A wall of thick, dark clouds, almost black, was moving in from the east, traveling low over the water. The front edge roiled in upward waves, like curling smoke; the interior flashed with voltage.

It was headed toward us like a giant plow.

Thea said, "Okay, now I'm scared."

Suddenly, the temperature plummeted. It was as if twenty degrees of warmth had vanished in an instant. The first peal of thunder rolled like the sound of some dark god clearing his throat. It built and built until it was almost continuous, the volume always increasing. Water was sloshing in the cockpit.

I told Thea, "Go below. See if there's a bailer."

"What's a bailer?"

"Something to get the water out."

She fought her way into the cabin. "There's a bucket!" she cried.

"That'll work!"

She scrambled back up and began to scoop water from the cockpit and fling it over the side—a losing battle. We dipped into the next trough, sending a cascade over the bow. I was so cold I could barely feel the tiller in my hands.

Rain began to fall.

Not "fall": it stabbed us like needles. We were inside this thing now.

"Help!"

A voice, but where? Ahead of us? Behind? I swiveled my head, searching for the source.

"Help me, please!"

"Do you hear that?" I yelled to Thea.

She was bailing frantically. She didn't even glance in my direction; probably in the chaos she couldn't hear me. The bow rose, crashed down, rose again. The dock was within sight now. How could I land the boat without smashing us to bits?

And then it was over.

It was inexplicable. One moment we were locked in battle with a raging tempest; in the next we were floating on a sea of almost perfect calm. Bright corridors of sunlight angled through clouds that had begun not so much to dissipate as to dissolve. It was as if I had wished the storm away. In silent astonishment, we glided to the dock and tied off.

"Proctor, you're trembling."

I was. I was so cold my shivers felt like spasms, coming from deep within. I'd already forgotten about the cry I'd heard—an illusion, no doubt, made by the storm.

"You need to warm up. Let's get you to the house."

She helped me from the boat, put her arm around me, and led me up the pathway. I felt utterly undone. We entered through the patio, into the living room.

"Where can I find a blanket?" she asked.

I directed her to the linen closet and commenced, clumsily, to peel off my sodden clothes, removing all but my undershorts. I was sitting on the sofa, hugging myself, trying to stop shaking, when Thea returned.

"I need to warm you up," she said, and proceeded to strip until she, too, was wearing only her underclothes. "Lie down and scoot over."

She positioned herself beside me, drew the blanket over us, and wrapped me tightly with her arms. It was all right there. The warmth of her, pressing against me. The soft brush of her breath on my face. The scent of her, her skin, her hair, exquisitely feminine.

"Is that better?" Her voice was soft; she was rubbing my back to warm me.

I nodded, still shaking. "Yes," I said.

And then, sometime later, "Much, thank you. Much, much better."

10

TWO A.M.

They come from all directions; they come from everywhere and nowhere; they simply appear, as they know how to do. They meet in the alley, Jess and Antone and six other boys, their bodies jangling, wiry as marionettes.

The Annex is quiet, no light or movement anywhere. Jess, kneeling on the pavement, pours the paint from one large can into four smaller ones. Thick paint, almost a goo, red as blood. The boys are eager to go. Each group is responsible for three signs, four if they can do it. The larger and more public, the better: thoroughfares, government buildings, shuttle stops, anything near the causeway. She reminds them again: No one can know, not even Mother. *Especially* not Mother. This is our thing, not hers. Is that understood?

It is.

The boys scatter in pairs. Jess looks at Antone. "Ready?"

Under hooded eyes, the boy nods. He's just as keyed up as the others but won't show it. He's steadier, more in control of himself. The stakes aren't lost on him; he's too smart for that. A natural leader. His day will come.

"Let's go," Jess says.

They make their way quickly through the alleys, emerging into a public market of shuttered stalls. They're about to step from cover when Antone holds up a hand. His hearing is keener than hers, able to parse the smallest sounds. There it is, coming from the left. The whiz of the drone. They duck beneath an awning. The drone glides over the tops of the buildings, away.

"Good ears," Jess whispers.

Their destination is an old watchman's kiosk at the end of the block. No longer used, it is still a symbol. It stands alone in the street, without easily available cover. So, a challenge, but worth the added danger. *We were here,* their message will say. *Right here. Right in the middle of everything, you fuckers.*

They skulk west in darkness, awning to awning. The kiosk comes into view, like an oversized tombstone in the middle of the intersection. A quick exchange of nods and they step out and move toward it. Jess is carrying the paint, Antone the brush.

"STRIKE," the boy paints.

He steps back, quickly eyes his work, dips the brush again, and adds an exclamation point.

"STRIKE!"

"Like we're yelling," he says to Jess.

Suddenly they hear the clap of boots on pavement.

"You there!"

They freeze.

"Stop what you're doing!"

"Go," says Jess.

They drop the paint and the brush and fly down the street, and at the first intersection they separate. Jess feels no fear; she is merely executing a plan. This is their world, not the watchman's. They know it cold; they know things he never will. Shortcuts.

Blind spots where a person can seem to vanish into thin air. Her destination is a certain basement window. Antone is a wisp, a wraith, far faster than she; the watchman has chosen Jess as his quarry. This makes her happy—no, delighted. Fuck this guy. She doesn't just want him to taste defeat; she wants him to gnaw on it like a piece of gristle.

She decides, perhaps unwisely, to have a bit of fun with him.

She passes the basement window with nary a glance. How she hates this man! And what power this hatred bestows upon her, what dark joy. Because that is the one true thing of the world—not Pappi's prayers, or Mother's schemes, or any of the rest of it. It's a world of boots and fists and sneering faces, and if you do things right—if you take all that hatred inside yourself and let its black tendrils wind around your heart—there's nothing that can stop you, and the next thing you know, half the Annex will be pouring down the causeway with a knife clamped in its teeth.

She enters another alley. The day's wash still hangs on lines above. The night feels empty, soulless. Even the stars are gone. A tall wooden fence blocks her path. But she feels invincible; she feels like she can fly. Far behind her, the watchman huffs and puffs. Jess takes three long strides, reaches up, grabs the top of the fence, and over she sails.

And comes down.

Hard.

Onto something.

That something is a two-by-four. The two-by-four is not the problem. The nail sticking out of it, *that's* the problem. The nail that passes straight through the bottom of her shoe and into the meat of her instep and out the other side.

The pain is so immeasurably large that she doesn't cry out. She cries *in*, her breath stopping in her chest. *Fuck! Fuck! Fuck!*

And the watchman is coming.

The pain rescues her. It gives her the will to act. Sitting on the ground, she pulls her knee to her chest, positions her uninjured foot against the two-by-four, fills her lungs with air, and pushes.

With a gush of blood, she's free.

There's no time to run, not that she could. The watchman is coming over the fence. At the top, suspended on his hands, he sees her.

Not a watchman. A suit. The one named Hanson.

"Well, look at you," he says.

She's sitting on the ground, clutching her foot. "I think I broke it," she says. She looks at him wide-eyed, teary, helpless, a broken-winged bird. "Please, don't hurt me."

He vaults over. He draws a baton from under his suit coat and snaps it to full length.

"Get up."

She raises her hands over her face. "Please, I'm sorry."

Hanson steps toward her. "I said get . . . the fuck . . . up."

When the baton comes down, she's ready for it. She lifts the two-by-four and swings, and as she swings she rises. The baton is suddenly gone, shot into the shadows. A moment of perplexity; Hanson just stands there, looking at his empty hand.

"What the hell—"

But that's where he stops talking. He stops because there's a nail in his temple. It's sunk three inches into the meat of his brain. Eyes wide, he appears more startled than anything else, a man for whom the greatest mystery of all is about to be solved. His knees fold and down he goes. Since he's still attached to the two-by-four, which Jess is holding in both hands, his carriage remains otherwise erect; his is the humbled posture of the faithful at prayer.

He closes his eyes. Dies.

She yanks the nail from his head and Hanson tips face-first onto the pavement. She's winded and shaking; her shoe squishes with blood. Yet the night's not done, not by a long shot. A body is one thing; there are others. There's a statement to be made, stronger than any word on a wall, and she is going to make it.

She raises the two-by-four over her head, takes aim, and brings it crashing down on Hanson's skull.

It takes a little while. Down goes the two-by-four, again and again and again. She bashes the man's skull to pieces, until there's nothing left. And when at last she's satisfied, and she tosses the two-by-four aside and hobbles down the alleyway, she knows just what she's done—that this is how and when a war begins.

11

Upon the twenty-four hours that followed, I shall draw a curtain of privacy. My feelings were, of course, my own; I cannot claim another's. But speaking for myself, it felt like I had entered a zone outside of time. I was under no illusion that Thea and I possessed anything that might be called "a future." I was married; my wife was the ward of Callista Laird, chair of the board; whatever difficulties lay between Elise and me were hardly a justification for bringing scandal down upon us all. But when I awoke in the middle of the night, bundled beside Thea on the couch from which we'd barely moved, I realized that to a week of unanticipated emotions I could add one more: I was happy.

Sunday morning broke sunny and clear. The heat had lifted, leaving behind cool, dry air and skies of the most arresting, depthless blue, as if the storm had cleansed the world of all impurities. It was apparent that neither one of us wanted to leave, to shatter the spell. Though I tried not to show it, I had also begun to worry—not so much about Elise as about myself. After such an experience, how was it possible to go back to the world? This happiness I felt—how could I endure without it, knowing what it felt like?

The moment came when we could delay our parting no longer. In silence, we drove back to town. Thea had left her car across the street from the restaurant; I pulled in behind it and shut off the engine.

"Will I see you again?" Thea said. She was looking straight ahead.

How bereft I felt! I could have cried right then.

"I understand if the answer's no," she added.

"I don't know what the answer is."

She turned her face toward me, took both my cheeks in her hands, and drew me into a kiss. Lingering, sensual, but also sad.

"You're a lovely man, Proctor Bennett."

She exited quickly and closed the door. I wished I'd found something more to say, words to capture how I felt; but I could not think, yet, what those words might be. I watched her get into her car. For an instant her eyes caught mine through her rearview mirror, but only for an instant, and then she drove away.

I had worried that Elise might beat me home, but this proved not to be the case, and she'd left no messages. Looking over the house, I saw I'd been incautious. My breakfast dishes were still sitting on the table; clothing was strewn around the dressing room; I'd left the bed unmade. I attended to these things and then commenced a general survey of the place, attempting to view it through the eyes of a wronged wife. I had entered a new state. I couldn't bring myself to regret what had happened; it had felt like a long drink of water after years of thirst. But I had also begun to grasp, for the first time, the darker psychology of my situation. In our world, adultery was hardly unknown, but it was widely frowned upon. In any divorce settlement, the offending party typically came away with nothing, and the social penalty was large. Even if I never so much as laid eyes on Thea again, I would forever be the keeper of a secret that, if revealed, would destroy us both. I could offer no defense for what I'd done; I was purely in the wrong. In other words, I'd given my wife immense power over me, and the thought was deeply uncomfortable.

I went to the patio to wait and sharpen my lies. Too vague and I'd look like I was hiding something; too detailed and I'd seem to be trying too hard. (It was also possible that, given Elise's distracted state of mind, she wouldn't ask about my weekend at all.) There was still the drone to worry about—game, set, match if it came to that—but this had begun to seem a little paranoid, and the matter was, in any event, out of my hands.

"Mr. Bennett?"

A hand rested on my shoulder; Doria was standing over me. I must have dozed off. When had she come in?

"What time is it?" I asked. The sun had set.

"A little after seven, sir. Mrs. Bennett is on the phone for you."

Odd, at this late hour. I took the call in the bedroom.

"*There* you are," Elise said.

The guilt, long delayed, was instantaneous, a cold stab. "Is everything all right? I thought you'd be home by now."

"I know—I'm sorry, honey. The time just got away from me. Don't be mad. Are you mad?"

"I'm not mad, Elise. I was just concerned."

"It's just, I'm getting *so* much work done. Two whole notebooks of new designs! Two!"

I saw where this was headed. "So, you'll be staying."

"Would you mind too much? I have some meetings in town tomorrow afternoon. I thought I'd go straight from here and see you at home after."

My first thought, I confess, was this: I could have had one more day with Thea. My second was the one I spoke aloud.

"Where's 'here'?"

"I'm sorry?"

"You never told me where you were staying."

"Oh." She paused. "It's way out in the middle of nowhere, I forget the name of the town. The house belongs to a friend of my parents'—I don't think you've met them. I'm staying in the guest cottage."

The explanation felt incomplete, even a bit evasive, but I was hardly in a position to question my wife's whereabouts.

"Oh, you should see it out here, Proctor. It's so peaceful. And the air. It does something to my brain, I swear. It just sweeps out all the cobwebs."

"It sounds nice."

"It got me thinking. What would you say to looking for a place of our own out here? I know, I know, it's a bit of a stretch, but I'm sure my parents can help us, and you've been so down lately, honey. And now this awful thing with your father. I don't like seeing you like this. It might be just the thing you need."

How did this make me feel? Like shit! At the same time I'd been doing my best to destroy my marriage, my wife had been shopping for vacation real estate to cheer me up.

"Proctor, what do you think?"

I had to swallow before answering. "I guess there's no harm in talking about it."

"Because this would absolutely have to be a joint decision. I totally get that."

I became aware of voices in the background—first a man's, then a woman's, then a different man's, although I couldn't make out what they were saying.

Elise, suddenly distracted, said, "I'm being called to dinner."

"That's fine. You go eat."

"And it's okay? My staying? I can come home if you need me to."

There was a burst of party laughter at the other end of the line.

"Sorry, honey," Elise said. "It's a little loud here."

“That’s okay. Don’t let me keep you.”

“So, I’ll see you tomorrow night?”

“Tomorrow night.”

And at precisely the same moment—as if by a mutual understanding we could not forswear—we hung up the phone.

III

THE LOST GIRL

12

"Where's Jason?"

It was Monday morning. The driver, a young man with a brush cut and acne scars, was, once again, no one I recognized. "Who?"

"Jason Kim, my trainee."

"I don't know, sir. They sent me."

Curious, but there was nothing to be done about it. At the Ministry of Human Resources building, the driver let me off at the curb. I showed my credentials at the watchman's station in the lobby and made for the elevator just in time to sidle through the doors and find I wasn't alone.

Three men and a woman, the last a fellow enforcement officer assigned to District Five, Regan Brandt. We didn't know each other well—just enough to exchange greetings in the halls and make a bit of small talk—though we'd served together on various committees and review boards. Thus, I was taken aback when she neither returned my "good morning" nor even so much as glanced in my direction. Clutching a stack of folders to her chest, she kept her eyes focused in a death lock on the doors. As the car began to climb, she darted a hand to the panel and jabbed the button for level two; the moment the doors opened, she marched briskly away. Regan's office, I happened to know, was on level four.

Flummoxed by this odd encounter, I disembarked on six. Something was off. I sensed this with gathering unease as I approached my office. The place was oddly quiet: no clicking typewriters or shuffling papers, no background hum of voices getting on with the day. In their stead was a kind of subaudible white noise of anxiety.

Oona was sitting at her desk outside my office door, which stood open. Her eyes met mine with a quick widening of alarm. *You don't want to be here.*

"Ah, Proctor." Amos was standing in my office doorway. He waved me in. "Join us, won't you?"

Us? I followed him inside. On the love seat below the windows was a second man, who rose.

"What's going on?" I asked Amos.

"Take a seat, won't you?"

"I'll stand, thanks."

"As you wish." He nervously jangled some change in his pocket. "You know Nabil, I believe?"

Nabil West, chief legal counsel to the Ministry of Human Resources. Thin and serious, the man was known equally for his impenetrable demeanor and his sartorial dash. That morning, he was wearing a chalk-striped suit, tight as a drum skin, and a resplendently yellow bow tie.

"I'm afraid I have some disquieting news," Amos said. "Saturday morning, we received word that the watchman you assaulted on the wharf sustained a mortal injury."

His words didn't seem to attach to anything. "What are you talking about?"

"The man has died, Proctor."

I looked at both men in turn. "I'm sorry," I managed, "I'm not following. Are you saying I had something to do with it?"

Amos cleared his throat. "It wasn't the . . . um . . . strangulation per se. According to the medical examiner, the cause of death was a cerebral hemorrhage brought on by a blow to the head. Upon review of the drone footage, it's been determined that the injury occurred when you dropped him."

The news that one has taken a life is not easily digested. *A murderer?* the brain cries out. *Me? But I'm perfectly nice! I was only just eating breakfast! How can you be talking about* me*?*

"There must be some mistake. He was fine when I left him. Somebody's getting this wrong."

Nabil spoke next: "I'm afraid there's no error, Director Bennett. The examiner's report and the drone footage leave little room for doubt. And, of course, there's the witness."

"Witness? What witness?"

"Jason Kim, your trainee."

That little idiot! "What did he tell you?"

"More than enough."

Now I *did* have to sit down. I felt almost ill.

"Take a moment, Proctor," Amos said. "Do you want some water?"

I didn't, but it would give me something to focus on. Oona appeared with a glass. My hand trembled as I sipped.

"The review board met over the weekend." Amos's tone had shifted—less officious, more personal. The voice of an old friend, helpless before the unfortunate facts. "The good news is, you aren't being charged with a crime."

"Ha! Why the hell not? You're telling me I killed a man."

"No, that's not what we're saying. Yes, you played a role. But in the review board's opinion, his use of the shocker was unwarranted, and he also disobeyed a direct order. Your response, albeit rather drastic, was provoked by the watchman's overuse of force, and his injury could just as easily be termed an accident. There's also the mitigating circumstance of your father's episode. We're all sympathetic. You were placed in a terrible position."

The idea that my life was over was beginning to sink in. "So, what's the bad news?"

"Under the circumstances, it's the board's recommendation that your employment by Social Contracts be terminated immediately. In exchange for your agreement not to pursue the matter, the review board will take no further action. Nabil?"

From his briefcase, the man produced a sheaf of paper and placed it on the coffee table in front of me.

"This is nuts."

"All very standard, Director Bennett. If you'll please sign by the arrow."

Director Bennett—not for long. "Mind if I read it first? Professional habit."

A flash of irritation showed in the man's face; he wanted to be done with this. "As you like."

> This Separation Agreement (the "Agreement") is entered into by and between Proctor Bennett ("Employee") and Ministry of Human Resources, located at Two Hundred Prosperity Plaza ("Employer") for the purposes of termination of employment and general release.
>
> WHEREAS the Employee of the Employer and the following parties wish to avoid any claims made by the Employee against the Employer, including all other existing differences, in an amicable manner. The Employee acknowledges that the terms made under the Agreement is made for the sole purpose of avoiding uncertainties, exasperations, and litigation. The parties hereby represent that both voluntarily enter into it with full knowledge of its entirety, including its terms and consequences . . .

Et cetera, et cetera, et cetera. I'd conducted my life by such documents, set store by the power of their communal glue. My life's work, the good I'd done, my very name—all would be irrevocably tarnished with the stroke of a pen. What bitter irony! Ten minutes ago, I'd been planning to quit. Now the very thing I'd intended to give away was being ripped from my hands, and I felt utterly destroyed.

I turned to the last page. "You're kidding."

Nabil said, "It's a simple nondisclosure clause. All very standard."

"I'm not even allowed to *talk* about this?"

"Candidly, Director Bennett, why would you want to?"

Amos held out a pen. It was one of mine. "I'm sure you can see that this is what's best for everyone."

"Where's Jason? I want to talk to him."

The two men exchanged glances. Amos said, "I'm afraid the boy's resigned."

"He *quit*?"

"He was very shaken up by the whole thing. You were something of a hero to him, apparently. We received his notice this morning by courier."

"Does Callista know about all this?"

Amos nodded.

"And she really signed off?"

"This was her idea, Proctor. The review board's initial feeling was that the matter should be referred to the court. Callista gave quite a speech on your behalf. She's the reason you're not in custody right now." He pressed the pen toward me. "Proctor, *please*. Be sensible. A public scandal is in nobody's interest. If you won't do it for yourself, do it for Elise."

What choice did I have? There was a body on a slab; I was lucky to be getting off so lightly.

I accepted the pen and scrawled my name.

Nabil scooped the contract off the table and returned it to his briefcase, which he sealed with a conclusive snap. Meanwhile, two watchmen had appeared at the door.

"For fucksake, Amos, are guards really necessary? What do you think I'm going to do?"

"Just the rules, Proctor." I was unaware of any rules regarding escorting a murderer from the premises, but never mind. "One last detail. I'll have to ask for your credentials."

Did it ever stop? I tossed them onto the coffee table.

"No need to pack up," Amos said. "We'll send your personal things along."

"Keep them. I don't give a shit." Not entirely true, but it seemed like the right thing to say.

"I'm sorry things had to end this way, Proctor."

"Yeah, you and me both."

Oona, wearing an expression of absolute misery, was standing by her desk. "Oh, Director Bennett—"

With tears in her eyes, she broke off, unable to continue. We embraced—the first time we'd ever done so and, presumably, the last.

"It's Proctor now," I said. "Just Proctor."

And just like that, it was over. The offices of District Six were silent, like a house after everyone has gone to bed. I nodded at the watchmen.

"Let's go, boys."

Something I'd never known: the distance from my office to the street was exactly one hundred and eighty-six steps.

A question to ponder: What does one do with the remainder of his day when his life has been annihilated before nine A.M.?

Call his wife and bawl into the phone? Bore every stranger in the barroom? Stare at the sea, contemplating eternity?

None of these. What I did instead was vomit into a trash can.

It felt as if something had come unbolted inside me. Once, twice, three times I hurled my meager breakfast into the detritus of discarded papers, cardboard coffee cups, mashed chewing gum, and bagged dog poop at the bottom of the bin. Passersby were staring, and why wouldn't they? Who could have ignored this revolting scene, this diorama of degradation? Gripping the sides of the can, I finally drew myself erect.

"The fuck you looking at?"

My question landed hard on the disturbed face of an older woman walking a minuscule poofy-haired dog. She stared at me in horror.

"Go on," I snapped, "get the hell out of here."

Alarmed, she scurried away. My mouth tasted foul; sweat dripped down my face. I inspected my tie, the front of my suit, the tops of my shoes. At least these had been spared.

I crossed the street and entered the plaza. Its lush green lawn, its meticulously trimmed trees, its hedges and topiaries and flowerbeds—all suddenly seemed laughable, part of some great cosmic joke. Wandering the pathways, I realized I had no idea where to go. Home was, of course, the obvious destination, but I had no car and was in no shape to ride a shuttle. The thought of storming Callista's office held some appeal, but only for a moment—I had endured enough public humiliation for one day. It had also occurred to me, belatedly, that Elise already knew. *The house belongs to a friend of my parents'—I don't think you've met them.* Callista had whisked her daughter away for the weekend while my fate was being determined.

What I needed was someplace private where I could collect myself. Thea's gallery was just five blocks away. Probably not what the woman had in mind, but I could see no other option.

The door was locked, but the lights were on. I rapped on the glass to no avail, then looked further and saw the bell. Thea appeared on the second ring.

"This is a nice surprise," she said with a smile, but in the next instant her expression changed. "You look—"

"Awful. Yes, I know. Would it be okay if I came in? I need to clean up."

For a moment she was silent, computing the ghastly sight of me. "Of course."

Cool, dry air washed over me as I stepped inside. I glanced around at the paintings on the walls: ocean waves, landscapes, street musicians.

Seeing my reaction, Thea made a wry face. "I told you."

"God, who does this stuff?"

"People with paint and too much time on their hands. Come back to my office. There's a washroom."

A desk piled with papers; crates stacked against the walls; a tiny kitchen. In the washroom I removed my suit coat and shirt, soaked a hand towel in cold water, and ran it over my face and chest. My reflection in the mirror was disturbing. My skin was washed out, almost colorless, my eyes sunk in their sockets like ogres in a cave. In the medicine cabinet I found a bottle of mouthwash, gargled, spat. I splashed more water on my face. An improvement, but I still looked like hell.

Thea was waiting outside the door, looking worried. "Better?"

"A little, thank you." How different this was from our last encounter.

"I can make some tea."

I nodded. "Tea would be good."

I took a chair beside her desk while she put the kettle on. "Want to tell me what happened?"

"I just got fired."

Her face fell. "Proctor, that's terrible."

"Want to know something funny? I was actually planning to quit. Turns out that doesn't make it any easier."

The kettle whistled. Thea poured the water into mugs, dropped a teabag into each, and carried them to her desk. "Milk? Sugar?"

"This is good, thank you."

My hand trembled as I raised the mug to blow over the top. Thea sat, facing me.

"Do you want to talk about it?"

"Technically, I'm not allowed to."

"Oh?"

"They had me sign a nondisclosure agreement." I made air quotes, adding, "'All very standard, Director Bennett.' In exchange, the whole thing gets shoved into the shredder."

"That doesn't sound good."

"Can't say I blame them. They say I killed a man. The watchman on the pier."

I expected this announcement to alarm her. A murderer, sitting in her office, drinking tea! But my words seemed to have no effect on her at all.

I said, "You don't seem surprised."

"Oh, I'm surprised. I just don't get it, is all."

"They say it happened when I dropped him."

"I saw him when they carried him off. He looked okay to me."

"That's what I thought, too. They say it happened later. Cerebral hemorrhage."

"And you believe them?"

"Do I have a choice?"

She frowned. "It just seems a little . . . odd, don't you think?"

"I won't say the thought didn't occur to me."

Thea rose and moved away before turning to face me again. "Your father was echoing, yes? Having bad thoughts."

I nodded. "Yeah. It was pretty awful."

"Is it possible he said something you weren't supposed to hear?"

I looked at her carefully. "Are you sure you want to know about this?"

"If you want to tell me."

There seemed little reason to be cagey. I'd brought this to her door, after all.

"The whole thing was pretty strange. At the time I thought it was just babble, but now I'm not so sure. It started in the car, when he suddenly didn't seem certain who I was. That by itself wasn't so unusual—I've seen it happen before. But it was the *way* he said it."

"How was that?"

I searched for the words. "It was like I was me, but also somebody else at the same time."

"Was it a convergence maybe? Something from an old iteration?"

"I guess it's possible, but the man was my guardian. Surely one of us would have felt it before. He also seemed very impatient to get to the pier. 'I would very much like to arrive soon' was how he put it."

"'Arrive.'" Thea was looking at me intently. "That was the word he used. You're certain."

I saw the connection she was making. "You mean like the man I met at the shuttle stop? 'Arrival come,' and all that?"

Thea shrugged. "I don't know. There could be something to it, though."

"I have to say, it doesn't really seem like him. I don't see him falling for that stuff. It was when we got to the pier that he completely fell apart. He started saying crazy things. 'You're not you.' 'The world is not the world.' That's when he got out of the car and took off running, which I guess you saw."

"How about after? Did he say anything then?"

In for a penny, in for a pound. "He used a word."

"A word?"

"He said, 'Oranios.' 'It's all Oranios.' He kept saying it, over and over, all the way to the ferry. I'll never forget it."

Thea frowned. "What do you think he meant?"

"I looked it up. It's the name of an ancient Greek god."

"My mythology isn't the best, Proctor."

"He was the father of the Titans. The god of the heavens. The name translates as 'celestial.' It means the sky, basically." I shrugged. "Not a lot to go on," I said.

"Have you told anybody about this?"

"You would be the first."

She smiled at me. "I'm honored."

"Don't be. If what you say is true, I may have just gotten you in a heap of trouble."

She made a dismissive gesture. "Oh, I'm a big girl. I can take care of myself. So, what are you going to do?"

I hadn't really thought that far ahead. "I'm open to suggestions. Going home doesn't seem like the best option at the moment."

"Oh?"

"Yeah, you could say my getting fired isn't going to make me very popular. Also, I feel like hell. I wouldn't mind lying down for a while, if that's okay."

Thea rose. "As it happens, I know a place. Come with me."

She led me through a back door to a lobby with an elevator, which whisked us to the seventh floor. We walked in silence down the hall.

"Here we are."

She keyed the lock and stood aside to let me enter. Her apartment was modern, with an airy, unfussy feel. Wide windows in the living area looked over the rooftops of lesser buildings toward the harbor—a view nearly identical to the one from my office, though I wouldn't be seeing that again anytime soon. Furniture with clean, low lines, a wall of bookshelves half-filled, small objects on tables. There was a scent in the air, distinctly feminine. It seemed strange that, given the intimacies we'd shared, I was only now entering this zone of her life.

"The couch is comfortable. Too comfortable, actually," she said. "I fall asleep there plenty of nights."

I turned to look at her. "This is very nice of you. I'm sorry to intrude like this."

"Just try to get some rest. I'll wake you up in a couple of hours. You can figure out what to do then."

But I'd stopped listening. I was staring at the wall behind her. Thea turned her head, following my look.

"Oh, that? It's by the man in the Annex I told you about."

I stepped toward the painting. Bluish, oversized, perfectly square. As I neared, the details emerged.

It hit me like a punch.

"I need to sit down."

I collapsed into a chair. What was I seeing? The ocean at night, a great black sea of doubled stars, and in the stars were faces. They were like ghosts, hovering in the blackness, a great and terrible longing in their eyes.

"Proctor, what's wrong?"

"I've seen that before."

Her eyes narrowed on my face. "What do you mean, you've seen it?"

"It's a dream I have." *This poor woman!* I thought. A harmless flirtation at a concert, and now she had a raving lunatic in her apartment. "I know, that sounds totally crazy. Call the watchmen—I won't fight them."

"You . . . dreamed it."

"Dreamed, dream. It happens all the time. I never saw the faces, though." I shook my head. "I'm not making sense. I should go."

"I don't think you're going anywhere, the state you're in."

I looked up. "Take me to the artist."

Thea shook her head. "I can't."

"Why not?"

"Because he wouldn't like it. He's very private." She paused, then added, "There's something else you might want to know about him."

"What's that?"

"The man can't see," she said, and when I failed to comprehend, she added, "I mean, he's blind."

"He's blind and he paints *that*?"

"Believe me, I've asked."

I looked at the painting again. How could anyone see these things, let alone a blind man?

Because of all the faces, there was one I recognized.

Caeli's.

13

Monday, 10:00 A.M.

The motorcade—a pair of security vehicles front and rear, with the black limo in between—glides down the hill toward the causeway. All other traffic has been cleared. They race ahead, the sea lapping the edges of the floating structure over which they pass; the sky is tall and blue. When they reach the end of the causeway, the gates open; the guards wave them through. In the backseat of the limo, Otto Winspear unclasps his briefcase to examine the evidence again. There are photos, of course, but it's the drone feed that tells the tale. He removes the portable viewer from his case, backs up the feed, and starts again.

The feed, time-stamped, commences at 2:13 A.M. A pair of running figures and, in the background, the defaced kiosk; Hanson has yet to enter the drone's field of view. The two are careful not to look up at the camera, or else they don't notice the drone that has begun to track them. One appears to be a child—a boy. The second is a woman, with short hair. The two make for an alley, where they separate. Hanson appears at the edge of the screen and follows the second figure—a mistake. A child would have been the smarter choice: faster, perhaps, but not capable of beating him to death.

For fifty-two seconds, the drone loses them in the maze of alleys; then, four blocks west, they reappear. The camera has yet to capture the suspect's face. She enters the fateful alley. It's a curious choice; surely the woman would know about the fence that stands in her way. Indeed, Otto has begun to think that this drawn-out pursuit is by design. She could have lost him long ago; she wants him to know how little she thinks of him. She makes for the fence without a hitch in her stride. Up and over she goes, as cleanly as a gymnast, and drops behind it, out of view.

Hanson, close behind, has more trouble. He's tired; the pursuit has gone on too long. As he approaches the fence, he hesitates. He manages to grab the top but barely holds on, and for a couple of seconds he hangs there, until he hoists himself to the top, where he pauses. What does he see that makes him stop? Another few seconds and he drops down to the other side.

The drone is programmed to seek two things: movement and the heat of warm bodies. Hanson and the woman, behind the fence, are now out of view. The drone is hovering, calculating its next move, when something else catches its eye. It turns sharply and follows. The other suspect? No. It drops between buildings and gives chase, and the next thing Otto knows, the screen fills with the image of a mangy dog digging through a garbage can.

The motorcade halts. There's a gathering of onlookers, in addition to a heavy security presence, both watchmen and S3.

"Madam Chair, I think it's best if you wait here," he says.

Callista, seated opposite, gives him a withering look. "I've seen blood, Otto."

"Not like this you haven't. But it's the crowd I'm thinking about. Best to keep you under wraps, I think."

Though his point is a reasonable one, Otto knows she hates being told what to do. She lets a moment pass before turning her face to the window.

"For now," she says.

Otto disembarks and enters the alley, which is cordoned off by tape. Three S3 agents are waiting at the fence. One is named Campbell; Otto doesn't know the other two. He ignores them and kneels beside the corpse, which someone's had the decency to cover with a blanket. The photographs should have prepared him for what he sees when he draws back the blanket, but it still comes as a shock. Pretty much everything above Hanson's neck has been reduced to a red stain on the pavement, encircled by an irregular corona of small smashed bits. The tropical heat hasn't improved the situation, either.

Campbell says, "Sir, we found what we believe to be the weapon."

"Show me."

From the trunk of his vehicle, Campbell produces a blood-spattered two-by-four with a protruding nail. Otto gives it a little swing to feel its weight.

"Witnesses?" he asks Campbell.

The man shakes his head. "We canvased the entire block."

Otto looks up at the wall of windows above the alley. What happened here couldn't have been quiet. "Do it again. Don't be nice about it."

Campbell signals the other two, and the three men exit the alley at a quickstep. Meanwhile, the van from the Ministry of Well-Being has arrived. Two men emerge and retrieve a gurney from the back. Otto watches as they roll the headless Hanson into a bag and lift him onto the gurney.

"Straight to the incinerator," he tells them.

They wheel the body away. Alone, Otto looks over the scene again, trying to reconcile what he sees with the images on the feed. It's Hanson's pause at the top of the fence that interests him. There's nothing on this side that could have served as cover for the woman; if she was waiting to ambush him, surely Hanson would have seen her. And yet the man chose to go over anyway, straight into a two-by-four with a nail in it. What did he see?

Otto mentally carves the end of the alleyway into squares and begins to walk them, eyes focused on the pavement. Litter, broken glass, the usual detritus. He approaches the fence. Something is here: a dark stain.

He crouches, takes a glove from his suit pocket, snaps it on, and touches his index finger to the stain. It comes away tacky. He casts his eyes around. Now he sees them: footprints, racing from the alleyway.

Otto crosses the barrier and summons a watchman.

"Yes, sir," the man says, standing at attention. He's older, with a bit of a gut. Otto pokes his thumb over his shoulder.

"Get a bucket and brushes and clean that mess up."

He gets back into the car. "Well?" Callista says.

"The woman was hurt. Quite badly, I think. Agents are canvassing the block again."

Callista looks out the darkly tinted window at the crowd of spectators. "Let me ask you something," she says. "Do they seem . . . different to you?"

In fact, they do. The presence of the S3 should have sent them scattering, but the opposite's occurred; the size of the crowd has increased, and their attention is focused on the car with a look of challenge. *You think we'll tell you anything? Guess again.* Maybe the woman who smashed Hanson's head to smithereens is here right now, concealed among the crowd.

"They detest us," Callista says.

"Some do," Otto says. "They always have."

"I mean all of them."

Otto tells the driver to go. Already he is calculating his next move. A blast of the horn from the first security vehicle and the crowd, in no particular hurry, parts to let them through. Otto settles into his seat.

Fine, he thinks, let them hate us. It's better if they do.

14

The drive to the academy took ten minutes. Located on the inland edge of the city, the campus was vast, with multiple classroom buildings, athletic fields, indoor and outdoor performance spaces, and a gymnasium complex.

There was also a significant security presence, starting with a pair of watchmen at the front gate.

"Don't worry," Thea said as we drove up. "I've got this."

She drew down her window. "Good afternoon, Officer. We're here for the new guardian information session? The name is Dimopolous."

He consulted his clipboard. "I don't see you on the visitor list."

Her face fell. "That's probably my fault. We didn't call until this morning. We got good news!" She took my hand and squeezed it so the man could see. "Our number came up!"

"Oh. Congratulations."

"We'll be getting a boy. I was, like, fine, either's great, but my husband was adamant."

Following her lead, I leaned forward to send the watchman my best new-dad grin through Thea's window. "It's true. What man doesn't want a son, am I right?"

"And that's fine, honey," Thea said to me. "A boy first, a girl second. Fair is fair." She turned back to the watchman. "I guess you can tell, we're pretty excited. He's coming on the ferry in two weeks."

"Let me check again."

He examined the clipboard more closely, sliding his finger down the list of names.

"This is totally sweet of you," Thea said. "I can't thank you enough."

He reached the end and looked up. "You're *sure* your appointment is today?"

"Absolutely. One hundred percent."

The risk, of course, was that he'd pick up the phone.

"It's okay," Thea said. "Totally get it. We can come back later."

The watchman sighed. "Oh, the hell with it." He directed his voice at the guardhouse: "It's okay, you can let them through."

"Really? This is so incredibly nice of you."

He leaned down to the window. "Somebody probably screwed up. You wouldn't believe how often that happens." The gate lifted. "Have a good day now."

We began our journey up the long driveway. "That was quite a performance," I said. "Were you ever an actress?"

She shrugged. "Just a girl who can make the sale."

The campus was exactly as I remembered it. The stateliness of the buildings, the lushness of the fields, the general atmosphere of the place, with its air of noble purpose. Thea steered into the lot as a line of uniformed first formers, led by their teacher, proceeded past us like a jostling parade of ducklings, en route to the day's next adventure in learning.

"My turn to do the talking," I said.

The reception desk was presided over by a young woman with

a blond pageboy, a pearl choker, and a dark, somewhat matronly suit.

"Good afternoon," I said. "Proctor Bennett, Department of Social Contracts. My associate and I are here to see about a student. There have been reports of delinquency."

"Delinquency?" She seemed unfamiliar with the word.

"Skipping school."

Her eyes widened with shock. I took things up a notch: "The girl's been seen off campus during school hours, consorting with support staff."

"Oh, my goodness."

"May we see her, please?"

"Of course." She rose briskly from her chair. "What's her name?"

"Her first name is Caeli. Unfortunately, that's all we have. She'd be third or fourth form, I believe."

The woman disappeared into the back office. A couple of minutes later, she returned. "Are you sure you have the correct name? We don't have a Caeli currently registered. Maybe the spelling's different?"

I doubted it, but I offered a couple of possible variations. The receptionist looked, to no avail.

"I wish I could help." She shivered faintly. "The support staff. I can't imagine."

"Perhaps you've seen her. Short blond hair, about so tall. She has a mark on her cheek."

"A mark?"

"A scar, actually."

"Oh, my. The poor thing." She thought a moment. "Doesn't ring a bell, and I think I'd remember something like that. Oh, wait." She'd hit on something. "Maybe her guardians withdrew her. That could explain it."

Withdrawing from the academy: I'd never heard of such a thing. "Does that happen?"

"It can. Every once in a while, the guardians decide to educate the iterant at home. It's almost always when a ward is giving them trouble. Sounds like it could be this girl, from what you say."

"Wouldn't you still have records for her?"

"We give them to the guardians." Something changed in her face. "Didn't you say you were from Social Contracts? Wouldn't that be your thing?"

I slid my eyes past her. There it was, positioned at the margin of the ceiling: the inevitable camera.

"We'll be certain to look into it," I said with a smile. "Thank you for your time, Ms. . . . ?"

"Beaufort. Florence Beaufort."

"Thank you for your time, Ms. Beaufort."

We beat a hasty retreat. The guardhouse presented a whole new problem: How to explain our quick exit? But as we approached, the gate swung open automatically. Thea tooted the horn and waved from the wheel. The last I saw of the watchman, he was standing in the middle of the driveway with his hands on his hips, watching as we drove away.

"That might not have been so smart," I said. "One phone call and someone's going to put that together."

"I know. Have you ever heard of a student withdrawing?"

"No."

"Me neither." She glanced at me sidelong. "And you're sure you saw her face in the painting? Really *sure.*"

"I'm not making it up. It was her, I'm positive."

"And this business with her name—"

"I admit, it's a hell of a coincidence."

She glanced at me again. "I'm not saying I don't believe you, Proctor."

"But?"

She took a breath before answering. "But it seems a little . . . out there."

"I don't deny it. Say the word and I'll get out."

We drove in silence for a time. I felt physically awful. The cold had returned; my mouth and tongue had a bitter chemical taste. I wondered if I was coming down with something, a distressing thought. I had almost no experience with physical illness, no baseline with which to measure my expectations: how much suffering was involved, how long it lasted. We banged over a pothole; my stomach lurched. The motion of the vehicle was suddenly intolerable.

"Stop the car," I said.

"What?"

"I'm serious. Pull over."

I was out of the vehicle before it had come to a complete stop. Hands on my knees, I waited to vomit into the ditch, but nothing came, and why would it? I'd emptied my stomach on the street just a few hours ago. Slowly, the nausea receded, but not the cold, which had become something else—less a physical sensation than a disturbing inner wrongness. Something strange was happening to me. I looked up. We were parked at the edge of a grassy field. There was something exotically vivid about it, almost psychedelic. A gentle breeze brushed the tips of the grass, tickling it in undulating waves of alternating hue. The sight was hypnotically involving; it entranced me utterly. The wind on my face felt cool and strange, not a single unified force but a pattering of microscopic entities, like a rain of individual molecules. It was as if the world around me were dissolving into its tiniest particulars. A peaceful feeling came. I was suddenly alone in the universe. No, not suddenly; this had always been so. I was merely discovering it.

"Proctor?"

A voice, calling to me from the farthest distance. A voice from over the sea, volleying across the stars.

"Are you okay?"

And just like that, everything snapped back into focus. The grass, the wind, the line of trees in the distance: it was all perfectly commonplace. Thea was still sitting at the wheel, watching me through the open passenger door. I got back into the car.

"Sorry, felt a little carsick."

She eyed me warily. "You don't look too good."

"How long was I out there?"

She frowned at this odd question. "I don't know. Thirty seconds maybe?"

Thirty seconds. It had felt like days.

"Maybe we should find a reader and check your number," Thea said.

"That's the last thing I want. I'm done with those fucking things."

Wind buffeted the car as a large truck sailed past. I'd almost forgotten that we were parked on the shoulder of an actual road that other vehicles might use.

"You really care about her, don't you?" Thea asked. She was looking over the wheel. "Caeli, I mean."

Did I? I had no real reason to—she wasn't my ward, after all—and yet it seemed so.

Thea said, "There's a man I know, someone who might be able to help you track her down."

"'A man.'"

"He's not S3, if that's what you're thinking."

"I wasn't thinking anything."

"Sure you weren't. But I trust him, and he's very good at what he does."

I was in no position to decline.

"It may take a day or so to get in touch with him. But if anyone can figure out what happened to her, believe me, he's the guy."

"All right."

There was a pause.

Thea said, "You should probably go home, you know."

She wasn't wrong; I couldn't hide forever. But there was one thing left to do.

We got Jason's address from the directory at a phone kiosk. It wasn't where I would have thought. Most young people preferred to live downtown, where the action was. But the complex where he lived was on the western edge of the city, with a busy roadway in front. The building was older, a little dingy. A second-story walk-up. I knocked, but no one answered. The drapes were drawn. We asked around.

Nobody had seen him, either.

15

It's not that he cannot see. He can, though barely. Vague, borderless shapes; diaphanous mists of color; shifting shadows of movement, contrailed like comets: that is the world in which he lives, his life of quotidian detail. The bathing and dressing, the pissing and shitting, the eating and sleeping and arising each day to do it all again.

There was a time when his eyes worked just like everybody else's. Then, in an alleyway, that ended. He was a young man, fierce and wild; he wasn't sure what he'd done to incur the watchmen's wrath. It had something to do with being in the wrong place at the wrong time among the wrong people, a story often told. *Fuck you!* He gave them nothing; he had nothing to give. Nor did they seem to want anything. *Fuck the fucking lot of you!* Their batons, their fists, the tips of their boots: they fell and fell, and when they stopped falling, the world had changed. It had become a place of little dancing sparks and dark, hemming walls, like the sides of a tunnel. He thought this might pass, but it did not. The walls closed in; the dancing sparks bloomed into great, gaseous flares. One morning he awoke and couldn't tell if it was night or day, if he was awake or still sleeping.

To be blind, though, was not to be sightless. That was something he learned. His vision merely changed direction: not outward, toward physical reality, but inward, toward the mind. New thoughts were born within him, and with these thoughts came a new way of existing. The world was something he *felt,* unencumbered by the tyranny of sight.

The urge to paint followed. How else to capture this new awareness so that he wouldn't be alone with it? He had no idea what he was doing. Back when he'd had two good eyes in his head, he'd never so much as picked up a brush; the idea had never even occurred to him. But in his new state of visual silence, he felt an expansive tenderness toward everything existing. As if he were forgiving the world for what it was.

Thus, the faces.

The first time he painted them, he wasn't even aware he was doing it. This was . . . when? Years ago. He'd begun his morning in the customary manner: running his hands along the blank canvas, taking measure and stock. With his face pressed close—he paints the way an ox plows, focused entirely on the small, rolling patch of ground beneath his nose—he began. He was painting the way the day felt: nostalgic, with a hint of restless boredom. Blue was involved, and also green; circles but also squares; shapes suggesting buildings but with a disordered cant, as if gravity were acting upon each one in a slightly different manner. He had very nearly achieved a kind of trance when suddenly the spell was broken; someone was standing behind him.

"Who *are* those people?"

Claire. She had come to bring him lunch. She placed the tray on the workbench where Pappi kept his supplies: jars of brushes, pots of color, thinners and oils, all arranged in rows his hands could navigate without thought.

"Who do you mean?" He spoke brusquely, annoyed by the interruption. It felt like something stolen from him.

"Don't be funny."

"I honestly don't know what you're talking about."

A gray streak moved over his vision; Claire was gesturing at the canvas.

"The people in the painting. It's weird."

"What are you seeing?"

"Are you seriously telling me you don't know?" He heard discomfort in her voice; the painting disturbed her. "They're everywhere."

"You don't like it."

"You never ask me that."

"I'm asking now."

She paused, then said, "Not really, no."

She went away. Pappi realized what was happening. He was a conduit. The world was speaking through him—no, not the world. Something unseen, a hidden plane. Did this make him a madman? He didn't care, just as he also knew that the painting was but a first glimpse, like a clearing of the throat before actual words emerged.

What were the faces? Were they the spirits of the dead? Shadows of those yet to be? Who were these people, peering out from the buildings and the trees and the ocean and the stars?

After what happened with Claire, Pappi decided that he would keep the faces to himself. He need not have bothered; no one cared. He became a fixture, nothing more: the old blind crank, covering canvases with the nonsense in his mind. It was an arrangement that suited him, even as he often felt the lack of someone who understood what he was doing.

But there was one who did.

He remembers the first day Thea came to him. (Ten years ago? Fifteen? He can no longer recall.) How young she was, how uncertain, though possessing a certain restiveness, a hunger inside her. All these things were in her voice, but not only there: Pappi sensed them in the air around her, a zone of jangling energy, like a humming swarm of bees. She was a student of aesthetics at the university, she explained; she was planning, someday, to open a gallery. She had heard of him through a friend of a friend of a friend; the road on which his name had traveled to her was obscure. It was as if she had found him by instinct, some force of fate. He did not trust her, yet. He bore no intrinsic malice to Prosperans—that urge had passed—but that didn't make him a fool. Well, he said, what are you looking for? He was sitting outside in the alley, feeling the sun on his face; that was where the girl had found him. She wasn't sure, she said. Her toe scuffed the ground. She would know it when she saw it.

He sent her away. He had no time for such foolishness. Nor did he imagine that a girl such as she, schooled in all the correct things and correct ways, the very flower of Prosperan society, could possibly see the value of what he did—that she would think anything about it at all. He painted for no one but himself; the world could think what it liked—it made no difference to him. Some rich girl. What could she possibly know?

A week later, Thea returned; once again, he sent her away. Twice more this happened, but the fourth time, he relented. She obviously wasn't going to leave him alone, so best to get it over with. (Though it was also true that he had begun to look forward to her visits; Claire, too, who sometimes sat with them in the yard.) He led her into the studio; the walls were empty, everything put away. He sat at his easel.

"So, what do you think?" he asked her.

"About what?"

"The painting, of course."

"But there's nothing there."

This was true. The canvas was blank.

"Oh, there's something there all right." He gestured to the far end of the room. "There's a chair over there, yes?"

"How did you know that?"

"Because there's always a chair over there. Bring it here."

She did as he'd asked, positioning the chair just beyond the easel.

"Now go on," he said. "Sit yourself down."

She seemed to intuit his intentions. His sense of her was coming into sharper relief. Her curiosity, her skepticism, the quickness of her mind. Inside her, boxes within boxes within boxes.

"Do you need me to be still?"

"Not especially, but stay where you are. And no peeking."

"How long?"

"Questions, questions."

They spent the rest of the afternoon that way, and the next two afternoons as well, the hours unspooling in a silence that was neither awkward nor enforced. It radiated from the companionable bargain between them: *You sit, I'll paint, we'll see what it all adds up to.* Thea made no comment on the absurd fact that she was posing for a blind man; neither did she ask to see the painting itself. She had nothing to say about the fact that Pappi, for prolonged stretches, would apply no paint to the canvas at all. When he resumed, often with broad, apparently heedless strokes, like a man painting a wall, this fact, too, passed without remark.

"What's going on in there?" Claire asked one night at dinner.

Others were seated around the table, including a new girl who had joined their number. She went by the name Jess.

"Just work," Pappi said. He spooned soup into his mouth. "I'm trying something new."

"You've never asked *me* to sit for you," Claire said.

Pappi smiled for the table. "That's because I've never needed to. I understand you just fine."

Claire scoffed. "I wouldn't be so sure."

He finished late the following day. He placed his brush in a jar and put his palette aside. A dizzying mental exhaustion washed through him. He felt as if he'd been standing for three days in the perfectly calm center of a raging storm. He allowed a moment to pass and then said to Thea, "Do you want to see it?"

He heard the scrape of the chair as Thea rose and came to stand beside him.

"That's me?" Her voice was tentative.

"I believe so."

Layers of color, dark and light. Vivid points of pigment with attenuated, neuron-like threads connecting them. Wild, emotional swaths of color swirling around and into one another like the currents of a whirlwind. And, underneath it all, a great, patient reservoir of oceanic blue, impossibly deep, shot with filaments of a darker tone, almost black, like a net of iron. The black of pain, though not a pain that couldn't be withstood. It was the painting's deep structure, its well of strength.

"That's you," he said. "All that you are and all the things that have ever happened to you and all the things that will."

Thea was silent. Pappi waited. Her presence was absolutely still, yet radiating waves of energy. More seconds went by and he heard a sudden gasp and then a choking sound.

"It's me," she said. "It's me, it's me . . ."

She fell into his arms. She wept.

She became his. Not in the father-daughter sense of things, though it possessed that element. An uncle and his favorite niece? Had anyone asked, Pappi would have said only that they understood each other, and that this understanding was innate, requiring no examination. That they were simply two like-minded souls who had collided in the world.

She watched him paint. All others were banished; only Thea was permitted. Curious, to him, that she didn't ask to paint herself; likewise, she declined all offers for him to teach her. But she would, from time to time, and then more often as she grew into the role, make observations about his work and offer criticisms.

"That red is too angry," she might say, or "I don't understand what you're doing in this corner," or "You're off today. Maybe you should take a break." She was not imperious; she was simply stating the facts as she saw them. More often than not the girl was correct, and even when she wasn't, she forced him into a deeper consideration of his work. To see it, as it were, with another's set of eyes.

And, of course, Mother was always hovering. Thea's powers of observation, her alert intelligence, her need, always, to know more, to get beneath the surface of life: the girl was a natural. Also, a danger to them all. The comings and goings of strangers at all hours, the whispers in the kitchen, the silences that fell when she entered a room: the girl was no fool, either.

The time came when the subject could be avoided no longer; she simply had to be told. They gathered in the kitchen one afternoon. Besides Pappi, Quinn was there, and Mother of course, and Jess, who was assuming more responsibilities in the day-to-day. The choice Mother gave the girl was stark: leave now and never come back, or sit and listen and be one of us.

A silence followed. Beneath the table, Pappi knew, somebody's hand was tightening on a knife.

"Thank you for telling me," Thea said. Her voice, though faint, was firm; she was addressing them as a group. "I think I always knew, though."

Thus, the moment.

"What do you want me to do?"

Pappi missed her when she went away. For two years, she was forbidden from the Annex: these were the rules Mother set. Thea would burrow into her life in Prospera, deeper and deeper, until she was in a position to be useful. But two years passed, and still Thea did not appear. Of her life, Mother told him nothing. She was doing a job; that was all Pappi needed to know.

One afternoon in the fourth year, Pappi was working in the

studio when he felt her presence in the room. So overwhelming was his sense of her, it was as if he'd traveled backward in time. Without words, they embraced. They didn't have long, she told him; her visit would have to be quick. A few short words with Mother and she would return to Prospera. But in that brief span she told him all she could—about her life in the city, the people she knew and the places she went, and her apartment above the gallery, which had begun to hit its stride. *The work, it's just awful,* she said, laughing brightly. *A bad joke. It flies off the walls.*

How wonderful to be near her again. The ice was broken; thereafter, she returned from time to time, always without warning, or none that Pappi knew of. A brief conversation, a treasure to him, and she would disappear down the hatch. He tried not to worry, but of course he did. Not that she'd be found out; the thought was simply inadmissible. It was her true self he feared for, her Thea-ness. How long could she be one thing while pretending to be another, without becoming that person? Or becoming nobody at all?

These are the things on his mind when, sitting at his easel—his morning has just begun—he hears someone enter behind him.

"Hello, Mother."

She has her own way of moving through space, like everyone. Hers is a state of partial presence, almost ghostly. She is there but also not; she's never quite where one looks, but has only just departed.

"How did you know?" she asks.

"Please."

She moves behind him to look at the canvas. "Now, that's interesting," she says after a moment.

"I can live with 'interesting.'"

He resumes his work. *Oh, you're here? Well, that's nice.* He dabs his brush onto the palette to apply more color—a pure, almost shocking white—and pushes his nose to the canvas, angling the brush on its thin edge to carve an arc, thin as an eyelash. He has no idea what he's doing, only that it feels right.

"Am I disturbing you, Pappi?"

He sculpts another line. "Is that an actual question?"

"Pappi, for godsakes, stop with the fucking painting."

He puts down his brush and swivels on his stool to face her. It makes no difference to him, but people like to be looked at, even by a blind man.

"I'm not sure who else is around," he says.

"Forget the others—it's you I'm here to see."

"Is that right?"

"I have a question for you."

"Now, that's new."

Her shadow dissolves into the general grayness of things. Her footsteps take her in no particular direction; she is moving only to form her thoughts.

"Where do you think they come from? The echoes. The bad thoughts."

"Isn't that more Quinn's department?"

"I'm asking you."

"All right." Pappi pauses. "Someplace else, would be my answer."

"That's not very helpful."

"That's because it wasn't the right question." He raises his brush like a conductor's baton. "Not where the echoes come from," he says. "*Who* they come from."

She sighs.

"You don't like my answer. Well, too bad. You want my opinion, though, somebody was trying to tell Bennett something."

"Such as?"

"I haven't the foggiest. You have to admit, though, it's an interesting question."

He can feel the frustration radiating off her. It's like somebody left an oven door open.

"So, I'll ask *you* a question," Pappi says. "Maybe Proctor knows something and maybe he doesn't. I won't say I'm not intrigued. But even if that's true, what would you do with the information?"

"It means something. Something that might help us."

"To do what, exactly? Hack the faxes, maybe? What would you do then?"

"We live. Like people."

"We live like people now," Pappi says. "If you ask me, the Prosperans are the ones who don't."

"They think they do."

"That's what they *think*. It doesn't make it so. So, tell me. Would you simply wipe them out?"

"A lot of people would. Jess, for one."

Pappi waves this aside. "Jess is angry, and she's young. She's also not in charge."

"The watchmen beat you blind, Pappi. How can you not want them gone?"

"Forgive me, but you're trying much too hard. That's not in you, not anymore. We both know that."

Silence, and she moves away.

"It's okay to be sad, you know," he says.

A small, bitter laugh. "Is it really?"

"Just listen to yourself. Of course it is." He allows her a moment, then says, "You and I aren't so very different, you know."

"Oh? How do you figure?"

Pappi shrugs. "Because neither of us hates them. Oh, we may have, in the past. I've had my moments. But mostly we just want to know why. Why this place, why Prospera? It may not make sense to us, but it does to someone. Now," he says, taking up his brush, "if it's all right with you, I'd like to get back to work."

"You know, maybe I didn't mean 'interesting.' Maybe I meant deranged."

He's already loading his brush. "And you wouldn't be the first to think so. Claire would probably agree with you. She's just too nice to say it. Are we done?"

He expects more from her, but nothing comes. A few seconds pass and she moves toward the door. A creak of old hinges and Pappi hears the aural wash of the outside world. The ocean bulging against the land; the hum of humanity going about its day; the wind carving along the sides of the buildings; and, somewhere far off, the repeated note of a bereftly barking dog.

"I know you're worried about her," Mother says from the door.

Pappi doesn't answer.

"She'll be all right, Pappi. She can handle it."

He is only pretending to paint. "You know where to find me."

16

And thus came the hour when the music would have to be faced.

I hailed a taxi from the plaza; it was after five when I returned to the house. Elise was sitting in the living room, a glass of wine, untouched, resting on the coffee table before her. She didn't look up at my approach; everything about her radiated barely controlled fury. I took a seat across from her.

"So, I guess your mother told you."

"I've been waiting here for hours, Proctor."

"It's a long story."

"Oh, I'm sure it is."

She rose with a burst of angry energy and moved to the patio door, where she stopped, facing away.

"Listen to me, Elise. There's more to this. The watchman was okay when I left. I barely touched him."

"There's footage, Proctor. You *attacked* the man."

"It wasn't like that. I'm telling you, something doesn't add up."

She tipped her face toward the ceiling. "God, why didn't I see this coming? How could I have been so dumb?"

"What are you talking about?"

"Please. The dreaming, the sleepwalking. You're not *well,* Proctor."

"I was just a kid, Elise. You're making too much of it."

She spun on her heel and jabbed a finger at me. Her eyes were filmed with furious tears. "You think I don't know? Night after night, thrashing around, charging through the house. It's like a circus around this place."

My stomach clenched.

"What, you don't have anything to say for yourself?"

I took a breath to calm myself. Nothing was going the way I'd planned it. "Elise, you have to hear me out. This all has something to do with my father's echoes."

"Great," she said, tossing a hand, "a couple of lunatics, the two of you."

"I know this all sounds a little paranoid—"

"A little? Proctor, you need *help.*"

"You remember Jason, my trainee? Amos said he quit, but I don't think that's what happened. I went to his apartment and nobody's seen him."

"Maybe he didn't want to see *you,* did you ever think of that?"

"Well, he's not the only one. There's also a girl. I think she's a part of this."

Elise looked at me pointedly. "A girl? What girl?" Her voice was accusing. "Proctor, are you having an *affair*?"

"God, no. Don't even say that. She's just a kid."

"Oh, fine." Her eyes rolled. She made air quotes. "'Just a kid.'"

I felt like I was digging my own grave with every word. "You have this all wrong. I met her on the beach last week."

"What are you talking about? What does some girl on the beach have to do with any of this?"

"Because it's all connected. I don't know how, but it is. The thing is, she's disappeared, too. I even went to the academy to track her down."

"You followed a girl to *school*?"

I took another breath. "Elise, you're not listening. I went to look for her is all. The thing is, nobody's seen her. It's like they've never even heard of her."

"Do you know how you sound? You sound insane."

"Okay, it seems a little crazy. I admit that. But probably you know her. She's the girl with the scar."

Elise's eyes darted around the room before landing on me again. "What scar? Why would I know a girl with a scar?"

"Because she lives around here. You must have heard something about her. Her name is Caeli."

A curious thing happened. The muscles of my wife's face went slack; her eyes grew heavy-lidded, as if she were on the verge of sleep. I had the strange sense that her mind had departed the room, leaving her body behind. This went on for several seconds until, with a jolt, she wrapped her arms around herself and shivered violently.

"For godsakes," she declared, "why does it always have to be so fucking freezing around this place?"

The room was, if anything, too warm. "It feels fine to me."

"Well, it isn't fine! It isn't fine at all!"

She turned abruptly and marched into the kitchen. What could I do but follow? I was desperate to be understood, to salvage whatever I could from this catastrophe.

"Elise, stop—"

"I just wanted everything to be nice. Is that too much to ask? For things to be nice? I can't deal with this with my show coming up. I can't!"

Now I was the angry one. "How can you think about your show at a time like this? I could be in real trouble here."

She spun to face me. "*You're* in trouble? That's rich. I have my new collection coming out in two weeks and my husband is a famous murderer."

"For the love of God, you know me. Do I seem like a murderer to you?"

I reached for her hand, but she recoiled. "Don't touch me."

The obvious thought finally occurred. My wife was afraid of me.

"I mean it, Proctor." She took a step back, pressing herself against the cabinets. "Just . . . don't."

Which was, naturally, the moment when Doria entered the room.

"Mrs. Bennett? Is everything okay?"

I was only too aware of how the situation looked: raised voices in the kitchen, the agitated husband cornering his tearful wife.

"Everything's fine, Doria," I said—a little too sternly. "Thank you."

The woman was having none of it. She took a step forward. "Mrs. Bennett?"

Elise snuffled and wiped her eyes with the back of her wrist. She seemed about to speak but didn't.

"She's okay," I said. "Just a little upset. Do you need something?"

"I forgot my purse."

There it was, resting in its usual spot on the counter. Doria scooped it up and tucked it under her arm. "I'd be happy to stay if you need me, Mrs. Bennett."

Elise, looking at the floor, shook her head miserably. "It's fine. You can go."

Doria glanced at me with frank suspicion, then turned back to Elise. "Well," she said finally, "if you're sure you're all right."

"Thank you, Doria," Elise said. "Good night."

"Good night, Mrs. Bennett."

We waited in silence until the front door closed.

"Elise, I'm sorry—"

But I got no further; my wife charged past me and down the hall. What was about to happen was perfectly apparent. I retreated to the living room and did the only thing I could think of, which was to pour myself a whiskey and toss it back. A sudden weariness washed through me; I felt as if I hadn't slept in ages, that I'd had all the thoughts that a mind could hold. I poured another glass and took it to the couch, where I lay down and closed my eyes, the whiskey balanced on my sternum. The sounds of Elise moving through the house reached me like a series of distant radio signals. I thought: *Now she is in the bedroom, opening drawers and closing them, tossing clothing into a case. Now the bathroom faucet is running as she washes her face, freshens her makeup and hair. Now she is gathering her purse, her wallet, her keys.*

"Proctor, I'm leaving."

I opened my eyes. Elise was standing above me, wearing a tan raincoat; resting on the floor beside her was a leather overnight bag. It had been an anniversary present from me a year before.

"It's okay," I said, and sat up. "I get it."

Her gaze was firm. "Do you really? I don't think you do. I just wanted a normal life, Proctor. Not this . . . madhouse."

"This isn't exactly what I planned on, either."

Sharp words, final words. Amazing, I thought, how swiftly life could change, and once it changed, it could never change back.

"Well," Elise said. "I guess that's that."

"I guess it is."

And to the sound of a closing door and the crunch of gravel in the drive, Elise, my wife, was gone.

I was sitting on the patio when the sun rose. My life, as I knew it, seemed done. I considered calling Thea but decided not to; it could only make the situation worse. I thought instead to call a friend, someone from the old days. We could meet for lunch, say, and when the moment felt right, I could tell the story of the last week, seeking an opinion. But when I thought of the people I knew, I realized I didn't really have any friends at all.

The day passed. I heard nothing from Elise, though I hardly

expected to. I was also increasingly convinced that I was coming down with something. I felt chilled and shaky; food held no appeal. My headache had settled in as a kind of physical white noise, a background hum of pain. Late in the afternoon I descended the stairs to the beach, thinking a swim might improve my spirits, but the moment I stepped into the waves, the cold shocked me away. The water, a reliable balm in the past, felt like a threat. I walked the shoreline, hoping in a half-formed way that Caeli might appear. But the hours went by, and I didn't see her. I was beginning to wonder if I ever had.

Upon my return, I heard human sounds inside the house. Had my wife come home? For a moment I dared hope that, a night and a day having passed, her feelings had softened. But it wasn't Elise; it was Doria.

We exchanged terse greetings. I retreated to the bedroom to wash and change, and when I emerged, the woman was finishing the last of her chores and preparing to depart. My embarrassment was acute; something needed to be said.

"Listen, Doria, I'm sorry you had to witness that awful scene yesterday."

The woman eyed me coolly.

"It wasn't good, okay. Neither of us was exactly at our best. But you don't have to worry."

We stood a moment without speaking. I was wholly aware that she hadn't believed a word I'd said; I wouldn't have believed me, either.

She asked, "Do you need anything else before I go?"

Some absolution would have been nice, but it was hardly a request to make of one's housekeeper. She gathered her purse and I walked her to the door.

"Good night, Mr. Bennett."

"Tell me, Doria, how is your family?"

She paused in the entryway. "My family?"

"Yes, how are they getting on? I hope they're well."

"Everyone's fine, sir."

I had no idea why I was talking this way. "Well, that's good," I said, when I could think of nothing more specific. "I'm very glad to hear it. Give everyone my best, won't you?"

"There's just me and my boy, Mr. Bennett."

I nodded. "Yes, of course."

"He's eight."

Did I know this about her son? Did I even know she had one? She was trying to jog my memory, to spare me further embarrassment, which only made me feel worse.

"It's a fine age," I said, though I knew nothing whatsoever of childhood. "I bet he gets into a lot of mischief."

"A bit." She shrugged. "He's a good boy, though." She regarded me with a kind of sad pity, which I absolutely merited. "You met him last year at the holiday party, remember? He came to help me."

And suddenly I *did* remember: in a room full of grown-ups, a small boy, dressed like a pint-sized waiter, patrolling for dirty dishes and forgotten glasses. Late in the evening, I'd stepped out to the patio for a breath of air and found him sitting in a lawn chair, leafing through a book he'd taken from the living room shelves: an illustrated history of nautical design. It had been an adoption-day present from my father—the sort of book one keeps as a memento, not necessarily as something to read, and I wasn't sure I'd ever cracked the cover. The boy and I chatted for a while about boats—he knew almost nothing, having never been on one—and I'd made a vague, unkept promise to teach him to sail.

"Of course. George, yes?"

"That's right."

"I still need to take him sailing."

"That's all right, Mr. Bennett. It was just nice of you to offer."

Was I really the sort of man to make a promise to a child and not only fail to keep it but forget about it entirely? Apparently so. "No, no, it's my fault I let it slip my mind. Let's find a time when we can do it, shall we?"

"That's kind of you. I'm sure he'd enjoy it."

An awkward pause ensued; the encounter felt incomplete.

"Good night, sir."

"What do we pay you, Doria?"

She stopped on the path. For some reason, I was almost frantic to prevent her from leaving.

"How much, I mean. Per hour, say."

"Eight dollars, Mr. Bennett."

The stinginess shocked me. "That's *all*?"

"It's the government rate, sir. Mrs. Bennett leaves the money on the counter every Friday."

I'd seen the bills but never counted them. "That doesn't seem like enough. Not with everything you do for us." I plucked a figure from the air. "How does twelve sound?"

"Sir?"

"No, sixteen. That sounds more like it. Or twenty." I wanted, suddenly, to fill the woman's hands with money. "Let's go with twenty. Would that help?"

She nodded, seeming more dumbstruck than happy.

"Good, it's settled. I'll let Elise know."

"Thank you, Mr. Bennett."

"You're very welcome. Good night, Doria. Be sure to say hello to your boy for me. Tell him I haven't forgotten."

She headed down the walkway, into the fading light. When she reached the street and turned left, headed for the shuttle stop, I waved to her—pointless, because the woman wasn't even looking in my direction.

Darkness fell. I took a blanket and pillows to the couch and arranged myself there. Outside, a flash, followed by a rolling peal of thunder; rain pattered the patio, and then the sluice gates opened. Great volumes of water began to hammer the roof; it flowed down the windows in sheets. The heavens clanged and shook. A storm, but what a storm! The chaos relaxed me; I settled into the powerful flow of it. So much water everywhere, I thought, and soon was fast asleep.

Someone's in Thea's apartment.

She knows this the moment she enters. The air is different, disturbed. She halts by the door. The sun has set; the room is sunk in shadow. Gingerly, she places her purse on the table by the door and sidesteps into the kitchen. The knives are stored in a block next to the stove. Carefully, so as not to make the smallest sound, she withdraws the largest of them—a chef's knife, eight inches from handle to tip. A quiet rustling comes from the dining area. Is it just one person or are there others? For years, she's waited for this day; now it is here.

Holding the knife before her, she charges around the corner.

"Greetings."

She lowers the knife. "Quinn, what the *fuck*."

The man is sitting with absurd casualness, crossed legs propped on the dining table, paging through a magazine. A satchel rests on the floor by his chair.

"You're about to say you could have stabbed me. I accept your apology." He holds up the magazine: *Society Times*. "Some exciting stuff here. Love the party pics. Never really ran in those circles myself."

Thea deposits the knife on the table. "I take it you got my message about the girl."

His eyebrows lift. "There was a message about a girl? I was not aware."

Fucking Sandra, Thea thinks. *The woman was probably too busy screwing her yoga instructor.*

"Well, whatever it was," Quinn says, "it'll have to wait. The situation in the Annex is moving a little faster than we expected."

"Why's that?"

Quinn tells her about Hanson. Thea has to sit down.

"Good God," she says.

"We're not sure who's responsible, but either way, the board isn't going to let this slide. Things are going to get ugly over there. It's a powder keg as it is."

"What's Mother's plan?"

"Evolving as we speak."

"Meaning she doesn't have one."

"Meaning we have to assume everyone in the network could be compromised. Where are you on Bennett?"

"I need more time."

"That, I have to say, is not on the menu."

"Quinn, there's something there. I can feel it."

He looks at her skeptically. "Something?"

She tells him about the watchman on the pier.

"I dunno," Quinn says. "Okay, it's an interesting development, but maybe he actually *did* kill the guy, you ever think of that?"

"I'm not buying it. If you met him, you'd think the same."

"Wouldn't hurt a fly, that sort of thing? Gotta be honest, that wasn't what *I* saw in the drone feed."

"You'll just have to trust me."

"And why frame the guy for murder just to fire him? What does that accomplish?"

"Exactly," Thea says. "That's the 'something.'"

Quinn takes a moment to think. "What about this girl you mentioned?"

"I need you to track her down. Her first name is Caeli, but that's all I have. Two, maybe three years off the ferry."

Quinn eyes her cautiously. "How does some girl figure into this?"

"It's too weird to explain, but I think it's important. Just do it and I'll go."

Quinn rises and hauls his bag from the floor. "I'm only doing this because we're kind of, like, friends."

"Can you get access to a CIS terminal?"

"Don't worry about that. I know a guy."

Of course Quinn knows a guy. Thea walks him to the door.

"We're out of here by dawn," he says. "No fooling."

Thea closes the door behind him and returns to the window. A minute goes by and Quinn emerges from the building and, head bowed, strides resolutely down the street. The neighborhood is quiet, with no one about—odd for the hour, when people should be heading out for the evening, meeting friends, filling the restaurants and bars. Looking more closely, Thea notices the signs. Uncollected trash at the curb. A popular café with its lights doused, sidewalk tables and chairs stacked for the night. A helper fax idling at the corner with no one to pester. The stillness has the feeling of a city holding its breath, braced for some calamity.

There's no knowing how long Quinn will be; Thea can only wait. She lies down on the sofa. Time passes; her thoughts grow indistinct; she sleeps. In her dream—for she, too, has dreamed her whole life, though always without knowing it—she is swimming in the sea. As she makes her way forward, her head erect above the surface of the water, she senses she is not alone. There are others in the sea with her, though she cannot see them; she simply knows they're there. Dozens, then hundreds, then thousands, all swimming in the same direction.

Rain begins to fall, needling the surface of the water. The effect is soothing, but then its force increases. Lightning jabs the sky; thunder rolls above. The wind kicks up and, with it, the waves. They grow to staggering dimensions. She is being tossed, hurled; the sea has taken her in its infinite grip.

I am having a nightmare, she thinks. *This isn't real. Wake up, Thea. Wake up.*

When she does, the phone is ringing.

17

And, once again, I was somewhere else.

I came to awareness to find myself standing in the rain outside my father's house. I felt no alarm—rather, a sense of urgency. The rain was pounding, the wind lashing. Lightning cleaved the sky. My father's house was but a stern shape against the deeper blackness.

There was something here for me. Something I was supposed to find.

I retrieved the key and entered the foyer. I was soaked and shivering; water sloshed in my shoes. I tried the lights; the power was out. From the front hall bureau, I retrieved a flashlight and followed its ghostly cone into the living room and up the stairs. A feeling of fate accompanied my every step as I made my way down the hall to my bedroom and opened the door.

It was like entering a mind gone mad.

The paint was gone, replaced by writing—a dense black scrawl that covered virtually every inch of wallboard from floor to ceiling. I was, I understood, somehow seeing the room in its original state, before it had been painted over. I selected a wall at random and stepped toward it. It was filled with mathematical computations: long chains of digits and symbols, interspersed with *x*'s and *y*'s and more esoteric characters I recalled only distantly from my academy days. These were interspersed with geometric shapes—triangles, trapezoids, circles, Cartesian graphs in three dimensions—with bisecting lines and labeled points.

It was apparent that my father's mind had been decaying for some time; none of this had happened quickly. I thought, with sad horror, of the weeks or even months that the man had abided here, gripped by some incomprehensible obsession.

But that wasn't all; the telescope had returned as well. The only object in the room, surely it was connected to my father's mysterious writings, though I did not see how. Outside, the storm had increased in intensity. The wind didn't howl; it shrieked. I stepped to the telescope and bent to the eyepiece.

Darkness. Waves of titanic height and breadth. The great storm, charging over the sea. A flash, and for an instant, I beheld a tiny shape. A sailboat? What lunatic would be out on a night such as this? Another flash and then another and another, and with each one, the image hardened in my eye. A huge sailing vessel, driving through the storm. Its bow was pointed tight to the wind; waves thundered over the deck as it plowed out to sea. At the ship's wheel stood the tiny figure of a man, and above him, the heroic white canvas, curved to catch and scoop the wind, propelling him forward. What insanity! What catastrophe awaited this doomed fool! The bow dipped sharply into a deep trough between the waves; the stern rose into the air.

I saw the vessel's name.

I lurched backward. Everything felt suddenly, deeply wrong. It was as if the world were simultaneously expanding and collapsing, every atom separating from every other and then contracting into an entirely new arrangement. And the cold! Cold beyond cold, the deepest cold that ever was, the cold the universe would be if it stopped.

A new scene resolved around me.

I was in a house. A single large room with a kitchen and a living area with couches and chairs and a dining table. Behind me, a flight of stairs ascended to an interior balcony, running the length of the room. Morning sunlight was streaming through the tall windows and the patio slider, which stood open.

"Hello?" I called. "Is anyone here?"

I received no reply. I moved through the space, which possessed a cluttered homeyness. The seating looked plump and comfortable; books and knickknacks occupied the shelves and tabletops; there was a basket of keys by the door and a pile of dirty dishes in the sink. On the kitchen counter, someone had left an open box of cereal and a carton of milk.

Who lived here? Where had they gone off to? I heard running water outside; I stepped through the slider. There it was, the pool; that was the source of the sound. A large kidney-shaped pool, with jagged stone edges and a tiled wall with a spigot, from which water lazily decanted.

I felt, strangely, that a great deal of time had passed since my arrival, though it could not have been more than a couple of minutes. I returned to the living room. The light through the windows had changed—that was the source of the impression. Morning had become late afternoon.

Footsteps?

I stopped. The sound came again—light, quick, coming from upstairs. I ascended to the balcony. Two hallways branched from it, left and right. I paused, willing myself into absolute stillness to trace the source of the sound.

The left.

There were two doors. I opened the first. It appeared to be an office. Positioned in the center of the room was a glass table with a CIS terminal, though it was unlike any CIS terminal I had ever seen, sleeker and more compact. Shapes of variegated color moved upon the screen like crystals in a kaleidoscope. I sat at the desk. From one of the many piles of papers on the desk, I removed the top sheet. I began to read, whereupon an unsettling thing occurred. I could read the words, but all sense of their accumulated meaning fled my mind. It was as if each word erased the memory of the one that preceded it. I tried a second sheet, then a third. The result was the same.

Exasperated, I looked up. On the wall facing the desk was a large drawing, pinned to a corkboard: a blueprint, depicting a vessel of some sort, with large square sails. I rose to get a closer look, only to discover that the more the distance narrowed, the vaguer the image became. By the time I was standing in front of it, I could see no image at all.

A figure darted past the door.

I entered the hallway as the second door slammed shut. "Hello, who's there?" I tried the handle, but the door was locked. As I raised my hand to knock, a blast of noise erupted from the far side: an aural detonation of laughter and explosions and something that sounded like a car horn, overlain with a manic cacophony of horns and cymbals, even a xylophone. The sound was agonizing; it aroused in me a sudden, nearly overwhelming anger. I pounded the door with my fists. "Goddamnit, let me in!" My head soared with fury, a force like possession. "Open this goddamn door right now!"

The noise stopped.

My heart was thudding, my pulse racing. I tried the handle again; it turned without resistance.

The room was empty.

The air was stale, as if the space had been sealed for months—years, even. Angled beams of sunlight fell upon the carpet, which was marked by distinct depressions, indicating where furniture had once been—the bed here, the dresser there. I moved to the window and looked out. The day was nearly gone; heavy clouds were moving in. As raindrops began to patter the glass, I looked down at the pool. Somehow, in just the few intervening minutes, the water had been drained. All that remained was a black puddle of scum and leaves at the bottom.

I turned away. Scanning the space again, I noticed a closet. At first inspection it appeared empty, but then I espied a cardboard box on the top shelf. On tiptoes I slid it forward and brought it down.

The box was full of toys.

Not the ersatz toys given to new iterants, which were toys only in the broadest sense, designed to acquaint them with the humble workings of the world—these were actual playthings. Colored blocks with letters and numbers etched into their surfaces. A wheeled wooden duck on a string. A stuffed otter, so worn it looked chewed. I worked my way through the box's contents until I came to the final item. It was a dress: small, sleeveless, with a flared shape and wide straps with buttons. I pressed the fabric to my face. There was a dusty smell, but also something else, almost milky. The feel of it on my cheeks was exquisite, possessing an unbearable softness. I had begun to weep. I wasn't sure why. Outside the heavens roared, the wind raged, rain battered the walls in torrents. The very timbers of the building shook; the floor below me heaved like the deck of a boat at sea. Holding the dress to my face, I cried and cried and cried, my body heaving with sorrow, while, simultaneously, a different part of me observed this fact from a distance. *There is Proctor Bennett, ferryman,* my mind said; *there he is, weeping into the dress. If only he could forget.*

Forget.

Forget.

A face was hovering above me. The face had something urgent on its mind. This was strange, as was the light, which had a greenish cast, and the sound I was hearing—a great, roaring engine, like a truck bearing down.

"Proctor, we have to get out of here!"

I was hoisted painfully onto someone's shoulder. Couldn't this person, whoever it was, see that I needed to gather myself? I attempted to speak, but my tongue was like a balled sock in my mouth. The roaring was increasing, as were other sounds, sounds of breaking and snapping and crashing.

"Keep moving!"

The voice was a man's. Out the front door and down the porch steps he carried me, and suddenly we were in a whirlwind. Small, sharp bits pelted me as my deliverer hustled me across the lawn.

I was dropped. Not dropped; unfolded. I grasped where I was now: the backseat of a car. I looked out the window. What was I seeing? The air was full of things, and all the things were rising—rising and twirling and spinning, like water in a drain, though the drain was upside down. The car began to move; we were backing up, fast. In the air above my father's house, the clouds had assembled into a cyclonic black mass. It was like a living thing, some great skyborne monster. It writhed and pulsed, spinning like a disk. From its center, a whirling tendril dripped downward.

"Drive faster, damnit!"

We spun in a one-eighty; I tumbled to the floor of the car.

"Look out!"

A crash of metal; the car shuddered, swerved first one way and then the other. At the end of the driveway the driver slammed on the brakes, turned left, and hit the gas again. The engine roared as we accelerated.

My mind was slowly coming to order. Looking up from the floor, I beheld a familiar face: Thea was at the wheel.

"Hello," I said, absurdly, and with tremendous effort.

She glanced at me quickly in the mirror. "Don't try to talk."

From the passenger seat came a man's voice: "Is that fucking thing *following* us?"

Who was this second person? There was a great whooshing sound, followed by a crash; the car veered left again and suddenly we were barreling through underbrush, branches and leaves whipping the sides of the car. With a lurch, the car went airborne and slammed back down onto the road with a squeal of tires and a fresh burst of speed.

"They saw us for sure," the man said.

"Shit!" said Thea, and pounded the steering wheel with her fist. "Shit, shit, shit!"

"We can't go back to your place."

"You think I don't know that?" Thea said. "How's he doing?"

The shape of a man's face peered around the passenger seat. "You heard the lady. How's it going back there?"

I tried to respond, but the effort proved too large.

"Still pretty out of it," this unknown man said. He faced forward again. "We need to get off this road. Up ahead, turn right."

The car slowed. We were creeping along a dirt road—I could hear gravel spitting from the tires. The madness of the last few minutes had yielded to an otherworldly calm, the roaring wind suddenly gone. I may have actually fallen asleep, because the next thing I knew, I was being hauled from the car. The man took me by one side, Thea by the other. My toes were skimming over the ground; a long pendulum of spittle swayed from my lips. I sensed dense foliage around me and then some sort of structure.

It was a house—more like a cottage or cabin. The space was cramped and rustic, with a plank floor and an ammoniac tang of mildew. Thea and her accomplice carried me across the room and into another, where they deposited me on a bed. Someone drew a blanket over me.

"What the hell are we going to do with him?"

Voices from the living room. Thea and the man were talking—not talking, arguing.

"We couldn't just leave him there."

"Oh yes we could. You've been at this too long—I've seen it before."

"What's *that* supposed to mean?"

Much as I tried, I was having difficulty computing any of it.

Their words existed without meaningful reference, even to each other.

"I'm not going anywhere."

"Thea, we're *blown.* We have to get out of here. What do I have to do to make you understand that?"

There was more, but I could distill no meaning from their words. The voices dwindled, as if the distance between us were elongating. Mumbles, then whispers, then nothing at all. A door opening and shutting again. Silence stole over the room. My eyes had closed. Again, I felt it—felt it all. The roaring wind, the driving rain. The ship far out to sea, and its tiny figure at the helm. The spray blasting over me, the white sail above, my hands gripping the wheel. The exhilaration of it, the wild terror, driving my ship, my *Oranios,* straight into the storm's black heart.

18

I awakened to morning light and the feeling that I was not alone. I turned my head against the pillow. Thea was sitting by the bed, reading a book.

"Any good?"

Her eyes lifted from the page.

"The book, I mean."

She closed the cover and put it aside. "A little corny. Boy-meets-girl stuff. I'm more of a mystery gal myself. How are you feeling?"

"I've been better." I glanced around. "Where are we?"

"The house belongs to some friends of mine."

"Is one of them the man who helped you last night?"

"You remember that? I wasn't sure you would."

"It's a little hazy." I tried to rise. My head felt like it weighed a hundred pounds.

"Let me get you some water."

She left me alone. A roar of unused pipes and she returned

with a glass that looked like it was half rust. I attacked it with fierce gulps.

"Easy now."

I drained it and handed it back. "So," I said, "I seem to recall a storm."

She placed the empty glass on the table. "That's a start."

"A tornado, actually."

Thea nodded.

"My father's house?"

"Gone." She shrugged. "A lot of things are gone. According to the radio, the power's out over half the island."

"Was anyone hurt?"

"I don't know. I imagine so."

"How did you find me?"

She drew back. "What are you talking about? You phoned me."

"What did I say?"

"You just told me where you were going and to meet you there." She eyed me skeptically. "Are you saying that wasn't you?"

"Oh, no. I'm pretty sure it was."

"But you don't remember doing it."

I shook my head. "How did I sound?"

"It wasn't a social call. You were pretty insistent." She paused, searching my face. "Proctor, what really happened last night?"

"If I knew, I'd tell you."

"Not good enough."

She had me dead to rights. "I think I might have been sleep-walking."

Her eyebrows rose.

"I did it a lot when I was a kid."

"You were asleep when you called me. That's your explanation."

"Asleep, awake—I'm not sure I know the difference anymore."

Thea rose and circled the room before turning back to me.

"I should ask. How did Elise take the news?"

"It's fair to say that part of my life is over."

"I'm sorry."

I shrugged against the pillows. "After the last few days, the woman's better off without me."

"Don't be so hard on yourself, Proctor."

"I promise, I'm not." I was silent a moment, assembling my thoughts, my memories of the night. "When you found me, was there anything else in the room?"

Thea frowned. "I don't think so. Should there have been?"

"What about the walls? Was anything written on them?"

"The place was blowing apart. I didn't exactly get a good look." Her gaze tightened on my face. "Proctor, what did you see?"

And just like that, the answer came. The telescope, the equations, the blueprint in the study. They added up to one thing.

"I think I know what my father was doing."

"*Oranios* is a boat?"

"More like a ship, actually."

"Which you saw through this . . . telescope. Which may or may not have actually existed."

"You make it sound worse than it is, but yeah."

"And the writing on the walls—"

"Navigational computations, using the stars. My father showed me, when I was young."

We were sitting at the table in the cottage's tiny kitchen, drinking tea.

"Do you think it's real?" Thea asked.

"He designed it, I know that much. But the thing's gigantic. If he actually built it, he'd need a lot of help."

Thea thought a moment. "Was he planning to leave, maybe? To sail away from here?"

"A boat that size, that would seem to be the point."

"So why would he want to leave?"

"That's the part I can't make sense of. It just doesn't seem like him."

"Your father wasn't just anyone. He was chief legal counsel. Maybe he knew something."

"Funny, my mother-in-law said exactly the same thing."

Thea's face showed acute interest. "When was that?"

"The night of the concert. She was pretty interested in what my father might have said."

Thea looked away, lost in thought. Then, turning back to me: "Hypothetically, if you built a boat that big, where would you hide it?"

"Not in the water—the drones would see it. You'd need a large structure, and it would have to be right onshore."

"Can you think of a place like that?"

"Not really. And like I said, he couldn't have done it alone. If you ask me, it was just something in his head."

"Still, he left the blueprint right where you'd find it. He wanted you to know." She drummed her fingers on the table, then looked up. "Could it have been an echo? Something from his past?"

"You mean, he didn't know he was doing it?"

"Or he did, but didn't know why. He left the drawing behind for you to figure out, because he couldn't."

"It would've been nice if he'd included a set of instructions."

"Well, if you're right about the S3 painting over those walls, it makes sense to someone. Your mother-in-law, for instance."

"I don't know, Thea. Callista kept me *out* of jail."

"For now, maybe. Sounds to me like your relationship has changed over the last forty-eight hours."

I had to concede the point.

"Which would explain the drones."

Drones?

"When I got to your father's house, they were all over the place. I counted seven before the worst of the storm hit."

"Why would there be drones?"

"Maybe they've been tracking you all along."

I thought back over the days. "I don't remember seeing any except the ones at the Nursery."

"That doesn't mean they weren't there. Either way, I'd say both of us are on somebody's list at this point."

A grim thought. Also, the correct one.

"I really am sorry," I said. "I shouldn't have gotten you mixed up in any of this."

"I didn't do anything I didn't want to do." She smiled. "Maybe I just like you—did you ever think of that?"

"I'm flattered, but it doesn't seem like such a good deal for you."

"Take it as a compliment. And who knows? Maybe you're doing me a favor. No more pictures of flowers and fruit. Tell you the truth, I was getting pretty sick of the whole thing."

"I don't see how you can joke about it."

"Did I say I was joking? I have people in the Annex. It's easy to disappear into the crowd over there. Enough time goes by, maybe the S3 will lose interest."

I was taken aback. "You'd actually do that," I said. "Just . . . walk away."

"You can come with me if you want. It doesn't sound like there's a lot holding you here."

I thought of the man on the shuttle, the blaze of loathing in his eyes.

"They're just people, Proctor."

"I'm sure they're fine. But I don't think it's for me, I'm sorry."

"If your father's boat is real, they'll lock you up. Or retire you."

"Probably."

"Well, you may not care, but I do."

We were quiet for a time. How long before the drones showed up?

"There's something else I should tell you," I said. "Caeli was there last night."

Her face drew back. "At your father's, you mean?"

The memory was hazy; it lurked at the edge of my thoughts. The house, the pool, the footsteps on the stairs. All amounting, somehow, to a sense of her. "Not exactly. I'd try to explain, but it wouldn't make much sense. All I know is, she was there."

Thea rose and moved away.

"I need to find her, Thea."

She turned to face me. "Why do you need to find her? Tell me that. What's so important about this girl?"

"I don't know. I just think I'm supposed to."

Thea waited.

"I think that's what the echoes have been telling me. That she's in trouble and I'm the one to help her."

Thea sat back down. "Well, there's a bit of a wrinkle there. My friend, the one who helped me last night—"

"I was meaning to ask about him."

"Quinn's the man I told you about. We were together when you called. He used to do data analysis at Public Safety, and he still has friends who can get him access to the personnel files on CIS. He ran a full background on the girl."

At last, some good news. "And?"

"And nothing."

"What do you mean, 'nothing'?"

"I mean no trace of her. No adoption records, no transcripts, nothing at Well-Being. He did a full historical survey. As far as he could tell, the name Caeli has never been used."

I was totally flummoxed. "He must have missed something."

"I don't think so. If it were there, he'd have found it. As far as CIS is concerned, Caeli doesn't exist."

"What are you saying?"

"I don't know, Proctor. You tell me."

"That she's some kind of ghost. A figment of my imagination."

"No, I'm not saying that. If you say you know her, you know her. The problem is, you seem to be the only one who does."

"I'm telling you, she's *real,* damnit. I taught her to swim."

"Then can you think of a reason she'd be purged from the system?"

Suddenly, I could.

It was the worst part of my job.

Three times in my career, I'd been tasked with the job of returning a new iterant to the Nursery. In the first two years following reiteration, any ward could be sent back, no questions asked, but the practice was widely frowned upon, and the social costs were high. When a couple could wait years for the chance to adopt, how did it look when someone simply tossed away the life-enhancing experience of child-rearing? Not good. In other words, it happened, but very rarely, and when it did, it always had the feeling of a tragedy.

Of the three returns for which I'd served as ferryman, the first two, while deeply unpleasant, at least possessed some semblance of rationality. In the first instance, the ward, a strapping and athletic boy, had been struck by a shuttle and paralyzed. The situation was a catastrophe all around, and he offered no reluctance; indeed, he welcomed the chance to start over. In the second, the girl had become completely unmanageable: stealing, fighting, acting out sexually. Again, no fun, and I presented the guardians with all the countervailing arguments—she's young, she'll get through this, everyone will laugh about it later—but it wasn't like they hadn't thought about it.

The third, however, left me deeply disturbed. The guardians, it seemed, had simply tired of parenting. "Turns out, it's not really our thing," the boy's father told me, as if he were doing nothing more noteworthy than sending an underdone steak back to the kitchen. The whole thing was a horror show from start to finish. By the time I got the boy into the car, he'd gone limp with terror and his feelings of absolute worthlessness. His one job, to be somebody's son, and he had failed. On the drive to the ferry, he spoke not one word to me, or I to him—a cowardly act I regret to this day—and in the end, he had to be carried onto the ferry like the burden he'd been told he was.

These cases, different as they were from one another, had one thing in common. All three wards were wiped from the Central

Information System, all documents that bore their names unceremoniously shoved into the shredder. They were made to disappear, not merely in person but in official memory, as if they'd never existed at all.

"Is there a telephone?" I asked Thea.

She led me to a second bedroom, in the back. I was in luck: the phone was an old-fashioned rotary, not requiring electric current. I tapped the receiver and got a dial tone. There was a clock on the bedside table: the time was just past eight. Oona would be sitting at her desk by now.

"Director Brandt's office."

Why was I surprised? "Oona, it's Proctor."

Silence on the line.

"Oona, are you there?"

"Yes, of course," she said stiffly. "How may I help you today, Mr. Smith?"

I was in even deeper trouble than I thought. "I need a favor. Can you tell me if there's anyone in remand?"

"I believe I can assist you. Would you mind holding?"

The line went quiet. "What's remand?" Thea asked.

"It's where we put compulsory retirements until the ferry comes to get them. A holding area in the basement of HR."

"A holding area. Like, a jail?"

It shamed me, suddenly, to think it; in two decades, I'd never once put it to myself in these terms.

"Yes, like a jail."

Oona came back on. "Mr. Smith?"

"Yes, I'm right here."

"You can expect one other person at the meeting."

My stomach dropped; I'd hoped I was wrong. "Male or female?"

"I'm afraid the information is incomplete. A young person, from what I understand."

One person. Young. Caeli.

"Thank you, Oona. Just so you know, whatever they're saying about me, it's not true."

"I never doubted you, sir. But I'm sorry to hear you're feeling poorly. Before you come to the meeting, you might want to check your monitor."

My monitor?

"Goodbye, Mr. Smith. I hope you feel better."

She hung up. I turned to Thea. "Is there a reader in the house?"

"I thought you hated those things."

"I do. Is there?"

She found one under the bathroom sink. An older model but usable, and the battery still held a charge. I sat on the bed, Thea watching me, and plugged in. The panel winked to life; the data began to flow. Thirty seconds later, the screen went blank as the reader rendered its final calculation.

My number appeared.

For some time, I just stared at it. *Of course,* I thought. It was the only thing that made sense.

"Proctor, what does it say?"

I held it up to show her: nine percent.

I wasn't just losing my mind. I was dying.

19

When a person's number fell below ten percent, this was no longer a private matter. A signal was transmitted from the wearer to the Central Information System, which forwarded it to Human Resources. This was known as a "warning ping." Drones were dispatched to triangulate the signal; a Writ of Compulsory Retirement was issued, a team of watchmen dispatched. If no ferry was scheduled, one would be summoned. Within a day, two at the most, the retiree would be off to the Nursery.

So why weren't the watchmen banging down the door?

The answer was the storm. No drones were flying. The ping must have gone out sometime in the night; the drones had tracked me to my father's house. But then the storm had hit, cutting the power. The watchmen had no way of finding me until it was restored.

Which could happen at any minute. And if they found me, Caeli had no chance.

In the cutlery drawer, I found a chef's knife, passably sharp; in a tool box under the kitchen sink, a pair of wire cutters; in one of the bedrooms, a sewing kit, towels, a box of matches, and a clean white T-shirt, which I tore into strips. To this I added a bottle of vodka from the freezer. The bathroom seemed like the best place for what I intended to do; I was going to make a mess. I poured the vodka over the knife and wire cutters and lined up my supplies on the edge of the tub.

Sitting on the toilet lid, I poured three fingers of the vodka into a glass and tossed it back. Not much of an anesthetic, but it was what I had. Thea was watching from the doorway with an expression of stunned horror.

"All things considered," I said, "you might want to look the other way."

She made no move to leave; I was secretly glad. One thing my swimming days had taught me: an audience gave you courage. Behind my eyes, the vodka registered its presence with a soft nudge. I picked up the knife and angled the tip against my skin at the edge of the monitor.

"Here goes."

Stars in my eyes. Whole pinwheeling galaxies, a cosmos of pain. Beneath the blade, a sudden, vastly red outpouring, the body's inner reservoir undammed. To continue seemed impossible, yet I knew that if I paused even for a second, my will would collapse. Like a chef trimming fat from a roast, I carved along the edge of the monitor and then slid the blade beneath it to pry it free, applying upward pressure until, with a slow sucking sound, it came loose.

With the tip of the knife, I pried it away, revealing a small rectangle of striated pink meat, which promptly vanished under a fresh gush of blood. I dropped the knife and reached for the cutters. All that remained was to snip the wires, and yet I could not manage this. My head was floating; my hands had lost their strength. I held out the cutters for Thea to take.

"Please," I moaned, "help me do this."

Thus did the worst sixty seconds of my life come to an end. Thea stood before me, monitor in one hand, cutters in the other. She tossed them into the sink and pressed a towel to the wound. The towel had been soaked with vodka. Pure fire.

"Sorry," she said with a wince.

I was gasping for air. She guided my hand to the towel and held it there.

"Keep pressure on this."

She removed a needle from the sewing kit and sterilized it with a match. The rest was all insult to injury. By the time she finished sewing me up, I could barely put two thoughts together. I was also solidly drunk from the vodka. I downed a glass of water while Thea bandaged my arm with the strips from the T-shirt.

She asked, "Do you think you can stand?"

I managed to. My shirt, my pants, my shoes—all were spattered with blood. The monitor still rested in the sink where Thea had tossed it. A bit of ceremony seemed called for. I opened the toilet lid, tossed it in the bowl, and flushed it into oblivion.

"I'll need something to wear," I said.

From the bedroom, Thea retrieved a long-sleeved shirt, cotton trousers, and a pair of canvas slip-ons. The pants were too short, the shoes too large, but they would get me as far as I needed to go. I returned to the bathroom to wash my face. My reflection appalled me. I was as gray-faced as a drowning victim.

"Your friend from last night," I said to Thea. "I just now figured out where I'd seen him before."

"Oh?"

"He was the man I told you about, the one with the book."

Thea looked at me but said nothing.

"You'll have to tell me more about that sometime," I said.

The plan, such as it was, was to somehow get Caeli out of remand and bring her back to the house. After enough time had passed for the trail to cool, Thea would smuggle her to the Annex. Outside, the evidence of last night's storm was everywhere:

downed limbs, torn leaves scattered over the ground, whole trees tipped over at the roots. And yet the sky was clear, the sun shining, full and hot in the sticky air. At the car, I held out my hand for the keys.

"No chance," Thea said. "I'm going with you."

"I appreciate the gesture, but that's not a good idea."

"Proctor, look at yourself. You're a total wreck. If you're going to get her out, you're going to need help."

The woman wasn't wrong; on the other hand, I had enough on my conscience for one day. "Thea, think. Right now, you're just someone who answered a phone call last night. That's it. A phone call."

"You said it yourself. She's a kid."

"This isn't your problem."

"And yet, I'm the one with the keys." She opened the driver's door, slid into the seat, and looked up at me. "Well?"

I got into the car.

20

First, a stop.

Two watchmen were standing guard at my house—one in plain sight by the front door, the other covering the rear. At the end of the block, Thea pulled the car over to the side.

"Wait here," I told her.

I got out of the car, ducked into the woods, and skulked around back, keeping low, moving tree to tree.

The rear watchman, bless his heart, was fast asleep in a lawn chair.

The thing about using my elbow to compress the carotid: it's my only trick, but it's a good one. I moved behind the lounger where the watchman lay, quietly snoring with his cap tipped over his eyes. He didn't fight me, or not much, just three or four seconds of spastic kicking and a shocked cry that went straight into my palm before his body stilled.

I freed his shocker and let myself in through the slider. The house had an off-key, alien quality; it didn't feel like my own. I wondered why this should be so until I realized it had, in the deeper sense of things, always been Elise's; I just lived there. I crept to the front windows and peeked through the curtains. Where had the watchman gone?

Right behind me, was the answer.

The struggle that ensued was ferocious, vague, and decidedly unsportsmanlike: a storm of punching and grabbing and clawing more like a schoolyard scuffle than a contest between two grown men. Objects were smashed; furniture was overturned; at one point, I swear this is true, I began pelting the man with books. Both of our shockers were gone, squirted away in the initial moments of the struggle. The fight spilled from hallway to living room to kitchen and back to the living room. By this time, both of us were heaving for breath.

What the hell, Proctor, I thought, *you're dying anyway.*

I charged.

Head down, leading with my right shoulder, I caught the watchman across his midriff in a battering bear hug that lifted him off his feet and sent the two of us caroming across the living room. We crashed into the patio slider at full throttle, glass exploding around us into a thousand twinkling chips. I somersaulted over him, two full rolls, before landing, faceup, on the lawn.

He was on me in a second.

Rivulets of blood were running down his slashed face; his eyes glowed with murderous rage. Probably the man was under specific orders *not* to kill me; I was, after all, the son-in-law of Callista Laird. But the last few minutes had thrown the rule book out the window. Straddling me at the waist, he gripped my throat with one hand while forming a fist with the other. It would crush my face like a sledgehammer.

He never saw Thea coming; neither did I. Suddenly the full, limp weight of the watchman was lying on top of me. I looked past his shoulder to find her standing above me with the shocker in her hand.

"I thought I told you to wait in the car," I said.

"These are the thanks I get?"

I rolled the watchman aside; Thea helped me to my feet.

"I heard a crash," she said. "Probably half the neighborhood did. We better move quickly."

I located my missing shocker, went to my office to retrieve the file I'd come for, then turned my attention to the first watchman, who was lying just as I'd left him in the lounge chair. I wriggled him out of his uniform and duty belt and put them on. By this time, the watchman's eyelids were fluttering.

"Sorry," I said, because I was, and pressed the shocker to his neck.

In silence, we continued into town. In the wake of the storm, the city appeared stunned. Traffic was nearly nonexistent; only a handful of pedestrians were about. Signs of the tempest's wrath were everywhere: broken windows, roof tiles stripped away, a car crushed beneath a fallen palm. Scanning the skies, I saw no drones at all.

As we neared my office, I instructed Thea to turn into an alley and stop the car. I'd explained the layout on the way over, but I wanted to go over it again.

"The garage is on the west side of the building. Go to the second level and park along the wall farthest from the door, away from the cameras. We'll be coming out there. Wait ten minutes, and if I don't show, assume I've been caught and get out of there."

"What if somebody approaches me?"

"They shouldn't, but if they do, tell them you're waiting for a friend. The second level is visitor parking, so people use it for that."

"I'm waiting longer than ten minutes."

"Let me urge you in the strongest possible way not to do that. This is going to work or it isn't, and either way, it won't take long." I held out the second shocker. "Keep this just in case."

She accepted the shocker and examined it, expressionless, before looking up at me. "Proctor—"

"It's okay, you don't have to say anything."

She took my hand and for a moment just held it. It was the nicest thing I'd felt in a long time. Nine percent, how long did I have?

"Good luck," she said.

I got out of the car and strode across the plaza. Beneath my arm was a leather portfolio containing a Writ of Release, taken from my desk at home, now fictitiously sealed and fictitiously signed by Regan Brandt, managing director. Ministry buildings all had backup generators; the badge I'd taken from the watchman would be scanned at the desk, and cameras would be watching my every move. I entered the lobby at a deliberate pace, not too fast and not too slow, head down, badge at the ready. A single watchman was manning the desk; two more were positioned near the stairs. Any one of them might recognize me; I'd been going in and out of the building for almost twenty years.

A stroke of luck: the watchman at the desk barely looked up. I strode through the gate without a hitch in my stride.

"Hey, Wyatt, wait a second."

Was that my name? Wyatt? I dared not turn around. "Yeah?"

"I was wondering, any luck with that guy?"

'That guy.' Me. "Not so far. He never showed."

"How about that storm, huh?"

How long could I talk to him with my back turned? Also, one of the watchmen at the stairs was beginning to take notice.

"Yeah, that was really something," I said.

I resumed my purposeful walking. *Gotta go! Things to do!* The atrium felt like a death trap; I couldn't get out of there fast enough. Ten strides, fifteen, twenty, each one a gift. I came to the elevator bank. One of the doors stood open, a welcome development. I would be riding solo to the basement. I entered the elevator and pushed "B." The doors closed.

The elevator began to rise.

Fuck! *Fuck, fuck, fuck!*

I frantically pushed the button again and again, but someone had beaten me to it on one of the upper floors. We passed two, then four. The car began to slow.

We were headed for the sixth floor.

As the elevator halted, I dropped to one knee and pretended to tie a shoe. The door opened; one person got on. A pair of red heels and dark slacks. The woman reached over my head and pressed a button on the panel. The car began to fall. I, meanwhile, was busying myself with the other shoe. How long could I get away with this charade? The car continued its descent. Three, then two. We kept on going.

The woman, like me, was headed to the basement.

I know those heels, I thought.

Thea brings the car around, up the ramp, and into the garage. Just a few vehicles are scattered through the space. She parks along the wall and kills the engine. By now, Proctor must be inside. The whole thing could already be over, Proctor in handcuffs, being marched away to his fate.

She watches the door through the rearview mirror. There's a camera, just as he said, but it's aimed downward, at the door.

You've been at this too long—I've seen it before. Quinn's right: she's tired of the game. She's tired of all the lunches and parties and pointless conversations. She's tired of being afraid, and she's tired of being someone she's not, though she's not sure who she's supposed to be instead.

But that's not the reason she's here. She couldn't say quite *what* the reason is, only that it's deeply instinctive and personal. Part of it is Proctor's concern for the girl; it's as if he cares about her precisely because no one else does. Thea wonders why this should affect her so, and then she knows. She was a girl like that once. A girl alone in the world.

The minutes go by.

Eyes locked upon the door, Thea knows she isn't going anywhere.

As Regan stepped clear of the car, I rose and exited behind her. I was unsnapping the shocker from its holster when she glanced over her shoulder and did a fast double take.

"Proctor, what the hell."

"Oh, hey, Regan."

I'd waited too long, and the woman was no slouch. As I raised the shocker, she blocked it with her left, swung her right up and behind my wrist, and gave my arm a sharp twist. The shocker jettisoned from my hand and skittered across the floor. Regan followed this up with a solid, flat-knuckled punch to the solar plexus that knocked the wind from my chest and shoved me backward into the wall.

"Fuck you, Proctor," Regan said, and reached behind to the small of her back to draw a shocker of her own.

The alarm began to blare.

In the parking garage, Thea is jolted by a blast of noise. She sits up sharply as three watchmen come running up the ramp, headed for the door.

She makes a snap decision.

She throws open the car door and takes off after them. One of them is swiping the lock. She catches up to them, breathless.

"Lady, you can't come in," one says.

She points at the open door. "My husband's in there!"

"It's for your own safety. The building's on lockdown until we know what's going on."

She grabs him by the arm. "Please!"

The watchmen exchange looks. They're in a hurry and in no mood for debate.

"Okay," the first one says, "but it wasn't us."

She follows them into the building. As they race down the hall, she slows her stride to put distance between them. The corridor is generic, lined with office doors behind which, Thea imagines, workers are sheltering in place.

With a thump in her stomach, she realizes she left the shocker in the car.

She comes to a stairwell. Footsteps clatter from above; a group of watchmen tear past, headed for the basement.

What can she hope to accomplish? Logic says nothing. But Thea's not running on logic. It's as if there are two voices in her head, one entirely reasonable, the other telling her to follow.

She heads down the stairs.

The cameras had caught up with me, or else one of the watchmen in the atrium had finally done the math. Bad news, but the alarm gave me the moment of distraction I needed, and I still had a baton. I drew it from my belt and snapped it open. As Regan drove her shocker toward me, I brought it down on her forearm, hard.

A crack. She howled.

I turned and ran. My brain was swimming; nausea burbled in my gut. My collision with the wall hadn't helped, either. The door to remand was at the end of the hall. I buzzed it open with the badge and blasted through. A single watchman was seated at the front desk.

Not just any watchman.

The one I'd strangled on the pier.

"Wait a sec," he said, recognition dawning on his face. "I know you. You're that fucking guy."

As he rose to his feet, I clocked him across the side of his head with the baton. Down he went, spiraling to the floor. I heard footsteps pounding outside, voices barking commands. With the butt of the baton, I smashed the door's control panel, locking myself in, and moved behind the desk, where I dropped to one knee, freed the cuffs from my belt, yanked his arms behind his back to slap the cuffs on his wrists, hooked my forearm around his throat, and yanked his head upward by the hair.

"Where is she?"

"What the fuck! You hit me!"

"You've got one person down here. What cell, damnit?"

"How should I know? I just came on duty."

I tightened my arm against his windpipe.

"Eight, okay? Somebody was in eight."

Fists were pounding on the door. "Keys?"

"Front drawer. Take 'em, I don't give a shit."

A fat ring, but the keys themselves were numbered. "Caeli, I'm coming!" I yelled, though my efforts were moot by this point. The army was advancing; the army was practically here. But my teeth were in this thing now; I would go down swinging. It wasn't enough, but it was all I had: to tell the girl she mattered, that someone had cared enough to try. "Caeli, hang on, I'm coming to get you!"

I'd expended the last of my strength; I stumbled down the hall like a drunk. As I got to number eight, a great crash sounded behind me: the door had been breached. "He's back in the cells!" Boots barreled toward me; I didn't turn to look. I shoved the key into the lock and pushed my way into the cell.

It was empty.

Which was precisely the moment the army arrived, a vast weight slammed into me from behind, and the last thing I saw was the floor rising toward me as my face and body fell to meet it.

Thea emerges into bedlam.

The far end of the hall is crowded with watchmen. She hears banging, shouts, a crash. Then a voice saying, "We got him!"

Him. Proctor.

The alarm goes silent. A woman is sitting on the floor with her back to the wall, her eyes squeezed shut in pain. Thea kneels in front of her.

"Are you okay?" she asks her.

The woman is cradling her arm.

"Here, let me help you," Thea says.

"Ouch! Don't touch it!"

"I think it might be broken."

"I *know* it's fucking broken."

Thea angles her head down the hall, trying to see what's happening, but her view is obscured by the watchmen. "What's going on down here, anyway?"

"A lunatic is what's going on. Tried to break into remand. He's the one who did this to me."

Thea does her best to look shocked. "Wow. That must have been terrifying."

"Looks like they got him, though, the crazy bastard."

"Where do you think they'll take him?"

She's gone too far; she sees her error in the woman's face.

"What department do you work in?" the woman asks. "I don't recognize you."

Thea answers with the first thing she can think of: "Social Contracts."

The woman's eyes harden. "No, you don't."

"I should go." Thea rises and backs away.

"Hey!" the woman yells down the hall. "Help! There's another one! Over here!"

Thea runs, not looking back. She takes the stairs two at a time and emerges into the corridor. People are cautiously stepping from their offices. *You think it's safe to come out? Does anybody know what happened?* Thea blasts past them, through the outer door and into the garage; she climbs into the car and roars away, and only then, as she races down the street—away from the building, away from the plaza, away from everything she's called her life—does she feel the tears rolling down her cheeks.

21

"Proctor, can you hear me?"

The glassy sea, the doubled stars. The blue drop suspended in the sky. With long strokes, I swam my way toward it. The blue star had a name, like all stars; it existed in my mind but was buried in the depths. I was alone, but did not feel alone; the woman was somewhere nearby. The feeling of her presence wrapped me with a great calm, drawing me forward.

"Proctor, are you there?"

Ahead, a light, and a dark silhouette. As I narrowed the distance, the shape proclaimed itself: a sailing ship. Its sails were down and furled along their booms; the hull rested at anchor, motionless. A solitary lamp burned in the cabin.

"I don't think he can hear us."

I completed my approach. The vessel, like the blue star, felt inevitable; I had only to discover its meaning. Across the lighted porthole, a shadow moved; someone was inside. I glided toward the ladder at the stern. Was it the woman who awaited me? But it could be no other. She would take me in, feed me, hold me in her arms to warm my bones. She would lay me down and wrap my body with hers beneath soft, clean sheets. She would whisper in my ear all the things I needed to know. She would tell me the name of the star.

"I don't think we can wait any longer."

I charted my progress along the vessel's hull. The ladder came into view. I was close, closer, the ladder was practically within my grasp . . .

"Epinephrine."

My body jolted; the sky exploded with white-hot light. No!

"Proctor, can you hear me?"

The boat was gone. The boat, the sky, the sea, all gone.

"Open your eyes now."

I was streaming away, falling and spilling and tumbling . . .

"Proctor, *open your eyes.*"

Daylight. A bed. Faces around me, the sense of a crowd.

"That's it. There you go, buddy."

I blinked into the light. Warren?

"Welcome back, old sport." He guided a straw to my lips. "Don't try to talk yet. Just drink."

The water was tepid and tasteless. I attempted to bring my surroundings into focus, but something was wrong with my eyes. My vision was fogged and flattened, lacking all depth. I detected other figures in the room, though I could discern no details. I heard a sucking sound; the cup was empty.

"What . . . happened?" My tongue was furry as wool.

Warren put the cup aside. "You're in the medical wing of the Ministry of Well-Being."

The medical wing. Had I been ill?

"You had a seizure. Do you remember?"

My mind cast around. Little things, small, disordered flashes, but that was all. This was when I realized that I couldn't move. I was strapped to the bed.

"Proctor, I have something to tell you. I need you to listen carefully."

"Why am I tied up?" Thick bands crossed my legs and torso. I was wearing nothing but a thin hospital gown. "What's going on?"

"When I examined you on Friday—" Warren hesitated. "Well, I found something."

I looked past him toward the foggy figures. "What do you mean, 'something'? Who are these people?"

"Try to stay calm. I don't want to sedate you."

I had begun to strain at the straps. "You have me trussed up like a chicken, for God's sake."

"You have a brain tumor, Proctor."

The wind went out of me.

"I'm sorry, buddy. When I ran the data at the office last week, I discovered a large mass in the occipital and parietal lobes. It's been growing for years, probably since early iteration. Everything that's happened these last few days, none of it's your fault, Proctor. You're simply not yourself. We've stabilized you, but I don't know how long it will last. We need to move quickly to get you to the Nursery."

Could it be true? I'll admit, I bought it for a second. But only for a second.

"I don't believe you," I said. "You're making this up."

"Trust me, old friend, I wish I were."

"Don't you 'old friend' me." I looked at his self-righteous face; everything was coming clear. "It was that shot you gave me, wasn't it? You did something to my monitor."

He shook his head sadly. "No, Proctor, no. Yes, I lied about the vitamins. That part's true. What I gave you was an angiogenesis inhibitor. I thought it might slow the tumor's growth. But it was obviously too late."

"You're lying."

"Proctor, you're not thinking straight. The paranoia, the self-mutilation, the violent outbursts. That's not the man I know. And scaring Elise like that. The woman who loves you more than anything. She told me what happened Monday night."

"Nothing is what happened. I got a little mad, so what?"

"That's not the way she tells the story. You terrified her, Proctor. And that's hardly the least of it. They found the watchmen at your house. How do you explain that?"

"They attacked me!"

"Like the watchman on the pier attacked you?"

"He's alive! I saw him in the basement!"

Warren sighed. "Nobody's in any basement. This is no good, buddy."

"It's because of my father's boat, isn't it? That's what this is all about."

"Come now, Proctor."

"Oh, don't look at me that way, all innocent. Don't pretend that you don't know." Suddenly, the whole picture revealed itself. It was as if a curtain had been lifted on a brightly lit stage. They were all in on it: Warren, Callista, Amos, Regan, probably half the department and the board, too. Everyone.

"You think you're so smart," I said. "I know just what you're up to."

"Please, just listen to yourself. This isn't you."

"Where's Caeli?"

"Who?"

"The girl, goddamnit!" I was straining at the straps again. My protestations were pointless; they'd give up nothing. Part of me knew I was raving like a lunatic; another part didn't care. "I taught her to swim! She was supposed to be in the cell!"

"Dr. Singh, if I may."

A figure cut through the haze. Nabil West, dressed in one of his risibly snug suits.

"Mr. Bennett, how are you feeling?"

"I don't know, how do I *look*?"

He opened a folder. "I have here a Writ of Compulsory Retirement. Though your signature isn't required, you may, if you wish, review the contents."

"Fuck you. Fuck you and that sausage skin you're wearing."

The man nodded curtly and closed the folder. "As you wish."

My vision had cleared enough to let me make out the other faces in the room: Amos, nervously shuffling change in his pockets; Regan Brandt, her casted arm in a sling; standing by the door, a pair of watchmen, who probably wanted to beat me to death with their batons right about now.

"Do you hear me?" I said to the room. "Fuck all of you!"

Warren took my chin in his hands and steered my face toward his. "Proctor, look at me."

I shook him off. "Leave me alone."

"I can see you're upset. I know you don't like this. But it's for the best, and if we're going to get you to the Nursery, we don't have time for this nonsense. Elise wants to say goodbye."

My stomach dropped. "Elise is here?"

"She's waiting outside. But I care too much about both of you to let her see you like this. You don't want her to remember you this way, do you?"

The thought stopped me cold. Whatever else was true, my wife was an innocent bystander. Almost a decade together, happy in our way: she deserved a dignified farewell.

"Can you keep it together, Proctor, yes or no?"

Chastened, I nodded. "Okay, yes."

"I mean it. For both your sakes, don't let this end badly."

The door opened; Elise came through. A knot lodged in my throat; all the difficulties between us instantly melted from my mind. She leaned down to wrap me in a sorrowful embrace that I, bound to the bed, could do nothing to return.

"Oh, baby, I'm so, so sorry." She was weeping into my neck. "If I'd known, I never would have left like that."

"I'm sorry, too."

She drew back her face and placed her palm against my cheek. "You were a good husband, Proctor. The best husband any woman could have asked for."

Guilt stabbed at my heart. Obviously, I hadn't been. But there was nothing I could do about that now.

"I'm sorry we never got that country place you wanted." It was all I could think to say.

She smiled through her tears. "Did I tell you? Warren and I saw the perfect little house this weekend. Just a rustic cottage, but surrounded by the most beautiful orchard. The blossoms smelled so wonderful. I know you would have loved it."

"That sounds really great," I said. "You should get it."

How strange and sad it was to talk this way—as if I were already gone, like a spirit speaking from beyond the grave. What pain I had caused her! How careless I had been with my good fortune, to have her in my life! I thought of my Elise in the days ahead, moving through her paces without me: awakening in an empty bed; opening the closet and seeing my suits hanging there; turning from the stove to ask me to open the wine and finding no one there. I wanted more than I could say to take back the last seven days; I would have rewritten the entire book of my life just to remain in her company, and do my very best to recover the love we'd mislaid.

Wait a second.

"What did you mean, 'Warren and I'?"

Elise startled faintly. "What do you mean?"

"Just now, you said that you and Warren saw the perfect house."

"I just meant . . ." She stopped. "Well. I don't know what I meant." She took my hand. "The important thing is what comes next for you. A whole new life. That's the thing to focus on."

"So, he was with you, this weekend."

She looked suddenly lost.

"Let me get this straight. Warren was with you, in the country."

Warren stepped toward the bed. "Proctor, buddy—"

"Oh, that's just *swell.*" I collapsed my head into the pillows. "That takes the goddamn *cake.*"

Elise said, rather desperately, "Baby, it's not what you think. It's Warren, sweetheart. He's our friend."

"It's exactly what I think." I shook off her hand. "How could I have been so dumb? Well, I wish you every happiness. You certainly deserve each other."

Elise, weeping, turned toward Warren and leaned into his chest. He put his arms protectively around her as she sobbed against him.

"For godsakes, Proctor," Warren said, "I warned you."

I turned my face away. "Go on, get out of here. Leave me alone."

Warren led her away; the door closed behind them. Amos, visibly shaken, stepped to my bedside. "Well," he said, and cleared his throat. "I guess that's it." He turned to Regan. "Director Brandt?"

I groaned. "For the love of God, anyone but her."

"Compulsory retirement requires a ferryman at the level of managing director. You know the rules, Proctor."

Did I ever.

Strapped to a gurney, I was wheeled to the loading dock at the rear of the building—a compulsory retirement wasn't a spectacle for the general populace to witness—and shoved into the back of a van. Regan climbed in behind me and took a seat on the bench.

"How's the new job working out?" I asked. "I bet this is a lot of fun for you."

"Save it."

There was no end to my vitriol. "I'm guessing that arm smarts. What did they promise you to play along with that little charade? Besides my office, I mean."

"Go screw yourself, Proctor. Oh, wait, you already did."

We rode the rest of the way in silence. The compartment was

windowless, affording me no way to watch the passing world I was soon to leave. Scant comfort, but at least I'd be spared any recollection of this.

The van halted; the doors opened to the sounds and smells of the waterfront. The watchmen rolled me out. I heard the gurgle of the ferry's props but nothing else—no fond cries, no white noise of well-wishers come to see their loved ones off; I would commence this journey alone. They wheeled me to the base of the gangplank.

"See you later, Proctor," Regan said with a careless gesture. "Bon voyage."

"Look, I'm sorry about before. I shouldn't have hit you. But if it's not too much to ask, I'd like to do this on my own two feet."

Regan scowled but said nothing.

"Ferryman to ferryman, at least give me that."

She looked away, shaking her head, then turned back to me with a tart little snort. "Fine, have it your way. Let's just get this over with."

One of the watchmen undid the straps; I rose to a seated position, dangled my bare feet over the side, and, using one hand to hold my gown closed over my backside, carefully stepped down. I was weak, and a little dizzy, but I realized that the worst had passed. Had the effect of Warren's shot worn off? One more reason to hustle me off to the Nursery. The ferry's horn gave two tart blasts: the two-minute warning.

"Let's go," said Regan.

"Mr. Bennett! Wait!"

Two figures were jogging toward us. As they neared, I saw that it was Doria and her son, George.

"We just wanted to say goodbye," Doria said, a little out of breath.

Of all the people who might have come to see me off, here was my housekeeper, a woman I'd taken scant notice of for years.

"Thank you, Doria. That means a lot."

"You've always been so good to us. George, especially."

I had? And, come to think of it, how had Doria known I was leaving, when no one else did? I couldn't imagine that Elise would have told her.

"George wanted to give you a goodbye hug."

I nodded, perplexed. "Okay."

Still clutching the back of my gown with my fist, I crouched before the boy; he put his arms around me. A lovely feeling, to be hugged by a child, but why this last-minute fiction that I meant anything to him at all?

"I'm sorry I never took you sailing," I said. "I really meant to."

He shrugged. "That's okay."

Regan huffed impatiently. "This is all very touching, but can we move it along, please?"

"Goodbye, Mr. Bennett," Doria said, and shook my hand.

"Goodbye, Doria. Thanks for everything."

I watched them walk off. "Enough already," Regan said. "Off you go."

I turned to her. "Know what? You're kind of a terrible person."

I headed up the gangplank. The ferry, of course, was empty; it had been summoned just for me. The ten-second warning sounded; the gangplank withdrew. I moved to the stern. The van was already pulling out of the lot. With a roar, the ferry began to move. I scanned the area around the wharf, still hoping I might see a friendly face. But there was no one.

Moment by moment, the city shrank. The buildings, the parks, the cars; the people of Prospera, those I'd known and those I hadn't; the life I'd led: all receded from view. I was shivering in my hospital gown. The ferry passed through the inner harbor, into a livelier sea. The sun shone down brilliantly upon the water, bejeweling the tips of the waves. I watched them for a long while, letting their peacefulness flow into me, and when I raised my eyes again, I realized that I'd missed it: the moment when the city disappeared.

22

They arrive in vans, one after the other. They emerge from the back, dressed for combat: helmets, chest plates, pads at the elbows and knees. They have shields. They have shockers. They have batons already extended to their full, pummeling length.

They do not go unnoticed.

The word goes out: *Something is happening at the causeway.* People emerge from their homes and places of business; they rise from the stoops and wander from the corners; they stop what they are doing and join the gathering crowd. Twenty people, thirty, fifty, a hundred.

The watchmen's presence is, at first, a novelty. A variation on the normal state of things, but that's all, and because the watchmen are just standing around, they seem to have no purpose. But as the minutes pass, the crowd realizes there's something different about these watchmen, and it isn't just their weaponry. It's the way they carry themselves. They flex and strut. They roll their shoulders. They pat their batons against their palms, feeling their weight.

They are waiting for something to happen.

Then it does: a distant rumbling, growing louder. All eyes point down the causeway. A cargo truck, with a tarp on arched poles covering the cargo bay, is headed in their direction.

The truck halts. At the rear of the vehicle, a pneumatic platform unfolds. From within comes a clanking sound, and a pair of security faxes wheel out and are lowered to the ground. The same process repeats four times. The faxes' upper bodies align with a whirring and a *click-clack* of gears and together they roll to the top of the causeway to take position behind the watchmen, who have also formed a line.

A single watchman steps forward and raises a bullhorn. A howl of feedback and his voice, shockingly loud, volleys over the crowd:

"Attention all residents of the Annex. By order of the Board of Overseers, a lockdown has been declared. Return to your homes at once and await further instruction."

The crowd murmurs but doesn't move. It's the suddenness of the announcement that stops them. A lockdown?

Another howl and the watchman booms, "You are ordered to disperse."

Jess observes these events from the rear of the crowd. She has no regrets about Hanson—her mind still hums with adrenalized joy—but she also wonders, How much does the S3 know? What clues might she have left behind? All those windows above the alley: Did anyone see? Her injured foot, dressed in thick gauze and shoved into her boot, throbs like a heartbeat. Any weight applied to it feels like the nail going in all over again. She cleaned the wound as best she could, but she's shaky and a little feverish; she worries that an infection has taken hold.

Antone appears at her side, all bouncy excitement.

"What the hell are you doing here?" Jess asks him.

"I want to watch."

"No, you really don't."

"Who made you the boss of me? Besides, this is gonna be *fun*."

"I repeat," the watchman commands. "Return to your homes."

"Antone, I mean it."

"Fuck these guys," a man in the crowd says, and then, lifting his voice: "Hey, fuck you!"

There is a moment of uncertainty. The watchmen seem not to know what to do.

"Are you listening? Go to hell!"

The energy of the crowd has shifted. There is fear, and anger, but also something purer—noble even. The sensation is electric. A hundred bodies joining in a circuit along which a current of righteous defiance flows.

"If you do not follow orders, you will be forcibly removed."

The threat is met with a chorus of jeers.

"This is your final warning."

"I mean it," Jess says to Antone. "Get the hell out of here."

The first bottle is hurled from somewhere in the middle of the crowd. It lobs over their heads in a clean arc—at its apex, the glass flares with reflected sunlight—before it descends with sudden speed to smash at the watchmen's feet.

Immediately the air is full of things. More bottles. Stones of various weights and sizes. They pelt harmlessly on the watchmen's upraised shields like a clattering rain. Everyone is yelling, shouting. Boos, taunts, obscenities.

"Strike!" someone yells, and then another and another.

"Strike! Strike! Strike!"

Things happen quickly after that.

Canisters eject into the air, trailing yellowish smoke as they fall into the crowd. Simultaneously, the watchmen, their faces masked, march forward in lockstep, shields up and batons raised. The smoke is noxious and obscuring. It's as if a cloud of stinging acid has occupied the square. Some in the crowd are immobilized, coughing and retching onto the pavement; others scatter, covering their faces. The air is split by screams and the sounds of boots and batons. Jess grabs Antone's arm and begins to run, but the venomous cloud overtakes them, filling their eyes and throats and lungs.

Suddenly, the boy is gone.

Jess can see nothing. Cries of terror bombard her from all sides. "Antone!" she calls. "Where are you?" But her pleas are smothered by the coughs that are pouring from her throat. Sweeping her arms, she plunges blindly through the fog, but between the coughing and the stabbing pain in her foot and the stinging in her eyes, she doesn't make it far. A dozen steps and she falls to her hands and knees, and when the watchman brings his baton crashing down on her head, Jess doesn't even see it coming.

IV

THE NURSERY

23

I roused from my fugue state to the sound of crashing waves. The ferry was approaching the reef; beyond it, the Nursery rose imposingly from the sea. How quick the journey had been! At a distance of several hundred yards, the ferry altered course, turning south to circle the island. There, on the far side, the reef was interrupted by a narrow channel, through which we passed into a sheltered lagoon. Great walls of unscalable rock surrounded it on three sides; the water was black with depth. An arched opening appeared in the far wall. The tunnel.

Inside, the temperature plummeted; the sound of the ferry's engine increased as it rebounded off the damp stone walls. A few minutes passed; ahead, a single light appeared. The space around me expanded; the ferry had entered a cavern. At the far end was a pier, where a single figure waited. We came to rest with a soft roar of reversing engines. The waiting figure was a woman. I made my way down to her.

"Welcome to the Nursery, Mr. Bennett."

I was astonished. It was Dr. Patty. The twinkling blue eyes, the glossy brown hair, the silver clip to hold it back: she was exactly as I remembered, right down to the sterling white lab coat and the clipboard she was clutching to her chest. The woman hadn't aged a day, though at the time of my first visit with her, being so young myself, I'd probably mistaken her for someone older.

"Do you remember me?" I asked her.

A smile dawned on her face. "Why, of course, Mr. Bennett. You came to see me about dreaming, if I'm not mistaken."

"That's right." I was strangely glad to find her here. "My mother brought me. I was quite young."

"How very nice to see you again."

Her tone was fond but colorless, exuding a kind of generic warmth. The effect was unaccountably relaxing.

"We'll have lots to talk about, Mr. Bennett. For now," she said, directing me to an opening in the wall, "if you'll kindly follow me."

An opening led to a carpeted hallway—clean, bright, rather sterile, like something in an office. At the end was an elevator. We entered and began to descend.

"Have you worked here long?" I asked her.

"Oh, for quite some time now. I find it very gratifying to work with retirees. As you yourself must know."

"Why's that?"

She glanced at me sidelong. "You needn't be so modest, Mr. Bennett. I understand there are very few managing directors with your level of success. An achievement to be proud of, if I may say so."

We'd been going down for a while, I realized. The elevator's panel had just a single button, which, presumably, took it both to and from its only destination.

"And here we are," said Dr. Patty.

The elevator opened onto a second hallway, identical to the first. We resumed our unhurried walking.

"You know," I ventured, "I'm not actually supposed to be here."

"The feeling is common among new arrivals. I assure you, it will pass."

"What I mean is, this is all a big mistake. They did something to lower my number."

"'They,' Mr. Bennett?"

"A lot of people were in on it. I'm not even sure how many. But Warren Singh was the one who did it. He gave me a shot."

"Ah, Dr. Singh."

"So, you know him?"

"Not personally. But I'm sure whatever shot he gave you was meant to help."

"That's the thing. It didn't help. It got me sent here."

We'd come to a door, which Dr. Patty opened, revealing a small, windowless room with a video screen and a row of reclining chairs.

"Not to worry," Dr. Patty said. "If you'd like, I can look into the matter."

"You'd do that?" I was pleased, and a bit surprised, that the woman would so readily take up my cause. "I'd be very grateful."

"Not at all, Mr. Bennett." She patted my arm. "I only want you to feel comfortable. In the meantime, why don't you take a seat? I'll come and get you when the orientation film is over."

She stepped out, closing the door behind her. I took a chair in front of the screen. The upholstery was wonderfully soft, instantly lulling me. I cast my eyes around at the posters on the walls. "A whole new life," said one, beneath a silhouetted couple sitting side by side, watching the sun set over the ocean. "A return to youth!" proclaimed another, with a picture of a man serving a tennis ball.

The lights dimmed; the screen flickered to life.

"Hello, and welcome to the Nursery. I'm Dr. Patty, director of Reiteration Services for the Ministry of Well-Being."

She was wearing the same lab coat and carrying the same clipboard.

"Today is a happy day. I and my staff are here to attend to your every need as you embark on your exciting voyage to a new iteration."

The camera pulled back to reveal the same hallway we'd just traveled. Tracked by the camera, Dr. Patty began to walk as she continued to speak.

"No doubt you have many questions. And, perhaps, not a few concerns! First and foremost, let me assure you that your comfort is our number one priority, and the restorative process you are about to undergo is one hundred percent pain-free. But what awaits you on the other side?"

She halted. "Imagine it," she said.

Her image was replaced by a series of quick scenes: a classroom of young iterants, hands raised, their faces aglow with learning; a slightly older girl, dressed in a black riding jacket and jodhpurs, crouched over the neck of a horse as the two of them sailed effortlessly over a fence; a bride and groom kissing under a gazebo wreathed with fat tropical flowers.

"It's the best, most thrilling time of life," Dr. Patty said in voice-over. "A time of growth. Of learning. Of romance. Of wonder and adventure."

Her face reappeared. "Several days will pass before the reiteration process commences. In the meantime, we invite you to enjoy our luxurious facilities, all designed with the needs of the active retiree in mind."

New images took the screen: silver-haired retirees playing cards before a roaring fire; a pair of women bobbing in a pool; a tuxedoed waiter presenting a flaming crêpe in a copper pan.

"As you can see," Dr. Patty went on, "here at the Nursery we have something for everyone. Fine dining. Relaxing spa treatments. Stimulating recreational activities."

Dr. Patty was now joined by two individuals, a man and a woman, both wearing peach-colored smocks as they smiled robotically into the camera.

"During your stay, each of you will be assigned a personal attendant to ensure that all your needs are met in a timely fashion. At the Nursery, your well-being comes first."

The camera cut to just her face. Her smile had subtly adjusted: less chipper, deeply earnest, with a probing quality. A smile of infinite concern and understanding—a smile, even, of love.

"Your long and fruitful iteration has come to an end. A wonderful new life awaits you. If you have any questions or concerns, feel free to speak to your attendant, or any member of our staff. And again, from all of us at the Nursery, welcome."

The screen went blank; the lights came on. It took me a moment to gather my thoughts, as if I were waking up from an overlong nap. Dr. Patty's hypnotic gaze; the packaging of a reiteration as something like a stay at an upscale resort; the images of happy young people in the flow of life. I knew that every frame was calculated to create in the viewer a state of almost animal surrender—yet despite these warning bells, I felt its pull. A whole new life: Why the hell not?

"Mr. Bennett?"

Dr. Patty had appeared behind me. The sight of her was disorienting, as if she'd teleported off the screen and back into the flesh. With considerable effort—my body felt as sluggish as my mind—I pulled myself up from the chair.

"Did you find our film informative?"

"Yes, thank you," I said dully. "It was very helpful."

She beamed. "Wonderful. Will you follow me, please?"

We stepped back into the hallway, where a man awaited us—the same man I'd seen in Dr. Patty's film, wearing the same peach-colored smock.

"I'd like you to meet Bernardo," Dr. Patty explained. "He'll be your attendant during your stay with us."

"And how do you do, Mr. Bennett?" He was a sturdy and attractive man, quite muscular, with wavy black hair, a well-defined jaw, and straight white teeth. "Anything you need, anything at all, I'm here to help."

"Okay," I managed.

He gestured grandly down the hall. "If you'll permit me to show you to your room, this way."

He led me to the end of the hall, where a second hallway branched to the left. This one was lined with numbered doors. A kind of aimless music burbled faintly from speakers somewhere in the ceiling.

"Where is everyone?" I asked.

"At this hour, I imagine most are enjoying the facilities. The pool is especially popular."

"I saw it in the video," I said, then added, nonsensically, "It seemed very nice."

"I understand you were a swimmer of great accomplishment in your university days, Mr. Bennett. Three records, was it?"

"Four, actually."

"What a pleasant recollection that must be for you. Of course," he added as an afterthought, "many wonderful new memories await you. A lifetime of fresh triumphs. That's the thing to focus on."

At number sixteen, he stopped and reached into his pocket, producing a ring of keys. He selected one and opened the door.

"After you, Mr. Bennett."

The room, more like a suite, looked like something in a hotel: a living room furnished in a pared-down, contemporary style and, separated by an arched entrance, a sleeping area with a king-sized bed. Where windows might have been, video screens showed various natural scenes in rotation: seascapes, mountain vistas, fields of quivering wildflowers. I ventured farther in, just a step ahead of Bernardo, who, in the manner of a hotel bellman waiting for a tip, walked me through each feature. Upon the bed's voluminously puffy comforter—the sight made me want to pitch face-first into its soft embrace—somebody had laid out a smock just like Bernardo's, though pale blue in color, with matching drawstring trousers. (I had, by this time, grown weirdly accustomed to my backside-baring gown—I'd all but forgotten I was wearing it, in fact.) There were also a pair of canvas slips-ons and a terry-cloth robe.

"The dinner bell will be ringing soon," Bernardo said. "I'm sure you'll want to tidy up. Is there anything else I can do for you before I go?"

I couldn't think of anything. Indeed, all I wanted to do was sleep. Hardly surprising, given the tumultuous events of the last twenty-four hours, though these things had begun to seem distant and somewhat abstract.

"Very good, Mr. Bennett," he said with a smart little bow. "Just relax and enjoy yourself. I'll be back to fetch you for dinner."

Off he went. I checked the door, finding it locked, though this fact, peculiarly, did not trouble me all that much. To the contrary, it made me feel protected, almost cocooned. I went to the bathroom, turned on the tub, and, while I waited for it to fill, sat on the toilet lid and peeled the bandage from my arm. My skin was stained with iodine; Thea's homemade sutures had been removed. In their stead, a flesh-colored patch of some foreign material had been used to fill the hole, its edges held in place by tape. Except for the iodine and tape, you'd never know that less than twelve hours ago I'd taken a kitchen knife to my own flesh.

I lowered myself into the tub and sank neck-deep into its warmth. Under its influence, my mind softened to my present circumstances. For the moment at least, there was really nothing to be done. Yes, I'd suffered a great injustice, but the thought of starting over didn't seem to lack all merit. *Just relax and enjoy yourself,* Bernardo had said. It wasn't the worst advice I'd ever heard, and when was the last time I'd done such a thing? I couldn't recall.

Content to let events unfold, I drifted off to sleep, awakening sometime later to a harplike trilling: the dinner bell. I rose, dried myself, and dressed in the blue smock and slippers. I realized I was profoundly hungry. I'd barely eaten a bite for twenty-four hours, and the images of the splendid food in Dr. Patty's video took root in my thoughts to the exclusion of all else. When I tried the door, it opened without resistance upon the sight of Bernardo, waiting for me with his hands serenely folded at his waist.

"Mr. Bennett, you're looking quite well."

"Thank you, Bernardo. I'm feeling a lot better." This was true: it had been ages since I'd felt so good, so at peace with life.

His face beamed. "That's wonderful to hear. Now, if you're ready for dinner—" He made another of his grand gestures. "This way, please."

He escorted me down the hallway of numbered rooms. Several intersections later, we came to a pair of swinging doors.

"After you, sir."

At last, here were other souls. The room was decorated in a chic, minimalist style, with perhaps a dozen tables, all with multiple diners dressed in blue smocks and slippers. The sound of lively conversation filled the air.

"I'll leave you in Danielle's care," Bernardo said. *"Bon appétit."*

Standing before me was the same woman I'd seen in Dr. Patty's video, although it took me a few seconds to recognize her. Her unisex, figure-dulling smock had been traded for a form-fitting black dress, sleek as a sealskin, with a plunging neckline; her hair, which had appeared rather frowsy in the video, was tinted with subtle blond highlights and fashionably cut to frame her face. A zone of scent—floral, with higher notes of something spicy—floated around her. The overall effect was almost sublimely sexual.

"Mr. Bennett, good evening. Will you be dining alone tonight, or would you like to join a group of our other guests?"

I realized I'd been staring at the woman—ogling her, in fact. Embarrassed, I wrenched my eyes away and surveyed the room, not expecting much, until I espied a certain morose figure sitting alone. *I'll be damned,* I thought.

I pointed. "How about that man over there?"

Danielle followed my gaze, then turned back to me. Her eyes were damp and astonishingly blue, seeming to possess a soulful depth that a person would gladly dive straight into. "Of course," she said, and gave a glossy smile. "A fellow new arrival. I'm sure you'll have much to talk about. If you'll come this way."

I followed her as she glided away, all elegant legs and sashaying derrière, the whole mesmerizing package proceeding across the restaurant atop the points of her tall, patent-leather heels. We were mere steps from the table when Jason finally noticed us. The boy startled like a fawn in a field. Before he could say anything, I thrust out my hand.

"How do you do?" I said, and bored my gaze into his: *Shut up, say nothing, we don't know each other, just play along.* "I'm Proctor Bennett."

A second's hesitation; then he took my hand. He swallowed hard and said, "Jason Kim."

"I'll just let the two of you get acquainted," Danielle declared. "Your waiter will be along momentarily." Addressing both of us, she dropped her voice to a conspiratorial register. "I just want to say, the lobster thermidor is *especially* good this evening."

I took a seat. "So," I said, when Danielle was out of earshot, "how are things?"

"Director Bennett, what are you *doing* here?"

"Same as you, being reiterated. And keep your voice down." Seeing the boy had nudged me from my watery mental state. "Let me guess. You have a brain tumor."

He stared at me, shocked.

"News flash. You don't have a brain tumor, Jason."

"I don't understand what you're saying."

"I mean that there's nothing wrong with you. You're perfectly healthy. We both are."

"But the doctor—"

"Was he named Warren, by any chance?"

His face retreated. "You know Dr. Singh?"

"Yeah. Or at least I thought I did. That injection he gave you—"

"How do you know about that?"

"He gave me the same one. It did something to us to lower our numbers."

The boy looked at me helplessly. "I'm so confused."

"Just take my word for it. You don't have a brain tumor or anything else."

A new character arrived. The waiter, dressed in a tuxedo, was a thick-bodied older man with upswept eyebrows and a snow-white Vandyke.

"Welcome, gentlemen," he announced, and proceeded to fill our water glasses from a sweating metal pitcher. "I'm Itzhak, your server for the evening." He presented us with menus. "Would either of you care for a cocktail before dinner? A glass of wine perhaps?"

"Water is fine," I said.

"And for you, sir?" he said to Jason.

The boy swallowed again, his throat visibly bobbing. "I guess water?"

The waiter offered a crisp bow. "Very good. I'll be back shortly to take your orders."

In his absence, Jason leaned over the table and said, with quiet uncertainty, "So, I'm not really dying?"

"Not today, anyway."

"Then why would Dr. Singh tell me I was?"

"They're getting rid of us because we were on the pier."

It took Jason a moment to process this. "So just because I *heard* something, I'm being reiterated?"

"That's pretty much the story, yeah." Seeing the boy's defeated expression, I felt a sudden heaviness in my chest. "I'm really sorry, Jason. This is all my fault. I never should have gotten you involved in any of this."

From a nearby table came a jolly burst of laughter.

"Let me ask you something," I said, leaning forward. "How long have you been here?"

"I got here last night. They called a special ferry for me. Dr. Singh said my number was too low to wait."

"And you were alone."

He nodded.

"Do you recognize anybody in here?"

He glanced around the room, then turned back to me. "No, should I?"

"Maybe not, but *I* should. I review every retirement in the district."

"Couldn't they be from other districts?"

"Possibly, but why are there so many? The last outbound ferry was Monday. Fifteen people were scheduled to be on it, including four from District Six. There are"—I did a quick head count—"thirty-seven people in this room, not including us."

"What about the retirees from last Wednesday? Couldn't they still be here?"

"Same story. I don't see a single person in this room I know. That includes my father, I'll point out. No, these people aren't from last Wednesday, either."

Jason scanned the space. "You're right." He squinted at me. "So, who are they?"

The conversation was broken as our waiter returned. "Ah, getting acquainted, I see." He withdrew a pad and pen from the pocket of his apron. "What can I get for you gentlemen this evening? Let me just say, the lobster thermidor is exceptional tonight. We have just a few portions left."

"Jason, how does that sound?"

The boy shrugged.

"Make that two," I said to the waiter.

"Very good." He scooped up our menus and walked away.

I asked Jason, "When you got here, Dr. Patty showed you a movie, right?"

He nodded.

"How did it make you feel?"

He thought a moment. "Sleepy?"

"Like you didn't care about anything."

"Pretty much, yeah."

"How about now?"

He puzzled over this. "Different, I guess. Seeing you and all."

I lowered my voice another notch: "Look around again, and be discreet. How do these people seem to you?"

He did as I'd instructed. "They look pretty happy."

"I've done this for years, Jason, and one thing I know, most retirees are scared shitless. They may not want to show it, but they are. So they get off the ferry, watch a movie, and just like that they're all smiles? I don't think so."

"And here . . . we . . . *are.*"

Too quickly, Itzhak had returned. Making a grand show of it, he presented us with our plates: on each, a split lobster shell stuffed with chunks of white meat, buried in a thick white sauce and swaddled in melted cheese and toasted bread crumbs.

"Enjoy, my friends," he said and, with a tip of his bearded chin, left us alone again.

"Wow," Jason said, eyeing his plate hungrily, "this looks delicious."

"Too bad, because you're not going to eat it."

The boy looked up, startled. "I'm not?"

"No."

His eyes widened. "Are you saying that it's . . . poisoned?"

"Oh, I seriously doubt that."

"Then what's wrong with my food?"

"What's wrong with it is that you don't like lobster. You told me the other day."

He stopped short. "You're right, I don't."

"And yet, all of a sudden, it's exactly what you want." I leaned closer. Other details were coming clear to me. "Do you hear anything?"

"Besides the other people in the room?"

"Yeah, some kind of music, very faint."

He paused to listen, eyes narrowed in concentration. "Actually, I do."

"I've been hearing it since I got here. I think it's doing something to our brains."

He was still listening closely. A few seconds passed and he looked up. "Not music," he said. "Voices."

The boy was right. The softest voices there ever were, murmuring at the razor's edge of audibility. The feeling they produced was less aural than tactile, as if my brain were being caressed. As I focused on the sound, a wave of well-being washed through me; I felt my breath deepen, my heart slow.

Think about your new life, the voices said. *All the new memories you'll make. That's the thing to focus on.*

"Whoa," said Jason.

Jolted back to awareness, I looked up. Jason, too, had felt it.

"That's fucked up," he said.

We were interrupted by a sudden cry. *"No!"*

Every head in the room turned. A woman had lurched from her chair, which now lay on its back on the floor. She was a tiny thing, though she did not seem frail. One could just as easily imagine her charging up a mountain trail or blasting a ball down the fairway as sitting in this upscale mausoleum, eating her final lobster.

"This is a *mistake,*" she said. "This makes no *sense.*"

Itzhak appeared at her side. "Madam, if you please, you're upsetting the other diners."

She looked frantically around the room, her head darting like a bird's. "Who are these people? What am I doing here?"

He took her by the elbow. "If you'll come with me, please."

She shook him off and backed away. From the far side of the room, Danielle and Bernardo were bearing down on her.

"I don't understand what you people want," the woman cried. She raised her voice to the room. "For godsakes, why is everyone just sitting there? Can't you see what this is?"

I did not so much decide to intervene as discover myself in the midst of doing it, quickstepping through the maze of tables. My intention, admittedly not well thought out, was to insinuate myself between the woman and the three individuals I now regarded as nothing less than her attackers.

But as I neared, something knocked me off my stride. The woman's eyes, searching the room, landed on my own, and in that instant, something changed—everything changed. Her body relaxed; her eyes softened; all fear seemed to leave her in a blink. It was like seeing a light go on—that was the look I saw on the woman's face.

"Director Bennett?" she said. "Is it really you?"

But that was the end of it. Grabbing her from behind, Bernardo wrapped his arms around her waist and hoisted her off her feet. She began to kick and scream—the wordless cries of a trapped animal. Meanwhile, Itzhak had moved to insert himself between me and the unfolding horror.

"Mr. Bennett, there's no need to concern yourself."

"It isn't right!" the woman screamed. Bernardo was hauling her across the room to the exit. "Do you hear me? This isn't right at all!"

Her last shrieks were silenced as the door closed behind them. A ghastly silence gripped the room. But then, just a few seconds later, a strange thing happened—strange and also eerie. As if on cue, all the other diners simultaneously resumed eating, filling the air with the tinkle of china and silverware and the buzz of conversation. It was as if nothing had happened at all.

"If you please, sir," Itzhak said, "why don't you return to your table? You don't want your lobster to get cold."

"Where are you taking her?"

"Madam is upset."

"Yeah, I got that. That was pretty obvious."

"I'm sure she'll feel better soon. There's no need to worry."

A second voice from behind me: "Mr. Bennett, how can I be of service?"

Bernardo had materialized at my side. That was fast, I thought. Where the hell had he come from?

"A straight answer would be nice."

"Madam wishes me to convey her regards to you. She appreciates your concern, and is very sorry about what happened. She's retired to her quarters to rest."

A twitchy silence followed, the two men taking me in with an altogether different sort of smile: not the robotic solicitousness of hotel staff eager to please, but something more in the key of a nightclub bouncer's final warning. *Don't fuck with us.*

"I'm sure this has been a challenging day for you," Bernardo said. His hand dropped to his waist, and that was when I saw the shocker, peeking from beneath the edge of his smock. "Perhaps you'd like to lie down in your room."

"You know, now that you mention it, I am a little worn out."

Itzhak said, "A fine idea, Mr. Bennett. It's important to take care of yourself. A little rest and you'll feel more like yourself."

"This is really kind of you," I said, eyeing each man in turn. "Everyone has been so nice."

"Would you like me to wrap up your dinner for you? We can send it along to your room."

"Sure." I nodded. "That'd be great."

With one hand on my shoulder, the other taking me by the elbow, Bernardo steered me across the room to the hostess station.

"Good night, Mr. Bennett," Danielle said. "Sleep well."

We were almost out the door when I stopped. "Hang on a second," I said to Bernardo.

His grip tightened a notch.

"I forgot to say good night to my dinner companion. I don't want to be rude." I jostled free of his grasp. "I'll be just a sec."

But when I turned to look, the table was empty.

The woman's name was Aurelia Voss.

She'd taken the Monday ferry. I knew this because hers was a long-scheduled retirement, and I'd reviewed her file some weeks before. Age one hundred thirty-one, monitor in the high teens.

She'd had a long career as first chair oboist with the City Symphony; her fourth husband, a book editor, had retired to the Nursery three years prior. She was in remarkably good health overall but showing signs of mental discomfort—distractibility, forgetfulness, mild depression; she missed her husband, could no longer play the instrument she loved, and had decided it was time. In other words, a model retirement, not quite at the top of her game but close enough. The kind of retirement that made people say: I should be so lucky.

But here was the thing. In the course of reviewing her case, I'd only seen the woman's picture. We'd never actually met.

And yet she'd addressed me by name. Had our lives intersected in some manner I failed to recall? Possible, but I didn't think so. And there was something about the *way* she'd said it—"Director Bennett, is it really you?"—that went deeper than casual recognition. She didn't just know who I was; I *meant* something to her. Like a long-lost relative or an old friend mislaid for years.

Alone in my suite, I took measure of my state of mind. By this time, the dulling effects of Dr. Patty's video had worn off. The voices were still there, but my awareness of them seemed to be forestalling their effect. How long could I hold out? There was nothing in the room to occupy me—no books, no television, nothing interesting to look at. The screens with their scenes of natural magnificence were, I knew, just one more trick to make me pliable. *Look at the pretty sunset. Look at the dancing poppies. Look at the morning dew on the grass, and, come to think of it, maybe I'll lie down and never get up.*

I paced my rooms to stay alert. My uneaten lobster—Itzhak had brought it by on a tray—had gone straight into the toilet. I was famished; barely a morsel of food had passed my lips for going on twenty-four hours. But to yield even to this ordinary temptation felt like a defeat, a first step on the road to psychological surrender.

And to what end? I had, strangely, never given specific thought to what actually *happened* at the Nursery. The retiree arrived in one state and departed in another; that was all I knew, and I had accepted this on its face, never probing any deeper. Surely something medical had to take place, yet apart from Dr. Patty, I'd seen neither medical staff of any kind nor any indication that the place was more than a luxury resort where people ate overly rich meals and lounged in mud baths.

I continued my restless pacing, trying to keep my thoughts busy, to hold the voices at bay. Could I really go on like this all night? To maintain my agitation, I sent my mind into the past—not to the happy moments but, rather, to the assorted disappointments and embarrassments that punctuate any life, that have the power to rouse a person in the middle of the night in a state of searing regret. An academy teacher who'd humiliated me in front of the class. A sexual failure of spectacular awkwardness. A college companion's sudden discarding of our friendship over a petty rivalry. My mother's suicide, and my father's coldness in the days that came after, and the awful scene on the pier.

The pier.

Doria and her boy, George, coming to see me off, and the boy's sudden, forceful hug even though the two of us were virtual strangers: I wondered anew, *What on earth was that about?* The whole thing made no sense; indeed, the encounter had made the boy visibly uncomfortable. Which could mean only one thing: he was acting under his mother's orders. So why would Doria command her son to embrace a man he barely knew?

Maybe the hug wasn't an actual hug, I thought. Maybe it was something else.

My hospital gown was lying on the bathroom floor. My memory wasn't wrong; the gown had a pocket. I removed the folded paper the boy had secreted there and opened it.

It appeared to be a technical drawing, rendered in miniature. Some of the lines, I saw, were labeled with tiny writing.

"Dining room." "Pool." "Residences." "Spa."

George's drawing: it was a map.

24

Thus did the night pass.

I remained awake, or mostly. Perhaps for a time I drifted off, but always I managed to jolt myself awake, whereupon I'd drop to the floor and do push-ups to clear my head, all the while thinking any awful thought I could come up with. (I was surprised how many there were.) I had no idea what time it was—the room possessed no clock—when the door opened to reveal Bernardo, looking fresh as a dewdrop and bearing a tray with a chrome lid.

"Good morning, Mr. Bennett," he said sunnily. "I trust you had a good night's rest."

Obviously not; no doubt I looked as crummy as I felt. Bernardo placed the tray on the coffee table and lifted the cover to unveil a stack of pancakes, drenched in butter and syrup, with two thick slices of bacon crisscrossed atop it. My stomach practically imploded with hunger.

"Dr. Patty thought you might be more comfortable eating in your room."

Not good news; I needed to get out to have a look around the place.

"Thanks," I said. "That's great."

Bernardo continued to stand there, staring at me with his empty grin. His message was clear: I would have to eat my breakfast in front of him. With doom in my heart, I took up my knife and fork, carved off a piece, and put it in my mouth. Just the feel of it on my palate, its pillowy softness, ignited pleasure sensors in my brain that made me swoon. Dear God, was it ever delicious! Did people know how delicious pancakes were? And bacon! The way it crunched between the teeth, its burst of fatty joy upon the tongue. Miraculous!

"You seem to be enjoying your breakfast a good deal, Mr. Bennett."

Bernardo's voice aroused something in me—a flicker of resistance. What the fuck was I doing? Pancakes: they were kiddie food. And yet my plate was practically empty, all but a couple of bites now lounging heavily in my stomach. I wanted them desperately; I would have licked the plate like a dog at his dish. It took all my resolve to put down my utensils and look up.

"Wow." I dabbed my mouth with the napkin. "Did that ever hit the spot."

"Aren't you going to finish, Mr. Bennett?"

"Honestly, Bernardo, I think I'm full. Thanks, though. That was really good. My compliments to the chef."

A moment passed before he nodded. "Very well." He lifted the tray from the table and headed for the door.

"Hey, Bernardo?"

The man turned.

"I was wondering if maybe I could grab that swim we talked about. You know, maybe work off some of those pancakes."

He considered this a moment. "Of course, sir. I'll ask Dr. Patty."

"Yeah, about that. The thing is, I'm feeling a little keyed up. You know, with the upcoming reiteration and all. It's kind of making me nervous."

"I understand, sir. I'll pass that along."

"So I wouldn't mind going right now. If that would be okay."

The question hung in the air between us.

"I'll inquire, sir," he said and stepped from the room.

The minutes passed. I'd about given up hope when the door opened again. Bernardo was holding a small bundle: swimming trunks, wrapped in a towel.

"I'll wait while you get ready, sir."

In the bedroom, I changed into the trunks and put on the robe. "Thanks for doing this," I said to Bernardo, as we proceeded down the hall. "I'm sure it'll put me in the right spirit."

"Not at all, Mr. Bennett."

We were, as far as I could tell from George's map, on the eastern side of the complex, which had two levels, connected by stairways at both ends. Housing and dining were located on level two, the pool and spa on level one. The complex also possessed a central vertical core, presumably mechanical in nature, that seemed to go all the way to the top of the island.

"You know," I said, "I was wondering, where exactly will my reiteration take place?"

"Oh, there's no need to trouble yourself with that, Mr. Bennett." At a leisurely pace, we were moving down the hall toward the eastern stairwell. "I wouldn't give that a moment's consideration. For now, I'd say just rest and enjoy the facilities. That's what I'd do."

It was like I was listening to myself spout the pablum I'd recited to retirees for twenty years. The feeling was not an altogether comfortable one. "They say it's like falling asleep," I said.

"Indeed, they do, Mr. Bennett. That is what they say."

"I was hoping you could elaborate on that."

"Oh, I really couldn't. That's not my area of expertise."

"So, what is your area of expertise, exactly?"

He shot me a sidelong smile. "Why, making you comfortable, of course! Your well-being is my only concern, Mr. Bennett."

We came to the stairwell and descended one flight. The air here was cooler and wetter, with a smell of chlorine. I felt a low, mechanical throbbing underfoot, which, based on George's drawing, I presumed to be some kind of pump or air exchanger.

"And here we are."

To my right, an opening appeared. Beyond, the space enlarged to reveal the pool: competition-sized, with glossy tile edges and a dark blue bottom that gave the water an inky density. I counted eight swimmers, a mix of men and women, not so much swimming as bobbing in the water, like human pool toys. At the far end was a burbling spa, where two women in bathing caps were lounging in a cloud of steam.

"Thanks, Bernardo. I can take it from here."

"I'd be glad to keep an eye on you, Mr. Bennett."

"That's nice of you, but you know? Four records and all. I think I'll be okay."

The man just looked at me, dead-faced.

"Okay, fine," I said, "you caught me. It's a little embarrassing, but it would mean a lot to me to, you know, relive those days one last time. By myself, I mean. If that's all right. If that'd be okay with you."

The man brightened. "Ah," he said. "I understand completely, Mr. Bennett." He leaned in, speaking more intimately: "And may I just say? I appreciate your being honest with me on a matter so personal. I want you to feel you can speak freely with me. On any subject. Any subject at all."

"I do. Absolutely I do."

He gave one of his little waiterish bows. "I wish you a very pleasant swim. I'll be right outside when you're done."

Off he went. I walked to the far side of the pool, where there was a bench, and removed my robe. None of the other bathers seemed to take notice of me, or even of one another; nobody was talking. I scanned the room for familiar faces. I thought I recognized one or two from the dining room, but I couldn't be sure, and Aurelia was not among them.

According to George's drawing, the central core of the complex was located behind the far wall. At first inspection the wall appeared disappointingly solid, but as I looked more closely, I noticed a panel about four feet off the floor and held in place by screws at each corner. Pretending to stretch out my calves, I placed my hands against the metal. It was pulsing like an artery.

"Help!"

I swiveled around in time to see a figure partially rising from the water. Not rising: thrashing. Just the crown of the person's head was visible, and a single, upstretched hand. The water boiled around them with their terrified flailing. For a fraction of a second, the person managed to tip their face toward the ceiling and lift their mouth above the water.

"Help me!"

It is a fact of drowning people that even to touch one carries great risk. In their panicked state, they can easily drag their would-be rescuer down with them. I say this not because this cautionary thought was on my mind, but because that was precisely what happened. Five long strides and I launched into the water. By this time, the victim had lost all traction on the surface; they were sinking fast. I dived down, the pressure squeezing my ears. The person appeared to be a woman, rather small, wearing the same blue pajamas. As I reached out to take her hand, she spun around and lassoed her arms around my neck from behind. I was caught completely off guard. An elbow hit me in the eye, then what felt like a foot. With each failed attempt to free myself, my own panic surged. It felt like an eternity had passed since I'd taken a breath. I tried to pry her arms off me, but the woman would have none of it. Every attempt I made only caused her to tighten her grip. *Can't you see I'm trying to save you?* I thought. *Let go of me, goddamnit!*

Suddenly, I was free.

My need to breathe had overridden all other functions. I pushed off the bottom, shot to the surface, and filled my lungs with a gasp so loud you could have heard it a mile away. I had expected to find a crowd of onlookers—even, perhaps, an outstretched hand or two—but there was none. I might have been alone in the room, so stark was the absence of concern from the other bathers. I hauled in two more breaths and dived. The woman was now lying facedown on the bottom. She would fight me no more; my only hope was to get her to the surface as quickly as possible and drain her lungs. I hooked an arm around her and began to draw her toward the stairs at the shallow end of the pool.

At last I was able to pull her clear of the water and onto the deck. No one had offered help; none of the other bathers was even looking in our direction. I positioned the woman on her side and pounded her between the shoulder blades. Still she failed to stir. I rolled her onto her back, revealing her face.

It was Caeli.

The rest was a blur, all my senses focused on the project of filling the girl's lungs with air—as if not only her life hung in the balance but my own as well. Cupping the back of her neck, I squeezed her nose and blew into her mouth, then did it twice more; I straddled her waist and performed thirty rapid chest compressions at one-second intervals. Some of the other bathers had, by this time, noticed what was happening, though none had offered assistance, and I experienced their presence only in the abstract, as an actor whose eyes are flooded by the spotlights is aware of his audience without actually seeing it. I was crying out. I was yelling her name. I was telling her in no uncertain terms to open her lungs and breathe. I was pushing on her chest when, miraculously, it happened: a hard spasm, followed by a gagging cough, and I rolled her onto her side as she commenced to disgorge great volumes of vomity water onto the pool deck.

I fell back on my haunches. My pulse was pounding; my heart felt like some huge swollen object in my chest, a balloon inflated to the edge of bursting. Beside me, Caeli coughed and coughed and coughed, and when she was done, I crouched down to meet her eye.

"Caeli, can you hear me?"

Her eyes were distant and unfocused.

"Do you know where you are?"

She blinked, then said, softly: "The pool?"

"That's right. You had trouble in the water, and I got you out."

She thought about this.

"You're safe now," I said.

"I'm safe," she repeated dreamily. "You got me out."

"That's right."

"I'm sorry."

"You don't have to be sorry, Caeli. It was just an accident, that's all."

I wedged a hand behind her neck and eased her to a seated position. My awareness widened at this point to include the other bathers, who had crowded around. The sight of them filled me with anger.

"What the hell is wrong with you people?" I barked.

Glances were exchanged, but no one spoke.

"Why didn't anyone help us? You all just stood there!"

A new voice: "Hello again, Mr. Bennett."

Bernardo was striding toward us from the entrance, carrying my robe.

"I apologize for the intrusion, but I was becoming concerned." He stopped before me and opened the robe, holding it out like a valet. "How was your swim, sir? I hope it was refreshing."

I shot to my feet and faced him squarely. "What the hell is going on around this place?"

He frowned and lowered the robe. "Mr. Bennett? Is there a problem?"

"She could have drowned, for godsakes. It was lucky I was here."

Pursing his lips, he followed my gesture, held his eyes there a moment, then lifted them to my face again. "Ah," he said. "You've found a friend."

"What's she doing here?"

"I couldn't say precisely, Mr. Bennett. But I imagine she's here because *you're* here. That's how these things usually happen."

I'd wearied completely of the man's obfuscation. "Don't bullshit me, Bernardo."

"Tell me, what can I do to help?"

"I need to see Dr. Patty. I need to see her right away."

"Of course, Mr. Bennett! You have only to ask."

His sudden acquiescence took me by surprise. "You'll take me to her?"

The man demurred. "Not directly, no. Dr. Patty is a very busy woman. But I'll be glad to make the necessary arrangements. Why don't you wait in your room?"

"I'm bringing the girl with me."

"Of course! Your friend is more than welcome to wait with you."

Bernardo's agreement seemed too easy, but I was hardly in a position to interrogate the man's largesse. I put on the robe and helped Caeli to her feet. In her wet clothing, she looked as frail and tiny as a bird.

"Do you have another robe?" I asked Bernardo.

The man's face fell. "Oh. I'm afraid I don't."

I removed my robe and held it out to Caeli, but the girl shook her head. "I don't want it," she said.

"Take it. You must be freezing."

"I said I don't want it!"

How to account for the passion of this weird refusal? "Okay, okay," I said, "whatever you want."

Bernardo chimed in: "So the matter is resolved? Very well." He gestured toward the exit. "After you, Mr. Bennett."

With Caeli clinging to my side, we returned to my suite in silence.

"We'll need a set of dry clothes for her," I told Bernardo.

"Absolutely, Mr. Bennett. Why don't you and your friend make yourselves comfortable."

"Her name," I said, "is Caeli."

"Of course. A lovely name, too. And what size, may I ask, is Caeli?"

Why was the man being so obtuse? "What does it look like? Small, obviously."

He nodded crisply from the chin. "If you'll both excuse me."

While we waited, I drew a bath to warm her up. Bernardo returned with a blue smock and matching pants, and more promises to talk to Dr. Patty, who, he said, was presently unavailable but would be free shortly. I placed the clothing, folded, on the vanity, beside the pile of towels and miniature bottles of soap and shampoo.

"Take as long as you need, okay?" I told Caeli. "I'll be right outside."

She nodded, but that was the extent of it. She hadn't spoken a word since we'd returned to the suite. Obviously, her guardians had sent her here; I'd been wrong about a lot of things, but not about that. I could also see that the experience had left her badly traumatized. Perhaps, when she'd had a chance to collect herself, she'd be able to tell me what had happened to her, but I didn't want to press. For now, what she needed was a friend.

I changed back into my scrubs and sat on the bed to wait. I heard the tap running as she reheated the water, but otherwise no sounds issued from the bathroom. Without a clock, I had no way of measuring how long she'd been in there; in this windowless place, time's passage had become a complete abstraction.

And just how long *had* I been here? In the video, Dr. Patty had said that "several days" would pass before my reiteration. George's map had so far proved itself correct, but Caeli's presence was a wrinkle. Swimming back to Prospera was off the table; no way could Caeli make it. And even if I could, what would I do when I got there? Try to find Thea's people in the Annex? Confront Warren and Elise? Perhaps I should march straight to Callista's office. That would be an interesting scene.

Eventually I rose and rapped my knuckles on the door. "Caeli? Are you okay?"

The door swung open. Caeli was standing before me, wearing the smock and with her hair turbaned in a towel. I had the sense that she'd been waiting there for some time.

"I was worried," I said.

She stared at me a moment. "I took a bath," she stated.

"I know. I drew it for you, remember?"

A key turned in the lock.

"Hello again, sir," Bernardo declared from the doorway. "I bring good news! Dr. Patty seemed very keen to talk with you. She asked that I escort you to her office right away."

It was hardly the moment to leave, but with Bernardo standing there, my conversation with Caeli would have to wait regardless. "I have to go for a few minutes," I told her. "Will you be all right here?"

She nodded faintly. "That's okay."

"I'm going to get you out of this place, I promise."

Bernardo led me down the hall of numbered doors. Once again, I was struck by the absence of any people. The place had the silent air of complete inhabitation.

"You know," I said, "I was wondering if I could see my friend from last night."

"Another friend, sir?"

"Yes, the man I had dinner with."

"Ah, you're referring to Mr. Kim. I believe he's using the spa facilities."

Jason in a mud bath: I couldn't see it. "Aren't you his attendant? Shouldn't you know?"

"I understand your confusion, Mr. Bennett, and I must apologize. I assisted Mr. Kim when he first arrived, but Danielle is his attendant now."

I wondered which of the two Danielles the boy had looking after him: the dowdy nurse of the video or the siren of the restaurant?

I asked, "Are there any other attendants or just you two?"

"Oh, there are quite a few of us. You met Itzhak last night."

"I thought he was a waiter."

"Right you are. Each of us serves in several capacities. We find that it helps us get to know our guests on a personal level."

"How many guests do you have at the moment?"

He shrugged good-naturedly. "Oh, it varies, day to day."

"I counted thirty-seven in the dining room last night."

"Perhaps that's the number then."

Talking to Bernardo: it was like trying to snatch a fly from the air.

He continued, "Perhaps this is a question best suited to Dr. Patty."

"The video said I should direct any questions to my attendant. So, I'm asking *you*."

"And I wish I could be more helpful. If you'd like, I can look into the matter for you."

"When?"

"When what, Mr. Bennett?"

"When will you look into it."

"Absolutely as soon as the opportunity presents itself."

He wasn't stonewalling, I realized. The man just didn't know. We passed the dining room, which was dark and empty, proceeded down another hallway, and came to a door with a sign that said CLINIC.

"I'll wait here for you, sir," Bernardo said.

Stepping into the room, I was instantly smacked by a wave of déjà vu. The examination table with its crinkling paper cover, the cabinet of gleaming instruments, the single wooden chair parked in the corner, and the flat, dimensionless lighting: the room was an exact duplicate of the one I'd visited with my mother all those years ago, and again when Warren had examined me.

"Won't you come in, Mr. Bennett?" asked Dr. Patty, who was closing the cabinet of instruments. Hands tucked in the pockets of her lab coat, she turned to face me with a sunny smile. "I hope you've enjoyed your stay with us so far."

There was something different about the woman, I realized. Different and also compelling. Her cheeks were flushed, her lips tinted and faintly swollen-looking. Her hair was done up in an elegant chignon; a frisson of black lace peeked from the neckline of her lab coat.

"I understand you've found a friend. Caeli, is it?"

"Yeah, and that's the reason I need to talk to you. She's just a kid. She doesn't belong here. It isn't right."

"I see."

"Neither do I. I tried to tell you before."

"You seem tense, Mr. Bennett."

"Yeah, I'm tense. I'm being railroaded. Both of us are."

Taking a slow step toward me, she unclasped her hair, freeing it with a coquettish toss.

"Dr. Patty, what are you doing?"

She bit her lower lip and took another step. "What can I do to put you more at ease?"

Good God. It was like some bad blue movie.

"Tell me, Mr. Bennett. Anything at all."

I won't deny it. As she slithered her hands up my chest, aligned her hips to mine, and went in for the kiss, my body responded. And not just my body. My head filled—literally filled—with an obliterating carnal fog. Her breath entered my mouth, and then her tongue—a gently searching presence of heavenly softness—and it was as if the whole erotic history of my life, every experience, real and imagined, came undammed inside my brain to form a rushing torrent of sex.

"Does that feel nice?" Dr. Patty murmured. "Isn't that the nicest feeling in the world?"

All volition had left me; my eyes were closed. Things were happening—surprising things, marvelous things—though I could not have said, exactly, how these things were being enacted. I had somehow come to be on the examination table, Dr. Patty above me—the motion was undulating and aquatic—but her role in these events possessed an abstract, even spectral quality; she could have been anyone or no one.

What happened next, I lack the words to wholly capture. The closest I can say is that I felt myself being disassembled, my personhood—that is to say, my subjective sense of reality—atomized into a great generality of un-being. No longer was I lying on the examination table being radiantly fucked by my boyhood pediatrician; I experienced neither pleasure nor pain; one might say that, in conventional terms, I experienced nothing at all; and what remained of the being known as Proctor Bennett—not much—understood that this was what it meant to die.

Whereupon a curious thing happened. I found myself standing in a room. I say "room," but the word is misleading. What I mean is, it felt like a bounded space, though its limits were unknown—a room without walls—and what light there was radiated not from any single source but from a surrounding cosmos of tiny, ever-separating points.

A room of stars.

I was not alone. Standing beside me was a woman. She was naked—as, I noted, was I.

"Director Bennett," she said, "is it you?"

This seemed to be the case.

"And I'm . . . Aurelia?"

I had no doubt that she was.

"Will we be arriving soon?"

"Arriving," I repeated. The word felt strange in my mouth. "Arriving where?"

She released a long, disconsolate breath, like someone on the edge of sleep. "Because it's been so very long," she said.

To my right, another figure had appeared: a man. He, too, was naked.

"Hello," I said, and added heartily, "I'm very glad to see you"—as, indeed, I was.

With exaggerated slowness, he swiveled his head toward me. What a kind, earnest face he had! There are people with such faces; one cannot help but be drawn to them, to give them one's absolute trust.

"Director Bennett," the man said. "Are we there?"

Things were changing. Form was asserting itself upon formlessness. New sensations moved over me. The tickle of wind in my hair. The salt perfume of the sea. The sound—low, throaty, rhythmic—of a ferry engine, and the presence of hard steel plating beneath my feet. A rush of youthful vitality poured through me.

"It's happening," the man stated.

"I believe that it is," the woman agreed.

But something wasn't right. As tempting as it was to yield to these new circumstances, a deeper part of me resisted. There was something I needed to do—something, perhaps, on which my very life depended—and being here meant that I could not do this thing.

"I need to leave," I told them. "I'm sorry. I have to go back."

But neither appeared to have heard me. Their faces were slack, their eyes staring into the middle distance.

"Hello," the man said, to no one. "I am Jason, your ward."

"Hello," the woman echoed. "My name is Aurelia. It's very nice to meet you."

I was becoming increasingly agitated. Around us, the scene continued to resolve, its details crystallizing like water into ice. The white-tipped ocean. The dazzling, sunlit sky. The bubbling churn of the ferry's props beneath the fantail. I knew that to surrender—to yield to this remade reality—meant I'd be forever lost.

"Are you listening? We can't stay."

"My name is Aurelia," the woman droned. "It's great to finally meet you."

"I'm Jason," the man went on. "How do you do?"

I seized him by the shoulders. "Can't you see what's happening?"

"It's a pleasure to make your acquaintance."

"Snap out of it!"

"And you must be my father."

I reared back and slapped him across the face. He stumbled into the rail, then drew himself upright with his back to the sea. "Thank you for the warm welcome."

"Goddamnit, there's no time! We have to jump! If we stay here, we'll die!"

"I am very much looking forward to our time together."

I rushed him, too late. I knew it the instant our bodies collided— or, rather, failed to. Jason was gone; my arms held only air.

And then I was falling.

Falling and falling and falling.

Down and down and down.

25

Dr. Patty, hovering above me: her skin shone with sweat; her hair swayed with her movements and the quick rhythm of her breath.

"Stop."

Arching her neck like a cat, she increased the speed of her pelvic undulations. The sensation was revoltingly mechanical.

"I said stop!"

I shoved her off me. Our separation was like the breaking of a circuit. Instantly I was cast into a full, horrified awareness. Good God, what was I doing?

"Mr. Bennett!" Dr. Patty cried. "What's the matter?"

The woman stood before me in a state of frank post-sexual disorder. I yanked up my pants and scrambled off the table.

The door opened: Bernardo. He cocked his head at me with an expression of dismay. "Pardon the interruption," he said, turning to Dr. Patty. "I thought I heard a noise."

Enough of this. I grabbed Bernardo by the wrist and moved

quickly behind him, twisting his arm behind his back while simultaneously pulling the shocker from his waistband and jamming it against the underside of his jaw.

"Mr. Bennett, this is completely unnecessary."

"Bernardo, I want you to reach down slowly and take your keys from your pocket."

"There's no need for any of this. You shouldn't excite yourself."

I pressed the shocker deeper into the flesh of his throat.

"Very well," he said and, with a sigh, dropped the keys.

"Jason Kim," I said, "where is he?"

"Danielle has taken Mr. Kim back to his suite, I believe."

"What's the number?"

"Twenty-six."

The boy had been just down the hall the entire time. I thumbed the safety off the shocker.

"Mr. Bennett, if I may. You really don't want to use that."

"Have to disagree."

"I'm only telling you this for your own safety. Application of a strong electric current to my person would be highly disruptive. *Highly.* I cannot guarantee the outcome."

For a second, the man's warning gave me pause. But only for a second.

Bang.

I found myself sitting with my back against the door. My ears were ringing; my body tingled, as if with a dissipating electric charge.

Bernardo and Dr. Patty were gone.

The keys were where Bernardo had dropped them, but the shocker was nowhere to be found. I scanned the room for something I could use as a weapon. Various medical instruments lay strewn over the floor.

A scalpel.

I took it in my fist and eased the door open. The hall was empty. Bernardo's keys were numbered. I'd get Caeli first, then Jason. After that, I didn't know.

Caeli was sitting on the sofa, exactly as I'd left her. "Honey, we have to go."

She looked up at me. The girl was crying, fat tears spilling from her eyes. "I'm sorry about the pool," she said.

I crouched before her and took her hand. "I know, sweetheart. It was just an accident. But we really need to get out of here."

She released an anguished sob and pitched forward into my arms, wrapping me in a fierce embrace. "I didn't mean to do it!" she cried. "I take it back! Let me take it back!"

"Ah, *there* you are, Mr. Bennett."

Bernardo had entered the room behind me, apparently none the worse for wear.

"I'm pleased I found you. Dr. Patty apologizes for the interruption and would very much like to conclude your examination."

The funny thing is, and speaking in hindsight, I had come to feel a certain fondness for the man. He was infuriating, yes, but his amiable manner made it impossible to dislike him. One rarely meets a person of such geniality, and I genuinely wished him no further ill.

Nevertheless, I stabbed him.

As he stumbled backward, I grabbed Caeli by the hand and pulled her from the room. I pounded on Jason's door, which promptly flung open to reveal Danielle, seductress of the dining hall.

"Mr. Bennett, I'm afraid you just missed him." She touched her hair and smiled. "I'm happy to see *you,* though."

"Mr. Bennett! Mr. Bennett!"

Bernardo was jogging down the hall toward me. But here was the thing. He wasn't coming from my room.

He was coming from the other end of the hall.

I spun around. The first Bernardo, knife still buried in his ribs, had just emerged from my room. A third Bernardo, two more Danielles, a pair of Itzhaks, and several Dr. Pattys were striding briskly from the direction of the dining hall.

A lunatic asylum; that's what this place was. A trip into absolute madness. Pulling Caeli by the hand, I bolted for the stairwell. Footsteps banged overhead; I looked up.

A throng of Bernardos was charging down the stairs.

We reached the bottom floor and raced down the hall. The smell of chlorine told me we were close. We swerved into the pool area and made for the far wall. I had little hope I'd be able to open the panel, having no tool of any kind, but it was my only hope. I fingered the edges, looking for a gap. A thin crack: I wedged my fingernails into it. It began to widen; I slid my fingers in and pulled.

The screws tore loose; the panel burst free. The space beyond was a dark hole. I helped Caeli in, then hoisted myself up and through the opening. The core was circular, maybe twenty feet wide, and packed with thrumming machinery. Fixed to the wall, a ladder disappeared into the gloom.

"You first," I told Caeli. "Don't look down. I'll be right behind you."

We climbed. I heard clanging on the rungs below. The first of the Bernardos was charging up behind us.

"Faster, Caeli!"

We had entered the nebulous region of our ascent where neither the top nor the bottom of the core was visible. How high would we have to climb? Would we have to go all the way to the top of the island? And what good would that do us? We'd be trapped at the top of a cliff.

A shape emerged above us: a catwalk, leading to a door in the wall.

"There!" I called to Caeli, pointing. "Hurry!"

As she hoisted herself onto the platform, a hand grabbed my ankle. The first Bernardo had caught up to me. I tried to shake him off, but his grip was unyielding.

"Goddamn you, get off me!"

I wedged the foot he was holding against the side of the ladder and kicked with the other, aiming for his head. Twice he dodged it, but on the third try I connected. Away he tumbled, into the darkness.

I pulled myself onto the catwalk. Where was Caeli? The door stood open; she must have already gone through. I entered to find myself in a large, low-ceilinged space. Caged bulbs were attached to the ceiling; the whirr of machinery emanated from the murk on either side.

I called out, "Caeli, where are you?"

"Mr. Bennett! Mr. Bennett!"

A gang of Bernardos, speaking as a grotesque chorus, was shoving its way through the door.

"Mr. Bennett, kindly allow me to assist you!"

"Mr. Bennett, come with me, please!"

I raced into the darkness, calling for Caeli. The room ended at another door—an imposing steel barricade with a wheel at the center, like the door of a safe. The Bernardos were closing fast; where would I emerge?

I stepped into starlight and the sound of waves crashing on the rocks below. I'd reached the top of the island.

"Caeli!"

My voice soared into the darkness. How had it come to be night? Was it the first night or the second? I was panting for breath; my face was drenched with sweat. I stumbled blindly forward. A maw of space opened before me: the edge of the cliff.

"Caeli! Answer me!"

But the girl was nowhere; Caeli was gone.

"Hello, Mr. Bennett."

I turned to see a single Bernardo jogging toward me, waving jauntily. He halted ten feet away, bent at the waist with his hands on his knees, and paused to take several long breaths. "I'm relieved I caught you, sir. You gave me quite a scare, running off like that."

"Where are the rest of you?"

"The rest of me, Mr. Bennett?"

"The other Bernardos!"

He turned his head from side to side, then looked back. "I'm afraid it's just me. And I have to say, you certainly gave me a run for my money!"

"Cut the crap, Bernardo. There were, like, twenty of you."

"I'm not saying there were, and I'm not saying there weren't. That's a matter for you to decide. Be that as it may, it's your safety that's uppermost in my mind. That's my only concern at the moment."

I could feel, from behind me, the tug of space, like some great gravitational field.

"So, if you'll kindly step away—"

"Hey, know what?"

He seemed cautiously pleased. "What's that, Mr. Bennett?"

"I owe you an apology."

"You do? I was not aware. What for?"

"Stabbing you, for starters. And kicking you off the ladder. Also that business with the shocker. You tried to warn me. I really should have listened."

He smiled benignly. "Think nothing of it. As you can see, I'm perfectly well."

For some number of seconds, five or ten or twenty, Bernardo and I stood in silent stalemate, each daring the other to make a move.

"Let me ask you something," I said.

"Of course, sir."

"There isn't any Caeli, is there? You can be honest."

"No, Mr. Bennett. I'm sorry. Perhaps there was, at some point in the past. But not now."

"Because as I'm standing here, I realize the whole thing doesn't make a hell of a lot of sense. I should have seen it before."

"You mustn't feel bad, Mr. Bennett. As you yourself must know, the prospect of reiteration can be quite stressful. Your friend was here simply because you needed her to be."

"Do you think she used to be my ward?"

He shrugged lightly. "A ward, or perhaps just a very good friend. Someone important in your life."

"Because that's how it felt. I've never had a ward before, but I think that's maybe what it's like."

"Indeed, sir."

"The thing is, the girl could be pretty difficult. She wasn't all that easy to get along with sometimes."

"They say that's often true of young people."

"But, you know? I actually didn't mind all that much. I kind of liked it."

"All the more reason, if I may say so, to keep your eyes looking forward, Mr. Bennett. To focus on the future."

"Yeah, about that," I said. "I don't think so."

His face drew back. "Sir?"

"Enough's enough. I'm good."

His body tensed. "Mr. Bennett, what are you—"

"See you around, Bernardo," I said, whereupon I turned my back to him, crossed my arms across my chest like a pharaoh in his tomb, and stepped off into space.

In gravity's grip, one ceases to experience gravity at all. One feels oneself floating, untethered to the world's binding force; it is as free a state of being as one can experience in life.

My aim was true. Toes pointed, arms folded, my carriage erect, I speared the surface like an arrow. The water's depth was unknown to me; it was possible I'd smash to bits on the bottom. But this proved not to be the case. I popped to the surface and was instantly hurled back toward shore. Wave after wave slapped me, threatening to crush my body on the rocks. I also couldn't see a fucking thing. I filled my lungs with air and dived down, pushing forward beneath the waves, and broke the surface again. I hadn't traveled far, but the principle was sound; the trick would be to time my descents to carry me below the waves' crests. Again and again I submerged, each time driving myself a little farther from the rocks but never quite enough. I was also quickly exhausting myself. The waves were overwhelming me; I felt my strength fading with every dive.

I saw a light, bobbing in the distance.

Not just bobbing. Flashing.

A signal?

I redoubled my efforts. The light was headed toward me. Friend or foe? All I knew was that if I didn't make it, I was going to drown for sure. The vessel came into focus. It was a fishing boat, with nets hung on outriggers from her flanks, like a pair of wings. A spotlight passed over me.

It was headed right for me.

It was going to run me over.

I ducked my head and dived. The roar of the propellers grew louder. I was prepared to be chopped to pieces when something scooped me up like a hand. I was caught in one of the boat's nets. I burst through the surface, tangled up like a fly in a spider's web.

"Okay, we've got him!" The voice was a man's. "Get us the hell out of here!"

The pilot swung the boat around at high speed. The net was pitching wildly above the water; I was helpless, unable even to cry out. The outrigger swung the other way, and I was dropped to the deck. Dark figures loomed above me.

"It's okay, Proctor. You're safe now."

Thea?

A bag was yanked over my head; someone rolled me onto my stomach and, with quick expertise, bound my wrists and ankles. I was rolled faceup again, lifted by the shoulders and feet, and the next thing I knew, I was being carted across the deck and down a flight of metal stairs.

"Okay, prossie, in you go."

They dropped me on the floor.

"Now keep quiet if you don't want us to throw you over the side."

A door slammed; a pin dropped in the latch.

V

THE ANNEX

26

I awoke to the sound of the door opening; somebody unbound my ankles, heaved me from the cabin, and pushed me up the stairs, across the deck, and onto a pier. I felt the warmth of daylight on my skin; we had traveled through the night.

"Let's go," a man growled.

I could see nothing distinct through the bag, just vague shapes. My scrubs, still damp from my plunge into the sea, clung unpleasantly to my skin; my shoes were long gone.

"Where are you taking me? Where's Thea?"

The man responded with a sharp jab to my left kidney that made me buckle at the knees. He wrapped his fist around my collar, yanked me upright, and shoved me forward.

"Walk."

I did as I was told. A door opened and we passed into a cool, damp space that stank of fish. I was by this time thoroughly disoriented. I heard a creaking sound coming from the floor, followed by a bang. Somebody—presumably the same man—cut the bindings on my wrists.

"Get down on your knees and crawl backward," he ordered. "You'll come to a ladder. There are twelve rungs to take you to the bottom."

"The bottom of what?"

The man snorted. "The bottom of the ladder, prossie."

I located the top rung with my feet and groped my way down. The acoustics changed; we had entered some kind of corridor or tunnel. The man spun me around and pushed me forward, another sixteen steps.

"Stop."

I heard a long series of bolts coming undone. A new voice, also a man's, said, "About time. I hope he was worth the trouble."

The voice, though muffled by the bag, sounded familiar.

"Nice work with the drones," the first man said.

"Yeah, funny how they all went down at the same instant. Somebody should look into that."

"Is she here yet?"

The door opened wider. "Take him to the bunkhouse."

I was led deeper into this underground world of hallways and doors. The feeling of space expanded again; we'd entered a room. The man stopped me by the elbow and ripped the bag from my head.

I blinked into the light. The room was a small, windowless chamber with two stacks of bunk beds, a sink and mirror, and a toilet shielded by a curtain. A table was positioned in the corner, where a lone figure was sitting.

"Hello, Proctor."

It seemed impossible. No, it *was* impossible. Time had passed, and it had not been kind. But there was no mistaking her.

I was looking at my mother.

"Stefano, will you leave us, please?"

With a grunt, the man left my side and closed the door behind himself.

"It's good to see you, Proctor."

I was frozen in place. My brain felt like it was whirling in my skull.

"I know this comes as a shock."

"What the *fuck*."

"I'm sure this is confusing for you."

"You're *dead*. You *died*."

"And I'll explain everything, if you give me the chance." She gestured to the chair across from her. "Please. Sit."

What could I do? One doesn't argue with a ghost, especially the ghost of one's mother. I sat.

"The first thing to tell you is that you're in no danger. You're among friends here."

"What friends? Where am I? What is all this?"

"You're in the Annex. This complex is one of several spread throughout the island. We're a clandestine organization connected to the movement you know as Arrivalism."

Her words were like gibberish to me; I could do nothing with them.

"I know this is a lot to take in."

"This is insane. You were my mother, goddamnit."

She nodded. "Yes, I was. I still am, Proctor. But you need to know that I'm not Prosperan. I never was. I was born and raised here, in the Annex."

I could say nothing to this.

"My parents were leaders in the Arrivalist movement. I was somebody who could look the part, so when I was eighteen, I was placed in the city as a university student, when the transition is easiest to cover. I was given a new name, a full personal dossier, a fake monitor, and a history that was impossible, or at least very difficult, to trace."

"Now you're telling me you're some kind of spy."

"I enrolled as a student of structures and societies with the mission of getting as close to the Board of Overseers as I could. As it happened, that was the Office of the Chief Legal Counsel."

The truth was sinking in, and it wasn't nice. "My father," I said.

She nodded. "Yes, Proctor. Your father."

I could sit no longer. I rose and moved about the room. I had no intention; I simply needed to use my body. It was like looking through an inverted telescope down the hallway of my life. Everything, a lie!

"Proctor—"

Facing away, I held up a hand. "Just wait a minute, will you?"

"I know this is difficult to hear."

I turned around and, for the first time, took full measure of her. Deep creases fanned from the corners of her eyes and mouth; her hair, for which she had once been known and admired, was mostly gray. Yet her eyes, as they met my own, were unmistakably the same: the same piercing green, with irises flecked by bits of a golden color, giving her a look of keen intelligence, as if she were party to all the mysteries of life. Part of me wanted to throw my arms around her; another part wanted to march out the door and pretend I'd never seen her.

"Just how is it you're not dead?"

"My suicide was staged. I'd been pretending to be a Prosperan as long as I could, but I was aging too quickly, and people were starting to notice. The anchor line was tied with a simple slipknot, and there was a length of hose stored under the boat. I used it to breathe until the drone left. A boat picked me up and brought me back here."

"So why cut out your monitor?"

"I needed them to think I was crazy, Proctor. I knew the drones would be watching."

"You certainly succeeded."

She regarded me a moment. "I know I hurt you."

"Do you realize what it did to me? What it did to *him*?"

"I understand you're angry, and you have every right. But with your father, the situation wasn't quite what you think. He knew who I was, Proctor. Knew *what* I was."

I was dumbstruck.

"Not at the start. I admit I deceived him. He was a good man and he didn't deserve that. But eventually I got tired of the lying, and one day I just told him." She paused. "You were part of it, actually. It was the day you won your first big race. Do you remember?"

I was unprepared for this sudden swerve into the past. "What does that have to do with anything?"

"You weren't supposed to know I was there, but I was. I was just so . . . happy for you. But a little sad, too. I knew my job being your mother was over. It's how things are supposed to work, but it still hurt. That may sound strange, given what you now know about me, but it's true. It surprised me how much." She paused with a wistful look, then said, "That was the night I told your father the truth. I was completely prepared for him to call State Security. Want to know what he said?"

"Could I even stop you?"

"He told me he already knew. He'd known all along. Before we signed our contract, he'd run a full background check on me. We're pretty thorough, but your father was a hard man to outsmart. He checked my recorded adoption date against the ferry manifest. Sixteen adoptees got on, but according to the record, seventeen got off. After that, it wasn't hard for him to figure out that my whole dossier was a fake."

"Then why in hell would he marry you?"

"Why does anybody marry anybody? He was lonely, he'd been on his own a while."

"Meaning he never stood a chance."

"That's one way to look at it. It's not the only way." She leveled her gaze at me. "Our relationship was . . . complex. At the start he was a job—I won't say otherwise. But we were together twenty years, and a lot can happen in that time. And once I told him who I was, he agreed to help us."

My mind rejected the notion outright. "That's impossible. Not him."

"You didn't know your father like I did. He'd been quietly

working to change things for years. Did you know he's been trying to get the board to shut down the S3? The man was a thorn in everyone's side, but especially them. He loathed those people, really *loathed* them. Coming over to our side was just one more step on a long road. Which is maybe why I liked him as much as I did, even from the start. I didn't ask him to join us—he offered."

What were my father's exact words? *This is all my fault. There were things about her, things you didn't know.*

"What about me?" I asked. "Was I just a job, too?"

"You were my son."

"Don't patronize me. You let me think you'd killed yourself. All these years, did you for one second think how that felt?"

"Of course I did. But there was no other way to keep you safe. Your father and I were in agreement. The S3 was bound to come snooping, and what would you have said? You were still a young man—you had your whole life ahead of you."

"A life based on a lie."

She considered this. "Was it? I wasn't who you thought I was, but what parents are? I'll tell you something else," my mother continued, "and you can take it how you like. You were the most important thing in that man's life. The Malcolm Bennett I met was all rules and regulations and protocols. 'Stiff' would be the word. But the day you stepped off the ferry, something changed. I know he wasn't always good at showing how he felt, but it's true. He would have done anything to protect you."

I realized something then. The distance my father had forged between us after her death: he'd done it for me.

I asked, "Did you ever contact him?"

She shook her head. "Once I left, I left. That was our deal, for all our sakes."

"So, is Cynthia even your real name?"

"That part's true. Around here, though, I'm known as 'Mother.'"

"You're kidding."

"It's more like a job title than a name. Each resistance cell has a mother. This one is mine."

The irony was simply too rich. "He named a boat after you, you know."

She nodded. "I'm aware."

"When I finally got him on the ferry, you know what his last words to me were?"

She eyed me stoically. "No, Proctor, I don't."

"He said, 'I didn't want to forget her.' Now I'm thinking maybe it was best he did."

It wasn't a nice thing to say; I wanted to hurt her. But when I searched her face for a reaction, I saw none.

"You can be as angry with me as you like, Proctor. As I've said, it's nothing I don't deserve. But I wasn't going to let the S3 have you."

"And Thea? Is she part of this little charade, too?"

"It was for your own protection, Proctor. We needed someone close to you."

"*'Close'?*" I barked a nasty laugh. "Well, the woman certainly did her job. You should give her a raise. Is she support staff, too? Just trying to get a fix on exactly how stupid I am."

My mother shook her head. "No. Thea came to us, years ago."

"Whew, what a relief. You know, for a second there, I thought I was sleeping with the help."

My mother gave me a sour look. "You're better than that, Proctor."

"Not right now, I'm not."

The door opened, revealing a lanky man with a beard.

"It's you," I said, amazed.

He grinned. "How you feeling, friend?"

"Like I'm not your fucking friend."

He lifted his chin toward my mother. "I just wanted to make sure everything was okay."

"Everything's fine. Thank you, Quinn. We'll be along."

He exited the room, closing the door behind himself. I turned to my mother. "Him, too?"

"We're very thorough, Proctor."

"Anybody else I should know about? Might as well have the full list."

"I'm guessing you know about your housekeeper. Also, your assistant, Oona."

The woman might have reached out and slapped me, such was my amazement. "Oona? *My* Oona?"

"She's been one of our most productive operatives. That's where the map came from." My mother looked at me pointedly. "There are a lot of us, Proctor. That's what I'm telling you. Mostly support staff, but a few Prosperans, too. People, like your father, who are fed up, who see the truth and are working for change. That man, Quinn? He used to be a data analyst for State Security. He was the one who reviewed the drone footage of my suicide, and it turns out I wasn't as clever as I thought. He tracked me back to the Annex and came knocking at the door. In his line of work, he'd seen a lot of things he didn't like, and he offered to help us. He's been with us ever since."

It was all too much to process. I felt like a chess piece being moved around the board, or the butt of some great cosmic joke that everybody was in on but me.

I asked her, "So, how did you know I wasn't really dying?"

"I didn't. Not for sure. But that shot Singh gave you—that's one of the things they do."

"'They' meaning the S3."

My mother nodded. "I know this is a lot to take in. You'll need some time with this. But time, I'm afraid, is a luxury we don't have. The situation in the Annex is deteriorating. Five nights ago, an agent of the S3 was beaten to death in an alley."

"Huh. Sounds like that'd be kind of your thing."

"I'm not going to shed any tears over the man, but it wasn't one of us, as far as we know. That's not what we do. It was also a senseless provocation in an already tense situation. The board responded with a lockdown, and a riot broke out at the causeway. Fifteen people were killed, and more are missing, including two of ours. We hope they've gone into hiding, but they could be in custody. If that's the case, it's only a matter of time before the S3 comes calling."

"And this concerns me how, exactly?"

"Because, like it or not, you're one of us now."

"Ha!"

"I wouldn't take it so lightly. By now they've realized who got you out of the Nursery, and they'll be looking for you."

I had to admit it: the woman had a point. Not that I was ready to hear it.

"So, tell me," I said, "as long as you're enlisting me to your cause, just what *is* it you're fighting for?"

"That's easy. Change. Justice."

"I think the word you're looking for is 'war.'"

"Not if it can be helped. Real change has to come from the inside, from men like your father. But I won't lie, Proctor. There are plenty of people who are willing to fight."

I'd heard enough. "Well, best of luck," I said. "I wish you great success. All right if I go now?"

"I wouldn't recommend it."

"That's my affair. Also, you've pretty much forfeited your right to give me advice on my life choices, wouldn't you say?"

"Think about it, Proctor. Where would you go?"

"I've got a score to settle with an old friend, just for starters."

"We need you, Proctor."

"Ah, here we go. Why *did* you rescue me, anyway?"

"I rescued you, Proctor, because I care about you."

"This would be the part of the conversation when you tell me what you want."

She settled back in her chair. "Well, you're right. I do want something. The answer is: information."

"I've already told Thea everything I know. Why don't you take it up with her?"

"Not everything. You've been to the Nursery. You've seen what happens there."

"Aren't you the people with the map? Shouldn't you be the experts?"

"Yes, but unfortunately, that's *all* we have. We've tried to get people inside. Nobody's ever come back."

I shrugged. "Okay, fine. Where should I start? The staff's very accommodating. The food's a little on the rich side, though. I'd give it three stars."

"Proctor, I'm not joking."

"Neither am I." I gave her a hard look: *That's all you're getting, don't ask again.* "So, are we done?"

My mother considered this, then nodded. "As you like. You're free to go, of course."

"I hear a 'but' in there."

"But," she said, "I'd like to offer you a trade."

"Not interested, thanks."

"I think you will be, when you hear what it is." She paused. "Do you remember when I took you to the doctor about your dreaming? It was long ago—maybe you don't."

"Of course I remember. What does that have to do with anything?"

"The doctor, what was her name? Dr. Patty, I think it was. You should know that I didn't tell her the whole story. Your sleepwalking wasn't just some occasional thing. It happened literally every night. I even started bedding down in the living room to keep watch over you. And it wasn't just the silly stuff I told the doctor about, the sandwich and the broken lamp and all the rest. Mostly it was the same thing, over and over."

This was news to me. "What exactly did I do?"

"You'd just go outside and stand there, looking at the sky. Always the same spot on the lawn, facing the water. I didn't want to wake you up, I thought it might upset you, so I'd wait there with you. It could be two minutes, or ten, or even much longer. One time you were out there nearly an hour. You'd watch the stars, and then you'd turn to me, like you'd known I was there all that time. Sometimes you'd shake your head, just a little, like the sky had disappointed you somehow. Then you'd march straight past me, into the house, up the stairs, and get back into bed."

"Did I ever say anything?"

"Not a word, though I always felt like you might."

I recalled none of it. And yet, it felt as if I had indeed done these things. "Why are you telling me this now?"

"Because you're different, Proctor. You're not like other people, content to just . . . go along with things. I think I knew it from the moment you stepped off the ferry." She paused. "And because the dreaming never stopped, did it?"

"Did Thea tell you that?"

"Yes, but I wasn't surprised. Something like that doesn't just go away on its own—it's part of who you are. You have questions, Proctor. I don't have all the answers, but I know more than you do."

"Such as?"

"That's the trade. The Nursery, for what I have to show you. After that, you can decide for yourself whose side you're on."

I had to admit it; the woman knew how to make a sale. On the other hand, how could she possibly let me go? She was making the offer to spare us both the problem of my walking out the door, straight into the hands of the S3.

I said, "Before I agree, one question."

She nodded. "Fair's fair."

"That day at the doctor's office, you told me you dreamed, too. Was it true?"

She shook her head. "No. I wish it were, but no."

"Then why did you tell me you did?"

"Honestly, it was so long ago, I don't remember. I imagine I just didn't want you to feel so alone with it." She paused, then said, "Thea told me about your monitor."

I held out my arm, with its flesh-colored patch. "Oh, this? I guess you could say carving yourself up with a kitchen knife runs in the family."

"It's not a small thing, Proctor, doing that. I ought to know—it takes a lot of courage. How did it make you feel?"

"Like I wished I'd drunk more vodka."

"I mean after. Knowing it was gone."

"How does a dog feel when you take off its leash?"

For the first time, she smiled. How strange, to see her smile. "A first step, then. So, do we have a deal?"

I was made to wait. Several hours passed; I couldn't be sure how many, as there was no way to know the time. The door wasn't locked, but my mother had asked me to stay where I was, and after my encounter with the man who'd taken me off the boat, I was in no hurry to meet more of her associates. As for escaping—all I knew was that I was underground, with a great many doors between me and the outside world. I doubted I'd get very far, and in any event, my mother was right: Where would I go?

I was dozing on a lower bunk when the door opened. Thea.

She stepped cautiously into the room. She was carrying a pile of fresh clothing for me, which she placed on the table.

"I brought you something to wear," she said.

"Ah."

"Would it help to say I'm sorry?"

I wanted to laugh. "Help who? You or me?"

"Both?"

"Save yourself the trouble. I'm still just trying to get used to the fact that my entire life turns out to be bullshit."

"I know you're angry, Proctor. You have every right."

"Yeah, that's what people keep telling me."

She gestured to my bunk. "Mind if I sit?"

I scooted up, back against the wall, as she took a place on the edge of the mattress. Gone were the stylish clothes, the understated makeup, the costumery of her class. Her clothing was practically shapeless: loose-fitting trousers and a plain dark shirt.

I said, "Just tell me one thing, and please don't lie."

"All right."

"This whole thing, you and me. It was all an act, wasn't it? I know the answer, I just need to hear you say it."

She took a long breath. "Well, you're right, it started that way. But I also meant what I told you the other day in the car. You *are* a lovely man. I don't think I've ever met anyone like you. Could we maybe leave it there?"

"You kind of broke my heart a little."

"And for that I couldn't be sorrier. Feel free to hate me forever if it helps."

"I won't, but thanks."

A silence passed.

"So, what about the rest of it?" I asked.

"You mean, how am I here? There's no simple answer. But what I told you at the restaurant was true—my parents, the opera, all of it. I just didn't feel the way about things that other people did. Everything seemed so . . . dull. Lifeless, really, like that woman's awful playing. All surface with nothing beneath it. I did my best to be happy, to get along, but I just couldn't manage it. That was when I started going to the pier on the days the ferry left. Here I was, barely off the ferry myself, thinking maybe if I got back on and started over, I could be different, normal. I can't tell you how many times I wanted to."

"But you never did it."

"No. It seemed weak somehow. Or maybe I just didn't have the courage. But everything changed when I met Pappi."

"Your blind painter."

"Yes, but he was just the first. These people, they're not like us,

Proctor. It's not just how they live. It's how they *are.* It's not all sweetness and light. I've seen a thing or two. But it's life, *real* life, and it's what kept me off the ferry."

"So, you're a believer. An Arrivalist."

She shrugged. "I'm not sure what I am. Maybe there's a promised land and maybe there isn't. But for now, what these people give me is enough—the rest can come out in the wash." She looked at me a moment, then said, "Your mother really cares about you, you know."

"Ah."

"'Ah' nothing, Proctor. It's perfectly obvious."

"Where is she?"

"Gone. The woman's pretty mysterious. You kind of never know when she'll pop up. She'll be back."

"I'll point out that her track record in that department isn't great."

"Now you're just being peevish. You think it was simple, getting you out? That she'd do it for anybody else? That woman had to call in a lot of markers."

"So, not everyone on the team was in favor? I ask because that first guy seemed like he wanted to kill me."

"Oh, Stefano? Don't take it personally—he wants to kill everybody."

"Imagine my relief."

An uncertain moment passed; she got to her feet.

"Anyway, it's time you met some people. Feel up to a walk?"

"I can just do that?"

"I don't see why not. As long as you promise to mind your manners and don't do something stupid, like take off."

I said, "Before we do this, there's something I should mention."

"Oh?"

"You were right about Caeli. She was just something my brain cooked up, some kind of echo. I imagined the whole thing."

Thea looked at me strangely. "You weren't *imagining* anything, Proctor."

"That's nice of you to say, but I'm well past that now. It's time I faced the truth."

"I *am* telling you the truth."

What could she mean? "I'm sorry, I'm not following."

"You actually don't know, do you?" Her eyes searched my face. "Caeli's here, Proctor. They pulled her out of the water, same as you."

27

The call comes at two P.M.; by two-thirty, Otto Winspear is in the basement of Well-Being, being greeted by the ministry's lead pathologist, a rather arid older man with small, wire-framed glasses. He offers a mask, but Winspear waves it away.

"Just show me," he says.

They pass through the doors into a tiled room with drains in the floor. There are fifteen steel tables, each bearing a body covered by a sheet. The air smells of urine, feces, and unwashed skin, and Winspear knows that the stink will cling to him for hours. He'll need a clean suit brought to his office.

"This way, Minister."

The pathologist leads him to a table in the middle of the room and pulls back the sheet. The corpse is a woman. She's naked, with skin mottled by settled blood, and flattened, saucer-like breasts.

"The cause of death was cranial trauma." The pathologist slides his gloved hands beneath the woman's head and gently lifts it from the table. "If you'll allow me—"

"How she died is of no interest to me."

The pathologist gives Winspear an empty look; he is a creature of protocol, used to doing things in a certain way.

"Her foot, Doctor?"

The pathologist nods and moves to the other end of the table and draws the sheet aside. "It seemed like the kind of injury you were looking for," he says.

One foot, the left, is swaddled in a thick, homemade-looking bandage. The surface is rusty with dried blood.

"Remove it," Winspear commands.

The pathologist unwinds the fabric, takes a probe from his pocket, and crouches slightly to examine the bottom of the woman's foot. "A small puncture wound, quite deep. See this here?" He presses the edges with the probe. "Necrotic tissue. The woman was well on her way to losing the foot, I'd say."

"How old is the wound?"

The pathologist purses his lips. "From the infection, I'd say five, maybe six days."

"Could a nail have done it?"

"I'd say so."

Winspear looks down at the woman's gray, lifeless face, mentally superimposing the image in the drone feed over what he sees now. It's her. He's certain of it.

"Thank you, Doctor."

Campbell is waiting for him outside. Winspear asks him, "What do we know about her?"

The man withdraws a small pad from his jacket pocket and flips back the first few pages. "Jessica Ordway, thirty-four. Her work permit says she works as a driver for a private company. But she hasn't shown up since Friday."

"Address?"

"We looked. Vacant building."

"Do we have any surveillance footage of her?"

"Data Analysis is going through the files now."

Winspear takes the car back to the office. The streets are quiet, with an anxious feel: *First the storm, now this.* The official word is that the Annex has been quarantined because of an outbreak of a waterborne disease—easy enough to believe—but it won't take long for people to suspect there's more to the story. From the steps of the ministry, Winspear counts sixteen watchmen patrolling the streets around the plaza; security faxes in groups of three are parked outside the ministry buildings; drones are flicking through the sky. He rides the elevator to the top floor, where he finds Callista sitting on the sofa in his office.

"Well?" the woman asks. "Was it her?"

Winspear takes a seat behind his desk. "I believe so."

"You don't seem happy about it."

"Why would I be?"

"Justice has been served, hasn't it?"

Winspear makes a dismissive gesture. "There's justice and there's justice. The woman may have acted alone, but there are plenty of others like her."

"We need to tone this down, Otto. It's getting out of hand."

"What happened at the causeway was unfortunate. But what Bennett saw or thought he saw adds a whole new wrinkle. We're up against people with more resources than I thought."

"And you're certain they have him."

Winspear shrugs: *Who else?*

"We have to keep him away from Elise."

"Our friend has seen to that. Proctor couldn't get within a country mile of her."

Callista rises. "Turn the place upside down if you have to. We need to get things back to normal."

Winspear gives her a thin smile. "I like my life, too, Madam Chair."

She strides toward the door, where she pivots sharply toward him, wrinkling her nose. "And for godsakes, Otto, it stinks in here. Open a window or something."

She closes the door, a little too hard. Day by day, his doubts about her magnify. The woman is simply too close to things; she's not seeing the bigger picture. The promised suit arrives; Otto changes and takes the elevator down to the basement, where Data Analysis is housed. In a dark room with a wall of screens, each showing a drone feed, he's greeted by the S3's chief data analyst, Hugo Abshire. He's a young man—surprisingly young, given his rank—with an animated face and rigidly parted blond hair.

"Do you have any matches on Ordway?" Winspear asks.

"Not so far, I'm afraid."

"What about the woman on the boat?"

Abshire smiles. "Better news there."

He sits at his workstation and calls up an image on the first monitor: Proctor and the woman, sitting in the cockpit of the *Cynthia,* their faces upturned to the drone camera. It's the first time Otto has seen it.

"Her name is Thea Dimopolous, an art dealer. Nothing of note in her personnel file, though we're still digging."

Otto knows just who she is. "Are there any other recent facial matches for her in the database?"

"Actually, yeah. We came up with two just within the past few days."

A new image appears: a pair of faces seen through the windshield of a car. Abshire freezes it. "This was captured the night of the storm, when Bennett went to his father's house. And look here." He zooms in on the second party. "His name is Quinn Dawes. And here's the kicker: he used to work here."

Otto needs a moment to collect himself. Then: "What do you mean 'here'?"

"I mean the guy was S3. Not a field agent, mostly data analysis and surveillance, but apparently he was really gifted."

First Jason Kim, then Thea, now this. Quinn Dawes, right under his nose! How had he missed it?

"What happened to him?" Otto asks.

"Up and left twelve years ago. Too bad, actually. You should see his evaluations."

"Do we know where he is now?"

Abshire swivels to a second screen and begins to scroll. "This is Dawes's personnel file. Since he left the department, the guy's been moving around a *lot.* Different jobs, different addresses, all of it changing every couple of months."

Winspear frowns. "Meaning what?"

"Meaning either the guy has ants in his pants or the file's been fucked with. I'd say the latter. Give this guy a CIS terminal, and he could do pretty much anything he wanted."

Of course he could. "You said you had a second match for the woman."

Abshire returns to the first terminal, strikes a few keys, and up pops a fresh feed: the shuttle stop at the base of the causeway, time-stamped a week ago.

"Last Wednesday afternoon, right after Bennett had his meltdown, Thea Dimopolous's badge was scanned on her way to the Annex. You can see her there, getting off the shuttle. She appears to be alone, right? Just watch."

The woman moves away from the unloading area and heads up the street. Behind her, a second person appears: a man, wearing a blue windbreaker and oversized dark glasses. It's Hanson. With feigned nonchalance—the man couldn't be more obvious—he begins to follow her.

When the woman is halfway up the block, a boy with shaggy hair bounds straight into her path, skipping backward to match her stride. Some street kid, Winspear supposes, hoping for a handout. And, in fact, that's precisely how things unfold. A brief exchange and the woman produces a bill. The boy snatches it from her hand—the kid's like lightning—and the next thing Winspear sees, at least a dozen more kids materialize from the nooks and crannies of the street to descend on Hanson like a cloud of flies. By the time he shoos them away, the woman's gone.

"The boy was definitely working with her," Abshire says.

"Who is he?"

"No matches yet, but with these kids, it's hard to keep track. A lot of the births aren't even properly registered."

The boy, Winspear thinks; the boy is the key. Find him and you find the rest. "Can you get a clear picture of his face?"

"I should be able to do something."

Winspear nods. "Clean it up as best you can and send it through the system. The kid's out there somewhere. Somebody knows who he is."

Winspear calls for a car, which is waiting for him when he emerges from the building. The ride home takes forty minutes, half of it on a winding switchback that ascends the ridge that backs the city to the west. With each turn, the view expands. The shadows of evening lay long and low across the land. The lights of the city are coming on as Winspear's car pulls into the drive, where a black sedan is parked. The agent in the driver's seat, who is reading a newspaper, acknowledges Winspear with a quick lift of his head as Winspear disembarks, then goes back to his reading.

Ramona, his young bride, is nowhere to be found. Perhaps she's shopping or has chosen to linger in town with friends. Winspear is undisturbed by her absence. Theirs is a loose arrangement, and the contract is brief, just five years. His attention span in these matters is short; his eye wanders; he has no illusions about this aspect of himself, and neither does she.

He fixes a drink in the kitchen and repairs to the den. It's a little after eight when the phone rings.

"It's Campbell, sir." His voice is excited. "This is going to be easier than we thought."

28

"Hey."

Saying nothing, Caeli glanced up from the kitchen table, where she was snapping beans into a bowl. Her eyes met mine quickly and fell again.

"Proctor," Thea said, "this is Claire."

We exchanged hellos. A woman somewhere north of fifty, thick about the waist, with graying hair tied back. The skin of her face was shining from the heat of the stove. She greeted me even as she remained in constant motion, moving about the kitchen.

"Thea says you'll be staying for dinner."

"Yes, thank you. If it's no trouble."

"Then here—" She passed me a bowl of potatoes on a cutting board. "Make yourself useful. The cousins will be here any minute."

I sat at the table with Caeli and got to work, peeling the potatoes and dicing them into cubes. She had yet to look my way for more than an instant.

"How are you feeling?" I asked, hoping to draw her out.

"Okay."

"I was really worried about you," I said. "I'm glad you're safe."

Thea came up behind us. "Proctor, I have to leave for a few minutes. Will you two be all right here?"

"Is that okay with you, Caeli?"

She answered with a shrug. I exchanged a look with Thea. *Who knows what it's all about?*

"We'll be here," I told her.

We resumed our quiet work. Behind us, Claire was stirring, tasting, pulling a roast from the oven to check it and sliding it back in again.

"Are you angry with me about something?" I asked Caeli.

Snap, snap, went the beans. "Why would I be angry?"

"I don't know, you just seem like it."

"I'm not angry."

"You've been through a lot. Anyone would be upset. Can we talk about what happened at the Nursery?"

She shrugged again.

"Let's start at the beginning. Do you remember how you got there?"

"No?"

"You're certain? You don't remember anything at all?"

Caeli didn't answer. She was staring at the table.

"How about the pool? What do you remember about that?"

"There was a pool?"

"Yes, there was a pool. You almost drowned."

"Whoops. Sorry. Fucked up there."

"Caeli, I really need you to try."

"Who said I'm not trying? Maybe I just don't remember the things you're asking me about. Who was that guy? The big guy."

"You mean Bernardo?"

"There sure were a lot of him. He really needs to get over himself."

"So, him you remember."

"Is Thea your girlfriend?"

I drew back, startled. "What? No."

"Because it kind of seems like it."

"Thea's a friend. She's helping us. Is that what this is about?"

She returned to her beans.

"Caeli, please. Look at me."

A moment's hesitation, and at last she raised her face. Not anger—something else. The girl was on the verge of tears.

"What is it? What's wrong?"

Her jaw tightened. "Nothing's wrong, okay? I'm fine."

"You don't look fine to me." A terrible thought occurred. "Caeli," I said, lowering my voice, "did somebody hurt you?"

"No, nobody hurt me, Mr. Ferryman. Why would someone hurt me?"

"Then why are you crying?"

She looked away.

"Talk to me, honey. Please."

"I just need to know one thing," she said, turning back to me. "Are you going to be the one to look after me now? Because if you're not, okay, but I really need to know if you are."

My heart cracked. Of course that's what she'd want to know. Who will look after me, now that I have no one?

"Is that what you want?"

She nodded through her tears. "I mean, if that's okay."

"Of course it's okay. It's better than okay. You don't have to worry about that, not for a second."

"Do you promise? Because I kind of need you to promise."

I drew an X over my heart. "I'm not going anywhere, I promise."

We worked together in silence after that. As dinner approached, Claire shooed us to the dining room to set the table. There were sixteen place settings; who else was coming? The table, like Claire herself, had the feeling of a hub: long but narrow to facilitate conversation, with a surface of pitted wood, worn smooth. There was a long bench on one side, chairs on the other, with two at either end. Caeli and I were putting out the plates when people began to file in. Not people: kids. They ranged in age from eight or nine to older teenagers. I was expecting their parents to follow them, but none did. Were they literal cousins, as Claire had said, or something else? Their surprise at seeing us seemed mild—they were accustomed to new people in their midst—while also containing an element of wariness. *What are the prossies doing here?*

Claire entered the room and clapped her hands. "Everyone, we have guests," she said, and gestured toward us. "This is Mr. Bennett and his daughter, Caeli. I expect you to be polite." She quickly scanned the room. "And will someone *please* get Pappi? The food's going to get cold."

His daughter, Caeli. Claire had obviously not been fully briefed; she had simply assumed this. But it was not the time to correct the error, and hadn't I just told Caeli I'd take care of her? While everyone took a seat, three of the kids followed Claire into the kitchen and returned bearing platters and bowls of food, which they arranged in a line down the center of the table. People were talking animatedly among themselves; I was unsure how to act, even where to point my eyes. Thea entered the room and took the empty seat next to me. She gave me a wary look.

"Everything okay with you two?"

But before I could answer, a new figure entered, being led at the elbow by one of the teenagers. He had the look of a street derelict, or some wise man from a children's story. He moved rigidly, his head swiveling from side to side. His eyes were dead and gray as stones. Nearing the table, he halted abruptly. He lifted his chin and aimed his face straight at me.

"Proctor." A smile spread across his unshaven cheeks. "There you are. Good."

All conversation around the table had ceased.

"I'm Pappi, the resident madman. Or so they tell me." He gestured toward the head of the table. "Come sit by me, won't you?"

All eyes now lay upon me, the interloper. I rose and changed places with a boy at the end of the bench, on Pappi's right side.

"And your young friend," Pappi commanded. "Her, too."

More shuffling of the players, as Caeli moved to sit beside me.

"Welcome," Pappi said.

Caeli looked confused. "Hi, I . . . guess?"

The man directed his attention to the assembly. "Everyone, if you please."

It took me a second to understand that we were all expected to join hands. I had never done such a thing before a meal, or ever. Yet, in the automatic way that everyone around the table formed this human chain, I felt the power of the ritual. I held up an open palm to Caeli, who gave me a "This is weird" look but took it nonetheless, and then accepted Pappi's, which was rough and thick and stained with paint.

Pappi cleared his throat and spoke: "Great Soul of all creation, you who fashioned the world we see and the world that we cannot, thank you for your many blessings and the chance to be together today. And thank you as well for the presence of our guests, Proctor and . . . ?" He aimed his face at the girl.

Her eyes darted side to side. "Um, Caeli?"

"Caeli," Pappi continued, "whom we welcome to our table and our company. Keep us safe in your hands that we may know the fullness of your Grand Design until the day of arrival, as promised in your holy writing. Till arrival come."

The table, in unison: "Till arrival come."

With the chain of hands broken, a burst of voices took the floor, as the serving bowls and platters proceeded around the table. I was a little stunned by it all: the warmth, the depth of feeling. Actual cousins or not, this oddball gathering was a family, and I had been invited to join them—I, a stranger, and technically their enemy.

I turned to Pappi. "That was nice, what you said."

He shrugged. "A little corny, but people like it."

"You spoke of a 'grand design.' I was wondering what that might be."

"Ah," he proclaimed, and rubbed his hands together, "here we are."

My question, evidently, would have to wait; the food had arrived. Fried potatoes, roasted vegetables, meat in thick pink slices, charred at the edges and swollen with juice. I filled my plate and, since the conversation at the table seemed to be on hiatus, began to eat, all the while keeping an eye on Pappi. I had never seen a blind person before—any Prosperan so afflicted would run, not walk, to the ferry—and I was struck by the sense that, despite his handicap, he seemed in full command of his surroundings. He ate in the most striking manner, his movements slow and exact as a jeweler's. Having carved an unseen piece of meat or speared an unobserved carrot, he would raise it to his mouth with deep solemnity, whereupon he would work his jaw in a circular motion like a cow at its cud, all the while ejecting tiny nasal coos of pleasure.

"I hope you're enjoying your meal," he said to me.

"Yes, thank you." This was true; the food was delicious.

"Caeli? How about you?"

Her plate had gone mostly untouched. "It's good, I guess," she stated.

"Do you want to know something?" Pappi asked her.

Her eyes darted around nervously. "O . . . kay?"

"It seems we've met before. What do you think of that?"

Caeli startled faintly, as did I.

"Oh, not the way you're thinking of. Not *in person.*" Pappi raised a finger and tapped his temple. "In here."

Caeli said, "I don't get it."

"That makes two of us. Nevertheless, Thea tells me that I painted your picture."

"How could you paint my picture if you don't know me?"

"*That* is a most excellent question." He wagged a finger at Caeli's plate. "You should eat something. You don't want to hurt Claire's feelings. The woman takes feeding people *very* seriously."

We ate in silence the rest of the meal, even Caeli, who, in the end, finished most of what was on her plate. As people were carrying their empty dishes to the kitchen, Pappi put his hand on my arm.

"Come with me."

I left Caeli with Thea and took Pappi's elbow as he led me deeper into the building, which seemed to serve as a kind of clubhouse or shelter—sleeping mats on the floor, belongings strewn or in piles, mismatched couches on which people had obviously been sleeping.

"I apologize for the mess," Pappi said, "though I can't say it bothers me much. One of the benefits of being blind—you don't give a rat's ass about the niceties."

It had begun to dawn on me that Pappi and Claire ran what amounted to an impromptu orphanage. "Just how many people live here?"

"How would I know? You'd have to ask Claire. The woman's a total pushover."

There was, suddenly, a strong odor of mineral spirits. We emerged into a large, high-ceilinged space that might have once served some commercial or industrial purpose. I released Pappi and stepped deeper into the room, coming to a stop at the center. So bright and expressive were the squares of canvas upon the walls that I had the feeling of being inside a kaleidoscope. They were like captured bursts of pure sensation, pure experience, so vivid they seemed to pulse. I was reminded of what Thea had told me about Picasso—how, looking at his paintings, one was actually seeing from several angles simultaneously. Within the paintings' cantilevered shapes and swirls of bold color, I detected the presence of familiar objects and scenes, but they were like shadows, ghostly reflections of some deeper, supernal realm, beyond the dull reality of the physical world.

My thoughts were broken by a sudden wash of sound; my mother stepped through a second entrance I'd failed to notice. She strode toward a table at the far end of the room, removed a small bundle from inside her jacket, and placed it on the table. A bag of soft cloth, tied with twine.

"What's this?"

"My end of the deal." My mother gestured to the satchel. "Go ahead, open it."

I unknotted the twine, unfolded the lip of the bag, and slid the contents free. It appeared to be a single sheet of paper, yellow with age.

GUIDELINES FOR ARRIVAL

This document has been introduced into your environment to assist you in the days ahead. Soon you may begin to notice changes in yourself and in the world around you. These may include:

- Meteorological disturbances, such as sudden storms
- Feelings of disorientation or panic
- Disruption to sleep patterns
- Memories that do not seem real
- Feelings of déjà vu
- Coincidences
- Hallucinations
- A sensation of intense cold that passes quickly
- Changes in the night sky, such as the appearance of unfamiliar celestial bodies

DO NOT BE ALARMED.
DO NOT SEEK MEDICAL INTERVENTION.
FURTHER GUIDELINES WILL BE ISSUED AT A LATER DATE.

"We call it the Artifact," my mother explained. "It's said that there used to be hundreds of them, thousands even. This is the only one left. We move it from house to house to keep the S3 from finding it."

"Where did it come from?" I asked.

"Nobody knows. All we know is, it's old."

So this was the sacred document, the so-called holy writing that Pappi had invoked at dinner. It didn't look holy at all; it looked like a public service announcement.

"And you really based a whole religion on this."

"People need hope, Proctor. They need something to believe."

"Meaning you don't." I looked at her. "That's completely cynical."

"Proctor, if I may," Pappi interjected. "I admit your mother and I have had our differences on the matter. But whatever else is true, Oranios is real. Arrival is real. The Artifact proves that."

"I don't think it proves a thing. Hell, this could be somebody's idea of a joke."

My mother said, "Tell me about Caeli, Proctor."

"What does she have to do with this?"

"That's what I'm asking *you.* For starters, have you ever noticed that the girl doesn't have a monitor?"

"What are you talking about? Of course she has a monitor."

My mother shook her head. "No, Proctor. She doesn't."

We were interrupted by the sounds of a commotion. Thea appeared in the doorway.

"It's Antone," she said. "He's back."

The boy was seated at the dining table, shoveling leftovers into his mouth. The cousins were crowded around. My mother shooed them aside and sat across from him.

"Where have you been?"

"Told Thea," he said through a mouthful of food. He took a long, throat-pumping drink of water. "Got arrested."

"At the causeway, you mean."

The boy nodded, forking more leftover roast into his mouth.

"Antone, stop eating for a second."

"I'm hungry! The suits barely fed us!"

"There'll be time for that later."

With a vast sigh, the boy put his fork down.

"Start at the beginning," my mother said.

His face was dirty, his hair matted with grease. His clothing hung on his bones like an old dress on a hanger. "It's what I said. The watchmen rounded us up. Put us in the basement."

"How many?"

"Don't know exactly. A lot."

"Did they ask you anything? Interrogate you?"

He nodded. "Some, yeah. Suits would come and take them away. Not me and some others, though."

"And what happened then?"

"Some big suit comes down, says to let us go."

My mother frowned. "Let you go? Just like that?"

"That's what the suit said."

"Did he tell you why?"

The boy looked up suddenly, his eyes scanning the room. "Where's Jess? Is she here?"

"We thought she was with you."

The boy shook his head. "I haven't seen her since the causeway. Lost her in the smoke."

My mother and Quinn exchanged a look, unspoken words passing between them. My mother turned to Antone again.

"The suit, what did he look like?"

"Gray hair. Had a beard, too. Kind of fussy-looking."

"Gray hair? Or was it white? Silver, maybe?"

"Silver, I guess."

"He let you go and then what happened?"

He shrugged again. "The suit told us to go home."

My mother's expression darkened. "You didn't come straight here, did you?"

"What, you think I'm stupid?"

"No, I think you may be the smartest person here, actually. But is there any chance you were followed?"

"I didn't see anybody. No drones, either. I took the long way, too."

She rose. "Thea, Quinn, can I speak to you privately? You, too, Proctor."

We retreated to the kitchen, where Claire and Pappi joined us. "Did that sound like Winspear to you?" my mother asked me.

"It could be."

"Quinn, go check the street."

The man strode from the room.

"What about Jess?" Thea asked.

"She could still be in custody," my mother said. "Maybe they weren't kept together."

Quinn returned. "Nobody out there I can see."

My mother said, "Which doesn't mean they're not there."

Thea said, "If Antone was followed, why aren't the watchmen breaking down the door right now?"

"Maybe they're trying to figure out who's here and who isn't."

Thea said, "Meaning you?"

"No," my mother said, and tipped her head in my direction. "Meaning Proctor."

Everybody looked at me.

I said, "So I'll turn myself in."

"You've been here, Proctor. You've seen us. You know who we are."

"You think I'd tell them anything?"

"That's not how these things work. Also, we don't know for sure that the watchmen are coming. It's possible Antone just slipped through the cracks somehow. It's happened before."

Claire said, "What do you want me to do about the cousins?"

My mother considered the question. "Let's play it safe and put everybody underground for the night. We can see where things stand tomorrow."

Claire left to get the cousins organized; in short order, everybody had gathered at the back door. Quinn went first to scout the situation, then whistled the all-clear. We filed out and headed down the alley at a quickstep, Thea taking Pappi by the elbow to bring up the rear. Once in the warehouse, everyone assembled at the hatch and descended one by one. Stefano was waiting at the bottom. My mother, the last down, drew the bolts.

"Let's get everyone settled for the night."

In the bunkhouse, we laid out extra mats on the floor. Quinn, meanwhile, had retreated to the lair to tap into the drone feeds. By now it was getting on toward midnight. Caeli had already staked out one of the lower bunks. I went and sat on the edge. Her left arm lay atop the blankets, the pale flesh of its underside partially exposed.

"Why are you looking at my arm like that?"

I raised my eyes, embarrassed to be caught. "No reason."

"Yeah, there was."

"It's just that . . . you don't have a monitor, Caeli."

She wrinkled her nose. "Like, in my *arm*? Gross."

Was it possible? Had I simply assumed she'd had one from the start—made her into the person I wanted, or needed, her to be? But I was so certain she'd had one. And without a monitor, what was she doing in the Nursery? It made no sense at all.

"Never mind," I said. "It's not important right now. Just try to get some sleep."

"Why is everybody so afraid?" she asked me.

"Not afraid. Nervous, maybe. We'll be okay."

"Are we staying here long?"

"In the basement, you mean?"

"No," she said. "Here with the cousins."

"Do you want to?"

"Kinda." She added, with a hint of a smile, "Thea can be your girlfriend if you want."

"Oh, so I have your blessing now?"

"In case you were, you know, looking for a second opinion." She studied me for a moment. "Is Mother your *actual* mother?"

"So, you heard about that, huh?"

"Is she?"

"It's a little more complicated than that."

"Doesn't sound like it to me. And if she is, you should, you know, probably be a little nicer to her."

"You're full of relationship advice, aren't you?"

"Just trying to pull my weight around here. Plus, you seem to need help with your personal life."

"Well, you're not wrong about that." I rose from the mattress. "Time for you to get some sleep, kiddo."

"Could I ask you a favor?"

I looked down at her. "Sure, name it."

She hesitated, as if embarrassed, then said, "Could you, maybe, rub my back a little? To help me fall asleep." She winced. "Sorry, that was weird of me, wasn't it?"

"Not at all," I said, and smiled. "Scoot over."

She drew her knees up to her chest and turned her body toward the wall. Sitting on the edge of the mattress, I moved my palm over her back in slow circles. It wasn't something I'd ever done before; it seemed strange, and a little sad, that I had somehow missed this simple task, helping a child to sleep. The room had quieted, all the cousins bedded down. A few minutes went by. When I lifted my hand away, Caeli didn't stir. I rose and crept from the room to find Thea waiting in the hall.

"The two of you are good together," she said. "I can see why you're so fond of her."

I wondered how much she'd heard. "Do you really think we'll be safe here?"

"I'd say we're okay for the night. The tunnel's been here a long time. The watchmen haven't found it so far."

"How long, exactly?"

"Some people say since the beginning. It goes under the bay all the way to the city, where it connects to the sewers. From there you can get just about anywhere. That's how Quinn taps into CIS." She gave a tiny shudder. "Tell you the truth, it's a little unnerving, all that water over your head."

"So, you've been down there."

She nodded. "It's how I got back here after they shut down the causeway." She paused. "I was there, you know, when you boarded the ferry. I don't think you saw me."

"I wish I had."

"Is it wrong to say I was proud of you?"

"What for?"

"Just . . ." She searched for words. "The way you handled yourself. Head high, shoulders back, that sort of thing. I thought you were very dignified."

"I hid it well, then. I was actually scared shitless."

The exchange ended there.

"We've got mats in the kitchen," said Thea. "You should get some rest yourself."

I glanced back into the bunkroom; Caeli was still out like a light. Curled up, she looked like she was about six years old. It wouldn't have surprised me to see her slide a thumb into her mouth.

I said, "I thought I'd go help Quinn keep an eye on things."

"And avoid your mother, maybe?"

"You don't miss much."

She angled her head down the hall. "Go on. It's going to be a long night. Quinn's an acquired taste, but I'm sure he won't mind the company."

The door was open, showing Quinn hunched over his terminal. I rapped on the frame to announce my presence. "Okay to join you?"

He waved at a chair. "Have a seat, friend."

I sat. On his monitor were a dozen gray-and-white squares, each with a different aerial image. The plaza. The guardhouse at the causeway. A section of rocky coastline, glazed by moonlight.

"What are you looking for?" I asked.

"Could be anything. What you don't see can tell you as much as what you do. For instance, right now? I'm not getting anything from the whole north end of the Annex."

"So?"

"So, they either don't know we're here, which is good, or they do and they don't want to tip us off. Which is, let's say, not so good."

"My mother said you used to work for the S3."

Still watching the screen, he grimaced. "Yeah, not my finest hour."

"What changed your mind?"

"That's easy. Working for the S3."

A few silent minutes passed as, together, we watched the images cycling on the screen.

"Mind if I ask you something?"

His mind still caught up in the drone feeds, the man nodded absently. "Mmm-hmm."

"My mother said you were the one who saw her in the boat that night."

"That was me, all right."

"How did you know she was faking?"

"I didn't. Not at first."

"But something must have tipped you off."

He swiveled in his chair so we were facing each other. "You really want to talk about this?"

"If you don't mind."

"What did she tell you?"

"Just that she staged it."

"Staged, yes. Faked, not so much."

I stared at him. "I don't get it."

"I'll put it this way. The woman I saw on my monitor that night was, in every possible way, in the process of killing *someone.* I saw it when she looked up at the drone. The eyes don't lie, and trust me, nobody's that good an actor. Which made me realize something else."

"What's that?"

"She couldn't be Prosperan. The slipknot, the hose—that was the easy part, once I started looking. I took a drone off the system and used it to track the boat that brought her to the Annex."

"So why didn't you report her?"

"Why would I do that?"

"Wasn't that your job?"

"Oh, I was never very much good at playing by the rules. Seeing your mother just sealed the deal. Doing what she did—well, you'd have to have a pretty good reason. I wanted to know what it was."

"And now you do."

He nodded. "That's right. Now I do."

"My mother showed me the Artifact."

"Did she?" he said, grinning. "And what did you make of it?"

"I really don't see how anyone could think it's some holy text."

"And why is that?"

"Have you looked at the damn thing? It's like a business memo."

He rocked back in his chair, placing the tips of his fingers together at his waist. For a silent moment, he regarded me serenely, then said, "You know what your problem is?"

"I'm guessing you're about to tell me."

"It's the same problem most people have, actually. You know a lot of things. You *believe* almost nothing."

"And you do?"

"What I believe, friend, is irrelevant. That's everyone's choice to make. Though, if you ask me, it's pretty obvious life's more than just the grimy details."

"How is it obvious?"

He smiled. "Because it has to be. Otherwise, what would be the point?"

"Your reasoning is a little circular."

"Maybe, but it gets me through the day. Which, believe me, is a pretty tall order when you've worked for the S3."

"So why *did* you work for them?"

"That's easy," he said. "Because I was good at it. At least until I wasn't. Why did you become a ferryman?"

"Something similar."

"And now you're here, the same as me."

"I didn't have anything to do with that."

"I wouldn't be so sure. These things that have been happening to you. Dreams. Visions. Sounds to me like the universe would like to have a word with you, friend."

"Maybe I'm a lunatic, did you ever think of that?"

He waved the thought away. "Oh, you don't seem like a lunatic to me. Just a man who hasn't opened his mind to other possibilities yet. Sooner or later, you'll come around."

"The day we met on the shuttle—"

"Ah."

"You tried to give me a book, *Principles of Arrivalism.*"

"A bit of a misnomer, in my opinion. There's really only one."

"Oh? What's the principle?"

Instead of answering, he spun in his chair, opened a drawer below the console, and produced a copy, which he handed to me. "Why don't you judge for yourself?"

I opened the cover. The first page was blank. I riffled through the whole thing, front to back. All the pages were the same, just white nothingness.

I said, looking up, "Is this a joke?"

"Not in the least. The opposite, actually."

"But it doesn't say anything."

"My point right there. Words just get in the way, like the world gets in the way. You have to see through it to find what's really there, underneath. The Grand Design. That's the principle."

My eye caught something on the screen behind him. "Hang on a second."

He swiveled back to his terminal. "What did you see?"

I pointed. "Top row, second from the left. Can you enlarge it?"

The image expanded. A small house, a cottage really, seen from above. Two figures stood outside, illuminated by the lights coming from the windows. The image was static; the drone was just hovering.

"Been like that a while," Quinn said.

"Where is that?" I asked.

He tapped a few keys. "Pretty much the boondocks."

"No, where *exactly*?"

A box appeared on the right of the screen and, within it, a map with a pulsing red dot. "Up in the mountains near Victoria." Quinn glanced over at me. "What's the big deal? You know them?"

The figures were a man and a woman. They appeared to be engaged in animated, even passionate, conversation. The woman abruptly turned her back to the man; he reached for her shoulder, but as his hand made contact, she shook him off and stepped away, hugging herself protectively. He stood his ground for a few more seconds until, tossing up his hands in frustration, he stomped into the house. All of this was viewed from above, their faces obscured; yet one does not always need to see a face to know a person's identity. The small gestures, the way a person carries themselves, their occupation of space, distinctive as a fingerprint: these are enough.

"Yeah, I know them."

And then the alarm went off.

"Goddamnit!" Quinn yelled, and slammed his fist on the desk. "*How did I miss this!*"

He began typing furiously. A new image ballooned on the screen.

The warehouse. And all around it, moving in lockstep, a line of watchmen in helmets and armor, backed by security faxes, gleaming chrome monstrosities.

My mother appeared in the door, Thea close behind. "What's happening?"

"Company's coming, is what's happening." Quinn was up and out of his chair, moving to one of the panels, throwing switches. "You get the cousins ready, I'll prep the system."

"How long?"

"Two minutes."

"Quinn—"

He turned from the panel with a look of exasperation. "Just *go*."

We went. In the bunkroom, my mother was handing out flashlights.

"It'll be dark, so stay together, no matter what. At the fork, go *left*. Everybody, say it. Go *left*."

"Go *left*."

"Claire and Pappi, you're with them. Stefano? I'm putting you in charge."

A great roar, and the whole building shuddered. Dust floated down from the ceiling as the cousins erupted in screams. Caeli grabbed my arm, shoving herself against me.

"Stay close," I told her.

"You're telling *me*?"

"Time to go, everyone," my mother commanded. "Quickly, but don't run."

She led us deeper into the complex. Where the hallway ended, there was another hatch. She yanked it open and motioned for everyone to descend. Stefano went first, to help get Pappi down, followed by Claire and the cousins. More concussive sounds—the watchmen had reached the inner door.

"Where's Quinn?" Thea said suddenly. The last of the cousins were descending. She called down the hall, "Quinn!"

"I'll go." This was Antone.

"No way, mister," my mother said. "You get down that ladder right now."

"This is my fault! I should be the one!"

"Antone, do as she says," I told the boy. "Thea, take Caeli."

I raced back down the hall. Quinn was wedged beneath one of the panels, poking around with a flashlight.

"Whatever you're doing," I said, "we have to leave *right now.*"

"Yeah? Something important going on?"

Another loud *wang.* Quinn reached a hand toward me, wiggling his fingers. "Do me a favor and pass me that wire cutter."

"What wire cutter? Where?"

"Take a breath, friend. The small one with the blue handles. It should be on the counter right above me."

I located the tool and, crouching, placed it in his hand. "Can you just please hurry it up?"

"See, this is what I've been telling you. Have a little faith, okay?" He was sorting through a bundle of multicolored wires. "Want to hear my philosophy about situations like this?"

"Not especially."

"It's pretty straightforward. Something will happen, then something else will happen. Sounds dumb until you think about it."

A new sound erupted—a high-pitched screaming, like sheets of metal being ripped.

Quinn said, "Those would be the saws."

"Is that the 'something else' you mentioned?"

"Nope." He wriggled free, popped to his feet, and stood before his terminal. A few keystrokes, and on the screen a clock appeared. "This is."

Not a clock: a timer.

Ninety seconds. Eighty-nine. Eighty-eight.

"What the hell did you just do?" I asked him.

"Ever wanted to visit outer space?"

"Not really."

"Then I suggest we run."

At a sprint we hit the hatch, where Thea and Caeli stood waiting.

"She wouldn't leave without you," Thea said.

Caeli descended first, followed by Thea, then me, with Quinn bringing up the rear. Antone was waiting at the bottom with my mother. Another dank hallway, with exposed timbers holding up the ceiling and walls; the air smelled of refuse and rot. I was counting seconds in my head: sixty-three, sixty-two, sixty . . .

"Hurry," my mother said.

We headed down the tunnel at a brisk jog. Brackish water, the source of the smell, sloshed at our shoes. I asked Thea, "What did she mean, 'go left'?"

"Left goes deeper into the Annex. We can get to a safe house from there."

"And right?"

"Prospera, north of the boat basin."

Fifteen. Fourteen. Thirteen.

"Quinn—"

"You think you're the only one counting?"

The fork appeared up ahead.

Four. Three. Two.

One.

Nothing happened.

"Maybe you did something wrong," I said to Quinn.

"Who do you think you're talking to?"

In the next instant, something changed. It was as if all the molecules in the air had begun to vibrate at a higher frequency. I felt a rippling jolt of energy through the soles of my shoes, the floor of the tunnel rolling underfoot like a shaken carpet, and then the shock wave hit, a blast of pure cacophonous power that popped my eardrums and sent me sprawling forward into the fetid water.

Suddenly, everything was dark. I was groping through the water for my flashlight when a beam grazed across my eyes, momentarily blinding me. A backlit figure crouched before me: Thea.

"Are you okay?" she asked.

It took me a second to assemble an answer. "Yeah, I think so."

Quinn was scanning the ceiling with his flashlight. Long, spidering cracks were spreading across it and down the walls. The cracks widened, dust sifting from them like sand through parted fingers.

"That's . . . not great," he said.

"Caeli!" I called. "Where are you!"

The girl was sitting on the floor ten feet away, water lapping over her legs. I crouched and took her by the shoulders to face her squarely. "Look at me, honey. Are you hurt?"

"God," she said with a sudden frown, "this water is *disgusting*."

A series of crashes erupted behind us. I turned my head to look, following the light of Quinn's beam. Struts were folding in and falling like dominoes in a line.

Quinn said, "That's not great at *all*."

Another crash, and a deep rumble—this time coming from the opposite direction. Quinn swung his beam.

The left fork was gone. In its place was a mound of rubble.

And then the ceiling began to come down.

We ran.

Section by section, the tunnel was caving in behind us. We were under the harbor now; frigid seawater sprayed from the cracked walls, fanning our bodies and faces, filling our eyes and mouths with salt. How far did we have to go? A mile? More? How could we outrace an ocean?

The water rose: our ankles, our shins. Quinn was yelling something, but over the roar of the rushing water I couldn't make out the words. Suddenly, he bolted ahead on long, splashing strides, waving us forward, the bright shaft of his beam ricocheting off the ceiling and walls. He was pointing at a shape up ahead.

It was a ladder, set in the tunnel's wall. Quinn ascended, shoved the plate aside, and scrambled free. As Caeli ascended behind him, he lay flat on his stomach and reached down to pull her up. Antone was the next to go, then Thea, leaving me and my mother at the bottom.

"Go," I told her.

She began to ascend. As I positioned myself at the bottom of the ladder, I looked up to see Quinn's bearded face, full of intensity, and past him, the night sky, resplendent, hovering over all.

A titanic force hit me from behind.

The tunnel had failed completely. As my hands bit into the metal, my feet left the ground, my body arrowing away with the current. My head went under. As my grip began to fail, a second force intervened: someone was gripping my wrist. With a yank, my mother pulled me clear of the surface and guided my hand to a higher rung. Now partially free of the current, I was able to reach my second hand up as well, then the first again, until one foot and then the other found the ladder.

I hauled myself onto the pavement. I was coughing and sputtering. We had emerged into an alleyway in an area of darkened buildings and huge storage containers filled with trash.

"Okay?" I asked Caeli.

Her jaw was trembling, her arms wrapped tightly around herself. "C-c-c-cold."

"I know. We'll find you something dry to wear."

Something strange was happening to the light. The sky was glowing with alternating hues of yellow and orange, flashing off the undersides of the clouds. Not clouds: smoke. Across the water, the warehouse had been replaced by a roiling mass of fire. It looked as if a whole city block was being consumed.

"Do you think the others made it out?" Thea asked Quinn.

"They were well ahead of us. They should be all right."

We were all a little stunned—mesmerized by the vision of destruction unfolding across the water.

I looked at Quinn. "What now?"

"What now is, we find a vehicle." He turned suddenly and looked back into the alley. "Wait a second. Where's Mother?"

We moved outward, calling to her. But the woman was nowhere. She was gone.

In our favor: there were no drones.

Not in our favor: everything else.

Before Quinn had set the charges, he'd uploaded a virus to the drone control system. This would, he estimated, buy us a few hours, perhaps the rest of the night. But the street-level cameras would still be operating, and, at this hour, anyone moving through the city was going to draw attention from the watchmen.

Unless they were driving a garbage truck.

In the depot garage, we stripped off our wet clothes and exchanged them for sanitation workers' uniforms we found hanging in the lockers. The cab was built for two; Thea and Caeli sat inside, while Quinn, Antone, and I took up positions on the rear platform, holding on to the handrails.

We rumbled out of the depot and headed inland, tracing the edge of the city to the north. Our destination was the safe house where Thea and Quinn had taken me the night of the storm. For the first ten minutes or so, we traveled unimpeded—not a single car in sight—and I began to think we were going to get away cleanly. Then, up ahead, a barricade appeared.

"Fuck," said Quinn.

As a watchman stepped into the roadway with his hand raised, Thea brought the truck to a halt with a hiss of air brakes. Four more watchmen, hands riding atop their belts, were positioned along the barricade. The first stepped up to the cab, holding a flashlight and a clipboard.

"Road's closed for curfew," he said.

"What curfew?"

"A state of emergency has been declared. Roads are closed until six A.M."

"But this is my regular route. Nobody told me anything about a curfew."

The danger, I realized, was that he'd use his flashlight to have a good look at her. Uniform or no, the woman hardly looked like a sanitation worker.

"Not my problem. You see anything suspicious?"

"Like what?"

The watchman pulled a sheet of paper off his clipboard and handed it up to her through the window. "Like this guy."

A moment passed. "Sorry, no." Thea passed it back. "I haven't seen anybody. Why are you looking for him?"

"Hell if I know. You'll have to turn around."

As the watchman stepped back, Thea put the truck in reverse, swung it across the roadway, and headed back the way we'd come. When we were well out of sight of the barricade, she pulled to the side, got out of the cab, and met us at the rear.

"I'm betting all the roads out of town are blocked," she said. "We need a place to wait until curfew ends."

"Got any ideas?"

Thea thought a moment. "Maybe I do know someone. Didn't we pass a phone kiosk?"

We continued down the road. There it was, next to a shuttle stop. Thea climbed down from the truck and returned a moment later with a page torn from the directory.

"We're in luck. It's close."

Quinn looked at the address. "I don't know—a lot of government officials live up there."

"Well, they have garbage, too."

He handed the paper back. "You said there's a husband. What do you know about him?"

"Nothing, except that he leaves his dirty socks lying around. We'll have to wing it."

We headed back toward town. We'd still seen no traffic on the road; even for the hour, the city seemed dead. At the first lighted intersection, Thea turned the truck north, ascending a steep grade into a neighborhood of winding streets and large homes set back from the curb. Not a single lamp burned in the windows; dawn was three, maybe four hours off. Thea slowed the truck, scanning for the address, and came to a stop in front of a center-hall colonial. We couldn't just leave a stolen garbage truck sitting on the street. We continued on, searching for someplace to dump it, and came upon a construction site—a half-built house, ostentatiously huge. Thea pulled in behind it, concealing the truck from the street.

We returned to the house on foot. While the rest of us crouched in the bushes, Thea stepped up to the door and rang the bell. No answer. She rang again, more insistently, and this time a light came on. Thea stepped back, so whoever answered could see her through the sidelight. The curtain pulled back.

"Sandra, it's Thea. Thea Dimopolous."

The door opened, revealing a sleepy-eyed woman in a bathrobe. "What are you doing here?" She looked Thea over. "Why are you wearing that?"

Thea glanced past her into the house. "Is your husband here?"

"He's asleep."

"We need a place to hide until they open the roads."

Something dawned in her face. "Who's 'we'?"

Thea gestured toward us. We stepped from the bushes and joined Thea at the door. "Better if you don't know the details," Thea said.

A masculine voice bellowed from upstairs: "Sandy, who's there?"

She directed her voice up the stairs: "Just a friend! Go back to sleep!"

"For crying out loud, it's the middle of the night."

She waved us inside. "Come in, quickly."

She led us through the house to the kitchen, then farther back to a large butler's pantry, and closed the door behind us.

"Tell me what's happened," she said to Thea.

"The warehouse is gone. The tunnel, too. We barely got through before it collapsed."

"Is Mother safe?"

"She was with us, but then she took off, we don't know where. We tried to get out of town in a sanitation truck, but the roads are blocked."

"What do you need?"

"Clothes. A vehicle."

She nodded. "Give me a minute."

We waited in silence until she returned.

"My husband's on the small side," she said to me; and then, to Thea, she added, "But you and the girl should be all right."

We dressed hurriedly. I could barely fasten the buttons on the shirt; the pants were like being squeezed in a vise. For Antone, the woman had selected a pair of athletic shorts with a drawstring waist and a floppy pullover.

"Take my van," she said to Thea, and held out a key on a leather fob. "You can hide in the garage until the barricades come up. My husband gets picked up by his office at six-thirty, so wait until he's gone."

Thea accepted the key. "You should come with us. You're not safe here anymore."

The woman demurred. "Oh, I think I'll be all right. The man barely notices me as it is."

"I don't know how I'll ever be able to repay you. All those years, I never knew . . ."

"Well, that's the idea, isn't it? Silly Sandra with her paint swatches, who would ever think."

Thea pocketed the key. "I meant to ask, how'd it go with your yoga instructor?"

The woman gave a sly smile. "Well, let me just say, *that's* a story. I'll tell you all about it when I see you again."

She led us through the back of the kitchen to the garage, a sparkling-clean space with a sedan on one side and the promised van on the other. On the door of the van was printed SANDRA WEST, CUSTOM INTERIORS.

"Remember what I said," she told us. "Once he's gone, don't wait. I'll report the van stolen at noon. That should give you plenty of time."

Quinn said, "In case the barricades are still up, are there any back roads open to the east?"

There were, she said. "Take Ocean Drive north, then turn left at Highland. You'll come to a dirt road on your right. Take it for a few miles, then another right, and that'll bring you back to Ocean on the other side of the barricade." She took Thea by the hands. "Stay safe, all of you. Arrival come."

A sudden clatter: the garage door lifted to reveal a solitary figure standing in its mouth, wearing a silk bathrobe.

The name on the van. The undersized clothes. The early A.M. car. It all made sense, suddenly, that the man standing before us was Nabil West, chief legal counsel to the Ministry of Human Resources, holding a shocker.

Not a shocker. An actual pistol.

"Don't try to run, Bennett—the watchmen will be here any second. And you," he said, waving the pistol in Sandra's direction, "you dumb cunt. I might have known."

"Go screw yourself, Nabil."

"I don't think it's the Nursery for you this time, Bennett. Well, too bad."

Beside me, Caeli made a whimpering sound.

"And who do we have here?" Nabil said.

"Please," she begged. "He made me come with him. He said he'd kill me."

Nabil's face twisted with disgust. "For godsakes, Bennett, taking a hostage? This is low even for you." He beckoned her with his free hand. "Come over here, young lady. You're safe now."

As she buried her face in the front of his robe, Nabil draped his arm around her back, looking past her shoulder at me. "How do you even live with yourself?"

Caeli didn't use her knee, as I'd expected. Instead, she dropped her right hand, formed a rather dainty-seeming fist, and drove it determinedly upward, right where it counted. Eyes bulging, Nabil stumbled backward, dropped the pistol, and folded like a pocket-knife, clutching himself.

"You little bitch!"

I grabbed the pistol off the floor. Right on cue, sirens began building in the distance. Thea was already at the wheel of the van, Quinn in the passenger seat; the rest of us, including Sandra, climbed in back. The sirens were coming from the south, blocking the route Sandra had described. Thea roared out of the garage, hit the street with a bouncy crunch, spun the wheel to the left, and raced away.

"How do we get out of here?" she said to Sandra, speaking toward the rearview.

"Next block, go right."

"That'll take us back to the main road."

"Everything else is a dead end. But there's another way."

We all slammed against the wall of the cargo compartment as Thea, barely decelerating, made the turn. "What now?"

Sandra said, "Four blocks, another right."

All of a sudden, the windshield blazed with twirling lights. Two patrol cars roared past us from the opposite direction. I looked through the back window of the van just in time to see their brake lights come on.

I said, "I think they made us."

Another high-speed turn sent everyone in the cargo area tumbling against the wall.

Thea yelled, "Open to suggestions here!"

I said, "Quinn, change places with me."

"What, *now*?"

I held up the pistol.

"Right you are."

He climbed over the console into the cargo area. I'd fired a gun before; the yacht club had a skeet range, and my father had taken me a few times. But that was years ago, and a pistol was a mystery to me, as alien a weapon as a jousting lance. Once in place, I opened the window.

"Thea, hold the van steady."

I had no desire to shoot anyone; I merely wanted to scare them off. I leaned out, extended the weapon, took general aim at the front of the first patrol car, and squeezed the trigger. The report was painfully loud; the pistol jumped in my hand like a thing possessed. I had no idea where the bullet had gone. I steadied my grip and fired again, this time making a satisfying flare of sparks on the front grill of the first patrol car.

"Hang on!" Thea yelled.

She swung the wheel hard to the right, sending me slamming against the side of the van. In the cargo compartment, bodies flew. Somehow, I managed to keep hold of the pistol. A squeal of tires and a fresh burst of acceleration and we were back on Ocean Drive. As I aimed the pistol again, a watchman appeared out of the passenger window of the first patrol car. Three loud claps, and something whizzed by my head. I ducked back in the van.

"What the hell!" Quinn yelled. "Since when do watchmen have guns?"

"Everyone, down on the floor! Thea, you need to step on it!"

The rear window exploded.

Shots pounded the van, round after round. With a roar, one of the patrol cars moved in beside us. Thea shoved the accelerator to the floor and swung the wheel to the left, clipping his front quarter and barreling past him. At least two more cars had joined the pursuit. We'd entered a stretch of open roadway—dense foliage to our left, on the right a steep drop to the sea, all of it sailing past at an incredible rate. How many bullets did I have left? I leaned out again, extended the pistol, and fired.

And fired.

And fired.

And fired.

It was the last shot that connected—a lucky shot, no, a miraculous shot, skewering the lead patrol car's right front tire like an arrow through a bull's-eye. The car began to swerve from side to side; with each motion, the arc of its swing grew wider. Through the windshield I saw the driver's terrified face as he spun the wheel, fighting to regain control, but by then the outcome was certain. His front end hit the guardrail, making the car twirl in a one-eighty; it flopped onto its side, skidded another fifty yards, then, like a whale breaching the surface, popped off the roadway and, with a great screech of rupturing metal and a splash of bursting glass, crashed down onto its roof in the middle of the road. There wasn't time for the driver of the second vehicle—and then the drivers of the third and fourth—to stop.

A sheen of light. A boom, loud as a thunderclap. The night's second fireball, ascending.

"Holy shit!" This was Antone. "You see that? Holy fucking shit!"

I realized my face was wet—why was it wet? I touched my cheek.

Blood.

Sandra was slumped against the wall of the van, Quinn pressing his hand to her neck. Blood was pulsing through his fingers. More was splashed against the walls of the van.

"Pull over!" Quinn yelled.

"Are you kidding me?" Thea glanced at the rearview; her eyes widened sharply. "Oh, God."

A choking sound rose from deep in Sandra's throat. More blood was dribbling from her mouth. Caeli and Antone, braced against the opposite wall, were staring in mute horror.

"There's a turn ahead on the left," Quinn told Thea.

"Where?" We were still flying, eighty miles an hour at least.

"Two hundred yards. It's a back way to the safe house."

She slowed the van and made the turn. A plume of dust rose behind us; gravel spat up into the wheel wells. Thea pulled off into a small clearing, surrounded by thick foliage. I burst from the van and met Quinn at the rear. Together, we lifted Sandra from the van and carried her into the clearing, where we lay her on the ground by the light of the open cargo compartment.

"What do we do?" Thea said. She was kneeling on the ground beside Sandra. Her voice was choked with angry tears. "We should *do* something."

Quinn shook his head. "I don't think there's any point."

The bullet had torn through her neck from behind. Her breathing came in a series of thin gurgles, each shallower than the last. Her eyes were open, floating without focus. The last breath caught in her chest and she was still.

Caeli was looking down at the body with an expression of puzzlement. "Is she dead?"

"Yes," I said. "I believe she is."

"I don't get it. I mean, she was here a second ago."

Thea used her fingertips to close Sandra's eyes. The night felt suddenly vaster: indifferent and irrevocable.

"We need to go," I told Thea.

Thea looked up at me. "*Go?* Where would we go, Proctor? There's nowhere *to* go."

The idea had sprung to my lips without thought. And yet it seemed not merely right but inevitable. As if I—as if all of us—had been headed toward this conclusion from the start. "I mean we need to leave, Thea. *Really* leave. And we need to do it now, before the drones come back on line."

She studied my face. "Are you saying . . . what I think you're saying?"

"Tell me what our other option is and I'll listen."

"We don't know what's out there."

"You're right, we don't."

"There could be nothing. Just . . . ocean."

"I'm not arguing. But they have guns, Thea, and there's nowhere to hide."

She looked toward Quinn. He was standing at the edge of the clearing, his back toward us and his face rocked skyward, like a man locked in silent argument with the cosmos.

"Quinn?"

His voice was quiet: "Yeah, I heard him."

"And—?"

A moment passed. His shoulders rose with a long, weary breath. Then he turned around.

"Where's this boat of yours?" he asked.

We crept through the countryside, Quinn driving. The clock on the dash said we had ninety minutes of darkness left. We'd used a furniture pad to cover Sandra's body—a meager gesture. Caeli had fallen asleep almost as soon as we'd gotten back in the van. She lay with her head against my side, her body slack, her breathing deep and even.

"You're okay, prossie," Antone said quietly. The boy was sitting across from me in the cargo area.

"Thanks."

"It wasn't your fault, what happened to the lady."

Caeli drew herself upright as we pulled up to the cabin. While Thea, Antone, and Caeli gathered supplies, Quinn and I carried Sandra's body from the van. There was no time to bury her; we brought her inside, laid her on the bed where I'd slept the night of the storm, and wrapped her body in a quilt. There she would remain until somebody found her.

We loaded the supplies: what food we could find that wouldn't spoil, gallon jugs of water, a pile of blankets and sweaters, a few basic tools, a couple of flashlights, and a small medical kit. I would have liked to bring some fishing gear along, but we couldn't find any; I substituted a ball of twine and some safety pins from the sewing kit Thea had used to suture my arm—an event that felt like something that had happened years in the past. We'd allotted twenty minutes to get ready; we pulled out of the drive in fewer than fifteen. We were racing the dawn now, and the drones.

My memory of the tornado, and the destruction of my father's house, was hazy at best. All came into focus as we made our approach. As the van's headlights fell over the wreckage, I saw that the building had been torn to matchsticks, nothing but its twin chimneys left standing; its contents were scattered as if the structure had exploded from within. But the boathouse, to my relief, stood intact, the *Cynthia* bobbing beside the pier, looking little the worse for wear. While I made ready, the others toted the supplies from the car and brought them aboard. My goal was to be well past the Nursery before sunrise. There was nothing official about this as a line of demarcation; it merely existed in my mind as a border between our world and whatever lay beyond the Veil.

We set off. Close to shore, the air was worrisomely light, but as we proceeded outward, it built to a steady ten knots. Still, with the weight of five people aboard and all our supplies, the boat moved sluggishly, its wide hull rolling in the swells. On the other side of the cockpit, I heard Quinn fill his chest with air and let it out with a soft moan.

"If you're feeling seasick, look at a light onshore," I told him. "It helps. And if you're going to puke, do it with the wind so it doesn't blow back into the cockpit."

"So noted."

The Nursery rose into view off our starboard bow. The air had stiffened; we were making decent speed now.

"If the drones are back up . . ." Thea said.

She meant they'd be coming from the Nursery. "I know."

Tiller in hand, I kept watch on the sky. The minutes passed as we plowed through the dark. Nobody was talking; there was nothing to say. Our fate was being decided elsewhere; all we could do was meet it.

We passed the Nursery with excruciating slowness. Still there was no sign of any drones. The island's black silhouette fell away behind us. Was that it? After everything, had we managed to slip away cleanly?

"Uh-oh," Quinn said. "Here they come."

Six drones were skating toward us from the stern. There was something strange about the way they moved. They seemed larger and less nimble, as if they were bearing extra weight.

Quinn said, "I don't think those are reconnaissance drones."

A bright point fell away from the lead drone and dropped toward the water. There was a blinding flash, and instantly it rocketed toward us at incredible speed. I grabbed Caeli and pressed her to the floor of the cockpit as it zoomed overhead with a hiss of fire and gas and hit the water off our bow with an earsplitting boom. Water cascaded over us.

"What was *that*?"

"Hell if I know," Quinn said. He, too, was pressing his body to the floor of the cockpit, hands covering his head. "Some kind of missile drone."

"A *what*?"

A second detonation, closer this time. The boat heeled at a forty-five-degree angle, lurched upward on the swell, and came crashing down again, rolling in the opposite direction. All of us were barely holding on.

"Please!" Caeli cried. The girl was curled in a ball, hands over her ears. "Stop shooting at us!"

Another blast, this time from behind. The swell lifted the stern high in the air, shoving the bow downward, the hull sliding sideways and threatening to broach. Seawater poured over the sides, sloshing into the cockpit and cabin.

"Quinn, I need an idea here! Tell me you've got something!"

"Wish I had one," Quinn said. "I don't know why they haven't taken us out yet."

We were, by now, settled deep in the water. Explosion after explosion encircled us, tossing us first one way and then the other. It was as if the drones were enjoying themselves, letting the sea do their work for them. I pulled Caeli close. The girl's sobs rattled into me, taking root in my bones. *Caeli, I'm sorry, I couldn't be sorrier, how I wish you'd never met me.* And with that thought, I waited for the end.

Which did not come.

How long before my mind registered the silence? The sea's sudden immobility? I released the girl and slowly got to my feet. Where had the sky gone? For I could see nothing at all: no drones, no lights from the Nursery, not even the stars themselves. The sea was flat, the air breathless, with a dense feeling on my skin.

The Veil?

Quinn was standing beside me. "Do you hear something?"

I did: rushing water. Simultaneously, the boat began to move; an unseen force was pulling us forward.

"What *is* that?" said Thea.

I turned toward the bow. A wall-like shape had appeared ahead of us, barricading the entire length of the horizon. Rippling lines moved upward over its surface, which was illuminated from behind by a trembling multitude of glowing points.

It was a waterfall.

Going up.

It was full of stars.

I grabbed the emergency oar from under the gunwale and tried to paddle us backward, but this accomplished nothing; the current was too strong; the boat, half-sunk, was heavy as a tank. The sound had expanded to an all-encompassing roar. A last, desperate pull and the oar was stripped from my hand. The waterfall loomed over us, closer and closer, a vision of insanity, blotting out the sky. Its peak, if there was one, lay far beyond sight; we would be sucked into the heavens. I pulled Caeli to my side, wrapping my arms around her.

"Hold on to me. Whatever you do, don't let go."

She pressed her face into my chest. "I'm scared," she said.

The distance narrowed. Fifty yards, twenty, ten.

"Everybody, grab ahold of something!"

I closed my eyes.

VI

THE ANTECHAMBER

29

I burst to the surface—sputtering, flailing, desperate for breath. My heart was crashing against my ribs. I spun madly in the water.

"Caeli!"

My voice volleyed into the void.

"Caeli! Thea! Quinn! Antone!"

My pleas met only silence. The waterfall, the *Cynthia*—both were gone. I was alone in an endless sea of perfect calm. I tilted my face heavenward, searching for a sign, some signal from the heavens.

The blue star.

Head above the water, I moved toward it. The sea gave easily to my efforts; it required only the slightest effort to keep my body afloat. Onward I swam, until I saw a light.

The great ship, lying at anchor. *Oranios.*

All seemed right, like the fulfillment of a grand design. With smooth, nearly soundless strokes, I made my approach. Details sharpened as the distance closed. The majesty of her length. The stateliness of her masts and prow. The meticulousness of her rigging and the sleek, womanly curves of her hull. With what care and measure she was made! How graceful she was, how grand! I stilled my body in the water, bewitched by the sight of her. That such a vessel had been fashioned by human hand was nothing less than proof of our indomitableness as a species, the unconquerable spirit of our kind. To cross the widest of seas, to launch into nature's starry immensity, to traverse the infinite darkness: that was our destiny, our only fate.

I pushed my way along the hull toward the stern. I had detected no movement aboard, no signs of life within. I rounded the hull; painted on the vessel's transom were her name and port of hail.

ORANIOS

ANCHORAGE, AK

I took the ladder in my grip and hoisted myself clear of the water. A small door in the transom opened onto the spacious cockpit, with its great chrome wheel and navigation instruments positioned at the center. Everything was neatly stowed: sails bagged along their booms, lines arrayed in Flemish coils on the deck. Details of lustrous teak and gleaming brass imparted an elegant feel. On one of the benches, someone had left me a towel and robe, neatly folded. I stripped off my sodden clothing, donned the robe, and descended the ladder.

The vessel's saloon was, like its cockpit, a feast of teakwood and discerning nautical detail. It was rather large, as befit a vessel of her size, and organized into smaller zones designed for the efficient use of space: a work area with chart table and instruments, an L-shaped galley with a gimballed stove, a pair of curtained berths tucked into the bulkheads, and, in the center, a cozy dining area, set at right angles to the bulkhead, with facing banquettes.

Sitting at the table, reading a newspaper, was a woman.

"Dr. Patty?"

She lifted her face and regarded me, bright-eyed, from above her paper. "Director Bennett, there you are," she said with a warm smile. "I'm glad you finally made it."

Gone were the alluring adjustments to her appearance. Dressed in her spotless lab coat, her hair in a ponytail, she had returned to the workaday version I'd met as a young iterant. Yet something was different about her—an aura of deep sincerity and care, like a friend worthy of trust. It was as if I were finally seeing the woman's true nature.

"Come sit, won't you?" She folded up the newspaper and put it aside. "We have lots to talk about."

I took a place across from her.

"How are you feeling?" she asked. "Warm enough? You found the robe, I see."

"I don't understand what's happened."

She nodded along. "And that's to be expected. That's why I'm here, to help you understand." She leaned slightly forward and placed her hands, neatly folded, upon the table. "Tell me, Director Bennett. Where do you think you are?"

I cast my eyes around the cabin. Now that I gave it my full attention, I noticed a number of signs of human occupation. An open chartbook at the captain's workstation and a mug of pencils; a pair of leather deck shoes discarded at the base of the ladder; a small hammock of fruit—bananas, apples, a single orange—slung from the ceiling above the galley counter; and a line of freshly washed dishes in the drying rack.

"*Oranios,*" I said, and returned my eyes to her face. "This is *Oranios.*"

Dr. Patty gave a closed-lipped smile. "Yes and no."

"But I saw the name on the stern."

She settled back, then said, "Do you remember when we talked about your dreams? It was very long ago."

"When I was young, you mean."

"I said, think of your dreams not as dreams but as echoes. The source is gone, but the sound lingers, ricocheting through the mind until it, too, fades away."

"I remember."

"Well, there you have it. There is the *thing*," she said, moving her hands to one side of the table, "and then"—she shifted them to the other side—"there is the *echo* of the thing, the *shadow* of the thing. Are you familiar with the parable of the cave? I think you'd find it helpful."

The name rang a bell; I sent my thoughts back to my university days. "Plato?" I said. "I think it was Plato."

"Precisely, Director Bennett. So, here is the story. A group of prisoners is chained in a cave facing the wall. Behind them is a group of puppeteers, and behind them, a fire. The puppeteers move their puppets back and forth, creating shadows on the wall. The prisoners can't turn around, so all they see are the shadows. Look at the dog, they say, look at the house, look at the lady walking her dog by the house. They have no way to know that the shadows aren't the things themselves, but reflections of them. Does this help you in any way?"

I considered her meaning. "So, none of this is real, is what you're saying."

"Oh, I wouldn't say that. More like a reality of a certain kind. A *shadow* kind, if you will."

I resumed my scan of the cabin. The more I looked, the more I saw. A trio of bright yellow slickers hanging by their hoods on bulkhead pegs. A box of cereal on the galley counter and an open carton of milk. A smell, not of varnish or the sea but a soft, living, human scent—"domestic" would be the word—of worn clothing and cooked food and the comings and goings of warm bodies in an enclosed space. A smell of life, but something more. Something familiar, etched in the bone.

"I think I know this place."

"It's likely you would feel that way. That makes sense."

"Like I've been here before." I looked back at her kind face. "I don't know when, though."

"I assure you, it will come."

"Does it have a name?"

"Does what have a name?"

I made a swooping gesture. "All of this. Being here, with you."

"It does, Director Bennett. You called it 'the antechamber.'"

"*I* called it that."

She nodded. "Yes, that was you. Are you familiar with the word?"

"It's a room outside another room. Like a waiting area."

"Exactly. Or, let's say, a dressing room. Consider yourself as someone dressing for the evening, for example, or preparing to go out for the day."

"So, I won't be staying here, is what you're saying. I'm on my way to someplace else."

She gave a patient nod. "Correct."

"Arriving, in other words."

"Yes, Director Bennett."

"Where am I arriving?"

She smiled. "That's always the question, isn't it? Now, tell me, is the robe all right? You're not too cold, are you? I want you to be comfortable."

This shift in direction was mildly disorienting. Also, the woman was right; I was suddenly feeling chilled. "A little," I confessed.

"Well," she said, and wrinkled her nose attractively, "perhaps a warm drink would be good." She unwedged herself from the dinette. "Why don't you just make yourself at home while I put the water on? I'll only be a moment."

She stepped into the galley and set about making the tea.

I asked, looking up from the table, "Is Patty your first name or your last?"

She was setting a kettle on the flame. "Neither, actually." She took a pair of mugs from the upper cabinet, blew into them to clear the dust, and placed them on the counter. "It's simply what you called me. You thought it would be easier for people."

Again, this claim of responsibility I failed to recollect. "Easier than what?"

On tiptoes, she reached up to the cupboard's top shelf and removed a small metal box. "Well, the whole thing is rather a mouthful, don't you think?" She held up the box to show me. "I hope Irish breakfast is all right. There was peppermint around here someplace, but I can't seem to find it. Why don't you have a look at the paper while you wait? The water should be ready soon."

I realized she was referring to the newspaper she'd been reading when I'd first arrived. I located it on the opposite bench and reached over the table to retrieve it. The feeling of cold had increased; naked beneath the robe, I was feeling an uncomfortable sense of exposure; I was quite looking forward to the tea. I expected the paper to be a copy of the *Prospera Times,* but when I unfolded it, I saw that it was something called *USA Today.* A huge banner headline read:

CRISIS ENTERS NEW PHASE

- Disruptions increase as superstorms, wildfires assail all continents.
- Food shortages become widespread, putting millions on the move.
- Riots erupt in urban centers across the nation.
- Officials warn of catastrophic "tipping point" as climate shift abruptly hastens.

"Anything interesting?" a voice said—Dr. Patty said—but I was barely listening. I wasn't listening at all, so disturbing were the words on the page. A shiver battered through me; my fingers had gone numb as wood. I both did and did not want to read further—the cataclysm in the headlines both captivated and repelled—but this proved irrelevant; although I could march my eyes across the page, each sentence evaporated from my mind as soon as I moved on to the next, leaving only isolated words and phrases behind. "De-civilization." "Mass starvation." "Ecological collapse." And, most ominously, "extinction-level event."

"I can't read it," I said, first to myself and then, lifting my face from the paper, to Dr. Patty. "Why can't I read it?"

But Dr. Patty was nowhere to be seen.

The kettle whistled. I unwedged myself from the table, moved to the stove, and extinguished the burner. The abrupt silence seemed to magnify the oddness of the woman's absence. Where had she gone off to? Why would she leave a kettle boiling on the stove like that?

"Dr. Patty?" I called. "Where did you go?"

I heard footfalls overhead; apparently she'd gone topside. I exhaled a breath I hadn't realized I was holding; to be alone here was nothing I desired. Feeling irritated, but also relieved, I climbed the ladder to find her sitting at the stern with her legs dangling over the side. Evidently, she had left the kettle and gone for a swim; she had changed into a white robe like mine and was squeezing out her hair.

"Dr. Patty, what are you—"

But that was all I said, as the words stopped in my throat.

Not Dr. Patty, not at all.

Elise.

"Oops," she said with an embarrassed laugh. "I guess you caught me."

I was staring at her in a state of absolute mental numbness.

"I know, I know," she said, "don't swim alone at night. *Especially* at night."

"Elise, what are you doing here?"

"I just told you, silly. Taking a swim."

I was having difficulty assembling my thoughts. "But you never swim. You hate the water."

"Not always. Sometimes I like it." She lifted her chin to the sky. "It was just so lovely. Like . . . drifting in a sea of stars." She looked back at me again. "Please don't be mad. You're not mad at me, are you?"

"No," I said. "I'm not mad."

"Well," she said and, smiling at me, nodded. "That's good. I'm glad you aren't." She patted the deck. "Come sit by me."

I took a place beside her, our legs dangling side by side over the inky water. She leaned her head against my shoulder and slipped her hand into mine, weaving our fingers together.

"Do you remember," she began, but didn't finish.

"Remember what?"

"Just . . ." She took a long breath and let it out with sleepy contentment. "How happy we were."

The warmth of her, the closeness of our bodies: the sensation swept through me like a wind. A new feeling came over me, erasing all others. It was a kind of sadness. A sweet, heartbreaking awareness of time's passage, all things lapsing into the past.

"We *were* happy, weren't we?" I said.

She squeezed my hand. "Yes, we were. So very, very happy." Then: "I'm sorry that I left you."

"Left me? You never left me."

"I did, though."

"Where did you go?"

Her voice seemed to come from some far-off place. "I was right there the whole time, but I left you all alone."

Some amount of time went by. The stars shone down in their infinite array upon us. The air, the sea, the bones of the great ship, *Oranios*—all was absolutely still, the only sound the audible silence of all vast things at rest.

"Do you see it, Proctor?"

The blue star. It presided over the night like the brightest jewel atop the crown of heaven.

"I remember when you first showed me." She draped her arm across my chest, drawing our bodies closer. "There it is, you said. Right there. That will be the one."

"When?" I asked her.

"When what, Proctor?"

I was trying to think, to remember. "When did I show you?"

She took another languorous breath, nestling against me. "Oh, it was very long ago."

The answer seemed right. Long ago, like everything. So very, very long ago. I set my eyes to roam among the stars. They weren't mere pinpricks of light in an infinite darkness but a dense, thrumming canvas, like a pointillist painting. I thought of the word "firmament." An old word, a forgotten word, from the Latin *firmamentum,* "that which supports"; the sky as God made it, to separate the waters above from the waters below, the heavens from the earth.

"How are you feeling?" Elise asked me. "You must be chilled."

This was so. The cold, briefly absent or perhaps merely forgotten, had returned. She rose and, looking down at me, held out a hand.

"Come to bed with me," she said.

I let her lead me below. We passed through the saloon into a narrow passageway with closed doors on either side. Everything was bathed in a soft, seemingly sourceless light. The passageway concluded at the vessel's master stateroom: a snug space with a double bed that narrowed at the far end where it tucked into the curve of the bow. Elise untied her robe, shrugged it from her shoulders—she was naked beneath—and let it fall to the floor, revealing the smooth arc of her pregnancy.

"Oof," she said, exhaling sharply. "She's kicking again." She sat on the edge of the bed. "Come feel her, Proctor."

She took my hand and placed it upon the taut, warm curve of her belly. A ripple moved beneath my palm, then a sudden jab, like the heel of a foot. Elise's eyes widened with expectant delight. "There?" she said, and "Did you . . . ?"

"Yes," I said, amazed. To think, this hidden life among us. "I feel her."

Another jab—*Hello out there, hello!*—followed by a tumbling sensation, as if the baby were somersaulting.

"My God," Elise said, with a roll of her eyes, "she sure is busy tonight. She's going to be a handful." She looked back at me, smiled. "Now, come here, husband, so I can warm you up."

I stepped from my robe as well. Elise pulled the covers aside, slid beneath them, and lifted them like a tent for me to join her, as I did. The sheets were cool and fresh, the weight of the blankets a soft cocoon, enveloping us—we three. Our bodies mingled, joined. The mechanics of sex, yes, but lacking any sense of the mechanical: it felt edgeless, absent all physical boundary, as if we had been atomized, our bodies dispersed each into the other's. Like drifting in a sea of stars.

"Do you know what we've done?" Elise above me, smiling in the dark. Another room, another life. So very, very long ago. "We've saved her, Proctor. We've saved everyone."

Now it is morning. Bright daylight streams through the windows. What time is it? My mouth is sour, my tongue thick; my head throbs like a heartbeat. What a night we had! A night of celebration, of corks flying and good champagne flowing, of glasses raised in victory. To Elise! To Proctor! To Malcolm! To Thea! To Oona! To Quinn! To all of us who've worked so hard, and most of all to *her:* to *Oranios*! Everyone was there; even a handful of people from corporate had shown up. Callista, of course ("on behalf of the investors"), blowing in on a wind of money and dragging Julian along, and the awful Regan Brandt, and just-as-awful Nabil from legal, though, in all fairness, hadn't he been the one to turn the music up? And before they knew it everyone was dancing, the party spiraling from living room to patio, patio to pool, first one person and then another and another stripping to their underclothes and hurling themselves in with a whoop.

It's okay, honey, the grown-ups are just having fun, I know you want to see but what time is it, my God, you should have been asleep hours ago, come on, I'll take you, do you need a glass of water? The small figure at the base of the stairs, yawning into her palm, old Mister Otter swinging from her fist. *Sure, of course, give Uncle Malcolm an extra hug good night, and one for Mommy, too, all right, one more look through Uncle Malcolm's magic telescope, just one, I love you baby girl, now off to bed with you . . .*

"Elise? Are you awake?"

From beside me, a voice muffled by a pillow: "What time is it?"

I rise on my elbows and look. The effort feels heroic. "Nine . . . something?"

"You can't tell?"

I flop back down, my brain sloshing against the walls of my skull. "Gimme a sec. My eyes haven't started working yet."

"Gawd," Elise groans, "my head is killing me. Call the front desk. Somebody needs to shut those drapes."

"We're at home, Elise. This is our bedroom. Those are our drapes."

"Right. I knew that. I was just testing you." She pauses. "Now, was Malcolm making out with some woman on the sofa or did I dream that?"

"Not just some woman, actually. His ex-wife."

Elise is silent a moment. "I'm sorry, I thought I just heard you say that your brother has an ex-wife."

"Pretty much, yeah."

She rises on her elbows. "And you never got around to mentioning this?"

"You forget how much older he is than me. They were divorced before I was out of middle school. To tell you the truth, I'd forgotten all about it. I thought he had, too."

Elise just stares at me. "I'm having difficulty processing this. Your brother, Malcolm, was *actually* married to a real live woman?"

"It doesn't seem like him, I know."

"I can't even picture it. I mean, no offense, but he's like the Tin Man."

"Her name's Cynthia. The plot thickens. She's a civil engineer, part of the sixty-third group."

"The woman's a *colonist*?"

"Mal saw her name on the manifest and called her up. Seems he'd never gotten over her."

"I'll say he didn't. That was some show they put on." Elise eases herself back down and nestles against me. "Malcolm with a girlfriend, who would've thought. Well, good for him. Good for both of them."

We stay that way for a time.

"I saw you and Thea talking," I say. "I'm glad you guys are getting along."

"We talk all the time, Proctor. It's not like I can just ignore her." She sighs. "Okay, fine, you caught me. The truth is, I'm actually beginning to like her. As it turns out, we have things in common besides, you know, *you*."

I can't tell if she's mad or just having fun; more to the point, I'm not supposed to. "Well, that's good," I say. "I'm glad you do. And the only reason I brought her on—"

"Is because she's the best at what she does. You've mentioned that."

"Because it's true. We wouldn't be where we are without her."

"The woman's still hopelessly in love with you, you know."

I scoff at the thought. "Please."

"Proctor, don't be dense. Are you telling me you *actually* haven't noticed?"

"That was years ago, Elise. We were practically kids, for godsakes."

"And that right there," she says, "is proof of how little you know about women. Or people, for that matter." She exhales into my chest. "Oh, look at you, you love it. Two women fighting over you. It probably gives your ego, like, this gigantic hard-on just thinking about it."

"I admit I'm intrigued."

"Ha-ha."

"Well, what about Warren?"

Elise groans comically.

"I know he flirts with you."

"The man flirts with everyone, Proctor. It's like being the victim of a drive-by shooting. *And* he's your friend. Your *good* friend. Aren't there meetings where you talk about this stuff? Isn't there some kind of code?"

"Which goes to show how little you know about men. We like a challenge. It's half of the attraction."

"I see. Well, best of luck to him."

I pull her closer. "Just to be clear, if you were somebody else's wife, I'd still take my shot."

"That's sweet of you. Depraved, but sweet. I might even be tempted." She pauses. "Come to think of it, I do have a bit of a thing for Warren's car, though."

"You're . . . attracted to his car."

"What can I say? That little red roadster is kinda sexy." She pokes my sternum with a finger. "Get one of those, bub, and I might just love you forever."

We lapse again into silence—the rich, contented silence of long marriage. The hangover notwithstanding, is there a better feeling than lying in bed with my wife after such a night? If there is, I haven't heard about it.

Elise says, "She's probably been up for hours."

"Probably."

"We're not being good parents."

"She knows how to pour milk over cereal. She can watch TV."

"Not all morning she can't. Whose turn is it?"

"Yours?"

"Nice try." Elise rolls away and, in a bit of hangover theater, pulls a pillow over her head. "Wake me up when she's packing for college. Or you've made the coffee. Whichever."

In this manner, the matter is settled, not that there was any doubt. I rise, put on sweatpants and a T-shirt, and descend to the great room. The place is a catastrophe: half-empty glasses and plates of wilting food everywhere, furniture at odd angles, dead champagne bottles like overturned bowling pins in a tub of melting ice, even an ashtray with the stubbed-out leavings of one of Otto's wretched Montecristo No. 4s. (And where *did* the man get Cuban cigars, of all things? With everything else that's going on? But of course there's a way—there's always a way—for a man like Otto Winspear to get the things he wants. Probably he's planning to smuggle a humidor along.) I pause at the base of the stairs, surveying the wreckage. *What a night,* I think again. *What a night.* And, come to think of it, what a morning, too. After a week of drenching rains, the clouds have parted: glorious sunshine is pouring through the room's tall windows; there's nothing but blue sky above. Out by the pool, Malcolm's telescope still stands on its tripod where he set it up at the beginning of the party so everyone could take a look. *There, I see it!* They stood in line, waiting their turns to press their eyes to the lens. *Look how blue, how beautiful, how magnificent it is!* The perfect party favor, this hopeful glimpse across the reach of space and even time itself when so much else was lost.

And what of Caeli? A stepstool has been dragged to the counter, where there's a carton of milk and an open box of too-sweet cereal; from the den comes the cheerful aural chaos of an old-school cartoon. She's been glued to it for hours, probably—but what, really, is the harm? Why shouldn't she do as she likes on a sunny Saturday morning with her parents still asleep? I put the coffee on—not real coffee, of course; oh, how I miss it—retrieve a garbage bag from under the sink, and set about cleaning up the mess, beginning with Otto's lethal-smelling cigar.

I am feeling much better.

I am feeling almost happy.

I'm not paying attention to the sky.

I'm depositing the last of the plates in the drying rack when two things happen, the second nearly on top of the first. The first is a crash from outside. I turn to look. Malcolm's telescope has pitched sideways to the ground. A blast of wind buffets the slider.

The second is the horn.

There are sounds that squeeze the heart. Such is the sound of the horn. I drop the dish I'm holding—its shattered pieces will remain on the floor, unswept, for days—and tear into the den, where, on the television screen, Wile E. Coyote is strapping a rocket to his back. On the floor, Caeli has constructed a kind of nest. A pile of pillows. Old Mister Otter, tangled up in a swirl of blankets. A cereal bowl, the last uneaten flakes floating in the milk she so carefully poured.

No Caeli.

The screen goes blank, replaced by a blare of noise, and then a robotic voice announces:

If you are hearing this, take shelter immediately, if you are hearing this, take shelter immediately . . .

"Proctor!"

Elise comes flying down the stairs.

"Where's Caeli?" I call to her.

"I don't know!"

"Did you check her room?"

"She's not there!"

We race through the house. *Baby, where are you, Caeli, answer us!* My heart is in my throat. A savage wind batters the walls; the morning has gone dark as midnight. New sounds come from outside: crashing, tumbling, tearing. The two of us reemerge in the great room at the same second from opposite ends of the house.

"Where did she go?" Elise cries. "She has to be here!"

Then I see it. I see it, and time seems to stop. And in a way, it does. Henceforth there will be two distinct eras in my life—the one before and the one after—cleaved by the moment when I notice that the slider to the patio is open, and know for certain that I wasn't the one to open it. This is the moment I now enter, a purely purgatorial state both infinite and instantaneous, in which part of me will dwell forever.

I fling the door wide and hurl myself into the maelstrom. The telescope is to blame: Uncle Malcolm's magic telescope, the evening's enchanted centerpiece. Bored with cartoons, and with her parents nowhere to be found, Caeli tried the door and, finding it unlocked, went outside to look. Yes, it was daytime, the stars were hiding, but surely such a charmed device could penetrate this inconvenience to reveal, once again, that wondrous, watery dewdrop in the sky.

I howl into the wind: "Caeli!"

And again: "Caeli!"

The air is choked with debris—twigs, leaves, pebbles—spattering my face and arms and legs like bird shot; overhead, the clouds have thickened into a churning black mass. These storms: they are phenomena of incalculable violence. They blow down forests, smash cities, redirect rivers, level whole towns. They can tear off the very roof of the world. They are the raging offspring of the atmospheric mayhem wrought by man, and into this one's maw I cast myself, wailing my daughter's name.

I see a dark shape in the pool.

I take a gulp of air and dive. A sudden silence envelops me; beneath the surface, it is as if the storm does not exist. And the cold: it shocks me like an electric current. Heart-stopping cold, as if I've plunged into a pond of Arctic meltwater. Caeli is lying on the bottom, drawn to the deepest part of the pool by gravity and the tidal tug of the drain. The pink fabric of her nightgown billows around her like the pulsing bulb of a jellyfish. The idea that I have arrived too late is simply inadmissible; so, too, the fact that I have just passed thirty minutes washing dishes while, steps away, my four-year-old was drowning. I scoop her up, find my footing, and rocket off the bottom. Elise meets me at the shallow end. The lightning sizzles, the wind shrieks, the air is cracked by thunder. Things of surprising size—the limb of a tree, a patio chair—fly past. As I pull myself from the water and lift my daughter into my arms, a vision comes to me: of the night when she was born, and how, in the hospital room, while Elise slept, I stripped off my shirt, lay down on the cot the nurse had left so that the three of us could be together on our daughter's first night in the world, and placed her on my chest, skin to skin (I had read about this in a book), so that the scent and sound and feel of me would imprint on her brand-new brain, and she would know I was her father. (*It's your daddy,* I murmured, over and over. *It's your daddy, right here.*)

I carry her into the house. I am so cold I am nearly insensate; my thoughts feel thick as soup. Elise is yelling at me, though I can't make out the words. I lay my daughter on the floor. There's blood on Caeli's cheek. Why is there blood on her cheek? And I see that my little girl has cut herself—a long gash, more like a scrape, extending from her right temple to the corner of her mouth. How did it come to be there? The edge of the pool is made of natural stone, irregular and, in some places, sharp. She must have cut herself when she fell.

"Proctor, she's not breathing!" Elise's face is twisted with terror; she is in a place beyond reason, even beyond thought. Kneeling on the floor, she takes Caeli's cheeks in her hands and shakes her. "Caeli, baby, wake up!"

CPR training: it's been years. Lifeguarding, high school, summers chatting up girls and scanning the water for a life-threatening emergency that never actually happened. Yet the memory, when I reach for it, is still at hand. I drop to all fours, pinch her nose, cup her neck to tilt her head, and press my large, ungainly mouth to her exceptionally delicate one. Her lips are cold, her body still; there is no trace of life. Part of me knows this; another part does not. Two breaths, twenty presses to her chest, repeated over and over, Elise howling, begging, the storm raging. Debris batters the walls of the house; somewhere, a window is smashed. I have entered a zone of absolute madness. I feel like a man on a stage of dark wings and no audience, a single spotlight stabbing my eyes. I press and blow and press and blow some more. There is no life, no breath, no hope, yet I cannot surrender. Caeli, come back to me!

"Director Bennett?"

Caeli, don't go!

"Director Bennett, are you there?"

Something is wrong with my throat—a sensation of thickness, with a bitter, chemical taste. I try to swallow it away but it fills my throat like a fist. I begin to choke. Raw, animal panic jolts my heart. Elise! Help me!

"All you have to do is open your mouth and breathe."

I am choking, wheezing, flailing my arms and legs. My frame convulses in a hard spasm, like a whole-body sneeze; viscous fluid spews from my mouth and nose. I cough and gag and wretch.

"That's it, Director Bennett. All you have to do is breathe."

What voice is this, speaking my name? Is it the voice of God, addressing me? And the light! It is an exquisite torment to my eyes, like staring into the brightest sun that ever blazed.

"Alley-*oop*."

I am lifted. I am lifted and put down again. Wheels clatter below me; I am being rolled on a gurney. My gut swirls with nausea; my brain is spinning like a drunk's. The cold has transmuted to a new impression—one of being lightly touched all over, as if an army of ants was marching over my skin. I hazard the light and open my eyelids to the thinnest slits. Above my face, a ceiling rolls by, but what ceiling, where?

"And here we are."

Once again, my body is hoisted and placed upon a new surface. It is unlike anything I've ever experienced, conforming precisely to the curves of my torso and limbs so that all pressure is equally distributed, and radiating a nourishing warmth that seems to heat my very bones. A pinprick: something, a needle, has been inserted into my forearm.

"Get some rest, Director Bennett." The voice elongates; the

speaker has moved away. "The worst part is over. You'll be feeling better soon."

Wait! my mind cries out. *Send me back! I have to save her, I have to save Caeli!* I think these things but cannot say them, and then a door seals, leaving me alone.

Caeli!

Silence. Darkness. I weep.

30

First water; then fire.

She finds a ladder and climbs onto the pier. The smoke and heat are intense. The fire roars and crackles; glowing embers pop skyward, riding winds of flame; ashes drift downward, impossibly light, like fat, gray snowflakes. She makes her way along the waterfront, searching for a route. Her feet are bare, her shoes cast aside when she left Proctor and the others behind and dived into the water. She draws her sodden shirt up over her nose and mouth to filter the smoke.

She finds a clear path. People are standing in the street, staring upward over the tops of the buildings at the pulsing orange glow that dominates the sky. Others hurry away from the flames, many pulling along small children or carrying sacks of possessions. She moves with them, deeper into the Annex. There are no sirens, no signs of emergency personnel. A decision's been made: *Let it burn.* Callista. The board. It doesn't matter who. No one is coming to help.

The sun is rising when she reaches the rendezvous—an old storefront, boarded up, with vacant apartments above. She lets herself in through the rear. A single room, empty, the walls stripped to the studs. She crouches to examine the floor; footprints, stamped into the dust.

A shadow falls over her. Her heart slams into her ribs; she springs to her feet. But in the next instant she relaxes. It's Stefano.

"Did everyone make it?" she asks him.

"We lost Pappi," he says.

"What do you mean, *lost*?"

"It was dark. He was there and then he wasn't. That's all I know." He tips his head at the stairs. "Everybody else is here."

They ascend to the second floor. In the front apartment, the cousins are sprawled on the floor, asleep, or mostly; Claire is sitting against the wall. Cynthia can tell she's been crying, though she's past that part now. She tells Claire what happened, that Thea and the others are safe.

The conversation is broken by clanking outside. Cynthia meets Stefano at the window. Security faxes are moving down the street, helmeted watchmen with their batons drawn marching in formation behind them.

"They're everywhere," Claire tells her. "Going house to house, pulling people out at random."

A scream slices the air. Down the block, a woman is being dragged by the arm from a doorway. A man, her husband perhaps, appears behind them and is instantly met by a crushing blow across the face. Two watchmen have begun to kick the woman, who is curled into a protective ball on the sidewalk. Watching the scene, Cynthia feels her fists curl into themselves. Her vision contracts; her pulse is throbbing in her ears. The two are dragged into a waiting van and shoved inside.

"Don't," says Stefano.

He means: *I know what you're thinking—you won't make it ten steps.*

She takes a breath to steady herself, letting the air out slowly. "We have to find Pappi."

"Mother, listen to me. I know what you're feeling. But we need to let things cool off."

Cynthia casts her eyes around the room. They're not safe here, but where else can they go? She feels utterly beaten.

"Get some rest," Stefano urges her. "I've got more hours in me. I'll keep watch."

It's as if these words have an incantatory effect; she is suddenly so exhausted she can barely stand. She is old, she thinks, an old woman; she feels it everywhere in her body, this betrayal. How did she become old? She tells Stefano to wake her if anything changes, sits beside Claire with her back to the wall, and closes her eyes. She can still smell the fire, hear the screams; she can still see Proctor's face as she reached down to pull him up from the raging water. It was something anyone might have done, but it wasn't anyone; it was her.

She thinks, yet again, of the night she left them. Malcolm at the table, his face in his hands; the firm, familiar arc of his body as she held him, guiding him into sleep; the soft dawn light as she made her way from shore, and the warm strength in her muscles as she rowed; the small shape of the house receding, then gone; the pain, and the blood, and the weight of the anchor in her arms as she fell into the water. For a moment, just one, as the sea closed over her, she'd considered not letting go. How swift it would be, how simple, how complete. To let the anchor's mortal weight drag her to the bottom, into an infinite darkness, free of all worry or care.

But she didn't, and now, all these years later, here she is. What was she hoping for, what did she want from life? Her exhaustion steals over her; as dawn light fills the windows, she sleeps.

Time passes. At length, she becomes aware of a commotion: shouts, cries, roars, the volume increasing. Her mind rises through this sound, slowly and then quickly; she opens her eyes. The room is dark; she has, impossibly, slept through the day. The cousins are crowded at the windows—Claire and Stefano, too. She gets to her feet and joins them. The street below is empty, no lights anywhere. The sound is coming from the direction of the causeway. What are they hearing?

"Arrival come! Arrival come! Arrival come!"

She looks at Stefano. His eyes tell her that he's thinking the same thing.

It's begun.

31

Elsewhere, Thea makes her own slow journey to consciousness. Blinking—her eyes are dry and painful; everything's too bright—she lies still a moment, attempting to assemble her sense of the situation.

A ship? she thinks. *Wasn't I just on a ship?*

But the memory fails to coalesce. Beneath the thin sheet, she's naked. She rises and pivots her feet over the side of the bed. Her joints are stiff, her limbs watery and slow; there's something wrong with her vision, making everything seem both near and far away. Gingerly, she places her bare feet on the floor. The surface is cold, like stone, though it appears to be some kind of metal plating. She is, she decides, in some kind of hospital; that would explain the whiteness: white walls, white floor, white everything. She pivots her head; sure enough, at the top of her bed stands a metal cart upon which is arrayed an assortment of medical devices—a small hammer, a blood pressure cuff, a stethoscope—and standing beside it, an IV pole. Recalling a quick prick of pain, she looks down at her forearm. Where her monitor should be, there's a small gauze bandage, taped to her skin.

Gripping the edge of the bed, she draws herself erect. Her head feels both light and heavy, like a great hollow stone. More of the room is coming into focus. On the opposite wall, there's a sink with a mirror above it and, hanging on a hook, some sort of jumpsuit, like a laborer's, also white, and, resting on the floor beneath it, a pair of matching boots. The sink is unlike any sink she's ever seen. It possesses no spigot, no mechanism through which water would flow to fill the bowl, which does not so much hang upon the wall as bulge away from it. It is so alien a device that the mere fact that Thea can identify its function seems to come from a compartment of her brain that has yet to fully open.

The mirror beckons her forth. As she steps up to it, the edges illuminate automatically with a soft, clear light. What Thea sees is nothing so simple as a reflection; it is more like a window into a three-dimensional reproduction of the room in which she stands. It is as if she is looking through a window into an alternate but identical reality, or into an enchanted mirror from a children's story.

She pushes her face close to the glass. Yes, it is her face, looking back at her, but there is something . . . odd about it. The same but also different. There are strands of gray in her hair; a web of small lines fans from the corner of each eye. She extends a single finger to touch the glass; the other Thea does the same. So persuasive is this illusion of a second Thea that she's momentarily startled when she feels not the tip of a finger meeting her own but the cool glass surface of the mirror.

She places her hands in the bowl; a flat stream of water ejects from under the lip to fill her cupped palms. She drinks, trying to clear the unpleasant taste in her mouth, then splashes her face. The water is cool and fresh and smells like nothing. Someone has left a hand towel on the curved counter and, resting upon it, a toothbrush and an unmarked tube that she correctly surmises contains toothpaste. She brushes for a long while, then turns her attention to the jumpsuit.

Obviously, it has been left here for her. She draws down the zipper of the jumpsuit and steps into it. The material, soft and stretchy with a waffled texture, conforms precisely to the curves of her body. She sits on the bed to put on the boots. Made of the same spongy fabric as the jumpsuit, they appear more like socks than actual shoes, yet the moment she slides them on, the fabric stiffens, encasing her feet in a structured grip.

She moves to the door. There's no handle or knob, but then she sees, on the wall beside it, a small unmarked panel. When she reaches out for it, the door whooshes open, disappearing into the wall.

She angles her head out the doorway. A hall, extending in both directions. She steps through; the door closes behind her. This is when she notices the sound: a faint, basal throbbing, like a heartbeat. She turns both ways, trying to isolate the source, but the sound seems to come from all directions simultaneously. Also, there is something peculiar about the hall. It's not level but, rather, curves subtly upward in both directions, with Thea standing at the low point.

She chooses a direction and begins to walk. Ahead of her, the hallway rises, yet, strangely, she experiences no sensation of ascent. It's as if she is stationary and the hallway is moving toward her, rather than the other way around. Everything is silent, save for the soft footfalls of her padded boots and the omnidirectional throbbing.

Up ahead, a human form appears. Thea halts, then steps cautiously forward. The person is a man; facing away, he, too, is wearing white coveralls. She clears her throat quietly, then, when the man fails to react, calls out:

"Hello?"

Again, he does nothing; his thoughts lie elsewhere. Thea moves closer. Twenty feet away, she stops.

"Quinn?"

He turns. The man standing before her is indeed her old friend Quinn. Yet part of her feels as if she is looking at a stranger. He, too, looks older—there are flecks of white in his beard—but also more healthful, with a muscled frame and clear, bright eyes.

He squints at her and cocks his head. "You look different," he says.

"So do you."

For a few seconds they just stare at each other.

"Where are we?" Thea asks.

"You've got me there."

"But you feel like you *kind of* know, right? Like it's just on the tip of your tongue."

"Yeah." Quinn pauses, then asks, "Do you remember a boat? I don't mean the *Cynthia.* Something else, much bigger."

The man's right: there *was* a boat. She remembers swimming in a great blue-black sea and then, emerging in silhouette against the sky, there it was. She remembers swimming toward it, the ease of her strokes and the ladder at the stern, taking the first rung in her fist and, as she hoisted herself clear of the water, seeing, written on the stern . . .

"Oranios," she says, startling herself. She looks at Quinn. *"Oranios?"*

"Yeah."

More is coming back. "And there was a woman on board. A doctor. She made me tea."

"Dr. Patty."

"Did she show you a newspaper? The headline said something about—"

"A crisis. 'Crisis Enters New Phase.'"

Another pause, the two of them standing in the presence of these inexplicable facts.

"Did you go anywhere else?" Quinn asks. "Besides the boat."

"How do you mean?"

Quinn doesn't answer her. There's something he's not saying; she can read it in his face. "Quinn, what is it?"

A moment passes. "This is going to sound weird," he says, "but I think I met my mother."

"Your guardian, you mean."

"No, Thea. My *actual* mother." Visibly disturbed, he takes a moment to compose himself. "We were in a hospital. I was sitting on the bed, holding her hand. I knew she was dying. Most of her hair was gone, her skin was like paper. I didn't think she was even awake, but then she opened her eyes and smiled at me. I'll never forget it, that smile. 'You're my good boy,' she said. 'My very good boy. I'm so proud of you.' I reached down to hug her, but when I did, she wasn't there. She was just . . . gone."

He's unable to continue. Thea doesn't know what to say. She's never seen him like this. She reaches out, meaning to comfort him, but he quickly steps back, almost in a panic, as he raises his hands. "I'm all right," he says, and again: "I'm all right."

Thea waits.

"This place," Quinn says finally.

Thea nods. "I know."

"It's . . ."

"Yeah."

Quinn looks first one way down the hall and then the other. He is deciding something.

"Come on," he says.

"Ah, Director Bennett. You're awake."

I was lying on a bed. How and when I'd come to consciousness, I didn't know; I could have been lying there for hours. My mind felt empty, drained of all thought; every part of me ached.

"Tell me, Director Bennett, how are you feeling?"

A shape hove into view. I blinked the sleep from my eyes. What I saw was a face, and not just any face. A certain pugilistic jawline and wide, masculine brow; the twinkling eyes and the ingratiating, ever-helpful smile.

"Bernardo?"

He both was, and was not. His face was rigid and artificial, like a mannequin's; below the waist, the man's body wasn't human at all; in its stead was the gimballed wheel of a helper fax.

"I'm pleased you remember, Director Bennett. That is an excellent sign."

My tongue was thick and dry in my mouth. "Am I in the Nursery?"

From deep within his mechanical body, Bernardo emitted a little whirring sound. "I am not familiar with the Nursery. To answer your question, you are, at present, in the recovery area."

Recovery from what? I tried to think, but all I seemed to remember was a boat.

"You are disoriented," Bernardo went on. "Not to worry—the effect is temporary."

"Help me up," I croaked.

"Director Bennett, you should rest. If I may—"

"Aren't you my attendant?"

More whirring. His head made a small, jerky motion, like a bird's. "Your attendant, sir?"

The line of discussion seemed pointless. "Never mind, I'll do it myself."

Which proved inadvisable. As I hoisted myself up on my elbows, my brain sloshed against the walls of my skull; the room tipped nauseously from side to side.

"Director Bennett, would you like a basin?"

I swallowed; my throat was raw, my mouth rancid-tasting. "Thanks, I've got this."

I steeled myself and pushed my torso upright, simultaneously attempting to swing my feet over the edge. It was even money if I was going to accomplish this without fainting, but the moment my bare feet made contact with the floor, my brain settled into place. This was also the moment when I realized I had not a stitch of clothing on. I took a series of slow breaths to steady myself and, when this was done, surveyed my surroundings. I did indeed appear to be in some kind of medical facility. The room reminded me of nothing so much as Dr. Patty's office, which it very much resembled. But beyond that, I could construct no wider sense of my circumstances. I sensed that I had, quite recently, been through a powerful emotional trauma, though I could not have said what this was, only that it had happened.

Equally unsettling was a curious . . . offness to everything: the floor, the walls, the bed, the very air, even my own naked self. Nothing in particular made this so; neither can I say precisely what this feeling actually *was,* beyond a mild, existential unease. It was as if everything had been subtly altered at some essential, even molecular, level.

"Director Bennett?"

I looked at his unmoving face.

"Would you like to resume your duties? I would be very glad to assist you."

"Duties," I repeated. "Help me out, Bernardo."

"I'm speaking of the duties of director."

"So, I'm still a director here, is what you're saying."

"Indeed so. You are *the* director. There is no other."

Before I could press him on the matter, a door slid open behind him. A second mechanical character wheeled in, this one bearing the ersatz face of Itzhak, the bearded waiter.

"Director Bennett, you are looking very well. I'm pleased to report that I've had the opportunity to run preliminary diagnostics. All systems appear to be nominal. I can also report that Drs. Dimopolous and Dawes are resting comfortably."

Doctors? "Thea and Quinn are here?"

"Correct, Director Bennett. Danielle just looked in on them. I imagine they will be up and about soon."

"What about Dr. Patty? Is she someplace around here, too?"

A hitch in time, and Bernardo said, "Ah. You are referring to the Personnel Arrival and Transition Interface."

Personnel Arrival and Transition Interface. PATI.

"Take me to my friends," I said.

"Friends, sir?"

"What did you call them? Doctors Dimopolous and Dawes?"

"Of course, Director Bennett. Though perhaps you would like to visit the dome first, to ascertain our status."

This seemed promising. "Yeah," I said. "That sounds like a good idea. Why don't you take me to the dome."

Itzhak spun on his undercarriage and zipped from the room, evidently en route to other pressing duties. Bernardo, meanwhile, presented me with a one-piece costume, like a laborer's jumpsuit or a child's pajamas. I stepped into it; the moment I drew up the zipper the fabric compressed, conforming to my body. The same was true for a pair of booties.

"Lead the way," I told Bernardo.

Proceeding along the endlessly ascending hallway, Thea and Quinn eventually come to a doorway, this one also with a panel on the wall beside it. Above the panel are the words STORAGE COMPARTMENT 1. Quinn waves his hand over the panel, opening the door.

Lights come on as they step through, revealing a long, high-ceilinged space. It seems to be some kind of warehouse. Tall banks of shelved crates recede into the far distance, which, like the hallway, curves subtly upward. The crates are identical, made of the same white material as everything else, and marked with long strings of numbers, which, Thea realizes, are ascending, moving top to bottom, row to row. She selects a crate at random and steps up to it. It is twice as tall as she is and half again as wide, and marked 2881.15. She quickly comprehends that the numbers after the decimal function as the crate's address: storage compartment 1, row 5.

"What's in all of these?" she asks Quinn, who, like her, is staring upward at the wall of crates. A few seconds go by; then, with a faint start, he breaks his gaze.

"Let's keep going," he says.

They pick an aisle and resume walking. Lights come on to meet them, while those to the rear extinguish, casting zones of darkness ahead and behind. Eventually they come to an area of parked machinery: tractors, forklifts, heavy trucks. There are smaller vehicles as well, with heavy cages and large, knobby tires. Thick chains fix their bumpers to eyebolts in the floor.

"Hmm," says Quinn, and says no more.

They keep going. Thea is thirsty and has to pee; she is growing increasingly exasperated.

"Does this place go on forever?"

Walking beside her, Quinn doesn't answer. Thea's not even sure the man's heard her. She is about to say more—something, perhaps, on the subject of her dry throat and bursting bladder—when, just like that, they reach the end.

Before them stands a massive door, like the portal of a garage. Beyond it, she assumes, lies the outside world. She feels a frisson of fear.

"Ready?" Quinn says.

"This way, Director Bennett."

I was following Bernardo down the hall. "What's with the hill?" I asked him.

"The hill, sir?"

"Yeah, the hall keeps going up."

"I apologize, Director Bennett, but I'm afraid I don't understand your question. The hallway goes neither up nor down, strictly speaking."

Was something wrong with my eyes? After what I'd been through, it was certainly possible.

"This dome you mentioned," I said, "maybe you could tell me a little more about it."

"The dome is where you work, Director Bennett."

"I see. And just what is it that I do there?"

"You are the director, sir." Bernardo paused, then went on: "I see you are still having some difficulty. Perhaps when you get to the dome, more will become clear. I happen to know there's a message waiting there for you. You should find it informative."

"A message? Who from?"

"From you, Director Bennett."

Quinn waves his hand over the control panel. With a bang and then a rattle, the door commences its long ascent to the ceiling.

A vast, impenetrable darkness waits on the far side. Thea and Quinn step through, their shadows stretching before them on the floor. The air changes—it's thin and cold, like the air of a crypt. As Thea's eyes adjust, she discerns small pinpricks of light, like fireflies, twinkling in the dark.

"Over here," Quinn says.

He's found a kind of desk, semicircular, with a swiveling chair at the center. He sits. Is it some kind of CIS terminal? But there is no keyboard, no screen. Everything is smooth and sleek and edgeless.

"Quinn, what is this thing?"

He is surveying the surface with the look of a man working out a puzzle—a puzzle just within his grasp, if only he can wedge the final pieces into place. A pause, and then he places a hand, palm down, on the surface of the desk.

Everything comes alive. The top of the desk transforms into a busy surface of variegated lights and, in front of Quinn, a keyboard. Above the keyboard, floating in space, a large lighted rectangle appears: a screen. It reads, in block letters:

ORANIOSSYS

WELCOME, DR. DAWES

"And here we are."

We'd arrived at a door. Positioned at eye level was a pane of glass embedded in the wall.

"Is this the dome?"

"It will take you *to* the dome, sir. If you will kindly step to the glass and look straight ahead."

I did as he'd said. A thin red line materialized across the top of the glass, moved to the bottom, then returned to the top. Words appeared:

BENNETT, P. DIRECTOR

ACCESS GRANTED

The door slid open, revealing the carriage of an elevator.

"Would you like me to escort you the rest of the way, Director Bennett?"

I felt a sudden urge to be rid of him. "Thanks, Bernardo, I've got it from here."

"Very well. Itzhak has activated the field. You should have no difficulty."

"I see." I had no idea what to make of this. "Tell him thanks, okay? Thanks for . . . activating the field."

"I will be sure to convey that, Director Bennett. As you may recall, to open the dome, you merely have to say, 'System, open the dome.'"

"'Open the dome.' Got it." I stepped into the car. "One last thing. You said I left myself a message. When did I do that?"

"I couldn't say for certain, Director Bennett."

"More or less, then."

"I'm disinclined to speculate."

"Well, get inclined."

"Based on the contents, I would surmise that you prepared it just prior to your integration."

More guessing games; did they have no end? "My integration into what?"

But Bernardo didn't have a chance to answer; the door had already closed.

"I remember," Quinn murmurs. He looks up, eyes wide with sudden shock. "Thea, *I remember.*"

He begins to type, fingers skipping rapidly over the surface, like a pianist lost in the throes of the notes. Data cascades down the floating screen, too quickly for Thea to parse.

He stops.

"Here we go," Quinn says.

One by one, the lights come on. They move from front to back, revealing all. Not outside, Thea thinks. *Inside.* And the people. Thousands of them, tens of thousands, more. The walls are honeycombed with people, though the walls are the ceiling and the ceiling is the walls, and the floor is all of these at once, the whole world spinning in a gyre.

Thea doesn't know what she's seeing.

And then, all at once—like a burst of light inside her mind—she does.

The duration of the elevator ride—less than half a minute—was one in which my thoughts went, entirely, to my father.

Why this was, I cannot say. Perhaps I intuited that the journey begun on the day I took him to the ferry was finally coming to its end. I thought of those final minutes with him: the horror and the sadness, and, in the last instance, the swell of love I'd felt for him in my heart. I thought of the blast of the horn and my leap from the deck, and the moment when the ferry vanished from sight, leaving me alone. At the time, I'd thought it was my father I'd wept for; now, as the elevator climbed toward its mysterious destination, I understood that I'd wept for myself as well: for a man who'd skipped upon the surface of life without ever plumbing its depths, who had lived without love, and for whom love had finally opened its hand when it was too late for him to take it.

The door disappeared into its pocket, revealing yet another hallway, like the inside of a tube, with a floor made of some lustrous material, like the interior of an oyster shell. As my feet touched the floor, a tingling sensation rippled through the soles of my boots; lifting them free, I felt a subtly adherent tug, as if my feet were sticking to the floor. Was this the "field" Bernardo had spoken of? The hall culminated at yet another door. I saw no panel on the wall; how would I enter? But then, as if sensing my approach, the door slid open.

I could discern nothing, just vague shapes—all was darkness within—but as I crossed the threshold, lights came on. Perhaps a hundred feet in diameter, the room was circular, with an arched ceiling fashioned of the same material as the floor of the hall. A large white console, in the form of a U, with a chair at the center, was positioned in the middle of the room; six smaller consoles surrounded it, all facing forward.

"Welcome, Director Bennett."

Startled, I spun in place. Simultaneously, the surface of the consoles bloomed with colored lights, like gardens bursting into flower. Above the center console, a floating square appeared, and upon it:

ETA: –137.82

An unsettled feeling washed through me, deeply strange. All that had happened to me since I'd awakened suddenly bifurcated in my mind, as if these things had happened to two different Proctors: one who understood none of it, who recognized nothing, and a second Proctor for whom these things were not merely known but central to his life. For an instant, these two versions of me coexisted in my mind with equal weight and presence, as twins are curled together inside a mother's womb; and then I felt them folding into each other, the two Proctors becoming one, making me a single being at last.

This place.

I knew it.

I knew it, because I was the director.

"System, open the dome."

They proceed at a quickstep down the hall. The first mobile unit they encounter is the one named Danielle.

"Where's Director Bennett?" Thea says.

"Dr. Dimopolous, how nice to see you again." The unit rotates her face toward Quinn. "And Professor Dawes. You are looking very well."

Why did they make these things so obsessively polite? Was it Quinn's idea? Warren's? Probably it seemed charming at the time. "Never mind that," Thea commands. "Where is he?"

"I believe you will find Director Bennett in the dome."

"Hello!" a voice calls to them. "Hey! Hello there!"

From the opposite end of the corridor, a man is waving energetically as he jogs toward them. He comes to a halt about ten feet away.

"Sorry, I didn't mean to startle you," he says, catching his breath. "I've been wandering around for hours. You're the first people I've seen."

The man is, by Thea's estimation, in his early thirties—tall and broadly built, with a lean, attractive face and wavy hair.

"Do you know who we are?" she asks him.

He frowns, perplexed, but in the next instant, something dawns. "Hey, wait," he says. "Aren't you Thea Dimopolous?" He turns to Quinn. "And you're Quinn Dawes. Wow. I can't believe it. *Executive staff.* I feel like I should ask for your autographs or something."

Thea and Quinn exchange a look. "It might not be the same for everyone," Quinn says with a shrug.

Thea addresses the man again. "So, you don't remember anything else."

He thinks a moment. "Just some fucked-up dream about drowning. Probably a lot of that going around." He scans the halls. "Where is everybody? Shouldn't there be, like, a lot of us?"

"There may be some . . . issues," Thea says. "We're on our way to the dome now to figure out what's going on. Why don't you come with us?"

"I'm not cleared for the dome."

"Well, consider yourself cleared," Thea says.

Together, they head down the corridor. At the elevator, Quinn positions his face in front of the scanner.

DAWES, Q. CTO
ACCESS GRANTED

They enter the car; it begins to climb. Breaking the silence, the man says, "Sorry, I should have introduced myself."

"You don't have to," Thea says, then adds, "We're old friends."

The man's face draws back. "We are?"

"Yes," Thea replies. "You're Antone Jones."

And in this manner did I, Proctor Bennett, ferryman, behold the heavens.

The dome's opacity melted away. Simultaneously, the lights dimmed, like those in an auditorium before the curtain rises. An abyssal blackness; then, as my eyes adjusted, I saw them, saw them all. Stars by the millions, the billions, more. Stars without number, bedecking the sky with their infinite, far-flung light. As was my habit, I scanned them for familiar arrangements, finding none. But the stars weren't wrong, as I had once been told. The wrongness was—had been—in the eyes I had used to see them.

"System, rotate dome," I commanded.

"Specify," the voice replied.

"Rotate dome one hundred eighty degrees horizontal, ninety degrees vertical."

"Acknowledged, Director Bennett."

Our biaxial turning commenced. The motion was so graceful as to be balletic; one could practically hear the music, which was nothing less than the music of the spheres. A vision of blueness crested over the dome. Caelus. The great, watery world that, once upon a time, I named for you, though you would not live to see it. My Caeli! My heart, my one! For you I bridged the depths of space and time to find humanity a home, and yet I could not save you.

A door opened behind me. "Proctor . . ."

The voice was Thea's. Thea and Quinn, my friends, had found me. They were but the first; others would join them, to stand and stare in awe. The dome continued its rotation, sweeping over the alien seas below us like the eye of God himself. Water, life-giving treasure of the universe! What fantastical creatures must teem within your depths, what wonders lurk beneath your storm-tossed waves! But that was not the only miracle my eyes beheld. A second cresting as the dome rose above the fuselage, and a long, cylindrical shape swung into view.

"Talk to me, please, Proctor."

My eyes were dazzled; my heart swelled like a symphony.

"Proctor, it's Quinn." I felt the touch of his hand on my arm. "Do you remember where you are?"

I did; of course I did. Her vast, smooth bulk, the rays of an alien sun pinging off her miles of metal plating. The patient turning of her hull, like a cradle to carry the multitude of sleeping souls within. The great gossamer sails extended outward to cup and catch the heavens' wind: a wind of light.

I thought again: *Of course I know her. How could I not know her?*

She was my ship.

My *Oranios.*

VII

THE MAN WHO BROKE THE SKY

32

PROSPERA CORPORATION
PROJECT ORANIOS

EXECUTIVE STAFF

PROCTOR BENNETT, DIRECTOR
MALCOLM BENNETT, NAVIGATOR AND CHIEF PLANETARY SCIENTIST
QUINN DAWES, CHIEF TECHNOLOGY OFFICER
THEA DIMOPOLOUS, DEPUTY DIRECTOR, CIS
WARREN SINGH, CHIEF MEDICAL OFFICER
JASON KIM, PILOT
OONA PRIOR, CHIEF OF STAFF
CALLISTA LAIRD, CHIEF EXECUTIVE OFFICER AND CHAIR, PROSPERA CORPORATION
OTTO WINSPEAR, CHIEF OPERATIONS OFFICER, PROJECT ORANIOS

"Proctor, I am Proctor."

Floating above the console, the face on the screen was my own, the setting identical, right down to the chair in which I sat.

"That you're watching this recording means that *Oranios* has arrived at Caelus, and that you have passed through the antechamber and awakened from long-duration sleep. In the days to come, you will have many decisions to make; I cannot tell you what to do. This is strange, as I say it. You and I are, after all, the same person. But many years, and many lifetimes, have passed for you. It's also likely that after such an extended time you are having difficulty reassembling your sense of where you are and all that has occurred. Perhaps, for you, this has all transpired in the blink of an eye. Perhaps you feel the weight of time in ways I cannot predict. What we are about to do has never been attempted. Thus, I am leaving this recording to help you, in the gentlest way I can, become reacquainted with your circumstances."

A new image appeared. This time I was sitting in an armchair beside a roaring fire, wearing a dark suit and a shirt open at the collar. Across from me, in an identical chair with her legs crossed, sat a woman—fiftyish, attractive, with a polished professional air. In the left bottom corner of the screen, a time stamp read, "April 7, 2132."

"Good evening, I'm Sally Blythe," the woman said, speaking into the camera. "I'm here at Prospera Corporation's Anchorage campus with Proctor Bennett, director of Project Oranios." She directed her next words to me: "Welcome, Director Bennett."

"Thank you, Sally. It's good to be with you."

"First, allow me to offer you my condolences on your recent loss. That must be very hard."

The Proctor on the screen, who was also myself, swallowed visibly. "Yes, it's been a difficult time for everyone, especially coming so close to our departure. We're all like family here."

"Your departure for Caelus. A planet which, if I'm not mistaken, you named for your late daughter."

The on-screen Proctor nodded. "That was my older brother Malcolm's idea, actually. It was a present for her fourth birthday. The two were very close."

"You're referring to Dr. Malcolm Bennett, Oranios's chief planetary scientist."

"That's right. Mal was the one who discovered it. Caelus is the first exoplanet that we can confidently say is capable of supporting human life, possessing both liquid water on the surface and a breathable atmosphere. The name Caeli comes from the Latin *caelus,* meaning 'from the heavens.' It seemed appropriate."

"That's lovely. But a little bittersweet, maybe?"

"That, too."

She glanced down at her notes. "In a recent interview, you said of your daughter, 'It's her I'm really doing this for.' What did you mean by that?"

"I meant I wanted her to have a future. I want our *species* to have a future."

"So, you adhere to the tipping-point theory."

"I do. The data is inarguable."

"Not everyone would agree."

"Not everyone would agree that the earth is round, but that doesn't change the facts. Our planet is a system, we've knocked that system out of balance, and the system is correcting itself with increasing speed and violence. This isn't a matter of 'if' but 'how soon.' Simply wishing the problem away solves nothing; we've done that for almost two centuries. There have been periods, tragically brief in my view, when the idea that we are guests of the planet had political clout. But the prevailing tendency of human society has always been to foul our own nest. Combine this with the consolidation of wealth in the hands of a select few, both individuals and multinational corporate entities, and you have a recipe for inaction. It will spell our doom."

"That's a pretty dire prediction."

"Believe me, Sally, I'm aware. I'd prefer it were otherwise, but wishful thinking is what's gotten us where we are. Unless we establish a sustainable human presence elsewhere in the cosmos, our species will become a footnote—a brief, unpleasant memory for the planet. I didn't want that for my daughter—for *anyone's* daughter."

"Doesn't it strike you as ironic, even contradictory, that Project Oranios is a private endeavor, financed by a wealthy investor class?"

The on-screen Proctor made a gesture of demurral. "It could appear that way, I suppose, but that's where the resources lie. Nearly all off-earth exploration and development has been in the hands of the private sector since the end of NASA, and Prospera is the biggest player. The corporate leadership, Callista Laird in particular, has been fully supportive. The two of us have always had a strong relationship."

"But what of the rumors that *Oranios* has paying passengers—these same so-called investors? And that the colonists are, in essence, a kind of support staff for them?"

"Let me be clear, Sally. Nobody's 'supporting' anybody."

She briefly consulted her notes. "Tech billionaires. Wall Street titans. Foreign oligarchs. Heads of state. Even some Hollywood actors." She raised her eyes, smiling generically. "According to my sources, they account for nearly fifteen percent of the ship's complement. I have a full list right here, if you'd like to look."

The on-screen Proctor offered his own bland smile in return. "That won't be necessary. I'm well acquainted with the ship's manifest."

"I imagine so. And surely you can see—"

"What I see, Sally—and excuse me for interrupting—is that it's only a small part of the picture, and a misleading one. It is true that some of the ship's complement are individuals who have a financial stake. We all have bills to pay, and *Oranios* wouldn't exist without them. But the vast majority are volunteers who've been rigorously vetted to meet the practical challenges of settling an alien world. There are engineers and agronomists, of course, but for every agronomist you need at least a hundred farmers, for every engineer, a hundred carpenters. This isn't going to be easy. We have some families with children, but the majority are either single individuals or couples between the ages of twenty-five and forty. And I'll repeat—nobody's 'supporting' anybody. Caelus is our chance for a clean slate, to start over and do a better job of it."

There was a short pause while the woman, once again, checked her notes. "Tell me about the craft itself, *Oranios.* I've heard her described as a giant sailing ship."

"Yes, and I've sailed since I was a boy, so the comparison feels apt to me. *Oranios* is the largest spacecraft ever built, more than twenty times the size of the seventh iteration of the International Space Station. Her method of propulsion is a pair of massive particle collectors, rather like sails, that measure nearly ten square kilometers each. To reach the speeds necessary for our journey, we'll slingshot around the sun, using the sun's energy to fuel the collectors and reach one-twentieth the speed of light by the time we reach the Kuiper Belt. From that point, the ship will coast until it comes within range of Caelus, when it will flip around and use the remaining fuel to create reverse thrust. All told, the journey will take us two hundred and thirty years. Two hundred thirty years, one hundred nineteen days, and fourteen hours, to be precise."

"Quite an undertaking."

"I'd say so. But most of the technology we're using is off-the-shelf; we're just enlarging the scale. The same can't be said for life support. How do you keep eighty thousand people alive on a journey of over two centuries? That's something entirely new."

"You're referring to consciousness integration."

"That's correct."

"How is it different from other forms of stasis?"

"Well, as you know, stasis, or long-duration sleep, has been around for some time. For short periods—say, traveling to our settlement on Mars or mining operations in the asteroid belt—it works quite well. What we've discovered, though, is that somewhere between the five- and ten-year marks, problems arise. We've seen this in some of the longer missions."

"You're referring to the Neptune Probe disaster."

The on-screen Proctor nodded. "There are others, but that's the most dramatic instance. Over time, mental well-being degrades. The crew of NP1 emerged from stasis perfectly healthy but showing profound mental distress—paranoia, confusion, hallucinations, catatonia. The onboard diagnostics found no physical changes to their brains or central nervous systems, and yet all of them, to varying degrees, suffered from a range of symptoms consistent with acute schizophrenia. The crewman who blew up the ship's reactor was in the midst of a paranoid delusion that the vessel was swarming with snakes. No one could figure it out. That is, until now."

"You're saying you have."

"Yes. The problem was quite simple, actually. They ran out of dreams."

The reporter frowned. "I'm not following."

"Think about it, Sally. Every night, while you sleep, you dream. Some of these dreams are vivid, some are easily forgotten, some pleasant, some disturbing. But in all cases, three things are true. First, the mind *needs* to dream. Dreams are absolutely crucial to healthy mental function. They're a kind of workshop for the mind, helping us sort and store memories, make important connections, and process the emotional data of our lives. Second, while you're experiencing these dreams, no matter how far-fetched they seem, the mind accepts them as reality. When, for instance, you dream you're being chased by a wild tiger, you experience the same feelings of alarm you would if such an event were to occur within your waking life.

"But it's my final point that's the most crucial. To put the matter simply: What are dreams made of? And the answer is, your dreams are made of *you*. Your memories, your experiences, your obsessions, all mixed together and staged in an organized symbolic landscape constructed by the unconscious mind. They are, in that sense, purely imaginative—not in the pejorative sense of being a lesser or subordinate reality, but in a loftier sense of being works of the imagination, as a concerto or a painting or a novel is a work of the imagination. You might properly liken your dreams to works of art. In other words, your dreams are a subconscious re-sorting of your waking life, which serves as the source material.

"But what if there's no source material? Or, in the case of long-duration sleep, what if the sleeper *runs out* of source material? In just seven years, the crew of NP1 exhausted the mental resources provided by lived experience. They continued to dream, but over time these dreams became repetitive and nightmarish, a mental hell from which they couldn't escape, even when they finally emerged from stasis. The crewmember who detonated the ship's reactor had been bitten by a rattlesnake as a boy and very nearly died—a profound trauma, which his unconscious mind unleashed on him repeatedly in stasis. Imagine what it would be like if the worst things in your life were reconstituted in your dreams and you were forced to relive them over and over for years."

"That sounds . . . horrible."

"Now, enlarge the problem to the scale of interstellar travel—in our case, a voyage of over two centuries. Obviously, conventional stasis wouldn't work. It would be, in fact, a form of mental torture. What we needed was a way to give the ship's complement eight hundred years of fresh material."

The reporter frowned. "Why eight hundred? You said the trip—"

"Will take two hundred and thirty years. That's true, but dream time is different from real time. It's a good bit faster, actually, with a ratio of three-point-five-two to one. Most people believe, as we did, that dreams and waking life are temporally contiguous, with dreams perhaps a little slower. But this turns out not to be the case."

"All right, go on."

"The key was a continuous refreshment of the source material as a stimulus. The obvious solution was to build a computer-generated simulation—a virtual space that the sleepers could inhabit as they slept. This worked, but only temporarily. Upon waking, all our test subjects reported that something felt wrong."

"Wrong? In what way?"

"Wrong in that they became aware of its falsity. They didn't know *how* they knew, only that they did. The simulation was completely persuasive in every detail, but it didn't *feel* alive. That was, in fact, the expression a lot of them used. And once they knew it to be artificial, that fact was deeply distressing. Many became profoundly depressed. Life seemed meaningless, a word that many of them also used."

"Did any of them engage in antisocial behavior? After all, if nothing mattered—"

"There was some of that, yes. The test subjects were quite embarrassed by it when they emerged from stasis, but it did happen."

"So, what was the problem?"

The on-screen Proctor placed the tips of his fingers together and sat back in his chair. "Well, we didn't know. We tinkered with the simulation, but nothing seemed to make much difference. Sooner or later, all the test subjects saw through it, with the same distressing results. That was when we decided to bring Thea on board."

Another quick check of her notes. "That would be Thea Dimopolous, yes?"

"That's right. I've known the woman for years. She and I were classmates at MIT, back before the East Coast inundation. She's an absolutely brilliant computer scientist, really pressing the envelope on philosophical questions surrounding artificial intelligence, but she's also a highly accomplished painter whose work is widely shown around the world."

"I know her work. I saw her show at the new National Gallery in Columbus."

"Marvelous, isn't it? She paints these large, wonderfully expressive canvases, quite abstract but in some way not, if that makes any sense."

"I found them . . . unsettling."

"That's the word. Which is why I called her. I wanted somebody who wasn't *just* an engineer, who could see the problem in a way we hadn't thought of. She quickly agreed to fly up and take a look. I'd arranged for her to interview some of the test subjects, but she said she wanted to experience the construct for herself. When I woke her up two weeks later—a little over seven weeks for her—you know what she said? 'Nice world you got there, but it has no soul.'"

The reporter frowned. "What did she mean by that?"

"The simulation felt artificial because it *was* artificial. Persuasively rendered, and thoroughly pleasant, but dead as a doornail. As Thea put it, it was décor, not art. It was like one of those paintings you see in hotel rooms. Nice enough to look at, and they fill the space on the wall, but that's about it."

"So how do you put soul into a simulation?"

"Tell me, Sally, who's your favorite writer?"

"I beg your pardon?"

"Indulge me."

The woman smiled. "Jane Austen."

"So, let's imagine you're sitting in a chair reading *Pride and Prejudice.* It's a wonderful story, totally absorbing. You're utterly caught up in its made-up world of people and events. The lavish settings. The complex social manners. The slow-burning romance between . . ." The on-screen Proctor made a "Help me" gesture.

"Elizabeth Bennet and Mr. Darcy."

"Thanks, it's been a while. The beautiful though pigheaded Elizabeth Bennet—no relation, I'll add—and the dashing but arrogant Mr. Darcy. The book is so good, so enchanting, that while you're reading it, you completely forget where you are. Your body is sitting in your living room, you have a to-do list a mile long, you need to call the plumber and the dog needs to be walked, but none of that touches you in the moment, because your mind is someplace else. Your mind—which is to say, your perceived reality—is on a country estate in nineteenth-century England. It's not really pressing the envelope to say that you are, in fact, having a kind of very vivid waking dream. Would you agree?"

A cautious nod. "So far."

"The story proceeds. It's masterful—the characters, the plot, the setting, the thwarted passion. Surely Elizabeth and Mr. Darcy must come together in the end! And, indeed, you have every confidence they will. The story would be meaningless, and cruelly so, if they didn't. The interest you take in Austen's novel isn't so much worry over how things will work out, because some part of you already knows, but the more subtle pleasure of watching that ending unfold. Would that be fair to say?"

"I suppose."

"So, let me ask you this: What is the *source* of that enchantment? What makes the story so enthralling that while you're reading it, the so-called real world ceases to exist for you?"

The woman shrugged. "I guess it's because Jane Austen is such a good writer. A genius, in fact."

Now it was the on-screen Proctor's turn to smile. "A genius: yes, exactly. You can, in fact, feel the presence of her genius in every sentence, can you not?"

"I'd say so," replied the reporter, Sally, whom I now recalled in more detail (a son finishing up law school, a daughter in college, husband a hand surgeon, two corgis; we'd chatted over coffee).

"So, to continue the analogy, would it also be fair to say that this quality of genius is distinct? That is to say, it belongs to a single mind that presides over the world of the story?"

"Austen's, you mean."

"I do. It's her artistry that enables you to lapse into the tale, which is itself a kind of shared dream. It's created by Austen but played out in *your* mind, temporarily blotting out the physical existence of the room, which your body continues to inhabit."

"I think I see where you're going."

"Good. Tell me."

The woman hesitated. "You're saying, and I think I have this right, that Austen is the soul of *Pride and Prejudice.*"

The on-screen Proctor smiled again. "And right there you have it. That's the principle behind consciousness integration. A world without a living intelligence behind it—a soul, in other words—isn't actually a world at all. It's merely a place. The result is the emptiness and despair experienced by our test subjects. Austen's novel feels alive because it *is* alive, just as the world that you and I profess to live in is alive. It's made by a mind, not a machine, and that mind is what gives it the sense of deep order and purpose. You may not see it, but you can sense its presence, and that's what makes life not merely endurable but also worth living."

The reporter paused with a troubled expression on her face. "What you're saying, the implications—"

"Are quite large, yes."

"You're talking about God."

"That's one word. There are others."

"Are you saying you've proven he exists?"

The on-screen Proctor shrugged. "Him, her, it. I'm not a theologian, Sally. And I certainly don't claim to have proven anything of the kind. These are matters beyond proof, beyond science. What I *can* say is that the construct lacked one, which is why it didn't work. It needed to radiate from a living source."

"Living? You mean a person?"

"Correct. A single individual whose consciousness would preside over the construct. A kind of . . . local god, if you will. We call that person the 'Designer.' The minds of the sleepers aboard *Oranios,* all eighty thousand of them, will be joined in what is effectively a collective dream, with a single dreamer, the Designer, acting as the organizing mind. The ship's complement will live whole lives within this dream world, completely unaware of its falsity. Memory-suppression drugs, administered prior to their integration, will eliminate any recollection of their waking lives.

In this state, the sleepers will be born, live out their days, and be born again, over and over, for the duration of the journey."

It took the reporter a moment to digest this. "So, you're saying that the sleepers are like the readers of the dream, and the Designer is the writer."

"That's very well put. The difference is that consciousness integration is like an entire library. Once you finish one book, you simply go to the shelves and get another, reentering the dreamspace to live a whole new life."

"And you've actually done this."

The on-screen Proctor nodded. "We have."

"Will it feel like a dream? Will people be able to fly, for instance?"

"Alas, no. I agree that might be fun, but the whole point of consciousness integration is to keep the environment as realistic, as *un*-dreamlike, as possible. The dream itself, as I said, is generated by the Designer, but it's mediated by the Consciousness Integration System, or CIS, an artificial intelligence that applies preestablished controls to the dreamspace—its setting, its basic social structures, its material assets, the kind of world it generally is. In all the important ways, it will be a world just like ours, except for the fact that it exists only in the sleepers' minds. No one will fly, or find themselves taking an exam in a class they've never attended, or walking naked through a shopping mall. People will even have their actual first names, although surnames will move around of necessity through the generations."

"Will people recognize each other?"

"That's an interesting question, and we've spent some time with this. What we've seen in our trial subjects is that the dreamers, to varying degrees, can experience something rather like déjà vu. They have a tendency, for instance, to organize themselves into familiar family associations and circles of friends. They don't know why they're doing this—they simply feel more attracted to certain individuals. When we arrive at Caelus, CIS will bring these individuals into closer alignment to prepare them to exit the dreamspace—a kind of psychological off-ramp. Original surnames will find their ways to their owners. No one will notice this; it will simply occur."

"What about the children on board? Won't it confuse them, to dream they're adults?"

"You're right to ask this, and the question of children was, indeed, a concern. We originally planned to restrict the ship's complement to adults for just this reason. But as it turns out, preadolescents have very little understanding of, or interest in, adult experiences, and their dreams are only scantly retained. They'll dream whole lives just like everybody else, but when they're awakened, their minds will return to their original childlike state. The things that happened to them in stasis, if they recall them at all, will seem like some silly game of dress-ups, none of it memorable or interesting."

"And what happens if any of the ship's passengers starts to wake up prematurely?"

"They won't."

"But if they did—"

"Then the system would reinsert them into the dream."

"They'd have to die, in other words."

"In the dream, yes. Die and be reborn."

The reporter paused. "You said that CIS provided certain . . . parameters, I think it was."

"Yes, the basic features of the dreamspace are preestablished."

"By whom?"

"By me."

"So, you're the *other* god."

The on-screen Proctor gave a smile of chagrin. "I hardly think of it that way, but I do play a role, yes."

"And what exactly are those parameters?"

"That I can't tell you. First of all, the controls we've established are, of necessity, rather broad. A lot is left up to the Designer, whose intentions CIS will interpret and then manifest. Second, we don't want any of the sleepers to know what's coming in advance. Those that do seem to have a little more difficulty functioning in the dreamspace. They struggle with it."

"Struggle? How so?"

"The test subjects have described it as a kind of ennui, a restless dissatisfaction with life. It's nothing terribly dramatic, but we see no reason to put people through it. The dream should be a good one, after all."

"Eight hundred years of good dreams," Sally said with a telegenic smile. "That doesn't sound so bad."

"No, it doesn't."

"Maybe I should sign up."

"I don't know, can you farm?"

"Honestly? I can't even keep a houseplant alive. Though, come to think of it, I *did* build a pretty good birdhouse in shop class."

"Sounds promising. Shoot me your résumé and we'll have a look."

There was a pause.

"One last question."

The on-screen Proctor, back to business, nodded.

"This Designer you spoke of, the person who acts as the living mind of the dreamspace."

"Its local god, yes."

"You didn't tell me who that was."

And with that, a memory rose with full, sensory accompaniment. Candlelight. The taste of wine on my tongue. A consoling hand reaching over the table to take my own, and a soft voice saying, *The important thing, Proctor, is for you to figure out what you really want to do. Take me, for example. All I ever wanted to do was be a designer.*

"That would be the person who's the true creator of consciousness integration. My wife, Dr. Elise Bennett."

33

Callista Laird—trench-coated, umbrellaed, her hair covered by a silk scarf—descends the rain-slickened steps of Overseers Hall and makes her way across the empty plaza. The hour is just past three, though you'd hardly know it; dense clouds, disturbingly three-dimensional, create a perpetual, colorless dusk. She reaches the abandoned waterfront, cheerless in the rain, and follows the pedestrian path along the parkway. At length the wharf appears and, with it, a lone figure standing at the rail, looking out over the chunky gray water of the harbor. Past him, the ferry lies snug in its slip.

The figure doesn't notice her approach, or pretends not to. It isn't until Callista takes her place beside him that Otto stirs, though he doesn't turn to look at her, continuing to aim his gaze toward the horizon, a line more theory than fact, made vague by the weather. A black sedan, presumably his, is parked at the curb.

"Callista," he says, with a small nod. He, too, is holding an umbrella. "Thank you for coming."

"Why are we here, Otto?"

"I thought it would be good to get away for a minute. Take the air." He gestures over the railing. "One should take a moment now and then to appreciate the view, wouldn't you agree?"

"I have things to do. And I don't like standing in the rain."

Otto frowns in a distracted manner; the man's mind seems only partially present. "Very well," he says. "We're here because the situation in which we now find ourselves is . . . untenable. The Annex is spiraling out of control. The staff is on the verge of full revolt. Proctor and the others have made it out, and I'm betting they'll be back in due course. The man's not going to let this go."

"Let me handle things, Otto."

"That's my point. You *have* handled them. And now look where we are."

"She'll calm down. Warren will see to that."

"Warren I have no trouble with. It's you I'm worried about. You don't have the stomach for this. You never did."

What she doesn't have the stomach for is listening to the man. "I've given you too free a hand, Otto. I see that now. I'm ordering a pullback from the Annex."

His eyebrows arch. "And then what?"

"Find out what they want."

"They want what they've always wanted, Callista. Our heads on a pike. Proctor made damn sure of that."

"Also, you're fired."

"Yes, about that." His eyes dart past her shoulder. "Director Brandt?"

Callista turns just as she feels a stabbing pain in her neck, followed by a cold thickness as Regan presses the needle's plunger. It all happens so fast, Callista is unable to react. The umbrella falls from her hand; she stumbles backward against the rail.

"What the—"

But she cannot finish. Her head swims; her tongue moves

slowly in her mouth. Her legs go soft beneath her; she reaches for the rail but misses and then she's on all fours on the pavement.

"You don't look well, Callista," says Otto. "Perhaps we should check your number."

She can do nothing to resist as Regan moves behind her, seizes her by the collar with her one good hand, and draws her to a sitting position, propping her against the rail. Otto wrenches away the left side of Callista's trench coat and pulls up her sleeve while Regan plugs her in. The reader chimes; Regan disconnects it and passes it to Otto.

"Oof, seven percent," he says with a wince. "Not too good." He passes the device back to Regan. "Thank you, Director Brandt. You can take the car. I'll walk."

The woman returns to the vehicle and drives off. Otto reaches into his jacket pocket and produces the inevitable document. Callista can barely focus on any of it.

"I have here a Writ of Compulsory Retirement. Care to have a look?"

At last, and with considerable effort, Callista manages to speak. "Go . . . fuck yourself . . . Otto."

"Be honest, you knew this had to happen someday."

"He was . . . right about us. About . . . you."

"Right? Of course the man was *right*. Why do you think I'm doing this?"

"She's my . . . daughter."

Otto barks a high, single-noted laugh. "Good God, is that what you think? No, she isn't. You really have lost it, Callista." He crouches before her and lifts her chin to make her look at him. "I'll let you in on a little secret, Madam Chair. You won't be coming back. I severed you."

Severed. The word brings bile to her throat.

"Did you honestly think I wouldn't keep an open back door to CIS? Somebody had to."

"Please," she breathes. "Don't do this."

Otto makes a two-fingered "Come here" gesture, as if summoning a waiter to his table. A pair of watchmen appear from the wings, hoist her up, and haul her away. Otto watches as they tote her to the ferry and up the gangplank, deposit her on a bench, and step clear. The engines growl to life; the gangplank retracts; with a basso profundo blast of its horn, the ferry pulls away.

Otto returns to his office. Lots to do, but first, a call. Regan appears in his office almost at once.

"Director Brandt," he says, "how would you like to be the new minister of Public Safety?"

Her face lights up.

"You'd report only to me, of course."

"I don't know what to say. This is such an honor."

"I'm assuming I can count on your discretion about today, Director Brandt. Or should I say, 'Minister Brandt'?"

She stiffens where she stands. "Absolutely, sir. Never happened."

"I'll need you to make a few arrests. I've prepared a list."

He takes the file from his desk and hands it to her. Balancing it on her casted arm, Regan opens it and reads.

"This is the entire board."

"I'm sorry to say, evidence has come to light that they are in league with disruptive elements in the Annex."

"Evidence?"

"Incontrovertible."

For a moment they just look at each other.

"That's unfortunate," Regan says.

"Indeed. The penalty is immediate reiteration."

She closes the file and tucks it under her arm. "I'll see to it, sir."

"I'll be relocating to the chair's office directly. You can reach me there when it's done."

The woman departs. In her absence, Otto rocks back in his seat, giving himself a moment to inspect his emotions. All of this: it's been a long time coming. It was, he sees, ordained from the start—ever since the day a somewhat rumpled scientist named

Proctor Bennett strode into the boardroom at Prospera's Anchorage HQ, took his place at the podium, and told everyone they were about to die.

"Ladies and Gentlemen, I have bad news. The end is coming. For me, for you, for the entire human race. For nine trillion dollars, let me show you how you can save yourselves."

The lights dimmed. On the screen behind him, an image appeared—majestic, visionary.

"This," he said, "is humanity's lifeboat. This is *Oranios.*"

Well, that was certainly a showstopper. But: nine trillion dollars! (The eventual cost, soup to nuts, was more like twelve.) You could run an entire country, and not a small one, on a figure like that. Yet Bennett had found the money. Watching the man operate—in boardrooms and penthouses, in the backseats of limos and the sleek salons of private jets—Otto could only think how Bennett had missed his true calling, selling life and casualty. Which was, in fact, more or less what the man was doing. Maybe the planet was dying and maybe it wasn't. (Though let's be honest: it was.) Opinions could differ, but for the select few, those with the accumulated contents of the world's treasure stashed in numbered accounts from the Caymans to Hong Kong, didn't it make sense to tuck some aside for the ultimate plan B? If only for one's peace of mind? Could you even put a price on something like that? (Answer: Yes, you could. A billion dollars.) And what if, along the way, these lucky individuals could go on living just as they had, and do it for, let's say, another eight hundred years? The ultimate first-class ticket, while the unwashed masses rode in coach?

Sound of gavel banging. Sold.

But who, in the end, was passenger, who cargo? Otto had his suspicions from the start, but it wasn't until Singh brought him out of stasis that he realized what Proctor was really up to. The man had given the investors exactly what they'd asked for, which was precisely enough rope to hang themselves with.

Well, time for a new dream, Otto thinks. This one has pretty much worn out its welcome.

The sky outside his windows has darkened, the rain returned in earnest. He picks up the phone.

"Campbell."

"What's the situation in the Annex?"

"All our assets are in position." A pause. "What's the plan, exactly?"

"The plan is for everybody to follow orders. Continue with the roundups and interrogations."

"You mean arrest just . . . anyone?"

"Somebody knows something. I need these people found. And bring the car around."

"Where are we going?"

"A little drive in the country."

The call finished, Otto logs onto CIS. He enters through the back door and calls up the ship's manifest. The board was just the start; it's time to properly clean house.

He begins to type.

Name after name after name.

The best thing about blindness, Pappi thinks, is that darkness doesn't frighten you.

In the chaos, something happened: a small mistake, a wrong turn, then another and another, and he was all alone. He heard their voices calling his name, tried to follow, failed. The voices dimmed and were gone. The smell grew worse; he was deep in the sewers. He heard, then felt, the presence of rats, their soft weight brushing his ankles. In the pitch-black darkness he cannot see, he's wandered for hours and hours, one hand scraping the wall, the other searching the air before him.

Then, a miracle: his fingers latch upon a ladder in the wall. With slow care, he climbs to the top, hooks his left elbow into a rung, and raises his right hand until he feels the grate. Rain is falling through the slats, soaking his face and hair. He pushes as hard as he can, but the grate won't budge.

"Hey!" he yells. He bangs the grate. "Over here! I'm trapped!"

He repeats his plea over and over. He's on the verge of abandoning hope when he hears a voice.

"What are you doing down there?"

The voice is a boy's. "Never mind that. Can you lift the grate?"

A moment of struggle follows. "It's stuck."

"Find something to use as a lever."

"Don't you know what's going on? We shouldn't be here—"

"You can't leave me like this. Please."

The boy moves away. Has Pappi been abandoned? He's been clinging to the ladder too long; his balance is nearly gone. He's not sure he could even make it back down safely. But then he hears a clang as the boy wedges a lever under the lip of the grate. With a slow groan, it comes free; the boy slides it back. He extends a hand and helps Pappi up.

"Your hand's bleeding," the boy says.

Probably it is.

"Mister, we need to get out of here."

"Where's here?"

But he's alone; the boy is already gone, a puff of smoke. The rain is pouring down. Pappi picks a direction. He walks five steps, and his hands meet mortared brick. Now, which way? He stills himself to listen, and what he hears is a wave of aural chaos—shouts, cries, human movement en masse. Something is happening, something large. He feels his way along the wall until he reaches the end, where his sense of space enlarges. A man brushes past him, nearly knocking him over.

"Please, can you tell me—"

"Come on, come on!" a woman says.

"I'm trying!" a child whines.

"We have to hurry!"

More people brush by. Pappi feels completely spun around. He thinks the crowd is moving one way, then the opposite, then both directions simultaneously. He pleads for help but no one answers. Somebody crashes into him from behind, knocking him to the ground.

"Watch where you're going!"

The man keeps moving. To be old is to be forgotten; Pappi is a being of no consequence to anyone. The world races by, a roaring river of humanity, and yet he is apart from it; it is a club in which he's no longer a member. Simultaneously, he becomes aware that the situation has altered. The tide of the crowd has reversed. People are yelling, crying out, screaming incomprehensible words. Somebody grabs him by the arm and hauls him up.

"What's the matter, old man? You need to get out of here!"

The man shoves him forward. Pappi hears a different kind of footfall: the synchronized concussions of an advancing force. He stumbles blindly forward. He falls twice more, each time rising and somehow pressing on. From up ahead comes the sound of chanting.

"Arrival come! Arrival come! Arrival come!"

The crowd thickens; bodies jostle against him, propelling him forward.

"Pappi!"

Who's there?

"Pappi, stay where you are! I'll come to you!"

It's Mother. Pappi tries to stand his ground, but it's no use; the current keeps nudging him forward.

"Arrival come!" the crowd chants. *"Arrival come! Arrival come!"*

"Take my hand!"

"Where are you?"

"On your right! Take it!"

But he can't; he can't so much as raise his arm.

"Pappi!"

Her voice grows fainter, subsumed in the chants of the crowd.

They are being corralled on all sides by the advancing lines of the watchmen. He can barely breathe, so intense is the crush. The mob suddenly surges forward, and Pappi feels his feet lift off the pavement. He's levitating, unbound from the earth, and then down he goes, swallowed by a wave of bodies.

"Arrival come!"

Fists pump the air.

"Arrival come!"

"Arrival come!"

34

"I'll start with the good news," Quinn said.

The four of us were seated in the executive conference room. Six hours had passed since our deintegration.

"First of all, we haven't lost many people. Of the total ship's complement of investors and colonists, the cabinet failure rate is less than three percent, which is pretty consistent with our predictions, and remarkable under the circumstances, which I'll get to. With a few minor glitches, all of the ship's systems are nominal, and the landing boats are powered and ready to go."

"Okay, what else?" I asked.

Quinn shrugged. "That's it in the good-news department, I'm afraid."

Thea leaned over the table. "That's *all*?"

"I'll move on to the so-so stuff, beginning with the planet's surface. It's kind of a mixed bag. Probes dropped successfully after we entered orbit. We lost two, but the other eight completed their descents. The atmosphere is fine, a little oxygen rich but nothing that's a problem. The planet completes one rotation every twenty-seven hours, which will take some getting used to, but everyone should be able to adapt. Surface gravity registers at .86 g, a hair under our calculations, which explains the two lost probes."

"What's so-so about that?" I said. "It all sounds pretty promising."

"Well, it turns out the place is cold. Like, *really* cold. Mean global temperature is forty-four degrees Fahrenheit, about the same as it was during Earth's most recent ice age. Glaciation extends all the way from the poles in both hemispheres to the twentieth parallels north and south."

"But it looks so blue," Thea said. "How can that be?"

"That's because the ice is so compacted. You see that in some types of glacier ice. Not enough air bubbles to refract the light, so it's passing undisturbed through the surface, which absorbs most of the light at the red end of the spectrum. Because it's blue, it looks like liquid water, but it ain't."

I asked, "Is there *any place* we can put down?"

"I was getting to that. System, call up probe images one-six-three through one-seven-nine."

The screen appeared over the table, with seventeen boxed images. Quinn moved briskly through them, waving his hand to enlarge and shrink them as necessary.

"Caelus is 88.7 percent ocean, more or less as expected. There are three major landmasses, one at the southern pole, one in the southern hemisphere, and one in the northern hemisphere. The first two are totally glaciated, but the third"—he spread his fingers to enlarge the image—"extends nearly all the way to the equator, about seven degrees north. The southern third, more or less, is ice-free. The terrain is mostly alpine forest, pretty consistent with the climate, with areas of sparser growth—lichen, mosses, that sort of thing. It's rugged, with a lot of glacial moraine at the northern tier, but we won't freeze to death."

"Just how cold is it?"

"I'd pack a sweater," Quinn said. "Think Finland."

"What about vegetation?" This was Antone—the street kid of

the Annex who was, in actuality, a thirty-three-year-old soil biologist. "Can we grow anything?"

"I'll send you over the sample data, but the short answer is yes. As for animal life, the data is a bit more sparse. We've got some small ground mammals, or at least they're mammal-like, a kind of cross between a rat and a chipmunk, and something antlered, like an elk or deer, that moves in large herds. There's obviously more, we just haven't seen it."

Thea said, "So, no intelligent life."

"The answer to that isn't quite so straightforward."

"Oh?"

"System, show drone footage one-eight-seven-zero, minute three twenty-four."

The boxes on the screen were replaced by a single, moving image: a rocky shoreline, huge waves crashing and foaming, with chalky cliffs rising in a white wall above.

Quinn said, "This is taken from probe seven's drone, which was launched shortly after touchdown on the continent's southeast coast. Just watch."

The drone, which had been skating along the face of the cliff, came to a halt, then descended vertically to just a few feet above the waves.

"Why did it stop?" Antone asked.

"Because it's programmed to look for certain things."

"Like what?"

"Straight lines."

"Why that?"

"Because nature doesn't *do* straight lines."

There was a shape under the water—long, rectangular, though at one end curving to a point. "What is that?" I said, leaning in. "It looks like—"

"Yeah, the hull of a ship," Quinn said. "It did to me, too. Hang on, the real show's about to start."

The drone lingered another few seconds before ascending and resuming its course along the cliff. Something was odd about the rocks along the shoreline. Scattered among them were strange, twisted shapes, like grasping hands. The room was dead silent; everybody's eyes were locked on the screen. The debris on the shoreline continued to accumulate, forming a tangled barrier against the base of the cliff, which had begun to curve northward while simultaneously declining. Ahead I saw a place where the cliff came to an abrupt end, opening onto some kind of cove.

Not a cove.

A harbor.

The drone swept in low over the water, which was filled with rusted hulks cantilevered above the surface. So dense was the wreckage that it was difficult to tell where the water ended and the land began—for there, too, filling the shoreline in great, tangled drifts, were the remains of what I took to be a once-great city. The drone popped skyward again, widening the view of the destruction: toppled towers, strange domed structures smashed to pieces, vast debris fields, which stretched for many miles inland.

"All the drones found something similar," Quinn said. "In toto, they located thirty-six cities in roughly the same condition, about half along the coast, half inland. They're connected by what appear to be roads, as well as trenches that might once have been waterways."

Thea broke her eyes from the screen and turned to Quinn. "Who were they?"

"Caelusians, I guess. We won't know more until we're on the ground. And even then, it doesn't look like there's much left. We might find remains, we might not."

It was heartbreaking. Here was incontrovertible proof of other intelligent life in the universe, but we'd arrived too late.

Quinn said, "I have a theory, if you want to hear it."

His tone was unsettling. "Do I?"

"Couple things. First," he said, lifting his chin smartly at the screen, "look closely at the center of the wreckage. What do you see?"

I did as he said. A shape emerged: a depression in the land.

"An impact crater?"

"Or a detonation. Every city has at least one depression like that, sometimes a lot more. That's the first item. Item two is the background radiation. Nothing especially dangerous, but it's higher than it should be, about one-point-five millirems per hour on average across the areas we've scanned, with hot spots, like this one, where it's as high as three-point-oh."

"You're talking about a nuclear exchange."

"We got through our own nuclear era. It still kind of amazes me that we managed not to blow ourselves to bits. Maybe the Caelusians didn't."

"And the ice—"

"Nuclear winter. All the debris in the air blocks the sunlight, putting the climate into a feedback loop. The planet surface gets colder and colder until whoever's left starves to death. Looking at the moraine patterns, I'd say the ice is only now beginning to retreat."

"You're saying the Caelusians did this to themselves. Like us."

Quinn nodded. "Different means, but yes. They fucked it all up. Just like us."

The four of us sat in silence for a time.

"Have the drones isolated a settlement site?" I asked.

"Not so far."

"So, let's get them in the air again."

"They lost power."

"Why would they lose power? Don't they just return to their stations and recharge?"

"The stations are all dead, too."

This made no sense. "*All* of them? How can that be?"

"Yeah, well," the man said, his voice suddenly careful, "I was coming to that. It seems that we didn't just . . . arrive. We've been parked in orbit for a while."

I felt a sinking in my gut. "Just how long are we talking about?"

He took a long breath. "A hundred and thirty-seven years, two hundred ninety-nine days."

It was Warren who had done it.

Warren Singh, chief medical officer, whose job it was to awaken first, in order to ascertain the health and safety of the executive staff and supervise our deintegration. All of which he'd done.

Whereupon, seventy-nine hours later, he'd left us just as we were and reinserted himself into the dream.

I think of the man during those three and a half days. How alone he must have felt, how unsettled and disturbed, to find himself shot from a dream of paradise to this arid container floating high above a frozen sea. I'd known the man for years; I counted him among the dearest of friends. In the physical world, he was much the same as the Warren of the dreamspace—confident and cool, with a cheerful, easygoing manner and a great vigor for life. Had he paced the halls, muttering oaths against his fate? Gazing down on the icy sphere below, had he cursed its very name? And how could I blame the man if he had? For never was a world more aptly suited to Dr. Warren Singh than the world of Prospera: its mild days and soft, tropical nights; its easy society and boundless enjoyments; its effortless romance and rapturous collisions in the dark. How could such a man, facing life on a frigid tundra, fail to consider other options?

But I'm being too kind. The man was a coward.

What I can say for certain is that twenty-eight hours after his deintegration, my old friend Warren Singh made a decision: the decision not to decide. This burden he left to others, higher on the food chain: Callista Laird and Otto Winspear, whom Warren subsequently awakened. Their shock and dismay were no doubt as great as his own, and not merely because of the planet's harsh conditions. Callista and Otto were many things, but they were no fools. Two days later, the three of them reintegrated themselves, but not before installing a constantly randomizing passcode on the system, thus preventing us from waking up anyone else, colonist or investor. We were totally locked out.

"What about waking people up from inside, using the back door?" Thea asked.

Quinn shook his head. "You remember how I couldn't get past that firewall? Same problem. I was totally wasting my time."

"So how is it that the four of us are awake?"

Quinn thought a moment. "In Proctor's case, I'd say he's been trying to wake up for a while. That's what the echoes were all about. It's why Warren and the others were in such a hot hurry to send you back to the Nursery."

"Which means the three of them *didn't* take the memory suppressors when they reintegrated. They remember what they did."

"That's not all," Quinn said. "Without the suppressors, they'd be static entities inside the dreamspace."

"Meaning?"

"They don't age. They're exactly the same as the day they went back in, a hundred and thirty-seven years ago, real time. They never have to reiterate."

Thea said, "None of this explains how the four of us got out."

"No," Quinn said, "but it's a clue. The dreamspace isn't infinite. It extends only as far as a single mind can hold."

"Elise's, you mean," Thea said.

Quinn nodded. "This is all a little theoretical, since we've never tested it. But I'd say we crossed the outer limit of the construct, a kind of border between dreamspace and real space. That triggered CIS to put us in the antechamber."

"So, there *is* a way to wake people up from the inside."

"In theory, sure. You want to convince eighty thousand people to hold hands and sail off the edge of the world? Sounds like a pretty hard sell."

Thea said, "There has to be something we can do."

"Trust me, I'm all ears. But that's not the only problem on our hands." Quinn turned to Antone. "Tell me something. How much of the dream do you remember?"

It was, I confess, still difficult for me to reconcile the smart-alecky street urchin I'd met in the Annex with the grown man sitting across from me. "Not much," he replied. "It's still kind of jumbled."

"But less so as time goes by."

He nodded. "I'd say so."

"Can you give us a minute, please?"

"You mean, you want me to leave?"

"Why don't you head down to the lab? I'll send the soil data over for you to have a look."

Antone glanced at me, then at Thea, and back at Quinn. "Right," he said, rising from his chair. "I'll be in the lab if you need me."

"Thank you, Antone."

He exited the room.

"Proctor," Quinn said the moment the door closed, "what the *fuck*."

I'd seen this coming, of course. "Say what's on your mind."

"All right, I will. You know what's going to happen in the next few hours? That nice soil biologist who wouldn't hurt a fly is going to think: I will *kill* those motherfuckers. All the test subjects remembered the dream, Proctor. *All* of them. Some sooner, some later, but the result was the same. What do you think's going to happen if we actually manage to wake the colonists up? They'll tear the investors to pieces."

"Let's cross that bridge when we come to it."

"Let's cross it now. You're the one who set the parameters. Eight hundred years of good dreams, wasn't it?"

"That's what the board asked for."

"So tell me, how do you get a police state out of that? The colonists living in squalor, while the rest of us played tennis and ate canapés off a fucking tray?"

"I can't explain it."

"I think you can. You just don't want to say it."

"I honestly don't know what you're talking about."

From across the table, Quinn and Thea exchanged a cautious glance.

"For Christ's sake," I said, "the two of you, out with it."

Thea leaned forward over the table to meet my eye. "I know you don't want to, Proctor, but we have to consider Elise's role in this. We all remember how she was."

"She was upset. We both were. We'd lost our *daughter*."

"I know this is painful—"

"It's not painful, it's irrelevant. It's Warren we should be talking about."

"The Nursery. The monitors. The faxes and drones. How do you explain them?"

"So, CIS interpreted the parameters." I was only too aware of how defensive I sounded. "A little freely, okay, I admit that."

"Not this freely," Thea said. "It takes its cues from the Designer."

I looked at the both of them. "Are you saying Elise is responsible for this?"

"Think about it, Proctor. A life without pain, without sadness, without even death. A world where people could forget all their troubles. A world without . . . children."

I rose from the table. "I can't listen to another minute of this."

"Proctor—"

"Let him go," said Quinn.

And that was what I did.

I retired to my quarters. I had yet to visit the stasis cabinets, knowing what awaited me there. For a while I dozed, but my mind seemed unable to penetrate the border between the sleeping and the waking worlds. I had been asleep for three hundred sixty-six years, so perhaps that was the reason. I wondered if I'd ever really sleep again.

Eventually I gave up trying and rode the lift down to the main body of the ship. I wandered the halls, wondering about Prospera, and what might be happening there now. Had our escape been noted? If it had, what would the consequences be for the people we'd left behind?

And my thoughts turned, as I knew they would, to Elise: not the Elise of the dreamspace, now alone in the country with Warren, but the *real* Elise: the Elise who'd swept into my life and changed everything.

In the dreamspace, we'd met at a party; in real life, it was much the same. Not some grand occasion in a ballroom but a small dinner hosted by a mutual friend, where Elise and I were seated together. I had just begun my association with Prospera Corp., working from their satellite campus in Berkeley; Elise had just completed her postdoc at Stanford in neurophysiology. The subject of our conversation was dreams—not just in the general sense of the things one hoped for in life, but the psychological mechanisms that shaped these thoughts into a symbolic landscape. (I was beset by nightmares of various coming catastrophes that only I knew about; when I tried to tell people, they ignored me. Elise dreamed often of being lost at sea, though experiencing no fear.) When dinner ended, we moved to the couch, where we continued to talk, long into the night. We were so absorbed that we failed to notice that our host had gone to bed—a marvelous joke we told, and that our friends told, for years afterward. How clever she was, how smart and funny and kind. There was within her a kind of incandescence, a life force, that I had never felt in another person. My enchantment was total; in my mind, I'd started to build a future with her right then, a future I wanted never to end.

And I thought, too, of the Elise I'd known after Caeli died. The Elise of those terrible months, which stretched into a terrible year; the grieving Elise, silent and inconsolable, the one who went so far into herself that I couldn't reach her, no matter how hard I tried. The one who went away and never came back, leaving me alone.

After the storm, we had departed our house immediately. To

dwell in the same place where our daughter had died—to see, every day, the ghost of her: the thought was unbearable. First a hotel, and when that proved too small for two ruined souls, Callista and Julian's guesthouse, which, in the storm, had somehow been spared. (The world was on the brink of disaster, but for people like Callista and Julian, with the resources to insulate themselves, the worst had yet to happen.) The guesthouse was quite lavish, with enough space for the two of us to avoid each other almost entirely. Outside our windows were riotous gardens, tweezed to perfection. (There was, thank God, no pool.) For hours, Elise walked their manicured paths, floating among the hedges, the prize-winning roses, the drooping, flowered trees. Seen from the window, her figure appeared almost intangible, as if the sheer magnitude of her grief had dispersed her corporeal form into a cloud of atoms. She was unable even to look at me, to acknowledge my existence; of Caeli, she spoke not a word, not even her name. For hours I would watch her from inside the house, thinking: *Where are you, where have you gone? You have only to tell me, and I will go there, too.*

I was a wreck, but of a different sort. With absolute absorption, I hurled myself headlong into my work, making our final preparations for departure. That our daughter would not be with us only magnified my obsessiveness and, with it, a terrible sense of foreboding. This premonition proved correct, and fell upon the world with astonishing swiftness. With such abrupt totality did humanity receive its final notice of eviction, there was barely time for the great minds of the era to reflect on our demise. The informational superstructure that bound us as a species—that linked Peoria to Palau, Boise to Bangkok—failed virtually overnight; this was followed in short order by the economy, the food supply, energy, transportation, common currency, and anything that might loosely be called a government. The world's militaries dissolved into their heavily armed parts; as nature bared its claws, humanity set upon itself like dogs snapping over a scrap of gristly meat. All went, in a word, dark, and did so virtually overnight.

Oranios, already built and awaiting us in high orbit, was secure from all catastrophe, careening around the planet and bearing silent witness to those terrible weeks of storm and starvation, fire and flood, disorder and death. The days leading to departure unfolded in a swirl of chaos as we rushed to launch the shuttles that would bear us to safety. We'd imagined that we'd have far more time to accomplish this; the process was meant to be deliberate, giving people the time to close out their affairs and make ready. Most of the investors weren't even on-site but needed to be retrieved—a complicated, time-consuming, and dangerous task, as by now the atmosphere—that thin, life-giving envelope—was in full, furious revolt.

Then the mobs arrived.

Project Oranios was no secret; it had long been a subject of public interest. We'd been forced to turn away thousands of volunteers—those who, like us, had heard the whistle of cataclysm's train barreling toward us. But in the main, media coverage had been skeptical; our endeavor was portrayed as a colossal waste of money by a handful of preening billionaires and alarmist cranks.

That sentiment now became a thing of the past. Prospera's Anchorage campus was separate from the shuttle launch site, which was a hundred miles north in Talkeetna, reachable only by river and a solitary road. Both facilities were protected by fencing and armed security, but they were hardly fortresses, unprepared for the horde of desperate humanity that descended upon us. They pressed against the fencing like cattle in a pen—yelling, screaming, pleading for their lives. They held up their children; they offered the most intimate acts; they waved fistfuls of valueless cash. A rain of ashes fell upon them; virtually the entire continent west of the Mississippi was in flames, an ever-advancing wall of fire marching toward the Atlantic, consuming everything in its path.

The last of us evacuated by air to the launch site just as the fences were breached and the first shots fired on both sides. With me in the lifter were Elise, Warren, Thea, and Oona, my chief of staff. We circled low over the campus, turned north, and followed the highway inland. The air was thick with smoke. Nobody was talking; strong winds buffeted the aircraft. Below I saw not a highway but a pulsing artery of humanity, everyone headed the same direction we were.

Elise's emotional distress had, in the months after our daughter's death, been subject to lengthy interrogation. The general feeling was that her mental state was now too precarious for her to serve as Designer. Our search for a suitable replacement (and Elise knew nothing of this) had led us to conclude that I should serve in her stead. But CIS was keyed to Elise; we would have to rewrite miles of code. Six months at least, perhaps as long as a year. It was time we suddenly didn't have.

Perhaps I should have told Elise about our plan; I'm not sure why I didn't. Lifting this burden from her might have lessened her distress. In any case, it was easy enough to conceal what we were doing. She barely spoke to me, and when she did, it was always a terse exchange on some entirely practical matter. We'd remained in the guesthouse, lacking the wherewithal to find a place of our own; I took to sleeping many nights on the couch in my office, telling myself this was a matter of convenience—I was working day and night—though the reality was starker: I simply didn't want to deal with the problem, or my wife, anymore. I was lonely; I was sad; my thoughts were the blackest imaginable. And yet when I sought her out—the one person who I believed could understand my feelings, having suffered an identical loss—I met only empty stares and silence.

I bring this up not as justification for what occurred, but simply to establish the context. What happened between Thea and me was the source of tremendous guilt, and that guilt was what prevented us from repeating the encounter. But guilt is not the same thing as wishing I hadn't done it. If anything, it saved me.

A night in June, mere weeks before everything came crashing down. Thea and I were alone in the office; Quinn had gone home. This was nothing new, though the feeling of it had changed. In

Elise's absence, I had come to rely on Thea more and more for the kind of emotional sustenance one usually takes from a spouse, and of course there was a history—a history of first, passionate love. We'd been graduate students back then, young and poor and full of life; our relationship, which lasted three years, transpired in a haze of youthful ardor and bohemian charm. Our apartment, in a dilapidated triple-decker near the MIT campus, was one part computer lab, one part art gallery (even many years later, the smell of oil paint always propelled my mind back to those enchanted days), and one hundred percent bedroom. I couldn't believe how happy, how lucky, I was.

Our affair hadn't lasted. Such things rarely do, their ends built into their beginnings. No one thing caused its collapse. Our separate ambitions, the time-consuming intensity of our work, our divergent temperaments and only half-formed sense of ourselves: each played its role. Cracks appeared, then more cracks, until one day we found ourselves standing on the sidewalk beside the open trunk of her car, both of us in tears.

Moving in overlapping professional circles, we'd kept in touch through the years, and over time, the forces that had driven us apart seemed small in comparison to the warm memory of our time together. That Thea had never married (she'd come close, she said, but never pulled the trigger) did not strike me as all that strange; her work, both as a theoretical computer scientist and as an artist of growing reputation, was always her first priority. (This was, in fact, one of the reasons we'd separated.) In other words, we'd grown to be friends, though of a certain kind: friends whose interactions always contained a squeak of remembered intimacy, of the closeness we'd shared at a formative juncture of our lives.

Sometime around two A.M., cross-eyed with exhaustion, the two of us went up to the roof for a breath of air. In southern Alaska, the June sun never quite sets; it skates flirtatiously along the horizon, casting a penumbral glow that was now augmented by the haze from the great fires that had already begun to consume the American West. For a while, five or ten minutes, Thea and I stood at the parapet, our faces aimed toward the waters of Cook Inlet and the shadowed mountains to the west. One of them, Mount Susitna, is also known as "the Sleeping Lady"; its curled shape unmistakably resembles a body at rest. My eyes were drawn to her that night, and the longer I looked, the more I was consumed by the pathos of it, this body frozen for eternity. The feeling consumed me so completely that I began to weep, then sob, my body shaking, racked with grief.

I had wept for Caeli many times. I had wept for my wife, now so unreachable she'd become a stranger to me. This was different. The tears came from a place so abyssal I knew I was grieving for something else. I was grieving for everything. The whole sad, doomed lot of us, and a world that could no longer love us, because we had not loved it.

And Thea: I realized that she'd taken me into her arms. She was weeping, too. No words passed between us, only the feeling of the moment: the memory of the people we'd once been, so alive and full of hope, and the life together that we'd chosen not to live. She kissed me then, or I kissed her; the distinction was meaningless. We weren't kissing but falling, back in time.

The rest was inevitable.

It was barely two weeks later that we found ourselves in the lifter, racing north. To our left, the river; below us, mortality's tide, its last, desperate army following the highway. The ashes thickened, whirling past the windows like blackened snow. The roar of the engines made talking impossible, but what was there to say? Elise was leaning against me, her body wilted. Across the aisle, Thea shot me a cautionary look, and I knew that both of us were thinking the same thing: What will it be like, to live for centuries inside a broken woman's dreams?

We were nearing the launch site as two of the remaining shuttles to *Oranios* took flight. Bullet-shaped, with gleaming steel skins, they rocketed skyward atop cones of orange flame. A sea of people, hundreds of yards deep, ringed the compound. Quinn met us when we disembarked. The perimeter was about to fall, he said. There was no time to waste; we needed to get aboard the last shuttle now.

What had been meant to be a solemn departure turned into a mad dash; there was no time to reflect on its significance. We were not humanity's first interstellar voyagers but common refugees, running for our lives. We piled into a cargo truck and sped toward the launch site. Gunfire erupted behind us, a series of quick pops; security had been overwhelmed, steamrollered by the crowd. That, or they had joined with them. We skidded to a halt at the base of the gantry. The crowd was closing fast. Pounding footsteps, voices, screams, more shots. Bullets whizzed overhead, pinging off the fuselage. Did they mean to kill us all? The shuttle, fully powered, was a flying bomb. I was shielding Elise with my body to make a run for the elevator when she suddenly pushed me away.

"No!"

"Elise, what are you doing?"

Her face was stricken with horror. "I'm not leaving her!"

She dashed away. I took three long strides, grabbed her around the waist, and pulled her to the ground.

"Goddamn you!" She was thrashing, clawing, fighting me like a wild animal. "Let me go!"

Warren slung his pack to the tarmac and rustled through it. Out came the needle and vial.

"I can't leave her!" Elise wailed. "Don't make me!"

I held her down as Warren drew aside the waistband of her pants and inserted the needle into the pale flesh beneath. Before the plunger had even reached the bottom, I felt her body slacken. The crowd was close enough now that I could make out individual faces—twisted, terrified, deranged. An immense, woolly-bearded man, like some great forest creature, with a rifle slung over his shoulder and a toddler bouncing in his arms. A woman running beside a leashed dog, some kind of hound, her gray hair flowing behind her from beneath an orange stocking cap. A boy and a girl, teenagers, holding hands as they sprinted toward us, yelling for us to wait, to save them.

I lifted Elise into my arms and raced to the elevator car. Quinn slammed the gate closed as the first of the pursuing mob arrived. They hurled themselves against the wires, shoving desperate fingers through the openings. More shots; bullets were ricocheting off the gantry's struts. Someone—it might have been me—pushed the button; we began to ascend. Ten feet, twenty, thirty. One of the teenagers, the boy, was still holding on to the wires. Our eyes met in a heartbreaking flash.

"Please," he said, and fell away.

We continued our ascent, but not fast enough; our pursuers had found the stairs. They scurried up the launch tower like an army of crazed ants. We'd reach the top first but not by much. Some in the crowd had turned their fury on the shuttle itself, pounding its gleaming flanks with bullets, as if this would somehow save them. We reached the access arm, piled through the hatch, and sealed it behind us, just seconds ahead of the mob. Everyone took their seats while I strapped Elise in. Her eyes were barely open, the lids fluttering like tiny wings.

"I can't leave her," she murmured. Her face was streaked with tears, her hair dusted with ash. "Please don't make me leave her . . ."

I scurried up the ladder to the cockpit, where Jason sat at the controls. Behind us, the passenger compartment rotated into position for launch. "Take off," I told him. "Do it now."

His face was horrified. "What about those people? They'll be incinerated."

"There's nothing we can do. Fire the engines or I will."

It would be quick for them, I told myself. A thunderous crack, and a wave of fire, and then nothing at all. It would be, almost, a mercy.

The engines ignited; I was thrust back into my seat. The moment of departure, indelible. We were leaving our planet, our lives, all that we had known. The shuttle had cleared the tower; we vaulted skyward, away from the great blue cradle of our race. *Goodbye, Caeli,* I thought, and closed my eyes. *Goodbye, my daughter, my truest heart, your body gone under the earth.* Seconds passed, then minutes, time indistinguishable, obliterated by the rocket's roar. The accelerating energy of the engines flowed through me like a tide of molten lead. Higher and higher we soared, the cabin shuddering, my senses blasted with sound, and only when the engines stopped, and I felt my body rising weightlessly against the belts, did I open my eyes again, this time upon the darkness and the stars.

Eventually, I gathered my courage and made my way to the stasis cabinets. The command crew was housed separately, in a small chamber not far from the dome. The cabinets were arranged in a line, like coffins in a crypt. The first three were empty, their lids open, interiors drained; these were the ones where Thea, Quinn, and I had slept. Next came my brother, Malcolm (for a second or two, I thought of him as not my brother but my father, and, in truth, he being the older by twelve years, our relationship had always possessed that quality); then Jason, the naval aviator turned aeronautical engineer, endlessly eager, with a sweet, earnest nature. The loyal, can-do Oona, my faithful adjutant. Warren, betrayer of us all. I walked down the aisle, pausing before each, though I could not see their faces; the viewing windows were coated with frost.

I came to Elise's. With the tips of my fingers, I wiped the frost away. The cryogenic fluid was not opaque, though neither was it wholly clear. It possessed a gelatinous density, with a sepia color, like the tint of an old photograph. It was through this frigid, yellow-brown murk that I beheld my wife's face—her *actual* face—for the first time in nearly four centuries. How still it was, how lacking in life! But this was an illusion, I knew. Inside the holy mystery of her mind, an entire world unfolded: a world of city and country, land and sea; of work and rest, sadness and joy; of sleeping and eating and fighting and fucking; of roses and teacups and bicycles and baby shoes; of time and matter and light. Over this vast entanglement she presided, dreaming her dream like a god at rest.

The last cabinet I came to was unoccupied; it had been intended for Caeli. But, strangely, it wasn't her I thought of. Instead, I thought of the boy who'd clung to the elevator on the day of our escape from Earth. What harm would it have done to reach out and haul him inside—to save this one arbitrary soul? But it had all happened so fast, and now he was dead. He'd been dead for nearly four hundred years. It might just as well have been forever and, eventually, would be.

My thoughts were interrupted by the feeling of a presence in the room. I turned to see Thea watching me from the floor, her ankles crossed and her back braced against the bulkhead.

"Sorry," she said with a wince. "I should have said something when you came in."

"I guess you couldn't sleep either, huh?"

"Yeah, you could say I'm pretty much slept out."

I took a place beside her on the floor.

"How'd she look?" Thea asked after a minute.

"The same, I guess."

"It's kind of weird to think that we've all been living inside her head."

"I know what you mean."

Thea sighed. "You know what really pisses me off?" She held up a thumb and forefinger. "I came about *this* close to sleeping with that asshole."

"Are you talking about . . . Warren?"

"Who else? The man was a total tomcat. Believe me, it wasn't anything serious. We were both pretty drunk at the time."

This was all news to me. "I don't know what to say."

"You could start with 'My condolences.' I kind of blame you for the whole thing, actually."

"How is your sleeping with Warren my fault?"

"*Almost* sleeping with him. There's a difference. And it's your fault because it happened the night of the party at your house. A party like that—I mean, everybody's going to end up in bed with *somebody.* It's like a law of nature." She stopped short, a look of sudden horror on her face. "Oh, God, Proctor. I'm sorry."

"It's okay," I said. "Forget it."

"No, that was really stupid of me. I shouldn't have brought it up."

"I told you to forget it, didn't I?" I tapped her side with my elbow. "And you're right. It *was* a pretty good party."

She gave a quiet laugh. "Do you remember when Jason pushed Warren into the pool?"

I smiled at the memory. "He wasn't too happy about it."

"The look on his face. And what in God's name was Nabil wearing?"

"I think it was some kind of jumpsuit."

"Honestly, I have no idea how the man could even breathe. He looked like a dick in a condom in that thing. And Otto's cigars—"

"The worst."

"And that bitch Regan. God," Thea moaned, "I couldn't stand that woman. She sure can dance, though. I have to give her that."

I couldn't place this. "Are we talking about the same Regan?"

"Are you kidding? The woman's a regular Ginger Rogers. Like, a kinky Ginger Rogers. Ginger Rogers if Ginger Rogers went to stripper school. She put on quite a show."

"I guess I missed it somehow."

"You'd be the only one who did."

A comfortable silence fell. For the first time since deintegration, I felt my spirits lift a little. Our situation was dire, but for the moment, it was good to sit with a friend, to revisit these old things, to turn my thoughts to better times.

"Want to know something strange?" I said.

"If you want to tell me."

"I was just thinking about Caeli. Not the real one, the one in the dreamspace. She didn't turn out at all how I thought she would. As a teenager, I mean."

"No? How was she different?"

"A lot more . . . willful, I guess would be the word. Don't get me wrong—she could be pretty stubborn. She always had an independent streak, and I liked that about her. But it was the sweetness in her that always got to me. Elise and I butted heads over it a lot, actually. She thought I was going to spoil her rotten. She always said, Lookout, bub, that girl's going to be a handful."

"Maybe she was jealous."

The notion was strange. "What on earth would she be jealous of?"

"Just how easy it was for you."

"Trust me, it was never easy. It's no picnic being a parent."

"That's just the surface stuff. I saw how you were with her, Proctor. I've never seen anybody love another person the way you loved her, with your whole soul. It's a rare and wonderful thing, to be loved like that. Not everybody gets it. Caeli did.She knew it, too."

"I hope that's true."

"I *know* it's true. Want to know something else? None of it surprised me in the least. I saw it in you from the beginning. You were born to be a father."

"Is that why we broke up?"

"We broke up, Proctor, because we were young."

"And foolish, maybe?"

"Not at the time. We had different destinations, you and I. Places to go, things to do. It wasn't wrong, it's just how it was."

I couldn't argue the point. "I guess you're right."

"Don't misunderstand me—I used to wonder what might have happened if we'd stayed together. You can't *not* think about something like that."

"What did you decide?"

"It was either true love to last a lifetime or we'd tear each other to pieces. But then Elise came along, and I didn't have to wonder anymore. Case closed."

There was a pause.

I said, "We never talked about what happened the night we went up to the roof."

"No, we didn't. Do we need to?"

"Not if you don't want."

"I'll put it this way. Speaking for myself, in a universe of pluses and minuses, it was a clear plus. You may think I was trying to cheer you up. That wasn't it at all."

"No?"

"I was remembering. Remembering you, remembering the world the way it was when I first knew you. I think both of us understood what was happening, even back then. We wouldn't be here now if we hadn't. But it mattered a lot less when we were young, and it mattered less that night on the roof. For a few hours, I got to feel that way again."

I almost told her. Perhaps I should have. Standing at the parapet, lost in thoughts of eternity, I'd been wholly prepared to jump—that is, to end my life before it could be ended for me.

Instead, I said, "Me, too."

Slipping her fingers into mine, she leaned her head against my shoulder. The gesture was not desirous; it came from a different sort of closeness, of being there at the start and giving each other a model for life. We had been lovers, then friends, then lovers again, both in reality and then in dreams; now we were something else. It had no name but didn't need one.

"My turn for a question," I said. "You're so smart about all this stuff, how come you never had kids of your own?"

"All this time and now you ask that?" She sighed. "There's no simple answer. Work was part of it. The state of the world. Some things just aren't in the cards."

"Do you regret it?"

"There were times I did. I'd have these visions of myself as a little old lady, all alone. But then I thought how I probably wouldn't get to *be* an old lady the way the world was headed, and the feeling went away." She twisted her head to look at me. "Actually, can we not talk about this?"

"All right."

"Let's just sit here quietly then," she said, and nestled against me once more.

The minutes ticked by. I was struck, yet again, by the awesome silence of the place. An army of souls was packed within its walls. Not a tomb but a house of spirits, caught between worlds.

Wait a second.

"Caeli really *wasn't* like I imagined her."

Thea craned her neck to look at me. "Proctor? Is something wrong?"

My mind was racing down a hall. "Tell me something. How do you think Caeli got into the dream?"

"I just assumed that was you, like Quinn said. One of your echoes when you were trying to wake up."

"But I wasn't the only one who saw her. You saw her, too."

She sat up straight. "That's right, I did. We *all* did."

"So, it couldn't have been me."

Both of us looked toward Elise's cabinet.

"We need to find Quinn," I said.

35

Elise is pretty sure she's losing her mind.

Such as now: Sitting at the table in candlelight, waiting for Warren to present her with the dinner he's been fussing over for hours, she feels like she can barely breathe. Like she is literally suffocating. It's the rain, she's told herself, the endless, cooped-up days—it's enough to make anybody go a little cuckoo—but she knows that's not the reason, not by a long shot. At the stove, Warren pulls a roaster from the oven, checks the meat thermometer before sliding it back in, stirs a pan in which something is fragrantly sautéing, lifts the lid from a pot to a little burst of steam, and samples the contents with a spoon. She's so irritated she wants to scream.

"And . . . here . . . we . . . *are.*"

He places her dinner before her. Beef tenderloin, sautéed greens, a cheesy polenta garnished with a sprig of thyme, standing at attention. The sight of it sends her stomach tumbling. He pours her a glass of wine. This, too, is revolting.

Settling back in his chair, he raises his glass. Perspiration shimmers on his brow from the heat of the stove. "So what shall we drink to?" He laughs. "Not the weather, anyway."

He's not wrong. When was the last time it rained like this? Never, in her experience.

"Elise?" His eyes abruptly narrow on her face; she's been silent too long. "Is everything okay?"

It isn't, not at all. She picks up her fork and puts it down again. "I'm sorry," she says. "I'm just not hungry."

He means well; she knows that. She shouldn't be so hard on him. After everything she's been through, it's Warren who's stood by her. And, in fact, he's been the perfect gentleman. Each night he's bedded down on the sofa without discussion; he's barely touched her, even in passing.

"You know you can tell me anything," he prods. His eyes practically glow with concern. "I'm here for you."

She has no idea what to say.

"You're going to need time. That's all. Just time. You've been through a terrible ordeal. It's okay to feel this way."

"I know it is. It's just . . ." She stops herself.

"What? Tell me."

Out it comes. "I've been . . . dreaming, Warren."

He nods, expressionless. "Dreaming," he repeats.

A feeling of fullness behind her eyes tells her she's about to cry.

"Elise, you can talk to me."

Can she? Can she talk to him, to anyone? Will he know she's going mad, and if so, what then?

"Tell me what you're dreaming about."

She shakes her head. "I don't remember. Not really."

"But . . . something," he says.

She closes her eyes. The gesture is involuntary. She closes her eyes and what she sees is the sea. A great black sea, and in it she is floating—lost, alone, abandoned to her fate. There is only her and the sea, stretching infinitely in all directions, when suddenly the water changes. She cannot stay afloat. She flaps her arms, she kicks her legs, but it's no use, and down she goes, into the darkness.

"Elise?"

"I said I don't remember!"

She bursts from the table, and next thing she knows she's slamming the bedroom door behind herself. She sits on the bed, shaking.

A quiet knock on the door. "Elise?"

"Go away."

Warren tries the handle. It's locked.

"Elise, you need to open the door."

It's all wrong, all of it. What is she doing here, way out in the country?

"Elise, please." The handle jiggles again. "Let me give you something to calm you down."

"Leave me alone."

"Is it Proctor?" Warren says through the door. "Is that the problem?"

It is. It's Proctor. How she misses him. How could she have left him alone like that, just when he needed her?

"I know this is hard, Elise. But it's for the best, you'll see."

She drops her face to her hands, tears flowing.

"Elise, are you there?"

She offers no reply.

"Well," Warren says, and clears his throat, "I guess I'll just be . . . out here. If you, you know, change your mind about dinner."

She listens to his footsteps fade, and then hears, from the kitchen, the clatter of pans in the sink. This goes on awhile, and when at last she hears him heading down the hall to make his bed on the couch, the sound makes her unclench with relief. She changes into a nightgown, slides beneath the bed covers, and douses the lights. The room is freezing. Why is the room always so fucking freezing? She draws the blankets tightly around herself and closes her eyes. Time passes; her breathing eases; she feels her thoughts disassembling. Impressions come to her—sounds, sensations, even smells. Soft carpet under her bare feet. A milky odor, warm as breath. A certain hush, deeper than silence. These things mix in her mind with the rattling of the rain and the rolling of the thunder and the trembling of the windowpanes in their frames until she hears a voice.

"Mama!"

What in the world?

"Mama! Help!"

Terror squeezes her throat. *Baby! Mama's coming!* But she cannot rise, she cannot cry out. She is frozen, immobile, as entombed as a corpse in a crypt. The lightning sizzles, the thunder breaks and rolls, the rain hammers the windows and roof.

"Mama, I can't find you! Where are you?"

She commands herself: *Wake up, wake up . . .*

"It's dark and cold and I can't find you!"

Wake up she's drowning your little girl is drowning wake up wake up wake up . . .

A crash; she opens her eyes. Warren is standing above her in his boxer shorts. "Elise, what's wrong? You were screaming."

"She's out there!"

A flash. For a split second, light slants across Warren's face. It makes him look sinister, even skull-like. It's as if his flesh has been stripped away, laying bare the angular bones. Thunder shakes the windows.

"There's no one, Elise."

"Get away from me!"

She leaps from the bed, shoves past him, tears through the living room and out the door, into the storm.

Mama!

She spins around, trying to locate the source of the voice. She is shivering, soaked to the bone; the storm is a wild force enveloping her. "Where are you?" she cries. "I can't find you!"

Mama, help!

Warren, negotiating a pair of pants, appears on the porch. "Elise, for godsakes get back inside. It's not safe out here."

"I have to find her!"

She picks a direction and begins to run. Something is happening to the sky. The clouds have congealed into a black wheel, rotating over the forest and fields. It is toward this gyring, airborne maw that she runs.

"Where are you?" she calls, but her voice is torn away on the wind. "Please, answer me!"

Mama, it's dark and cold and I can't see you . . .

She stumbles and falls, hard, into the mud.

Mama Mama Mama . . .

She tries to rise, but it's no use; she can't continue. She sobs into the mud. Her daughter! Her little girl! (What daughter? What little girl? She cannot recall.) She rolls onto her back. Above her, the wheeling clouds have opened like a porthole, revealing a single star, with a bluish tint. She knows, suddenly, that this is where the voice is coming from.

Suddenly, someone is there. It's Warren. He kneels beside her in the mud.

"Elise, I'm sorry," he says.

There is a feeling of defeat about him, like a man who has given up on life.

"This is all my fault. I never should have let it come to this."

He slides his hands beneath her and lifts her up. His touch has a new quality—tender, as if she were a child, even a baby. In the cradle of his arms, she feels almost bodiless; it's as if she's floating. She looks up at his face, dripping with rain, and what she sees is strange. The man is crying. Why would he be crying?

"I'm s-s-so c-c-cold," she says.

Warren plods forward through the mud. "I know. Let's get you warm."

Lights suddenly blaze behind them. Warren stops short.

"Oh, shit," he says.

A commotion unfolds around them. Men, lights, the sound of engines.

A voice says, "Warren! I was beginning to wonder. A romantic stroll in the rain, is it?"

"Leave her be," says Warren.

"Leave her be? What is this I'm hearing, Dr. Singh?"

"She's been through enough, Otto. This has to end."

"No argument there."

Footsteps splash toward them. Spinning, Warren backs away. "Fuck you, don't you touch her!"

The first man says, with a tone of irritated boredom, "Do we really need to do this?"

"Look around you. She's falling apart. This whole *thing* is falling apart."

"All the more reason," the man says. "I'm afraid, Dr. Singh, that the time has finally come for a change in management."

"Who? *You?*"

"Let's just say it's a sacrifice I'm willing to make."

"I can't be party to this anymore."

"Very high-minded of you. This was all your idea, if I'm not mistaken."

Warren says nothing. The rain pours down.

"Allow me to add a fresh data point. Bennett got out."

Warren stiffens. "What do you mean, 'got out'?"

"I mean the man sailed right off the edge. No doubt he's on his way back here as we speak, burning with self-righteous fury. That would put you first on his to-do list, my friend."

Warren is silent.

"So, how about it?" the man says. "Are we all back on the same team here?"

Warren hesitates, then says, "Let me go with her to the Nursery. At least I can keep her calm. Isn't that what you want, Otto? To keep her calm?"

"You'd actually do that? Reiterate yourself after all this time? You amaze me, Dr. Singh. I thought you rather liked your life."

"I just want to forget all this."

"Your choice, I suppose. Who knows, maybe I'll adopt you!"

"I'll pass, thanks."

"Oh well, can't say I didn't make the offer. All right, everyone, you heard the man. Let him through."

The door of a vehicle opens. Balancing her weight, Warren ascends into a small metal space—the rear compartment of a van. He lays her gently on the bench.

"Is there a blanket?" he asks someone.

A blanket is produced. Warren drapes it over her body and tucks the sides under her, swaddling her in a cocoon.

"Hey, what's this?" Warren says.

Elise feels a sudden, jabbing pressure on her right wrist. A handcuff? She forces her eyes to focus on Warren: he, too, has been handcuffed to the rail.

"Just a little something to make sure you get where you're going," the other man says.

Warren tugs at the handcuff: a pointless reflex. "Fuck you, Otto."

The door slams. The van pulls away.

36

"Yes, I could have imagined I saw Caeli, but if that were true, I would have been the only one who saw her. I couldn't fully manifest her inside the dreamspace. Only Elise can do that."

We had returned to the conference room. Quinn, sitting across from me, leaned back in his chair, placing the tips of his fingers together. Thea and I waited.

"Okay, it's an interesting hypothesis," he said finally, "but how exactly does this help us?"

"The two times I saw Caeli on the beach, I was alone. Then the Nursery, then the Annex. Elise is manifesting her, but not where she can see her directly. I think she wants to remember but can't bring herself to do it. There's also the weather. From the moment Caeli showed up, we had storm after storm, each one worse than the last. That's not CIS—that's her."

"You think she's trying to wake up, same as you."

"Only she's afraid to. Part of her wants to, another part is terrified. And why wouldn't she be? And there's something else. The night after I got fired, I told her about Caeli. She completely locked up. It was like she went into some kind of trance, and when she came out of it, you know what she said? 'This house is fucking freezing.' "

Quinn looked at me with acute interest. "She really said that?"

"I'm telling you, she *is* waking up. Or at least trying to."

"What happened then?"

"She packed up her suitcase and left. To be with Warren, I assume."

Quinn thought a moment. "Those were the two people you saw on the drone feed that night in the Annex, weren't they?"

I nodded. "Warren's been watching both of us from the beginning. Callista and Otto, too."

"And you think that if Elise actually *sees* Caeli, she'll wake up and the dreamspace will collapse?"

"I think it's the only way."

Thea asked, "So, if she's trying to wake up, why don't they just send her back to the Nursery and reiterate her? Clean the slate and start over?"

"I wondered that, too. Maybe for some reason they can't."

Quinn said, "Or can't *yet.* She might be too unstable to send her through. Maybe that's why Warren took her to the country."

"Which means we don't have a lot of time. Once she's reiterated, she'll forget again and we'll lose our chance. I have to go back without the suppressors and somehow make her see our daughter."

Thea said, "Can we still do that? Send someone back in?"

" 'In' isn't the issue. Once Proctor goes into stasis, the system will reintegrate him automatically. But if he can't wake up Elise, or this doesn't work, he'll be trapped there. I can't get him out."

I said, "Trapped there or trapped here, I don't see what difference it makes."

"Fair point, I suppose."

"Assuming Elise is still with Warren, how close can you get me?"

"That's the easy part. How about the living room?"

The door opened. It was Antone, but something had changed. Gone was the mild-mannered soil biologist. His eyes, burning with fury, grazed quickly over Quinn and Thea before landing, hard, on me. Before any of us could react, he took three long strides to the table, grabbed me by the collar, yanked me from my chair, and hurled me against the bulkhead.

"You think I wouldn't figure it out, you bastard? You made us their fucking *slaves.*"

He came at me again, reaching for my throat. I put out my hands to keep him at bay, but I wouldn't be able to hold him off long. Thea wrapped her arms around his waist, trying to pull him away and, when this failed, began to pummel his back with her fists. Antone's eyes bored into mine, bright and wild and full of hate. The man was entitled; in every way, I had it coming. This was when Quinn appeared with a shocker, which he shoved against the base of Antone's neck. For a few seconds, he seemed to take no notice, such was his fury, but then I felt his body soften against my hand; with a groan, he melted to the floor.

"Be prepared, is my motto," Quinn said. "You can thank me later."

We carried Antone to my quarters and locked him in. "He's not going to be the only one, you know," Quinn said.

"Believe me, I know."

In the stasis chamber, I stripped and lay down in my cabinet. Thea molded the cap to my head, then exchanged a nod with Quinn, who was sitting at the control panel. I felt a slight pressure, then a wave of dizziness, as my connection to CIS was initialized.

Quinn said, "Without the suppressors, it may take you a few minutes to get your head straight once you're inside. But after that, you should be okay."

I looked up at Thea. "If I can't wake up Elise, the three of you should take the suppressors and go back into the dream. Enter through the Nursery. You can at least have some kind of life."

"Until we die and molder in our cabinets. No thanks."

From the console, Quinn said, "All set here. Say the word."

Thea gave me a wan smile. "You know, something just occurred to me. What if *this* is the dream? Maybe I'm in my apartment right now, sleeping on the sofa. Or maybe we never left Earth in the first place."

I couldn't tell if she was being serious or not. "It's an interesting idea."

She took my hand and squeezed. "Ready?"

I had no memory of my first time going into stasis; one isn't supposed to. It was said to be quick, though not quick enough.

"Yeah. I'm ready."

She stepped back; the cabinet door slid into place. Through the small window, I could see Thea, watching me from above. There was a gurgling sound; the stasis fluid—viscous, frigid—began to pool around my body like a fast-lifting tide. My muscles stiffened; I was suddenly unable to move. As the liquid rose to my chin, I experienced a moment of pure physical panic; I wanted to cry out but could not. *Don't breathe!* I thought, but that was all, as my face went under, the fluid crashed into my lungs, and my heart stopped in my chest.

I plunged.

37

Darkness.

Wind.

A night sky of clouds and no stars, and the sound and feel of rain.

I was lying faceup on the ground. The earth was damp and loamy-smelling; above me, the branches of the trees were tossing wildly, making a rustling sound. How had I come to be here, lying on a forest floor in the rain?

Rising gingerly, I looked down at myself. I was wearing a dark suit. I had a lingering memory of intense cold and a bad taste in my mouth. I was thoroughly disoriented yet also sensed, beneath my confusion, a feeling of purpose. There was a reason I was here; it was my job to remember what it was.

I took stock of my surroundings. The trees were of a type found at higher altitudes; I was nowhere near the coast—rather, in the country, high in the hills. More facts were coming clear. My name was Proctor Bennett; the island was called Prospera. I was, or had been until recently, a person of some importance. That I could assemble these basic biographical details reassured me, and for several minutes, as I stood in the pouring rain, something rather like a filmstrip played in my mind, a chronological presentation of my life. My father was Malcolm, my mother Cynthia. The home where I'd lived my early days was a large house with gardens by the sea, which explained my love of the ocean. At university, I'd studied human transitional dynamics, which led me to a career as a human resources enforcement officer. All of this revealed itself, with one salient exception, forming a hole in my thoughts: Wasn't I married? Wasn't there a person in my life whose very existence gave ballast and meaning to my own? I felt certain this was so, this unnamed person forming a distinct though negative presence in my mind: a presence of absence. I bore down upon it.

Elise.

My wife was Elise.

Our daughter was Caeli.

I was a sleeping body aboard *Oranios.*

None of this was real.

I chose a direction and began to walk. Quinn's promise of the living room had obviously been overstated; still, I assumed the house was somewhere close by. I made my stumbling, directionless way through the dark forest. Shadows lurched around me; the rain had increased in intensity, stinging my face and eyes. *Elise,* I thought, *is that you? Are these drops of rain the tears you cannot shed, is the wind the storm of bottled grief within you?* I had failed to see this world for what it was: a mirror to a mother's woe.

I entered a clearing. It appeared to be some kind of orchard. Flowering fruit trees were planted in rows, like a battalion of soldiers at attention. A hundred yards distant stood a cottage. A flash of lightning revealed a vehicle parked in front: Warren's roadster.

The storm would keep the drones away, but doubtless the house was being watched. Darting from tree to tree, I hopscotched across the field, then skulked around back and peered through a window, though it was too dark to see anything—the power was out. I waited for any indication that my presence had been detected, and when this failed to come, I raised the sash and hoisted myself inside.

I was in a rustic kitchen: a large, claw-footed stove, a sink with a pump, knotty pine cabinets. In the corner was a small dining table; one of the chairs lay on its back, as if in a swoon. Stilling myself to listen, I heard a faint shifting sound, like turning pages, coming from the other end of the house. I glanced around the kitchen, searching for something that might serve as a weapon. On the counter by the stove was a block of knives. I withdrew the largest one and stepped into the hallway. There were closed doors on both sides, and to my right, a narrow flight of stairs leading up. A light was coming from the front room, pale and flickering; I detected a faint scent of burning oil. At the end of the hall, I pressed myself flat to the wall and craned my head around the corner to look. A single figure was sitting by the fireplace, legs crossed, reading a book by lantern light.

Otto Winspear.

He looked up suddenly, meeting my eye with a smile. "Proctor! Good of you to drop in." Marking the page, he closed the book and placed it aside. "How was your trip?"

I stepped into the room. "Where is she?"

"Elise, you mean?" He shrugged. "Gone, alas." He wagged a finger at the knife in my hand. "You should be careful with that. You don't want to cut yourself."

"Tell me where she is, Otto."

"Or what? You'll kill me? You know that's not how things work around here."

"Maybe not, but I could take my time with it."

He waved this away. "Oh, please. You're forgetting—I know you. The *real* you. Stabbing me is not exactly in your repertoire."

"You might want to check with Bernardo."

"Ah. Lovely fellow, our Bernardo. I'll be sure to send him a get-well card."

No surprise: in three hundred sixty-six years, the man hadn't changed one whit. His arrogance was supreme.

"Tell me something," he went on, "and please be honest. You were never going to let the investors off the ship, were you?"

"They never belonged there in the first place."

Otto's eyebrows arched. "'They,' Proctor? It seems to me your hands aren't exactly spotless. You rather enjoyed the comforts of our largesse."

"At least I tried to do something about it."

He laughed. "I'll say you did! Conning the world's richest people out of a few trillion is no mean feat. You really ought to write a book."

"Maybe later. My plate's a little full at the moment."

"They *paid* for all this, Proctor. In case that slipped your mind."

"Somebody had to. Why not the people who ruined the planet?"

"So, for them, a sentence of death by nightmare, is it? That seems a little cruel."

"I'll be the judge of that."

"And of *them*, apparently. Do you ever get tired of playing God? No, of course you don't." He settled back, smoothing the tops of his trousers. "So, a clean break with the past, was that your plan? A world of honest, hardworking men and women coming together to give humanity a second chance?"

"Something like that."

"Proctor, Proctor, Proctor. Don't be so naïve, it doesn't become you. You think just because you start out with a bunch of farmers and ditch diggers that things will actually *stay* that way? Human nature is what it is, my friend. There are always haves and have-nots, and that's code you can't rewrite. It might take a hundred years, it might take a thousand, but you'll end up right back where you started."

"I don't have time for one of your lectures, Otto. Where is she?"

"Right now, you mean?" He glanced at his watch. "I'd say the woman's well on her way to her exciting new life of wonder and adventure. Don't worry, she's not alone. Our friend Warren will be joining her." He gave a little manufactured wince. "Callista, bless her heart, was not in favor. It seems she's grown rather attached. But you could say she's no longer part of the decision-making chain."

I raised the knife. "This conversation is over. I need the keys to Warren's car."

"You saw that planet. It's an ice ball. You should be thanking me."

"Okay, thanks. Now give me the fucking keys."

He breathed a heavy sigh. "Very well. I see you're quite determined." He reached into his jacket pocket, produced the keys, and tossed them to me. "Just so you know, trying to wake her up won't work."

"You don't know that."

"I'm afraid I do. The woman's defenses are a fortress. Also, and you may not remember, we've been down this road before."

"What's that supposed to mean?"

He shrugged carelessly. "Just what I said. Always the same thing happens—you and Elise find each other, Caeli shows up, the weather goes haywire, we shove you back in the freezer, everything goes back to normal." He paused in thought. "What is it, five times now? No, six. I'm pretty sure it's six."

Could it be true? And I thought: Of course it could. We'd been playing out this scenario ever since we'd arrived at Caelus—maybe even longer. It would have been strange if we hadn't.

"Before you go," Otto went on, "there's one thing I can't figure out. Why make the crew Prosperan? You I understand, you'd want to stay close to her, but why the others?"

"I didn't."

He considered this, then, with a sudden smile of recognition, looked up. "Yes, of course. More of Elise's shenanigans. I should have seen that coming. Anyway," he said, and slapped his knees, "it's nice to see you again, Proctor. Believe it or not, I've missed you." He straightened in his chair. "Gentlemen! If you please!"

The watchmen weren't as quiet as they thought; I'd been aware of them since I'd entered the room. As they pounded down the stairs, I took three steps forward. For a split second, I saw fear in Otto's eyes. But it wasn't Otto I was interested in; it was the lantern. I grabbed it from the table, spun around, and hurled it at the base of the stairs.

A crash.

Fire.

Lots of it.

As the room filled with oily smoke, I flew through the door, leapt from the porch, and jammed myself into Warren's roadster just as a phalanx of headlamps and twirling lights blazed from the edge of the orchard. I swung the car around in a one-eighty and punched the gas; the car leapt forward, its undersized steering wheel jerking in my hands as I bounded across the field. A flash of lightning revealed a rutted dirt track and, beyond, a break in the trees.

I aimed toward it, the watchmen's patrol cars swinging in behind me.

"This is . . . strange."

Sitting on the floor of the stasis chamber, Thea perks up at the sound of Quinn's voice.

"What's wrong?"

He's sitting at the terminal. "Hang on a second."

More tapping of keys. He halts, squinting at the floating screen.

"See this?" He points at a line of code. "The first alternate—it's been changed. Just a few hours ago, in fact."

It was something they debated at length in the months leading up to their departure from Earth: What if Elise were to die of natural causes in her cabinet? Because anyone could; there were no guarantees. They decided that, in such an instance, CIS would defer to the next person in line, designated as the alternate, to serve as the Designer of the dreamspace. The transition would be rocky—CIS would have to rekey itself to the alternate, using Elise's coding as a baseline—but the idea was sound. Because the code for Proctor was already mostly written, he was the clear choice for first alternate. Thea was chosen as the second alternate, Quinn the third.

"Who's the new first alternate?" Thea asks.

"Otto."

Good Christ. "Can he do that from inside?"

"We can't be sure it's him. It could be Warren or Callista. But somebody has an open back door. I'll bet it's Otto."

"Meaning he still has access to CIS."

Quinn nods.

"It doesn't make sense. What's he up to?"

Quinn goes back to work. A minute later he says, "He's severed Elise from the system. Not just her—the whole executive staff, even Warren and Callista. The board, too. Any of us dies while we're inside the dreamspace, or gets sent to the Nursery, we won't be reiterated. We'll be locked out."

To be severed: it was nothing less than being condemned to a living hell. An eternity of nightmares, trapped in the prison of one's own mind.

"He'll have to send Elise through the Nursery to reset the system. But once that's done, Otto's in charge."

"We have to get Proctor out of there."

"We can't. His only way out is to wake Elise up." Quinn pauses. "That's not the only thing Otto did."

"Good God, what else?"

"He severed the colonists, Thea. Every single one of them."

Two quick turns and I was back on asphalt, descending a winding mountain road—downshifting into the turns, tires squealing, engine roaring as I worked my way up and down the gearbox.

Elise was right about Warren's car. I could certainly see the attraction.

Lights below: a town. I hit bottom and raced through with nary a glance. The wind had increased, forcing me to clutch the wheel in a death grip. What was the hour? When would dawn come? I glanced in the rearview, expecting the patrol cars, but all I saw were the fading lights of the little town I'd just departed. I was speeding across a flat plain: vineyards, farms, houses and barns set back from the road. Had I lost the watchmen for good? A sign appeared in my headlamps: COAST HIGHWAY 12 MILES.

I shoved the accelerator to the floor.

The mob at the causeway has ceased to move, for it can go no farther. Driven from the rear by the advancing line of watchmen in full riot gear, it has been brought to a halt by a second barricade of watchmen and security faxes, blocking their path. Behind them, a long line of vans and cargo trucks snakes down the causeway, making cones of light in the rain.

"Arrival come!" the people in the crowd chant. Their raised fists pump in time with the words. *"Arrival come! Arrival come!"*

Cynthia rises on her toes to search for Pappi but can't see past the heads of the crowd. Stefano is somewhere nearby, and some of the cousins, but Cynthia has lost track of them, too. Strangely, the watchmen have made no pronouncements. There have been no orders to disperse. There is, in fact, no clear indication of who's in charge. There are only the two lines, one before and one behind, faceless in their riot gear, hemming them in.

Cynthia needs to see what's happening. She angles her shoulders and tries to slide forward, then, when this fails, muscles her way through. Many of the people in the crowd are armed, and not just with bottles and bricks. She sees lengths of pipes, clubs of scrap wood wrapped with wire, knives and hammers and wrenches.

She is nearing the front just as a woman in a raincoat, her right arm in a sling, steps forward from the line of watchmen. She raises a bullhorn to her mouth.

"This is the minister of Public Safety. I hereby place all of you under arrest. Lay down your weapons."

Her words are smothered by the chanting of the crowd, which, if anything, has grown louder and more defiant. The woman glances over her shoulder at the line of watchmen, as if to reassure herself that they haven't run off, and then raises the bullhorn again.

"I repeat, lay down your weapons."

The crowd ignores her. Suddenly Cynthia knows: the threat of arrest is meaningless, a polite ruse. They have been herded like animals for slaughter.

"This is your final warning," the woman says. "You *will* be fired upon."

Two things happen. The first is a blinding flash. A bank of lights behind the watchmen flares into the faces of the crowd. Holding their hands over their eyes, everyone surges back.

The second thing is a man.

He's on all fours, his body exposed by the mob's retreat. It's Pappi. He turns his head from side to side as if to measure his surroundings; then, tentatively, his balance barely maintained, he rises to his feet. There's blood on his face and clothing; his shirt and pants are torn. All of this Cynthia observes with a feeling of absolute helplessness. In the press of bodies, she cannot reach him, to stop what is surely about to occur. He stumbles forward, toward the lights and the woman with the bullhorn.

"Get back, old man!"

He extends his hands beseechingly. "Help me."

She drops the bullhorn and from her waistband produces a pistol, which she levels at his chest. Pappi, of course, can see none of this.

"I said get back!"

"I've done nothing wrong." Reaching out, he takes another step. "Please. I'm blind. I don't know where I am."

The shot, when it comes, seems to surprise the woman as much as anyone. Her face says: *Did I really just do that?* Pappi shudders but does not fall. Like the woman, he seems uncertain, puzzled by the swiftness of events. With searching tenderness, he reaches up, touches the wound in his chest, and draws his hand away. For a moment he stands there, rubbing his bloody thumb and fingers together. Then he drops to his knees and pitches sideways onto the pavement.

A silent moment follows, everyone wondering what's going to happen next.

And then, at last, it does.

Otto, standing in the rain, watches the final act of the house's incineration. You'd think the rain would slow it down, but no. The heat is intense, waves of it washing over his face. The walls, the roof—all are engulfed. Black smoke boils into the sky. It won't be long before nothing's left standing but the chimney.

You have to give the man credit, Otto thinks. The lantern: he didn't think of that.

Campbell, who has been sitting in the car, walks up to him. "Sir—"

"Did they get him?"

"Lost him on the mountain road. The man was driving like a maniac. No way could they catch him in that car he was driving."

Otto isn't worried. "It doesn't matter—we know where he's going. Put roadblocks on the coast road and send a squad to the ferry. Ten men—no, make that twenty."

"That's what I came to tell you. It seems no squad's . . . available."

"What do you mean they're not *available*?"

"They're all at the causeway," Campbell says. "It looks like half the Annex is coming across."

"Wake up, Elise."

Someone is shaking her by the shoulder. A voice is calling her name.

"Elise, please, you have to snap out of it."

She's not asleep, exactly. Neither could she properly be called awake. She isn't quite sure *what* she is. Sometimes she's in a van; others, she is floating in the sea, which is also time itself, extending eternally in all directions.

"Can you hear me? You need to listen to my voice. Follow my voice, Elise."

How terrible everything is, how sad. If only Proctor were here. He could explain what's happening to her. He could wrap her in his arms and bring her back to herself so that the world makes sense again. But then she remembers that she left him. Why did she leave him? It was stupid. It was cruel. She left him and walked the paths of the garden (Callista's garden) (Julian's garden) (they had gone there after the bad thing, the awful thing) and she knew he was watching her, she could feel his eyes following her as she walked. And yet she could not go to him, or even raise her head to meet his eye, because then she would remember.

She doesn't want to remember.

"I need you to wake up *right now.*"

And so she does; she opens her eyes. The sea, the garden—both vanish; in their stead, the confines of a bouncing metal box, and the dark silhouette of a man's face, backlit by the small window. Warren? It is.

"Elise. Thank Christ."

This is when she notices the man's right wrist is handcuffed to a rail set into the wall. Has he committed a crime?

"Do you think you can sit up?"

Sit up?

"Let me help you."

He extends the hand that isn't cuffed and gingerly draws her to a sitting position. She, too, is handcuffed to the rail. So, whatever Warren's done, she must have done it, too.

"Where are we going?" she asks him.

"You don't remember?"

She shakes her head. Dear God, the cold! Will it never stop?

"They're taking us to the Nursery," Warren says.

There's a nursery? And now that he mentions it, Elise *does* remember a nursery. Down the hall, second door on the right, the one with the hinges Proctor oiled so that it wouldn't squeak; walls a sort of dusty pink with a bit of gray, white carpeting underfoot, a view of the pool from the windows (the pool?). And everything quiet, so quiet, and the soft, small weight in her arms as she stood in the window swaying back and forth, back and forth, whispering, *Hush now, it's time to stop your fussing and be quiet now, baby girl . . .*

"Elise, are you there?" The sound of fingers snapping in front of her face. "Elise?"

Her mind rockets back. Warren. The van.

"We need to end this."

Her awareness widens. She sees it in his face: the man is afraid.

"I'm sorry for what I'm about to do," he says. He takes her hand and holds it firmly. "Look at me."

She does. She looks.

"I'm going to tell you something. I'm going to tell you something and I need you to listen very carefully."

Elise nods.

"She's gone."

Who is gone?

"Caeli." Warren's eyes bore into hers. "She died. Your little girl. Your little girl is gone."

"I'm not leaving him alone in there."

Thea is stripping down, tossing her clothes aside, her shoes. Naked, she sweeps her hair back and wedges the sensor cap onto her head.

"Thea—"

"It's not a vote. Where is he now?"

Quinn, with evident reluctance, works the screen. "Coast highway," he says after a moment. "Looks like he's in motion. Going pretty fast, too. He must be in a car."

"Can you drop me straight in?"

"You mean *into the car*?"

"No, I was thinking you could send me to the movies." The man just stares at her. "Yes, Quinn, into the car."

He blows out a puff of air. "That's not going to be easy. To be honest, I kind of fucked up with Proctor. Missed by half a mile."

"Half a *mile*?"

"Okay, maybe I was a little overconfident. This isn't simple."

She opens her cabinet. A little bit of the old fluid leaks onto the floor. "Just do your best."

"Thea, you know I won't be able to get you out. If anything happens to you, and Proctor can't get to Elise before Otto does—"

"I get it. An eternity in hell. Let's not dwell on that part, okay?"

She lowers herself into the cabinet, plugs in the headset, and settles back.

The door seals. The fluid rises. She closes her eyes.

Slam.

38

I hit the outskirts of the city going like a rocket. The roads were practically empty. What few cars I encountered, I roared around heedlessly, never touching the brake. My speed was blinding, everything around me smeared to a blur.

Elise, I'm coming.

Lights flared in my rearview; the watchmen had found me. I pushed the speedometer to ninety, then ninety-five, then one hundred. Still the lights did not recede. I was approaching an intersection. I downshifted and braked hard, felt the rear of the car sway outward as I jerked the wheel to the right. The car tipped ominously—I thought I was going to roll for sure—but then it crashed down again, all four tires biting into the asphalt and shooting me forward. I glanced at the rearview; the watchmen had made the turn, but at least I'd put some distance between us. Another turn, and then two more. The gap increased until I saw no lights at all.

Except the ones ahead of me.

A roadblock. I skidded to a halt and shoved the car into reverse. Patrol vehicles were now racing toward me from two directions. Between them lay an alleyway, if I could get there in time. I jammed on the brakes and made the turn. Tight quarters: the buildings were just a few feet away on either side. At least I was headed back toward the waterfront. I hit the coast road, swung the car into the turn, and raced ahead, the watchmen moving in behind me.

Which was precisely the moment that Thea arrived.

Elise screams.

She opens her lungs and the sound that pours forth is like no sound she has ever made, that anyone has ever made. A scream of pain so vast it could knock a planet off its axis, crack the heavens, unwind the fabric of reality itself. She is so far inside this scream that she cannot hear it, as the ocean cannot hear its roar; she is the scream and the scream is her, a pure continuum of pain.

The van is rolling. The van is tumbling, banging, bursting. She is, for a few seconds, airborne. She is floating and flying and then it all stops; she comes crashing down upon the ceiling of the now-inverted van and is thrown against the doors by the centrifugal force of its rotation, which goes on and on until it, too, comes to a halt.

For a while, a minute or an hour or a year, nothing happens. She lies there, listening to the wind and rain battering the overturned van and the small sounds coming from the wrecked vehicle—pops, creaks, the hissing of steam from the exploded radiator. She doesn't seem hurt except for her wrist, which feels broken, maybe, or sprained. The handcuff is still there but attached to nothing. She turns her face to the side. Warren is hanging one-handed from the rail, his legs folded under him and his head slumped forward onto his chest. There is blood in his hair, on his lips, a bit of it dribbling down his chin. Is he dead? But no, the man is breathing.

The watchmen haven't been so lucky. One of them is both in the van and also not, his torso shoved halfway through the windshield; the other is impaled on the steering column.

The doors of the van are jammed kitty-corner in their frame. Lying on her back, Elise kicks at them; to her surprise—she's stronger than she thought—they bang open. The weather swarms in. Cradling her wrist, she crawls free.

Where are the ambulances, the police, the helpful onlookers? Shouldn't somebody have come by now? But the streets are empty; the crash has gone entirely unwitnessed. Kneeling on the pavement, she hangs her head and begins to cry.

Mama!

She lifts her face.

Mama, here I am!

She peers into the dark and rain. Is that a shape she sees—a small human form in the distance?

"Hello?"

Mama, come find me!

"Who's there?"

The shape darts away.

"Wait!"

She rises to her feet. She runs.

Thea announced her presence with a groan.

"Fuuuuuck . . . *me.*"

I glanced over. She was sitting in the passenger seat, facing the windshield. "Right," she said after a moment. "Thea Dimopolous. Prospera. Got it." She turned toward me. "You know, that's just as bad as they say."

"What are you doing here?"

A crunch of metal and a sudden lurch: one of the patrol cars had made contact with my rear bumper. I floored it. The watchman did the same.

Thea swiveled in her seat to look back, then faced forward again. "Where the hell's that lever?"

Another *whang*. For a split second, I felt the tires losing their grip. "What lever?"

"Warren took me for a ride once. God, the man was such a show-off. Okay, here we go." She reached under the dashboard. "Keep it steady."

"What are you—?"

The car's canvas roof disengaged from the top of the windshield, filled with air with a loud pop, and sailed over our heads like a giant kite cut from its string. I glanced in the rearview in time to see it wrap around the windshield of the lead patrol car. Suddenly blind, the driver slammed on his brakes, causing the vehicle to skid broadside on the rain-slickened pavement.

The pileup was spectacular.

"Ha!" Thea was looking behind us. "Bet you didn't think of that, assholes!" She faced front again. "Proctor, hit the brakes!"

The van. It materialized from the rain with arresting suddenness, lying upside down in the middle of the road. I stomped the brake pedal to the floor.

It wasn't enough.

39

"Proctor."

I was in the shuttle. We'd reached high orbit; Jason had just shut down the engines. There was a feeling of buoyancy as my body pressed against my harness. But something was wrong; the pressure of the belts against my torso was too great. Also—and this was strange—it seemed to be raining in the cockpit. Since when did it rain in the cockpit?

"Proctor!"

I rocketed back to awareness. Not the shuttle: Warren's roadster. The car was lying on the passenger side, leaving me suspended in the air in the driver's seat, my body held in place by the shoulder harness. Every part of me hurt.

I looked down. By the lights of the dash, I saw that Thea had managed to belt herself before impact, but the dashboard on her side of the car had been shoved forward into the cabin, pinning her in place.

"Thea? Are you okay?"

The question was ridiculous. Her face was a rictus of pain, all gritted teeth.

"I think my legs are broken."

"Hang on, I'll get you out."

If I released my seatbelt, I'd fall straight on top of her. I rotated my body and extended my right hand to pull myself up by the driver's door, but now I couldn't reach the button to unfasten the harness. A flash of lightning lit the scene. We'd skidded off the road onto a grassy knoll.

"Thea, can you reach my seatbelt?"

"What?" She seemed only partially present.

I'd pulled myself high enough to brace one foot against the gearshift. "My seatbelt. I need you to release it."

I could hear her breathing hard against the pain. "Okay, got it."

The belt released. I pulled myself up and slithered down to the pavement. Thea's legs were wedged below the crumpled dashboard. I took her by the armpits, but the moment I began to pull, she released a scream so bloodcurdling I had to stop.

"Thea, I can't."

"Please, Proctor. Just get this over with."

The seat was the problem. If I could move it, I might be able to get her legs clear of the dash. I tried to ease it back, but the lever wouldn't budge; I would have to resort to brute force. I set my feet, placed my palms against the headrest, and pushed. I rocked it back and forth, each time feeling a little more play until, with a snap, the back of the seat broke loose and I was able to ease Thea free of the dashboard.

I lifted her into my arms, lay her on the grass, and knelt beside her.

"You have to find Elise," she said.

"I'm not going to leave you like this."

"You don't have a choice, Proctor." She explained what Otto had done. "That's what I came back to tell you." She reached for my hand, squeezed it once, and closed her eyes. "Just go."

The woman was right: unless I could wake Elise up, none of

this would matter. I jogged back to the wrecked van. It was still lying on its roof, although the force of our impact had spun it around to face the opposite direction. My hope was that I'd find Elise inside, but all I saw was Warren, dangling by one wrist from the railing.

I shook him by the shoulders, hard. "Where is she?"

"I don't know."

I shook him again, making his head bounce like a marionette's. "Yes, you fucking know!"

"I don't, I swear to you. When I came to, she was gone." He licked his bloody lips. "I'm sorry, Proctor. About all of it."

"Save it."

He let his head rock forward. "You know what's funny? I don't know what I thought I was doing. I don't even remember all that well. It was so long ago. All I know is, I'm sick of the whole thing." He looked up. "I told her, Proctor. About Caeli. That's what made the van crash. I think Elise has gone to look for her."

I moved to the front of the vehicle and dropped onto my stomach. The ring of keys on the driver's belt was just within my reach. I returned to Warren and unlocked the handcuff.

"I don't get it," he said. "You're letting me go?"

"Thea's over on the grass. Two broken legs and I don't know what else." When Warren said nothing, I added, "Well? You're still a doctor, aren't you?"

He was rubbing his wrist. "Yes. I'm still a doctor."

"Then go take care of her."

I stepped back out, into the wind and rain. *Elise, where are you, where did you go?*

Above the center of town, hovering low over the buildings, a whirling black mass had taken shape. Not a funnel cloud—more like a hurricane in miniature, with a distinctive eye at the center. Faster and faster the clouds wheeled; the eye widened, revealing a circular patch of unblemished, predawn sky, starless but for a single blue point.

There, I thought, and took off running.

The mob that swarms over the causeway is not the kind to bother with prisoners; nor does it linger on the watchmen, whom it quickly overwhelms. The watchmen are merely an obstacle, like a fence to be o'erleapt en route to a greater prize; so too the security faxes, which, absent anyone to give them orders, stand at mute attention as the crowd smashes them with bats and rocks and pisses on the pieces.

The drivers of the vans and cargo trucks are given no quarter, either. A few manage to escape, but the remaining twenty-three vehicles are seized by the mob, their drivers dragged from the cabs and beaten and hurled into the sea. As many people as can fit climb aboard the trucks.

The Annex is emptying. The Annex is on the move.

The first vehicles to reach the end of the causeway are met by a hastily assembled force of watchmen, which, caught on its heels, has no chance at all. They barrel through the roadblock, propelled by the force of their own momentum. How quickly it's all unfolding! To think that such freedom has always lain within their grasp, if only they had seen it!

At the wheel of the seventh vehicle in line, Cynthia is having some doubts—but not very many, and fewer by the moment. Yes, there is going to be more bloodshed—a massacre isn't out of the question—but it is also true that she was the one to hold Pappi in her arms as the last trace of life drained from his old blind eyes.

"Do you know how to use that thing?" Cynthia asks Stefano.

Riding in the passenger seat, the man is checking the magazine of the rifle he took off one of the watchmen. The windshield wipers slap at the rain.

"It doesn't look hard." He shoves the magazine back into the well.

"Please try to avoid it."

"If you say so." He means: no chance of that.

They cross what remains of the roadblock at the causeway's entrance. The watchmen are, by this time, in full retreat. Her head feels a little floaty, as if she's on something, making her both more focused and somehow less.

"We have to take the plaza," Stefano says. He pulls the bolt on the rifle, putting a round in the chamber. "Once we do that, it's over for them."

The line of vehicles has passed the top of the hill and is moving toward the center of town when the truck ahead of them comes to a halt. The tailgate opens; everybody in the rear compartment scrambles out and fans out into the streets. They move down the sidewalks, shattering windows, kicking in doors. One man, rail-thin with a dusting of pale beard, is holding a bottle with a rag in its mouth. He lights the rag and, with a satisfied smile, rears back and hurls the bottle into the nearest storefront, which bursts into flame.

"Time to move," Cynthia says.

They climb down from the cab. All the trucks are emptying; there are men, women, even some children. More are marching up the hill. They flow into the streets of Prospera like the waters of a flood—chanting, smashing, burning, throwing bottles and bricks. Smoke billows from all directions; terrified residents are bursting from the doors, fleeing ahead of the advancing mob.

"Come on," she says.

They join the crowd and move at a quickstep toward the plaza. The rain pours down, the wind howls around the corners of the buildings. It was never going to end any way but this, right here, right now. Jess was right after all.

The only question is how many bodies there will be, how high the pile, and who is going to be in it.

It was Otto's plan come to life.

Incite the malcontents, the provocateurs; let them reveal themselves. And once they did, be done with them, in the most permanent of fashions.

What Otto didn't count on was that it would be . . . everyone.

He arrives at the plaza as the watchmen are forming a defensive line in front of Overseers Hall. The men are visibly shaken by the swiftness of their defeat. The city is in chaos—people running, buildings in flames, the sounds of destruction coming from every direction. No one knows where to go. On top of it all, the storm has abruptly worsened; the fate of Prospera will be determined in a tumult of rain and wind, lightning and thunder, the sky in no less a state of revolt than the Annex itself.

"Where's Minister Brandt?" he asks Campbell.

"She was at the causeway. Apparently, she shot some guy. That's how the whole thing got started."

Amateur hour! Why the hell would she go to the Annex? Wasn't the whole *point* of being minister maintaining a certain distance?

"What should we do?" asks Campbell.

"Get the faxes in position in front of the hall."

"Um, they seem not to be . . . working."

"What the hell do you mean, they're not working?"

"No one can figure it out. When the rioters took out the ones at the causeway, the rest shut down."

Otto strides forward to the nearest watchman. "Give me your sidearm."

The man, with evident reluctance—now is not the time to surrender his weapon—releases it from his belt and hands it over. The watchmen aren't cut out for this, Otto knows; they're unaccustomed to the slightest resistance, more like schoolyard bullies than a dedicated fighting force. Complicating matters, most hadn't touched a firearm until three days ago, when Otto opened the armory. A mistake, he now sees: he's always kept the guns locked away to prevent the kind of senseless provocation that's put them where they are, staring down a mob in the rain—a mob now armed with those very same weapons.

But what's done is done. Otto faces the line.

"Gentlemen, the fate of Prospera is in your hands!"

At the far end of the plaza, the enemy has appeared.

"Fire on my order!"

So intent is Otto's focus on the task at hand that he fails to notice what's happening in the sky.

Mama!

"Baby, where are you?"

Mama, come quick!

Her bare feet splashing through the puddles, Elise tears down the street.

It's dark and cold and I can't see you!

The dense rain obscures her vision like a curtain. The small figure races ahead, never any closer, and never quite where Elise looks. Here? There? Her foot catches a curb and she stumbles but keeps going.

"Please," she cries, "wait!"

What is this feeling within her, this mad compulsion? She doesn't know who, or even what, she's chasing, only that she must.

Mama, help!

She looks up, and what she sees brings her to a halt. The porthole in the sky and the blue star at its center have returned. Elise thinks: *A blue star. Wasn't there something about a blue star?* A memory washes through her: the patio, and the warmth of a summer night and the energy of friends all around, and everyone saying, *See how blue, how beautiful it is?* as they press their eyes to Uncle Malcolm's (Malcolm's?) magic telescope.

The star has a name. What is its name?

Her face angled upward, she takes a slow step. It's true: the star is, indeed, beautiful. It is the most beautiful star in the history of stars, which is the history of everything. She cannot take her eyes from it, even as she also senses an ever-expanding human presence on all sides.

Mama, Mama!

The voice, like all things, is descendant; it comes from above. She continues walking forward, drawn by its call. When she reaches the fountain at the center of the plaza, she stops; she has reached the end of her journey. The star lies directly overhead, pouring its blue light down upon her like a spotlight falling on a stage.

"Yes," she says, "I'm here, baby. Mama is here."

Every story must reach the convergence of its elements—the moment when all the forces of the tale collide within a single space and time. And what is a dream if not a story we must tell ourselves?

Which is to say: I, Proctor Bennett, ferryman, ran straight into a war.

I emerged into the plaza. I had, by this time, sensed what awaited me there, or the kind of thing it was. What I'd failed to anticipate was the true scope of events—that I would suddenly find myself between two opposing armies.

And, in the middle of it all, Elise.

I almost made it to her.

Cynthia feels it first as a sensation of abstract slowing. The energy of the crowd has abruptly dissipated, but that is not the only change. It's as if something has gone slightly wrong with gravity. She feels a little seasick; the air is suddenly freezing. She turns to Stefano, meaning to ask him if he feels it, too. The man is still as a statue, rifle dangling at his side, his head rocked back to the sky.

Everyone is staring at the sky.

This thought is interrupted by a shout coming from the far side of the plaza. A lone figure is racing toward the fountain.

Stefano barely acknowledges her when she strips the rifle from his hands.

"Shoot him!" Otto yells, pointing. "Somebody, shoot that man!"

But nobody's listening. All the watchmen, slack-jawed, are gazing upward.

Otto sets his feet and raises the pistol. It feels unnatural in his hand, overly metallic and too heavy by half. At this distance, hitting a man in motion will be just about impossible; better to let Proctor come to him. Otto picks a spot along Proctor's trajectory and levels the sights.

As Proctor passes through them, he fires.

An interesting fact of being shot—one I was not aware of at the time—is that it's possible not to notice right away.

I did feel *something:* a nudge of pressure on my left side, as if I'd been bumped in a crowd, followed by a pricking sensation, no more noteworthy than the sting of a bee. I did not, as yet, connect these things to the crack of Otto's pistol, which itself had failed to fully register as anything pertaining to me. Thus, I ran on—five steps, ten, perhaps a few more—and then the pain arrived.

Down I went, onto my hands and knees.

A second shot: something whizzed by my head. I looked downrange and saw Otto marching toward me. A flash and my left hip exploded in a burst of blood and bone.

Otto fired again. This time the point of impact was unknown, as I had ceased to feel very much at all—or, rather, felt far too much to parse the details. I was a body being shot, that was the extent of it. I dug my fingers into the grass and began to crawl. I had no destination in mind; my direction was simply "away."

"Good God," Otto said, "will you please just die?"

He jammed his foot beneath my rib cage and flipped me over. I expected to be staring straight down the barrel of the man's gun, but I wasn't. The gun wasn't pointed at me at all.

It was pointing at Elise.

Otto was standing behind her, one arm wrapping her waist, the muzzle of the pistol pressed against the side of her head. Her eyes were wide with fear and mute astonishment. I tried without success to speak through the blood that was filling the back of my throat.

"Having trouble talking, Bennett?" Otto said. "That's new."

My sense of my surroundings had begun to dissipate; I felt a great weariness in my chest, as if the soft, pink tissue of my lungs were solidifying. I was, I realized, drowning in my own blood—drowning at last. I coughed, spraying a nimbus of red droplets, and tried again to form words.

"What's that you say?"

Each syllable was a stab of agony. And yet, it had to be endured.

I said, "Look . . . up."

Cynthia, racing toward the fountain, doesn't understand what she's seeing. There's Proctor, lying on the ground. There's a man with a pistol, which he is pressing to a woman's head. The man with the pistol doesn't seem to have noticed her, which gives Cynthia some advantage, but as long as he's holding the woman, she cannot use it. And the rifle: How, exactly, does it work?

She is twenty yards away when something happens. Suddenly, the man cries out—she hears the word "No!"—and, releasing the woman, stumbles backward, looking at the sky.

The man: it's Otto Winspear.

Cynthia drops to one knee, steadies the rifle, and fires.

The butt of the rifle crashes into her shoulder like a brass-knuckled punch. She's missed him by a mile. Goddamnit! Not only has she missed; she's tipped her hand. Otto, following the sound of the shot, turns and looks right at her. He raises the pistol as she puts him in her sights.

At the same moment, they fire.

The impulse to follow a simple command is strong; our first instinct is to obey, especially the wishes of a dying man.

And so did Otto Winspear lift his eyes to see what mine beheld: the depthless clarity of space and, at the center, drinking up the heavens' light, the great blue curve of an ice-bound world.

Caelus.

My brain, in its state of imminent dissolution, could no longer follow what was happening with any precision. There were gunshots. There were sudden, animalistic cries. There was Elise covering my body with hers, the most welcome embrace of my life, and also, I believed, the last.

Then: silence.

Silence but for my own gurgling breath, and the quiet sound of Elise's crying. She was kneeling beside me, cradling my head in her hands, pressing her cheek to mine.

"Proctor, I'm sorry, I'm sorry, I'm so, so sorry."

"She's here," I said, for I felt this to be so. Our daughter, Caeli, was here.

"I can't, I can't."

"Yes," I said, "you . . . can." She was a woman on the precipice, afraid to leap. "Say it."

"Please."

Above me, Caelus continued in its expansion, its grand assertion upon the heavens. It filled my eyes and mind with the glorious sight of it.

"All you have to do . . . is say . . . her name."

There is power in a name. It is through names that we bring all things into this world, and when they leave, it is names we carry with us, so they are never truly gone.

Elise's voice was a whisper: "Caeli."

"Again."

Her voice broke with a sob: *"Caeli."*

I knew without looking—for I could not so much as turn my head—that our little girl was there. Not the wisecracking, teenaged Caeli of the beach, but the one we'd lost and left. She was sitting on the grass with her legs crossed beneath her, still in her nightdress, old Mister Otter resting in her lap; and I knew as well the moment when Elise took our daughter in her arms, weeping softly, saying her name over and over and over. A new sensation swept my body, strange and still. I would know death in this place. What did it mean, to die in a dream? Would it be the same? Would it be a plunge into unbeing, or would I yet find myself passing into some new realm? And the thought came to me that maybe Thea had been right after all, that it was and always would be impossible to know what was dream and what was not; that all creation was boxes within boxes within boxes, each the dream of a different god.

I sensed, then, a new presence. Unshouldering her rifle, my mother—for that is how I thought of her—dropped to her knees beside me. There were dark streaks on her face, which, after a moment, I understood to be blood; she was pressing one hand against a wound in her upper arm, from which more blood was flowing. I did not then know that Otto was lying on the grass with a bullet in his chest, or how my mother had come to be shot. I was sorry for her pain, but also glad, so very glad, to see her.

"Proctor," she said, and took my hand, though I could not feel this. The blood on her cheeks was streaked with her tears. "I don't understand what's happening."

"It's . . . all right," I told her.

She hung her head and wept. "Oh, Proctor, Proctor."

The dream was dissolving around us; my breath had all but stopped. I hardly minded. It seemed fitting, as did the final words I would speak in this world.

"You've arrived."

But I was speaking to no one. Mother, like everyone else, was gone.

VIII

THE DEPARTED

40

This is a story in which no one dies.

Not Otto Winspear or Nicholas "Pappi" Pappier, chief administrator for resettlement operations; not the firebrand Jessica Ordway or the awful Regan Brandt or Sandra with her paint swatches; not Callista Laird, whose brief stay at the Nursery, with its soporific food and piped-in platitudes, was so rudely interrupted before she could travel its erotic off-ramp to oblivion; no Prosperans, no colonists, not even any watchmen, who were never real to begin with. Like gentle Bernardo and sashaying Danielle, they were features of the dreamspace itself—setting, not character.

No one. Not even me.

There were things to sort out. Sixty-eight thousand colonists couldn't be yanked from stasis simultaneously. *Oranios* was a cargo vessel, not a passenger liner; imagine a stadium's worth of men and women, naked as Michelangelo's David, in a state of profound disorientation, ejecting an oceanic quantity of vomitus onto the floors by their cabinets—and, when that was done, needing clothing, food, sanitation, medical care, and a place to lay their heads. The original plan had been to awaken the colonists five hundred at a time and relocate them to the planet before arousing the next group from stasis; full exodus was expected to take place over a period of two Earth years. But the sudden, total collapse of the dreamspace radically hastened this schedule. All the colonists still in stasis were now caught in the limbo of their own minds; after such an extended sleep, it wouldn't take long before their dreams turned on them like a pack of wild dogs.

The problem was compounded by other factors, two in particular. The first was the condition of the reactor, which provided primary propulsion for low orbital maneuvering. The core was down to forty-two percent of reactive mass—within the margin of safety, but barely. The second issue, more dire, was breathable air. A human being in stasis consumes no oxygen and, therefore, produces no carbon dioxide; too many breathing bodies, and the CO_2 scrubbers on *Oranios* wouldn't be able to keep up. In other words, the more colonists we awakened, the faster we'd have to get them off the ship, in a constantly accelerating feedback loop.

Thus: sixty days.

None of this would have been easy under the best circumstances, but there was one more variable to contend with: who remembered what. Some of the colonists, like Antone, awakened with a clear sense of where they were and their expected roles, the things and people and events of Prospera only vaguely recalled; others, like me, at first had no understanding of their surroundings, their minds still caught in the dream world. But sooner or later, just as Quinn had said, the memory of the dream caught up with everyone, with predictably chaotic results. Those preexisting, Earth-bound relationships—spouses, lovers, colleagues, friends—that had formed the backbone of people's lives and identities before departure: all were scrambled, and in some cases completely upended, by the things that had happened in the dreamspace.

Partners who had been together for years suddenly found themselves drawn to wholly new people, or riven by one or the other's relationship with a third party. Lifelong friends discovered sudden mutual hatreds over a remembered injury. People suffered crushing shame over the realization that they'd done horrible things. Some managed to laugh these matters off—who could be held responsible for their behavior in a dream?—but many more could not, and the rapid re-sorting of these various alliances and antipathies preoccupied the ship. There was jealousy and guilt. There were recriminations and arguments. There were fistfights, two suicides, and, in one instance, an actual murder. It was something we'd anticipated but had failed to find a solution for—all the assurances in the world that "none of it was real" barely moved the meter. By the time we'd awakened a quarter of the colonists, we'd begun to wonder if they'd ever be able to form a cohesive social unit again.

But then a funny thing happened. Everyone forgot.

"Forgot" is, perhaps, not the correct word. While the things that had happened in Prospera remained clear in most people's minds, as time went by—hectic, frantic days of making ready for departure—they seemed to matter less. In many ways, the psychological effect proved rather like the sensation of convergence in the dreamspace—a fleeting, déjà vu–ish awareness of past events, not terribly important in the day-to-day.

None of this was true for the colonists' memory of their treatment at the hands of the investors. As with Antone, their hatred was foamingly visceral. The cabinets where the investors remained in stasis—all twelve thousand of them, including Otto and Callista—were separate from the colonists'; we placed guards at all the access points to this area of the ship. With Cynthia and Pappi to vouch for them, the rest of the executive staff managed to avoid being targets of the colonists' ire, but I did not; I was the author of their remembered misery. I kept to the dome, delegating most responsibilities to Quinn and Thea and the others. My job was over anyway. I had led the colonists to their new home; the rest was theirs to figure out.

There was happiness as well, of course—joyful reunions, relationships restored, the anticipation of a new life in the making. It was on the eve of his departure for the planet surface that my brother, Malcolm, paid me a visit in my quarters. By this time, both of us had managed to work through the confusion of having been, for a time, father and son. We'd even laughed about it, though with a core of seriousness: the acknowledgment that my brother had always been, in every way that mattered, a father figure to me. (With Cynthia, it was a different story. I simply couldn't separate her from the role of mother, and stopped trying. She confessed she felt the same.)

"Mind the interruption?" he asked at the door.

"There's nothing to interrupt," I said, and smiled. "Please, come in."

He sat on the edge of my bunk. I sensed that he was troubled by something.

"Mal, what is it?"

He cleared his throat. "I think I'm here to apologize, actually."

"What for?"

"That whole"—he made a nervous gesture—"*episode* on the pier."

"There's nothing to apologize for. And it all worked out in the end. We wouldn't even be here if it hadn't happened."

"It's not just that." He paused, gathering himself. "We haven't really talked about it, but I don't think I was always the best father to you. Is that strange to say?"

"No stranger than anything else." I smiled to reassure him. "You were fine. Any shortcomings, all is forgiven."

He was looking at his hands. A moment passed.

"What you said to me, just before you left me on the ferry . . ."

"Listen, Mal—"

"No, let me finish. I didn't answer you then, and I should have.

It's just not a thing I'm good at, I guess. So, I'm answering now. I love you, too." He lifted his eyes. "That's what I came to say. That, and I know what you're planning to do."

So here it was. "You've been talking to Quinn."

"Everybody *knows,* Proctor. We've all been trying to figure out how to talk you out of it."

"And what did you come up with?"

"That I should come to your quarters, pull big-brother rank, and tell you not to. Which I'm not going to do."

"Why not?"

"Because of what I just told you." He rose and put his hand on my shoulder. "One last thing. This comes from both me and Cynthia. You're the captain of this ship, am I right?"

"Director, but I suppose it's the same thing."

"Then, as captain, would you marry us?"

From among the colonists, Oona tracked down a minister, who wrote out the words for me; we gathered in the dome, Quinn serving as best man (since I was already spoken for as officiant), Thea as maid of honor, and when it was done—the ceremony took all of thirty seconds—toasted the happy couple with one of the last remaining bottles of champagne in the universe.

No one mentioned Elise. How could they?

And so, one hundred and thirty-seven years late and far too soon, came the time to say goodbye.

The last landing boat was docked and loaded. My brother and his wife were already gone, as were Pappi and the rest of the colonists. The settlement site was a grassy plain on the continent's southwest coast, along the shores of a wide, glacial river. According to sources on the ground, the water was clean and cold and teemed with fish, including something rather like a trout, with a white, peppery meat.

I didn't want to go aboard the final shuttle, lest I lose my nerve, so I said my last farewells at the air lock. From Oona I received a long, weepy hug, followed by Jason, who snapped to attention and gave me a crisp salute like the naval aviator he was. I recalled a time, not so long ago, when, just a boy in his first-job suit and brand-new wingtips, he'd told me, *All I've ever wanted is to be like you.* It was a touching thing to hear at the time, and even more touching to recall now. Anything I might have said would have felt inadequate, so I embraced him instead, flummoxing the poor man completely. I'd never had a son and never would, or a younger brother to teach the ways of life, as Malcolm had taught me; and the thought came to me then that who we are to one another isn't so easy to categorize after all: that fathers can be sons, and lovers friends, and daughters mothers, and that such words as these tell only half the story, maybe not even half.

"I'm proud of you," I told him.

He entered the air lock and boarded the boat. Only Quinn and Thea remained.

"I wish I could change your mind," Quinn said.

"You can't, but thank you."

"I'll say it again: you don't have to do this. The investors don't deserve it. You don't owe those people a thing."

He was wrong; I did. They had done everything I'd asked of them, and more.

I said, "Do you remember the night we were together in the lair? It was just before the watchmen showed up."

"It's a little hazy, but sort of."

"You said, 'You have the same problem everybody else has. You know a lot of things. You believe almost nothing.' I didn't understand it at the time, but I understand it now. This is what I'm meant to do. It's been that way from the start."

To bring the matter to a close, I offered him my hand. For a moment, Quinn just looked at it; then, with a small sigh of defeat, he took it in his own. His grip, as we shook, was firm and final.

"Goodbye, Quinn. Thanks for everything."

"Goodbye, Proctor."

He turned away and headed through the air lock.

"Well," Thea said, and cleared her throat, "this is it, I guess."

She was standing apart from me, arms crossed over her chest.

"I guess it is," I said.

"I'm not going to cry, you know. I'm saving up for later."

"That's probably best."

"Damn you, Proctor."

"I know," I said. "I'm sorry."

"Aw, fuck it." Looking away, she rubbed her eyes with the back of her wrist. "I don't know how to do this. How do you do this?"

A knot had lodged in my throat. "What you do is, you get aboard the shuttle and go live your life."

"Really? That's what you've got? 'Have a nice life'?"

"A great life. The very best life there is."

"Promise you'll write, okay? Because I will if you will."

I did my best to smile. "Sure thing. What else would I do with all these extra stamps?"

"Goddamnit, Proctor. This *hurts.*"

She hugged me then, wrapping me in a fierce, fast embrace—the kind that's over before you know it but remember all your life.

"I understand," she said. "I don't have to like it. But I do understand." She held on another few seconds, as did I, both of us afraid to let go and also not to. "Go be with them," she said. Then she broke away, stepped into the air lock, sealed the door, and strode away without looking back.

I made my way up to the dome. How strange was the sensation, to be the only waking soul aboard her—aboard my ship, my *Oranios.* The screen was open. Below me, the great blue planet turned in the vastness. How many generations would pass before the story of *Oranios* would pass into history, into myth? Would humanity's children even remember her? And if they did, what story would they tell themselves? *We came from above, from far away; we traveled here aboard a great ship that sailed across the heav-*

ens, which are the stars at night; and that is known as the day of arrival, when all things of the world began.

I watched the shuttle as it fell, traveling down and away. In space, all things move with perfect grace; they are joined to the deepest of forces, caught in the very current of existence. The image receded. Its details were subsumed. The gleaming fuselage. The upswept, avian wings. There was a small burst as the engine fired, the craft orienting itself for reentry.

A streak of light.

So, at the last, a confession. I was the one who did it.

Not the Nursery; that was Elise. But the rest of it. The Annex. The drones and watchmen. The splendid houses and grand edifices and endless, temperate days for the privileged few to pass in gentle ease while the unacknowledged masses labored in the shadows of their masters' pleasure. The dream of Prospera may have been Elise's; the design was mine from the start.

Why did I do it? What thought possessed me that I should make one person's happy dream another's ceaseless nightmare? Better to ask: Who, having slumbered centuries in paradise, would willingly awaken to build a life from nothing, to hew it from the rock and ice of an alien world? To the colonists I say: I gave you what you needed, which was a weight to push against. A life you would be glad to leave, and a life to make you ready.

Do you hate me for this? Surely I have earned your loathing. I will not ask you for forgiveness. For such a crime as mine, there can be no pardon, save for God's alone.

And to you, the sleepers in my keeping: you have lived for countless lifetimes; you shall live for countless more. They will be different from the ones you've always known; your days of idleness and ease are gone. This is not a punishment—far from it. It is my gift to you, that you should be redeemed.

I will give you childhood, so that you might know innocence.

Age, so you will know the prize of youth.

Children, so that you will care for the future.

Toil, so that you will know the value of a day.

The body's failings, so that you will know its worth.

Death, so that you will cherish the bittersweet beauty of life.

We are, each of us, born a sparkling soul, clothed only in our newness; it is life that makes us what we are. You have been one thing; now you will learn to be another.

And so we voyage out once more. What will we find at our final port of call? What orts of mankind yet remain upon the plate? Shall we discover only the wind-scraped remains of a ruined world, none but ourselves for company? Not all of us will live to see that day. Time's nibbling jaws can be slowed; they cannot be stopped. Circuits will fail. Mechanisms will falter. Others among you will die in your cabinets of time itself—that is to say, of age. A friend, sitting across a table, will look up to find a vacant chair where you had sat. A spouse will turn to you in bed and discover only empty space, the sheets still warm with the heat of your vanished body. A shock, yet your absence will be met with perplexity above all else, the dreamspace quickly subsuming your memory, like waves over a drowned man. *Whatever happened to . . . ? Has anybody seen . . . ? Wasn't she right here . . . ?* They will shake their heads in puzzlement and then, with only the vaguest feeling of disturbance, go on about their business. *How strange, how very strange . . .*

We are indeed such stuff as dreams are made on, our little life rounded with a sleep.

Thus I beam this tale into the cosmos: this message in a bottle, tossed into the heavens' waves. Perhaps there is no one to receive it. Perhaps there is but one mind left to listen: the mind behind all things, like a face beneath the painter's canvas. Whoever you are, in whatever form you take—time, matter, light—I ask one thing only: that you leave us as we are. Let us sleep, and dream, and do the work of being human.

The engines fire; the great sails spread their canvas to catch creation's breath; my ship, my *Oranios,* drops its mooring and slips away from shore. In the stasis chamber, a friend is waiting. He greets me with good, masculine cheer and shows me to my cabinet, which stands open. Beside it, Elise sleeps, dreaming her own dreams. Soon I will give her another.

"Director Bennett?"

I am in the process of undressing. The cold of the room prickles my skin. "Yes, Bernardo?"

"Am I to understand that we will be returning to our point of origin?"

"Yes."

"To Earth."

"That's correct."

"And am I to further understand that you will be serving as Designer of the dreamspace?"

Indeed I am, I tell him.

"Very good, Director Bennett. May I ask if you have designated an alternate?"

I am nothing if not a believer in redemption. "That would be Dr. Warren Singh."

"And is there a second alternate, if Dr. Singh is unable to continue in that role?"

"Callista Laird."

"Very well."

Perched on the edge of my cabinet, I tie off my arm with surgical tubing and inject myself with the suppressors.

"May I assist you with the headset, Director Bennett?"

It is hardly necessary. "You may."

I lie back in the cabinet. Bernardo affixes the array to my skull like a crown of thorns.

"You've always been a good friend to me," I tell him. "I just wanted to say that."

"That's kind of you, Director Bennett. That's most gratifying to hear."

"Before we do this, mind if I ask you something?"

"Of course, sir."

"Do you dream, Bernardo?"

His circuits whirr, and then he says, "Since I do not sleep, Director Bennett, in the proper sense of the term, I cannot say that I've had the opportunity to do so. Although when I come out of hibernation mode, I often feel that I am returning from a journey of some kind."

"Well, there you go," I tell him. "That's dreaming."

"But I am a machine, sir."

"Maybe, maybe not. Maybe you're a person like me, you're just *dreaming* you're a machine. Did you ever think of that?"

Whirr, whirr. "It's an interesting thought, Director Bennett."

"Anyway," I say, "take it for what it's worth. It's just an idea I had."

"And I thank you for sharing it with me. I will give it some consideration. Will there be anything else?"

"I don't think so, no."

"Very well." He backs away. "Shall I proceed?"

I nod. "Arrival come, Bernardo."

"Sir?"

"Sorry, it's an expression. It means I'll see you when we get there."

"Ah," replies Bernardo, delightedly. "Then allow me the privilege of saying 'arrival come' to you as well, Director Bennett. I wish you pleasant dreams."

"And I you, my friend."

The lid seals. With a gurgling sound and a cold shock, the fluid rises, swirling over my body. I close my eyes.

My name is Proctor Bennett. I am a ferryman.

And I'm gone.

41

Thea has never dug a latrine before. Or driven a backhoe. Or stood in a line a hundred people deep to fill a metal tray with plain, nutritious food she cannot get enough of, since she's starving half the time, famished for the rest.

She's never done most of the things she does now.

The days are cold, the nights still colder. The wind tears through the seams of her coat; it shakes the walls of the tent like a bedsheet on a line, a tent she shares with a dozen other women, sleeping cheek by jowl. One of them is Sandra—the same bright, cheerful presence (she does yoga every morning on the floor of the tent) but also a mechanical engineer with a specialization in hydraulics (hence the digging of latrines). She is, as Thea learns, from Minnesota's Iron Range: a woman used to the cold. She'd signed on as a colonist when she'd seen Proctor interviewed on television. Her parents were gone; she was recently divorced, childless, without even a dog for company. In college she'd worked summers as a mountain guide in Idaho, leading groups of high schoolers into the wilderness, back when there still was one. Proctor's pitch had struck a nerve. The world was in deep trouble; anyone with eyes and half a brain could see that. She'd already thought of doing a stint off-world—Luna, maybe, or one of the mining stations on Mars. (A sure sign, she said, that she was in a depressive tailspin.) She rewatched Proctor's interview, then watched it again, and by the fourth viewing felt a spark of hopefulness. *What the hell,* she thought, *why not? There's nothing here for me. I'd take a whole new planet, any day.*

There's nothing here for me. How many times has Thea heard those words from the colonists she's met? *There was nothing; now there is something.*

In the free time she has—not much—she walks. Most days are cloudy, but Thea doesn't mind; the clouds make the sky interesting, full of depth and movement, unlike the skies over Prospera, with their relentless sunshine. She has found a route she likes, following the bank of the river to the sea. The beach is wide, with fine, dark sand, almost black. Wide waves unfurl metronomically upon the shoreline; behind her, crenelating the horizon, are mountains, their jagged faces glinting with ice.

She has seen little of Quinn and the others. Everyone is simply too busy with their allotted tasks. For this reason, Thea has yet to tell anyone her news, though it's also true that she's content to bide her time: to be alone with her secret as long as she can, like the answer to a question she's not sure anyone has posed.

She makes her way down the beach. When she first went exploring, the smallest sounds or the tiniest movements at the periphery quickened her heart with fear. But as the weeks have gone by, she's adjusted. More than adjusted—she craves it: the solitude, the peace. Her perceptions of the place have likewise deepened. Not merely the small things—the birds and plants and animals—but certain macro-truths as well. Caelus, for instance, has a certain smell. It is neither good nor bad—there is a slightly burnt quality to it, and something of ginger—and she wonders if this is true of all planets, that each has its own distinct odor, the way people's houses do. A thought that, naturally, turns her mind to the Caelusians. The colonists have yet to find any remains, though neither have they had occasion to look; Thea supposes this will happen in due course, once buildings are built, fields planted, and septic systems dug. She wonders: Who were they, these departed beings, lost in time? Were they creatures like us, with our symmetrical arrangements of arms and legs and ears and eyes, or did they follow a different evolutionary playbook entirely? Did they have feelings like ours? Did they love, hate, long, be longed for? Did they have families? Did they love and care for children? And did any among them see the end coming and, looking aloft, plot their escape? There are times, such as now, when Thea can almost feel them: spirits in the ether, like a portrait of the past laid atop the present moment.

There's a point where the beach narrows to nearly nothing, where she likes to sit and watch the night come on. But as she nears, she sees her spot's already taken. A figure rests on the sand with his back against a boulder, looking out to sea. She first supposes it might be Quinn—he, too, has a habit of wandering off—but it isn't. It's Pappi.

Thea's barely seen him—or, more accurately, barely seen him in private. As director of resettlement, the man is both everywhere and never in one place for long. So, finding him now, all by himself, seems a little incongruous, though not, on second thought, surprising; surely someone in his position needs doses of solitude. Indeed, he's so lost in reverie that he fails to notice her approaching until she's just a few feet away, when, with a faint start, he looks up at her.

"Thea." He offers a bright smile. "This is a welcome surprise."

No longer the wild-haired derelict of the Annex, he is a hale, rugged-looking man with sharp blue eyes and a neatly trimmed beard.

"Sorry to disturb you," she says. "If you'd rather—"

"Not at all. It's nice to see you." He pats the sand next to him. "Take a seat."

She does. The sand is cool and moist beneath her. The sun is receding behind them, deepening the gray of the sky.

"I didn't know you came down here," she says. "I thought it was just me."

He shrugs lightly. "Sometimes I do. It's good to get away once in a while."

"How's Claire? I haven't seen her."

The woman, a nutritionist, is assigned to the kitchens. She's also not a day over thirty.

Pappi says, "Happy as a clam, as far as I can tell. Feeding the multitudes agrees with her."

"If you don't mind my asking—?"

"Are we together?" Pappi shakes his head. "No. I'm sorry to say, that's over."

Thea had a feeling. "A lot of that going around, I guess," she says. "Honestly, though, that makes me a little sad."

"Me, too. But it was time. Remember, the two of us were together almost thirty years. I'd say that's more than enough."

They sit quietly for a few minutes, watching the waves unfurling beneath a darkening sky. As often happens at night, the clouds have thinned and separated. Soon there will be stars.

"You know what's strange?" Pappi says. "It surprises me to say it, but I actually miss being blind sometimes."

Thea startles. "You do?"

"There was something . . . I don't know, freeing about it. And I don't just mean that nobody expected anything from me, though that certainly had its advantages. It's probably the reason Claire's so sick of me. But the thing was, I *did* see. I just didn't see what everybody else did."

"What did you see?"

Pappi pauses. "Something truer, if that makes sense. Like I could get past the surface of things." He turns his face toward her.

"Remember when I painted your picture? It was when we first met."

"How could I forget?"

He aims his gaze over the sea again. "To be honest, at the start I was just screwing around. I thought if you got bored enough, you'd leave me alone. But then you did something strange. It was the way you sat, actually."

"Sat? Like in the chair?"

Pappi nods. "You were just so *still.* I don't mean that you weren't all fidgety, like I thought you'd be. It was something more than that. It was like your body had left the room but the real you was still right there. The rest was just illusion."

"Well, technically, it was."

"Maybe. I'm not sure I know what's what anymore. Which is probably the reason I come down here. To try to figure that out."

Thea asks, "Do you think you'll paint again?"

Pappi shakes his head. "I think I'll quit while I'm ahead. What about you? You're the real artist around here. You always were."

Thea shrugs. "Turns out I'm actually pretty handy with a backhoe. I think I'll put my talents there for the moment."

"We'll need other things eventually. The thinkers, the artists, the writers."

"Key word 'eventually.'"

"So, the backhoe for now."

She nods. "Yes, for now."

Another silence goes by.

Thea says, "Do you ever think about them? The Caelusians."

"What makes you ask that?"

The notion is crazy, she knows, yet the need to ask is strong. "It's just . . . do you ever wonder if they're somehow still here?"

"I don't have to, Thea. I *know* they're here."

The statement is strange. "You do?"

"Yes, I do," he says and, turning toward her, smiles. "They're here, because they're us." He gets to his feet. "It's late—I should be getting back. You coming?"

"I thought I'd sit a while longer. Watch the stars."

He thinks a moment, then nods. "Well, just be careful."

"Oh, I think I know the way well enough by now."

"I'm sure you do." He begins to leave but stops himself, turning toward her again. "I meant to ask. Did you tell him?"

Thea, momentarily confounded, is about to say: Tell who what? But then she remembers who she's dealing with. She shakes her head: No.

Pappi says, "Because you knew he was going to leave."

"Because he *had* to leave. I didn't want to make it any harder than it was."

"Who else knows? If you don't mind my asking."

"Nobody so far."

Pappi pauses, then says, "Well, I wouldn't wait. Claire's going to figure it out just by looking at you. You don't want to hurt the woman's feelings." He regards her a moment. "It'll be all right, Thea," he says.

"I know it will."

He smiles at her. "Just mind your step in the dark, you hear?"

Thea watches him make his way down the beach. The sun is gone; she watches as, one by one, the stars come out. She is looking for Proctor, trying to parse the lights of *Oranios* from the heavenly multitude. It's impossible, of course—the ship is long gone, making its long arc around the sun before hurling away—and yet she has to try.

She is pregnant; it happened that night on the roof. She has known this since the antechamber, when, in the wake of Dr. Patty's sudden departure, she heard a sudden sound. For everyone else, the antechamber was a place of memory, but not for her; for Thea, dreaming for two, the antechamber was something else entirely. She followed the sound to the end of the passageway, opened the door, and there beheld the source: a crib, and in that crib, the small, mewling bundle of a baby, swaddled in blue. A boy. She lifted him into her arms; the baby fussed a moment and then, nestling against her, fell quiet. A miraculous feeling, to hold this sparkling new being in her arms! The curtains of the nursery glowed with morning light; birds were singing in the trees outside. She carried her baby to the window to show him. There is the world, she whispered. Do you see? There is the grass, there are the trees, there are the birds singing in the trees. She began to sing herself: a lullaby, the only one she knew. *Dreams are flowing like a river, since the comforter has come . . .* It was an old song, a remembered song; where had she heard it? But she had been a baby once; someone must have sung it to her. *Everything is turned to gladness, all around this glorious guest. Banished unbelief and sadness, all is perfect peace and rest.* At the window Thea swayed and sang, the small, sweet bundle of her baby snug against her; and she abided there, full of peace and gladness, until everything was dark.

It will be all right, she thinks. That is what she'd say to Proctor now, if she could. That everything will be all right.

Epilogue

THE FACES IN THE STARS

Gentle breath of yours my sails
Must fill, or else my project fails
—Shakespeare, *The Tempest*

Director Proctor Bennett leans back in his chair, places the tips of his fingers together, and, with patient solemnity, regards the two small figures before him. He allows a little time to pass and then, with a dramatic, weary sigh, says:

"Well? What do the two of you have to say for yourselves?"

It's Nabil who leaps in. "She hit me! I wasn't doing anything!"

"That's a lie!" Regan cries. "He totally started it!"

"Did not!"

"Did too!"

"Enough."

They freeze.

Proctor says, "I'm not particularly interested in who started it this time. It's only September, and Mr. Cordell has already had it with the two of you. *Had* it. Am I making myself clear?"

Eyes downcast, they nod.

"Here's what's going to happen. As far as I'm concerned, the two of you are best friends from now on. You will eat lunch together. You will walk together between classes. You will play together at recess. If I look out my window or walk down the hall and see one of you without the other, I will not be happy. You *will* work out your differences and you *will* be friends, like it or not."

Their faces are aghast. "But . . . you can't!" Regan sputters.

"That's totally unfair!" cries Nabil.

Ignoring their protests, Proctor continues: "The other thing is that you owe Mr. Cordell an apology. Tonight, you are each to write him a letter. In your letter, you will describe, in painstaking detail, the nature of your error, and precisely how sorry you are. Which, to give you a hint, is very, *very* sorry. You will deliver those letters to me first thing in the morning, and I will pass them along to Mr. Cordell. Understood?"

The looks on their faces are so abjectly wretched, Proctor wants to laugh. Being friends! The horror! What a punishment!

"Regan?"

"Yes, Director Bennett."

"Yes what?"

"Yes, I understand."

"And what exactly do you understand?"

Speaking the words visibly pains the girl. "We're going to be friends. We're going to write a letter."

He shifts his eyes to Nabil. "What about you?"

"Fine, whatever," the boy huffs.

He expected as much from Nabil—always the clubhouse lawyer, quick to point out the ways he's been treated unjustly. Proctor arches his eyebrows in his most teacherly manner. "I beg your pardon?"

Nabil opens his mouth, perhaps to launch more words of protest, but then thinks the better of it and tries again: "What she said. We're supposed to like each other."

"And?" Lord, it's like pulling teeth with this boy.

"Tell Mr. Cordell we're sorry."

Studying the two of them over the tips of his fingers, Proctor allows another short silence to pass: a bit of stern-teacher theater, as he calls it.

"Now scoot," he says.

Off they go. The thing is, Proctor thinks, they're good kids, which is to say, good in the way that all kids can be good if you show them how. It's something he learned from his own years in the classroom, before he took on the job of academy director. They're also bright—the smartest in their class, Amos tells him—which is, of course, the reason they can't stand each other.

Proctor returns to his paperwork—attendance records, equipment requisitions, a short note to the faculty to remind them about first-quarter grade reports, which are right around the corner—and by the time he's finished, the final bell has rung. He makes his way through the empty hallways, still tangy with pre-adolescent sweat, past the walls of student artwork, the inspirational posters ("Be a friend to make a friend!"), the bulletin boards tacked with announcements. He is about to exit the building when a voice calls to him from behind.

It's Warren, carrying his leather bag of instruments, a stethoscope still swinging from his neck. The man has spent the day giving physical exams to the students, and it shows. His hair is askew, his clothing rumpled; there's a brown stain on the front of his shirt that Proctor decides not to ask about. The physicals are part of a new program out of the community health department, which Warren heads. He's moving through one grade per day.

"How'd it go?" Proctor asks him. "You look like you got dragged from a horse."

"Oh, this?" Warren says, fingering the stain. "Not what it looks like. Things got a little out of hand at the party is all."

"There was a party?"

"Proctor, Proctor, Proctor. You want to ask a line of thirty first graders to open up and say 'Aaah,' you better give them cupcakes."

"I was not aware."

"It's, like, the second thing they teach you in doctor school. The first is how to keep small children from pulling on your stethoscope when it's in your ears. You wouldn't believe how much that hurts."

Proctor laughs. "Are you really sure you want to do every grade yourself? You can send somebody else, you know. My feelings won't be hurt."

Warren waves this away. "Nah, forget it. It's nice to do some actual doctoring for a change. Plus," he says with a grin, "when else would I get the chance to be in a cupcake war?"

"Who won?"

"Everybody but the cupcakes."

They head outside and part ways—Warren back to his office, Proctor to catch a bit of a soccer game in progress. The campus houses grades K–8, but they share athletic fields with the high school; today it's District 6 versus District 4. It's a good game, surprisingly close, given that District 4 has all the best players this year, and Proctor lingers a few minutes before heading to the rear of the school building, where scaffolding has been erected. He looks up, shielding his eye against the glare.

"Otto," he calls, "how's it going up there?"

The superintendent's face peeks over the edge of the scaffolding. "Hang on, I'll be down in a second."

He leaves his two assistants, Hanson and Campbell, to keep working and clambers down.

"We've got a problem," Otto tells him.

"Don't say that."

"Better if I show you."

Otto walks to the base of the building, where debris is scattered. He picks up a board and carries it back.

"See this?" he says, displaying the wood, which is soggy and stained. "The sheathing's totally rotted. My guess is, water's been running up under the shingles for years."

"So, patch it. Can't you patch it?"

"I could, but we'd be chasing our tails. I've pulled shingles on all sides of the building. Same story. The whole thing's a goner. It has to be replaced."

It's the worst conceivable news. "I've got nothing like this in the budget, Otto. Not even close."

"This really can't wait. If we start now, we'll be lucky to finish before winter. You don't want ice dams with a roof like that."

Proctor steps back to get a better angle and once again looks up, as if looking at the roof will somehow fix it. Hanson is sitting on the peak, fearlessly eating a sandwich. Campbell is standing on a cleat a few feet below him, prying off shingles with the claw of a hammer.

"So, what do you want me to do?"

"I guess I can talk to her," Proctor says.

"Talk fast," says Otto.

"Hello, Sacha. Is she in?"

The woman swivels in her chair. "Callista! Your son-in-law's here!" She angles her head toward the door. "Go ahead."

He steps through. Callista's office is small—tiny, really, given the breadth of her responsibilities—and as cluttered as a kindergarten. Behind her desk, which is barricaded by tall stacks of paper, his mother-in-law is sitting at an angle, a pen tucked in the waves of her white hair, her feet propped on a stool to take pressure off her lower back, as she pages through a legal pad. Without looking in his direction, she holds up a palm to tell him to wait till she's done, and when she is, she swivels in her chair to face him, pulling her glasses down to the tip of her nose to look at him over the rims.

"Proctor. What can I do for you?"

"Got a second, Madam Mayor?" he asks.

"When did I have one of those?"

He takes the old leather armchair across from her and props his feet on the corner of her desk.

"Please," she says wryly, "make yourself at home."

"Thanks, I will. I have a bit of not-great news."

"Oh?"

"It appears that the roof is worse off than we thought. The entire thing needs to be replaced."

Callista sighs wearily and puts down her pen. "For goodness' sake, I just finalized the annual budget."

"Then you'll have to unfinalize it. This comes direct from Otto."

She shakes her head. "My God, that man."

"Oh, Otto's not so bad."

"I don't mean he's *bad* bad, Proctor. I mean everything's an emergency with him."

"He showed me how extensive the rot is. That roof's not going to fix itself."

"Also, I find him thoroughly annoying on a personal level."

"What is it with you two? Never mind, that's none of my business. I'm just the messenger." Something catches Proctor's eye. "Callista," he says, and points at one of the piles on her desk, "is that . . . a coffee cup I see?"

"Where?"

He rocks forward and lifts the pile to reveal a chipped white mug, suspended at an angle between adjacent stacks. He passes it to her over her desk.

"Oh," she says, with a sheepish little wince. "Thanks. I was wondering where that went."

"How long has it been in there?"

She's frowning into the bottom of the cup. "Hard to say from the looks of it."

"You know, just my two cents, but you might feel a little less stressed if things around here were a little more organized."

"Who said I'm stressed? Besides," she adds, "I like it this way. It's sort of homey, don't you think?"

"So what should I tell Otto?"

"Tell him whatever you like."

"I'd *like* to say, 'Go ahead and fix the roof before the water starts pouring in.'"

She takes a long breath and lets it out sharply. "Fine, I'll look into it. The budget committee meets next week. Will that satisfy you?"

"It'll have to do, I guess. Anyhow," he says, rising from his chair, "and speaking of home, I'm expected. Big doings planned."

Callista sits up a little straighter. "Wait, that's tonight, isn't it?"

"Yup."

She rocks back in her chair, shaking her head. "I can't believe it. How time flies."

"So they say."

"I'm sorry we can't make it to dinner. It's completely Jules's fault. We have to go to that thing."

Proctor has no idea what his father-in-law has done wrong, or what "that thing" is, though probably they've discussed it. "Don't worry about it," he assures her. "It's not like she never sees you."

"I'll think of something we can do with her over the weekend."

"That's nice of you. I know she'd enjoy that."

"Tell her we're thinking of her, okay? Give her our love. Our *special* love."

He gives a two-fingered salute. "Special love. Got it."

"And, Proctor?"

Halfway to the door, he turns. His mother-in-law has already resumed her paperwork, not looking at him as she speaks. "Tell Otto I'll find his goddamn money."

He heads home. The walk isn't far—just a couple of miles, though he's never bothered to measure it—through the heart of town and, when that ends, fields of corn and vegetables, all ready for harvest. The heat of late summer still lies on the land, though Proctor can feel, at the edges, the season starting to turn—a certain exhausted look to the trees, the way the shadows move and fall. It's always this way at the start of the school year, a change he welcomes. He doesn't look forward to the cold—nobody does—

but it's the days in between, crisp and fair with high blue skies, that he loves best of all.

He enters via the garden gate and goes straight to the backyard studio, where he finds Elise at her loom. The walls are covered with her work: tapestries, quilts, batiks, some framed like paintings. The room smells pleasantly of wool and melted wax. What began as a hobby—his wife started out as a teacher, like him—has grown into a thriving business. Every few weeks she sells her work at the craft market in town, making more money in a single morning than he makes in a month. He steps behind her and kisses her neck.

"Yikes!" Elise says, spinning. "You startled me!"

"You just looked so appealing, sitting there."

She touches his cheek. "Also, you could stand a shave, Director Bennett. Lord, what time is it?"

"Almost five. Where is she?"

"Still off with Mrs. Beaufort. I told her to be back by five-thirty."

Mrs. Beaufort lives down the road. A retired civil servant, she never married or had children of her own, keeps elaborate gardens and a constantly changing number of cats, and isn't a day under eighty. Her demeanor can come across as rather crusty and disapproving, but Proctor sees right through it; beneath the surface, the woman is as soft as the insides of a jelly doughnut. Still, calling her by her first name, which is Florence, is impossible. She is and always will be "Mrs. Beaufort."

Elise gets off her stool and says, excitedly, "Come here, I want to show you something."

She leads him to the storage closet, where she takes a rolled rug off the shelf. She unfurls it on the floor of the studio to show him.

"What do you think?" she asks.

The rug isn't big, maybe four by six, and made of a series of small, interlocking diamonds of blue and orange and white, with a single larger diamond in the center. The way the colors mingle is subtle and extraordinary, creating a sense of constant movement within the weave; it doesn't seem inanimate but strikes him more like a living thing, spawned in nature.

"Wow," he says.

"You really think so?" Her eyes shine with pleasure. "Because I'm kind of proud of it myself."

"You should be," Proctor says and, smiling, kisses her quickly. "It's just beautiful, sweetheart."

While Elise cleans up, Proctor goes to the kitchen to finish the preparations for dinner, a simple stew that Elise started earlier and that their daughter had requested. The cake, cocoa with white icing, is already made and waiting on the counter. Proctor is setting the table when he hears the front door open and Caeli bounds into the room, Mrs. Beaufort bringing up the rear.

"Daddy!"

"Happy birthday, kiddo." He crouches to hug her; her body is warm and moist, smelling of earth and sunshine. "It's not every day a girl turns eight. How's it feel?"

His daughter is all smiles. "Pretty great."

Proctor glances up at the old woman. "Thanks for looking after her, Mrs. Beaufort."

"Oh, it was no bother. She helped me in the garden."

"Do you want to stay for dinner? We have plenty."

"Please!" Caeli begs. "Stay!"

"That's kind of you, but not tonight." Mrs. Beaufort looks at Caeli with her soft, old eyes. "Thank you for the help, young lady. And happy birthday."

When Caeli doesn't respond, Proctor prods her: "What do you say, Caeli?"

"Thank you, Mrs. Beaufort."

The woman replies with a pale-lipped smile. "You're most welcome. Good night, Mr. Bennett. I'll show myself out."

"Good night, Mrs. Beaufort."

She takes her leave. "So," Proctor says to Caeli, "supper's almost ready. What do you want to do after?"

"Sailing!"

The request is unexpected. "Really? It'll get dark pretty soon, honey."

"That's when it's best," the girl says. "You can show me the faces."

Elise has entered the kitchen. Proctor glances her way to get a read. "It's *her* birthday," Elise says with a shrug.

Thus is the matter settled. "Well, all righty then," Proctor declares, and tousles his daughter's hair. "Sailing it shall be."

Dinner, cake, singing, the lighting and blowing out of candles; after they've finished, Caeli opens her presents, and by the time they're ready to go, sunset is thirty minutes away. They follow the boardwalk through the dunes to the pier, where the vessel, a small catboat, bobs in the evening light. Proctor named her *Cynthia*—for no reason whatsoever, except that the name seemed right to him, as if the boat were naming herself. As the temperature falls, the night will grow calm, nearly windless, but for now, a steady breeze is still coming off the water.

"Caeli, raise the sail like I showed you."

While the girl gets to work, Proctor attaches the rudder and drops the centerboard. Elise, who isn't much of a sailor—"That's your thing," she always says, "I'm just along for the ride"—has taken her customary position on the port bench, where she can observe the goings-on. Once Caeli has tied off the halyards, Proctor frees the dock lines, gives the nearest pylon a shove, and returns to the helm. The bow veers slowly off the pier, crosses the wind, and with a snap, the sail fills, sending them off and running.

"Caeli, take the tiller," Proctor says.

"Really?" she asks, elated.

"Sure," he says. "You're the birthday girl."

They change places. Proctor moves forward to the windward bench, across from Elise.

"How's it going back there?" he calls.

"Great." The girl is biting her lower lip; her eyes are intently focused over the bow.

"You'll want to head up a bit. Remember what that means?"

"Sail closer to the wind?"

"Exactly. Keep the point about twenty degrees off your port bow. We'll tack once we're past it."

Moving the tiller toward the sail, the girl draws in the mainsheet, clamps it in her teeth, then pulls it in some more and sets it in the block. The boat heels in reply.

"Nicely done," Proctor says.

Elise looks over at him. "I didn't know she knew how to do all that," she says. "When did that happen?"

Proctor can't help himself: he's grinning like a fool. He lifts his voice toward the stern: "Still good? Need any help?"

Caeli brushes a wind-tossed wisp of hair from her face and gives a quick shake of her head, never taking her eyes off the bow. "Nope."

"What can I tell you?" Proctor says to Elise. "The girl's a natural."

Onward they sail. Past the point, Caeli tacks the boat with crisp precision. Eight years old, and here she is, skippering like a pro. Proctor realizes what he's seeing: a memory in the making, of the night when her father handed her the tiller and put her in charge. The thought delights him, though not without an underlying twinge of melancholy: his little girl is growing up so fast. The day will come when she'll leave him, leave both of them, behind; friends, boys, new experiences, all will take the stage until, one day, he'll look up to find her gone, off with a family of her own. But isn't that also something to look forward to? To watch his daughter, whom, not so long ago, he held in the palm of a single hand, step into the flow of life? It's all very complex, and it seems to him that within this complexity lies the true essence of loving a child: a joy so intense that it can feel like sadness. Elise, sensing something in him, reaches across the cockpit to take his hand.

"I know," she says.

A chill has descended. Proctor directs his attention to the sky, where the sun is unleashing its final colors: purples, reds, oranges, great swaths of them blending into one another like strokes from a painter's brush; and behind the colors, the stars, asserting themselves upon the darkness like the lights of a celestial city coming on. The wind has died and, with it, the waves. Darkness falls in full. They are nearly motionless, bobbing on a sea that spreads around them like pooled ink.

"Show me the faces, Daddy."

He joins his daughter in the stern. On the small bench he wedges himself beside her and puts his arm around her back, pulling her close for warmth.

"What's the rule?" he asks her.

"You can't see them if you're trying to."

"That's right. You have to let the faces show themselves. Now relax your eyes. Not only your eyes, your whole body. Just breathe." He fills his chest with air and lets it out slowly. "In, out, in, out. Like that."

The girl does the same.

"Are you relaxed?"

"I . . . think so?"

"Good. Now just wait. It may take a minute. You have to be patient."

A pause, and then she says, excitedly, "I see them!"

"Tell me."

She's scanning the sky. "They're everywhere." She turns her face to look him in the eye. "Who are they?"

"*That* is a most excellent question. And no one knows for certain. I'll tell you what I think, though. I think they're all the souls who ever lived, watching over us."

She frowns. "You mean . . . ghosts?"

"No, not ghosts. Ghosts are scary. Do you feel scared when you look at them?"

She shakes her head. "Nuh-uh."

"So, what do you feel when you see them?"

She looks skyward again. "Happy," she says.

"What else?"

The girl thinks a moment. "Safe?"

"Well, there you go. That's how they make me feel, too." Then: "You're up there too, you know."

"I am?"

"Sure. Everybody is."

"Where am I? Show me."

"Well, that's the thing," Proctor says. "I could show you, but you wouldn't be able to see it. You can see other people, but you can never see yourself."

"Do *you* see me?"

"All the time. You and Mommy both. You always see the people you love."

The girl sets her eyes roaming once more. "There!" she cries, pointing overhead. "I see you!"

"Perhaps you do. I'll have to take your word for it, though."

"And there's Mommy!"

Proctor cranes his neck to look. "Where?"

"Right there!"

Proctor follows her finger with his eyes. "Now, I do believe you're right. I do believe that's Mommy."

She moves her finger to the left with a swooping gesture. "And there's Grandma Callista," she says. "And over there is Grandpa Julian."

"So that's who loves you," Proctor says. "That's your family, right there."

She sees others: teachers, friends at school, Mrs. Beaufort, even the man who delivers the mail. The more she looks, the more she finds. How thoroughly enjoyable to end the day, this *special* day, the day his little girl turns eight years old, scanning the skies for all the people in her life. Caeli looks and looks, each discovery a fresh excitement to her eyes, and when she can find no more, and the looking is done, they drift in silence for a time, just watching the stars.

"I think Mom's asleep," says Caeli.

So she is. Without Proctor being aware of it, Elise has taken a blanket from the cabin and is now curled on the bench beneath it.

"What about you?" Proctor asks. "Getting tired? It's pretty late."

Trying not to, Caeli yawns. Whenever she does this, she looks much younger than she is. "A little," she confesses. A small shiver runs through her. "It's cold."

Proctor goes below, and by the time he returns, Caeli has moved to the starboard bench. He lays her down and wraps her in the blanket, tucking the sides under her.

"Better?"

Her eyes are closed, her voice soft and sleepy. "Uh-huh."

He moves a wisp of hair from her cheek with his fingertips, curling it behind her ear. "You did well with the boat," he tells her. "I'm proud of you."

"Can you rub my back?"

It's been a long time since she's asked this. It was something she loved when she was little and going to bed.

"Sure thing," he says.

Moving his hand in slow circles, Proctor watches as the emotions of the day drain from her body and face. Her breathing grows deep and even; she sleeps. He bends and kisses her on the forehead.

"Happy birthday, baby girl," he whispers.

He returns to the helm. A perfect stillness lies around him; all is bathed in starlight. He could easily doze off himself, so profound is his contentment. How like a dream it all is, he thinks; a perfect dream, this life. He sits that way for a time, watching over his beloveds as they sleep, and, when the moment seems right, brings the bow around, finds the air to fill his sail, and steers his boat toward home.

Acknowledgments

For guidance, encouragement, faith, and, most of all, patience, I send my heartfelt gratitude to Ellen Levine, Jennifer Hershey, and the fine crew at Penguin Random House, my publishing home of twenty-five years.

A shout-out to my students at Rice University, for the gift of their energy and esprit de corps. "Write the pages," y'all. I will do the same.

Thanks yet again to my daughter, Iris, who graciously let me steal the name "Prospera." Darlin', I owe you a proper noun.

Love and appreciation to my son, Atticus, my boon companion in all things sci-fi, and all things generally.

Thank you, Leslie. Thank you, thank you, thank you.